Plain Perfect

A Daughters of the Promise Novel

BETH WISEMAN

QUAKER SUMMER

LISA SAMSON

THOMAS NELSON

Since 1798

NASHVILLE DALLAS MEXICO CITY RIO DE JANEIRO BEIJING

ISBN: 978-1-59554-745-3 (FCS Ed)

ISBN: 978-1-59554-740-8

Printed in the United States of America

09 10 11 12 13 HCI 5 4 3 2 1

Plain Perfect

To Reneé Bissmeyer,
my best friend.

Glossary

ach—oh

Aemen—Amen

appeditlich—delicious

baremlich—terrible

boppli—baby or babies

daadi—grandfather

daed—dad

danki—thanks

Deitschi wege—Dutch ways

Die Botschaft—a weekly newspaper serving Old Order Amish
   communities everywhere

dippy eggs—eggs cooked over easy

eck—special place for bride and groom at the corner of the
   wedding table

Englisch or *Englischer*—a non-Amish person

fraa—wife

guder mariye—good morning

gut—good

haus—house

hochmut—pride

in lieb—in love

Kapp—prayer covering or cap

kinner—children or grandchildren

kinskind—grandchild

mamm—mom

mammi—grandmother

mei—my

naerfich—nervous

Ordnung—the written and unwritten rules of the Amish; the understood behavior by which the Amish are expected to live, passed down from generation to generation. Most Amish know the rules by heart.

Pennsylvania Deitsch—Pennsylvania German, the language most commonly used by the Amish

redd-up—clean up

riewe—red beets

roasht—traditional main dish at an Amish wedding, consisting of cut-up chicken and stuffing

rumschpringe—running-around period when a teenager turns sixteen years old

rutschich—squirming

schnitzboi—snitz pie

schnuppich—snoopy

verhuddelt—confused

wedding nothings—dessert reserved for weddings; fried pastries sprinkled with confectioner's sugar

wunderbaar—wonderful

ya—yes

yummasetti—a traditional Pennsylvania German casserole

LILLIAN PEELED BACK THE DRAPES AT THE FRONT WINDOW and squinted against the sun's glare. She'd called the taxi almost an hour ago. If her ride didn't show up soon, she would have to forego her plan and spend another night with Rickie. Biting her lip, she worried if she had enough cash to change her flight if she didn't make it to the airport on time.

She lowered the drape and paced the living room in Rickie's house, silently blasting herself for ever moving in with him in the first place. Her stomach writhed at the thought of one more day under the same roof with him. And yet her window of time for her departure was closing, she realized, glancing at her watch.

She tugged at the drapes again. Relief fell over her when she saw the yellow cab pull into the driveway. Snatching her red suitcase and purse, she bolted for the door, shuffling toward the driver as he opened the trunk.

"Please hurry," she said to the driver, handing him her suitcase.

The driver stowed her luggage without comment and was climbing into the driver's seat when she saw Rickie's black Lexus rounding the corner and heading up the street. Her heart sank.

"Where to?" the driver asked.

"Bush Intercontinental Airport," she answered. "Hurry, please."

As the driver made his way down Harper Avenue to make the long drive to the northwest side of Houston, Lillian watched out the rearview window. Rickie's car slowly neared the house.

The cab driver turned at the corner. She'd made it. A clean getaway.

Irma Rose Miller couldn't help but notice the bounce in her husband's steps. The cancer kept him down and out on most days, but not today. Today Lilly was coming, and his anticipation and joy were evident.

"*Danki,*" Jonas said as Irma Rose poured him another cup of coffee.

"You're welcome."

Her tall husband, once muscular and strong as an ox, sat hunched over the wooden table between them. His healthy load of gray locks and full beard were now thinning and brittle. Dark circles under his eyes and sunken features revealed the many sleepless nights of pain he had endured over the past few months. God had given her husband of forty-eight years a challenging road to travel, and he was making the trip with dignity and grace.

"Our Lilly will be here this afternoon." Jonas smiled and raised the cup to his mouth. His hands trembled, but his eyes twinkled with a merriment Irma Rose hadn't seen since the first mention of their granddaughter coming to stay with them. She hoped he wouldn't be disappointed. They hadn't seen the girl in seventeen years, since she was ten years old.

Irma Rose stood to retrieve some doughnuts from a pan atop the wooden stove.

"It will be *wunderbaar gut* to have her here."

Irma Rose placed two doughnuts on her husband's plate. "*Ya*, that it will. But, Jonas, you must keep in mind how different our ways are. We will seem like foreigners to our *Englisch* granddaughter."

"These doughnuts are *appeditlich*," Jonas said.

"*Danki*. But, Jonas, you need to prepare yourself. Sarah Jane raised Lilly in the outside world. We don't know her. As a matter of fact, we don't know exactly how Sarah Jane raised her."

The thought twisted Irma Rose's stomach in familiar knots. It had been hard enough when her daughter chose to leave the Old Order Amish community at the age of eighteen, but even more difficult when she wrote to tell them she was in a family way soon thereafter . . . with no husband.

"She was a glorious child," Jonas said. "Remember how quickly Lilly learned to ice-skate? What a joy she was. What a *gut* Christmas holiday we all had."

Irma Rose shook her head at her husband's ignorance of the obvious. Lilly wasn't a child anymore. She was a grown woman. Jonas had talked about that last Christmas together until the next season came and went. When Sarah Jane and Lilly didn't show up the following year, he merely shrugged and said, "Maybe they will visit next year." And each Christmas thereafter Jonas anticipated a visit that never happened.

Jonas never uttered a negative word about Sarah Jane's choices. But she'd seen the sadness in his eyes when their daughter left home, and she knew the pain dwelled in his heart over the years. But he only said it was impossible to always understand God's direction for His children—their child. Their *only* child. The good Lord had only seen fit to bless them with one. A beautiful daughter who had chosen a life rife with hardship.

Irma Rose had prayed hard over the years to cleanse herself of any discontentment with her daughter. Sarah Jane's choice to leave the Amish faith was prior to her baptism and church membership. Therefore the community never shunned her daughter. She had chosen to avoid visits with her parents. From the little Irma Rose gathered over the years, Sarah Jane and Lilly had lived with friends and moved around a lot.

An occasional letter arrived from her daughter, to which Irma Rose always responded right away. More times than not, the letters were returned unopened. It was less painful to assume Sarah Jane had moved on and the postal service returned the letters. Although sometimes it cut Irma Rose to the bone when she recognized her daughter's penmanship: *Return to sender.*

She was thankful her last letter to Sarah Jane wasn't returned. She couldn't help but wonder if the news about Jonas's cancer had prompted her granddaughter's visit. When Lillian's letter arrived over a month ago, Irma Rose had followed her instructions not to return a letter but to call her on the telephone if at all possible. She wasted no time going to the nearby shanty to phone her granddaughter. The conversation was strained and the child seemed frantic to come for a visit.

"I'm a teacher and when school is out in May, I'd like to come for a visit," her granddaughter had said on the phone. "Maybe stay for the summer. Or maybe even longer?" There was a sense of urgency in the girl's tone.

Irma Rose feared her faith was not as strong as her husband's and that a tinge of resentment and hurt still loitered in her heart where Sarah Jane was concerned. She didn't want any of those feelings to spill over with her granddaughter. She would need to pray harder.

As if reading her mind, Jonas said, "Irma Rose, everything will be fine. You just wait and see."

* * *

It wasn't until the plane was high above the Houston skyline that the realization of what she'd done hit Lillian. After landing in Philadelphia, she caught a train to Lancaster City and hopped a bus to Paradise, which landed her only a few miles from her grandparents' farm. She was glad there was a bit of a walk to their property; she wanted to wind down and freshen up before she reacquainted herself with her relatives. Plus, she'd had enough time on the plane to wonder if this whole thing was a huge mistake. Her mom hadn't wanted to be here, so why think it would be any better for her?

Not that she had much choice at this point. She had no money, no home, no job, and she was more than a little irritated with her mother. When her mom had begged Lillian to loan her money, Lillian reluctantly agreed, with the stipulation she got her money back as soon as possible. But her mom had never repaid a loan before. Lillian didn't know why she thought it would be any different this time, and she was determined to move away from her "boyfriend" Rickie. So Lillian quit her job and made a decision to distance herself from her mother and Rickie by coming to a place where she knew neither of them would follow: Lancaster County.

Lillian shook her head, wondering if she was making a bigger mistake by coming here. She didn't know if she'd ever understand what ultimately drove her mother from the Plain lifestyle. From what she read, it rarely happened—Amish children fleeing from all they'd ever known. The circumstances must have been severe to drive her mother away.

Although . . . it didn't look so bad from Lillian's point of view, now that she was here. Aside from having a dreadful wardrobe, she thought the Amish men and women strolling by looked quite content. They seemed oblivious to the touristy stares. The women wore simple, dark-colored dresses with little white coverings on their heads. The men were in cotton shirts, dark pants with suspenders, and straw hats with a wide brim. Box-shaped, horse-drawn buggies were abundant.

Ironically, it all seemed quite normal.

She took a seat on a bench outside the Quik Mart at the corner of Lincoln Highway and Black Horse Road and watched the passersby. Clearly, Paradise was a tourist town, like most of Lancaster County, with everyone wanting to have a look at the Amish people. Watching them now, she wondered if the Amish were all as peaceful as they appeared. Despite her initial thoughts, she decided they couldn't be. Everyone had stress. Everyone had problems. Surely the Plain People of Lancaster County were not an exception.

But they could have fooled Lillian.

Samuel Stoltzfus gave hasty good-byes to Levina Esh and Sadie Fisher and flicked his horse into action, hiding a smile as his buggy inched forward. The competitiveness of those two widow women! First Levina had presented him with her prize-winning shoofly pie. Not to be outdone, Sadie quickly offered up her own prize-winning version. Stalemate. The two of them had stood there glaring at each other while he tried to think of ways to escape unhurt . . . and unattached.

He might have to rethink his shopping day. Both women knew he went to the farmer's market on Thursdays . . .

Once he cleared town, he picked up the pace. The road to his farm near the town of Paradise was less traveled, and he was particularly glad of that on this day. It was a glorious sunny afternoon, perfect for a buggy ride through the countryside. Pleased he had chosen his spring buggy instead of his covered one, he relished the warmth of the late afternoon sun. Rachel had loved this time of year, when spring gave way to summertime and all the world felt full of promise.

God's soil was tilled, and he had planted corn, alfalfa, and grain. Life would be busy as he awaited the bountiful rewards of spring's labor. There was the garden, with peas to pick. The strawberries would be ready. Lots of canning and freezing. Much time went into preparing a garden for harvest.

And Rachel's garden had always been lush and plentiful. Gardening was work for the womenfolk, but Samuel had done the best he could the past two years. He was thankful his sisters took care of most of the canning and freezing.

He closed his eyes, his shoulders lifting with his sigh. He missed Rachel the most this time of year.

Lillian felt like a fool. Didn't "down yonder a spell" mean right down the road? The friendly Amish boy had pointed down Black

Horse Road and uttered those exact words when she'd asked for directions to her grandparents' farm. She'd thought the walk would do her good—help her shed some of the calories she ingested while sitting at the Quik Mart with a large cinnamon roll and cola.

Evidently, she'd mistranslated "down yonder a spell." There wasn't a farmhouse in sight.

She really should have considered the strappy sandals she was wearing before opting to venture down the road to nowhere. Her capri blue jeans and short-sleeved, pink-cotton shirt were good choices, however. The clement sun mixing with a soft breeze made for a perfect day. An excellent day for a walk . . . if only she'd worn better shoes.

Setting her red suitcase on the grassy shoulder of the paved road, she plopped down on top of it and scanned the farmland surrounding her. It was so quiet. Peaceful. She could only hope that some of the peacefulness the Amish were known for would rub off on her during her stay. She needed it. Life had not been easy on her the past few years.

Her mom's idea of parenting had left much to be desired—jumping from one man to the next, looking for something she never seemed to find. All the while she'd toted Lillian along. Lillian had grown up changing schools, saying good-bye to friends, and continually hoping Mom's next boyfriend would be better than the last. At the first chance, Lillian had bailed on the situation, telling herself she could do better.

Despite her good intentions, she'd ended up close to following in her mother's footsteps. After putting herself through college while living with three other girls in a small apartment, she'd landed a teaching job. There were boyfriends, and she'd definitely made her own share of mistakes.

But always, something had whispered to her that there was another way to live. Sometimes she'd listened, sometimes not. But she never felt comfortable enough to ask herself just where that voice was coming from—she just didn't know enough to form an opinion. She didn't listen to the voice when it cautioned her not to move in with Rickie. But when the voice became too strong to ignore, she knew it was time to get out of that situation.

Despite the complete lack of religious upbringing, she always suspected there might be a God looking down on her. But in light of her mom's thoughts on church, she couldn't ask her about it. Her mother seemed angry at religion. While she heartily encouraged Lillian to attend various churches with her friends when she was a child, she herself would have no part of it. It was a huge contradiction in parenting, and Lillian didn't understand it to this day.

Now, knowing the Amish to be solid in their faith, Lillian decided it might be best to keep her suspicions about God to herself around her grandparents.

"Guess I better get moving and find out how far 'down yonder a spell' really is." She jumped off the suitcase, gave it a heave-ho, and started back down the paved road, gazing to either side where the acreage stretched as far as she could see. The sun pressing down on the horizon left her a tad worried about how much farther the farm was.

"Whoa, boy!" Samuel yelled to his horse. The animal slowed his pace to a gentle trot, bringing the buggy alongside an *Englisch*

woman cumbersomely toting a bright-red suitcase. She was minus
a shoe . . . if you called a flat-bottom sole with two small straps a
shoe. Certainly not a good walking instrument.

"Can I offer you a ride?" He pulled back on the reins and
came to a complete halt, as did the small-framed woman. When
she turned, he was met by radiant green eyes in a delicate face.
Delicate, that is, until she grimaced and blew a tendril of hair out
of her face.

Then she smiled, and her face transformed, lighting up like
the morning sun. He was momentarily struck dumb.

It didn't matter. The woman was focused on his horse. Deserting
her suitcase on the side of the road, she stumbled over to Pete
and reached out to stroke his nose without so much as a "May I?"
Thankfully, Pete was a gentle giant.

"He's beautiful," she said, glancing briefly in Samuel's direction, eyes sparkling.

He cleared his throat. "*Ya*. And a fine work horse too."

What an interesting woman this was. Unafraid. And beautiful, he had to admit. He watched as her long brown hair danced
in the wind, framing her face in layers. She wore no makeup
and seemed lacking in the traditional *Englisch* look, although her
brightly colored blouse and calf-length breeches certainly gave
her away. A tourist, most likely. But a tourist walking alone down
Blackhorse Road?

The woman's mouth curved upward in delight as she cooed
over Pete. The horse gently snorted, nudged her, and she laughed
heartily, her head thrown back. It was a thoroughly enchanting
scene.

Suddenly uncomfortable at his thoughts, he straightened

and coughed. It was enough to bring the woman's attention back to him.

"I would love a ride!" With a final kiss on the old horse's muzzle, she went back for her suitcase. "Where should I put this?"

"*Ach*, my manners." Samuel jumped out of the buggy and made his way to the woman. "Let me." He took the suitcase from her, quite surprised at how heavy the small bundle was. After stowing it behind the double seat, he offered his hand to assist her into the buggy.

"Thank you." Now she was studying him . . . seemingly from head to toe. At her open glance, he felt a flush tint his cheeks.

"I'm Samuel Stoltzfus," he said, extending his hand but avoiding her questioning eyes.

"I'm Lillian Miller."

Her hands were certainly that of an *Englisch* woman, soft and void of a hard day's work. The Plain women in Lancaster County tilled gardens, shelled peas, kneaded bread, and a host of other necessary chores uncommon to *Englisch* women from the city. City women's hands were not only smooth and manicured, but pleasing to the touch.

Returning to his seat, he started up the buggy again. The woman was obviously tired and happy to be resting; with a slight groan she stretched her legs out. He found his eyes wandering her way and silently remonstrated himself.

"Where are you from, Lillian? Or, more important, where are you going?"

"I'm from Houston."

"*Ya*, Texas," he said, slightly surprised. They didn't usually get

Texans walking the roads out here. "Lots of farms in Texas. What brings you to Lancaster County, Pennsylvania?"

"I'm coming to stay with my grandparents for a while." She smiled. "They're Amish."

Amish? He was once more at a loss for words. Not to worry—the *Englisch* woman wasn't.

"Actually, I guess I'm Amish too," she added.

Discreetly glancing at her *Englisch* clothes, he wondered how that could be so.

"My grandparents are Irma Rose and Jonas Miller. I'll be staying with them for a while." She looked his way as if waiting for a response that never came. "I'd like to adapt myself to the Amish ways. I need a peaceful, calm lifestyle away from the city. Anyway, I've decided to be Amish for a while."

Samuel had been trying to connect this vivacious outsider with the staunch Irma Rose and Jonas he knew, but these words jostled him out of his musings. "You'd like to be Amish for a *while?*"

"Yes. Although I don't plan to wear one of those dark-colored dresses or white caps like the women I saw strolling by earlier."

In spite of himself, Samuel chuckled. "Do you even know what being Amish means?" He didn't mean the remark as harshly as it sounded.

Lillian slanted her eyes in his direction, as if slightly offended.

Unexpectedly, the buggy wheel hit a rut. With an *oomph*, his new friend bounced in her seat. She was a tiny little thing. Luckily, she didn't catapult right off the seat and onto the pavement.

"Yikes!" she said when her behind returned to the seat. And then she giggled. As Pete's ears swiveled back to catch the commotion, Samuel couldn't help but grin. The woman's enthusiasm was contagious.

He decided to drop the subject. He knew Irma Rose and Jonas well enough to figure they'd set her right about being Amish and what it really meant. Samuel reckoned they'd have their hands full with their granddaughter.

As Samuel righted the buggy, he asked, "When is the last time you saw your grandparents?" He hadn't even known Irma Rose and Jonas had a granddaughter.

"When I was ten. Seventeen years ago. It was the first time I saw snow. *Real* snow." Her eyes twinkled from the memory. "Anyway, I know things will be different from what I'm used to. But I can live without television. There's too much bad news on TV anyway. And I know Amish women cook a lot. I'm a great cook." She shrugged. "I'm a hard worker in general. I know Amish get up early and go to bed early. I know they work hard during the day. And if that's what it takes to feel peaceful and calm . . . I'm in!"

Samuel found her enthusiasm charming, no matter how misdirected it was. "Lillian, I'm sure Irma Rose and Jonas will appreciate you helping with household duties, but it will take more than chores and giving up worldly things to provide you with the peacefulness you're lookin' for."

"Well, it's a start," she said, sounding optimistic.

As for that . . . who was he to argue?

Lillian remembered the Christmas visit with her grandparents at their farm, especially the snow. Unlike the icy mix of sludge found rarely in her hometown state, snow in Lancaster County glistened with a tranquil purity. Almost two decades later, she could still recall the towering cedar trees blanketed in white and ice skating on the crystalline pond in her mother's old ice skates.

There were few presents. She remembered that. And while she recollected her grandparents as warm and loving, she also remembered the tension between them and her mother. Her grandfather had kept the mood festive, suggested the ice-skating, and seemed to make it his mission for Lillian to have a good time—even carting her to town and back in his gray, horse-drawn buggy. It had been the highlight of her trip.

"I remember liking the way my grandparents talked," she recalled to Samuel. "I didn't understand a lot of things they said. Things like '*Outen* the lights until sunrise when we'll *redd-up* the house.' And 'It wonders me if it will make wet tomorrow.' Mom translated those to mean '*Turn out the lights until in the morning when we'll clean up the house*' and '*I wonder if it will rain tomorrow.*'"

"That would be right," Samuel said.

Grandma and Grandpa both spoke another language she'd later found out was *Pennsylvania Deitsch*. Lots of times they would comingle their language with English. "*Danki, Sarah Jane, for bringing our little kinskind for a visit*," her grandfather told her mother that Christmas. To which Sarah Jane Miller forced a smile and nodded.

"*Grandma, why are you and Grandpa wearing those costumes?*" Lillian recalled asking her grandparents.

Grandpa had just laughed and said, "*It is our faith, my* kinskind.

We wear these plain clothes to encourage humility and separation from the world."

At ten, Lillian had little understanding of what that signified. Except somewhere in the translation she knew it meant they couldn't have a television or a phone. Several times after their one and only trip, Lillian had asked her mother if she could call her grandparents. Mom reminded her that Grandpa and Grandma did not allow phones at their house.

"Evidently, my grandparents came to Houston a couple of times before our visit at Christmas, but I don't remember," she told Samuel. "That Christmas was my last trip to Lancaster County and the last time I saw my grandparents. Until now."

"I reckon Irma Rose and Jonas are really looking forward to seeing you."

"I hope so."

Lillian tried to keep her gaze focused on the road in front of her. But her eyes kept involuntarily trailing to her left. Samuel Stoltzfus was as handsome a man as she had ever seen in the city. His plain clothes did little to mask his solid build and appealing smile each time she glanced in his direction. But it was his piercing blue eyes Lillian couldn't seem to draw away from.

"So, how long have you been married?" *Nosy, nosy.* The astonished look on his face confirmed her worry. She was crossing the line. "I'm sorry. I just noticed that you have the customary beard following marriage." She'd done her research before arriving here. "And . . . I was just . . . curious." *And curious why? He's Amish, for heaven's sake.*

"I'm not married. I'm widowed."

"Oh," she said softly, thinking how young his wife must have been when she died. " I'm so sorry. When did your wife die?"

"*Mei fraa*, Rachel, passed almost two years ago," he answered without looking her way.

"Again, I'm so sorry."

Samuel continued to stare at the road ahead. "It was God's will."

There was no sadness or regret in his tone. Just fact. Lillian knew she should leave it alone, but . . . "I'm sure you miss her very much."

He didn't glance her way. "There's Irma Rose and Jonas's farm," he said, pointing to their right. "I better take you right up to the house." He coaxed Pete down a long dirt drive leading from the road to the white farmhouse.

"Oh, you don't have to do that. I can walk." She wondered if Samuel Stoltzfus was ready to be rid of her.

His eyebrows edged upward beneath his dark bangs and he glanced at her shoeless foot.

Point taken. "A ride to the house would be great."

As Pete trotted down the dirt driveway toward the farmhouse, reality sank in. This would be her new home for the summer—or however long it took to accomplish her goal. At first glance, everything seemed lovely. Neatly mowed, prodigious fields were on either side of the lane, and the white fencing in good repair. But unlike the farms she passed on the way, there were no signs of new life planted. It wasn't until they drew closer to the farmhouse that she spotted a small garden off to her left enclosed by a wire-mesh fence. Parallel rows of greenery indicated vegetables would be forthcoming.

There was a large barn off to her left, the paint weathered and chipping. Another smaller barn to her right also was in need of a fresh paint job. She recalled the barns they had passed on her journey down Black Horse Road. Most were a bright crimson color.

The white farmhouse appeared freshly painted, but with flowerbeds absent of flowers or shrubs. They must have been beautiful at one time. But now they—and the rest of the yard—lent an air of neglect to the farm.

A wraparound porch with two rockers looked inviting. But while the idea of curling up with a good book in one of the rockers was appealing, Lillian knew it was the inside of the house and its inhabitants she feared most. Her grandma had seemed pleasant enough on the phone, but what if she and her grandfather were too set in their ways to make room for her? And what if she couldn't adjust to their ways? No electricity meant no hair dryer, curling iron, or other modern conveniences she considered necessities. How would she charge her cell phone? And she couldn't imagine a summer without air conditioning.

Grimacing as the thoughts rattled around her head, she reminded herself why she'd come. She'd had a month to consider all of these factors. She thought she had. But as her fantasy of leaving everything behind for *this* became absolute, her tummy twirled with uncertainty.

She was still attempting to envision her new way of life when Samuel brought Pete up next to a gray buggy parked on one side of the house. Samuel moved quickly to get her suitcase from behind the seat and extended his hand to help her out of the buggy. Towering over her, he promptly released her fingers.

"Thank you for the ride. Maybe I will see you again." She

could only hope. But his lack of response as he quickly jumped back in the carriage left her wondering.

Lillian waved good-bye and watched until horse, buggy, and man were back on the paved road. She knew she was stalling. Her grandparents would be strangers to her, and she would be a stranger to them. Yet they had encouraged her to come and stay with them. *"For as long as you like,"* her grandmother had said.

Striving to cast her worries aside, she turned around, picked up her suitcase, and headed up the walk toward what would be her new home . . . for a while.

2

"THE BOPPLI IS HERE!" JONAS EXCLAIMED. HE CLOSED THE window blinds and staggered to the door to welcome their grand-daughter.

"She's hardly a *baby*, Jonas. She's a grown woman." Despite her confident tone, Irma Rose fiddled with her apron strings as she followed her husband.

"Irma Rose, there's no need to look so *naerfich*. I reckon things will be just fine. The Good Lord will see to it." Jonas winked at her as he reached for the doorknob.

"I can't help but be nervous, Jonas. We don't know this girl," she whispered.

Jonas flung the door open and walked onto the front porch. Irma Rose followed her husband and noticed immediately that the young woman before them looked nervous as well. But, as was his way, Jonas plowed through the tension by making a joke.

"Irma Rose, this poor girl must have walked here all the way from Houston, Texas," he teased, his eyes narrowing in on his granddaughter's shoeless foot. "First thing to do is get her some proper walking shoes."

Irma Rose shook her head at Jonas as she scooted past him and toward the stranger in her front yard. Jonas didn't move. Hunched over, he kept his hands on his hips and continued studying the girl's feet with a wide smile.

"Welcome, Lilly," Irma Rose said. She embraced her granddaughter for the first time in seventeen years.

"Lillian," the young woman said as she awkwardly returned the hug. "I go by *Lillian* now."

"Oh, I'm sorry. We called you Lilly when you were young and assumed . . ."

"It's okay. I just grew out of 'Lilly.'"

"Well, Lillian—" Irma Rose began. Jonas interrupted her.

"I like *Lilly*. I am going to call you Lilly," he said firmly, with a boyish grin still plastered from ear to ear.

"Now, Jonas, if she prefers to be called *Lillian* . . ."

"No. I like *Lilly* better," her husband insisted. "Now, Lilly, let's get you into the house. We've got warm brownies and lemonade ready for you."

"Jonas!" Irma Rose tried to intercede. She often wondered if her husband's various medications had caused his already strong personality to escalate over the past few months. Sometimes he seemed to swing whatever way the wind was blowing and other days . . . Well, it was either his way or nobody's way. Today was clearly the latter.

"Brownies and lemonade sound great," Lillian said. She shot Irma Rose a soft look, assuring her Jonas's persistent ways didn't offend her.

Irma Rose watched Jonas struggle to tote the bright-red suitcase up the porch steps. She knew better than to assist him. His determined look left no question that he wanted to appear as much a man as he had ever been to his granddaughter. Irma Rose knew he'd pay for it later.

"Whatcha got in this thing . . . bricks?" he asked as he maneuvered through the front door ahead of the women.

Irma Rose studied the suitcase with curiosity.

"Mostly books," Lillian said, grabbing the suitcase from Jonas. "I like to read. I was an English teacher for several years . . . until recently."

Irma Rose considered asking Lillian what *"until recently"* meant, but stopped short, sensing regret in her granddaughter's tone. Perhaps Lillian had been fired from her job and had nowhere else to go. Or some other such embarrassing situation.

Lillian took in her surroundings and was pleasantly surprised. Not remembering much from her last visit, she'd built up an image in her mind. But the room was not as sparse as she'd envisioned. Dark-green blinds that were drawn halfway up covered the windows, and the whitewash walls were bare. But lovely furniture was placed throughout the room, including two high-back rockers with blue cushions, an oak sideboard and matching hutch, and a shelf that held four lanterns. Intertwined between the lanterns was a leafy ivy plant that was draped across the length of the shelf. There was even a worn brown recliner in the corner. No television, of course. The aroma of freshly baked goods lent even more warmth to the room.

Following her grandparents into the kitchen, she noticed the same dark-green blinds covering the windows. Unlike the den, there was definitely a focal point in this room: the wood-burning stove nestled against the far wall, the keeper of the fabulous smells permeating throughout the house. This room was more of a step back in time.

"Welcome to our home, Lilly," her grandfather said, beaming. She couldn't help but smile at his gleeful energy. Her grandmother was another story. Irma Rose seemed guarded and hesitant. Even her hug felt strained. Lillian knew she herself was partly to blame for the tension.

"Thank you for having me." She glanced at the pan of brownies atop the stove. Normally, she would shy away from such caloric luxuries, especially since she'd already blown it for the day with the big cinnamon roll she wolfed down earlier. But her grandmother offered her the biggest brownie in the pan. She accepted, deciding the walk had evened out the caloric playing field again.

"Lillian, Jonas and I already ate supper. We eat at four-thirty. But I saved you some chicken and mashed potatoes."

As her grandmother headed toward the refrigerator, Lillian shook her head while trying to quickly swallow the above-average bite of brownie. "No, no," she said, gulping the last of the warm dessert down. "This brownie is fine for me."

"I should have offered you some supper, I suppose, before brownies," her grandmother said, sounding regretful. She returned to one of the long wooden benches facing Lillian.

"Propane gas, Lilly," her grandfather belted out, seeing her eyes go to the gas bottle next to the refrigerator. "We use propane. No electricity. No connection of wires to the outside world."

"Oh." Lillian glanced upward at the gas lantern hanging above the table.

"We have an indoor bathroom," her grandmother added. "In case you were wondering."

"Yes, I remember that." The old outhouse was still outside, but she remembered indoor plumbing from her last visit.

"How did you get here, after your plane flight and train ride?"

Lillian recalled her journey with fondness. "I took a bus to Paradise and then Samuel Stoltzfus brought me in his buggy."

It was hard to miss the look of bewilderment on both their faces.

"Really?" her grandmother asked, her eyes lighting up with interest.

Lillian shrugged. "I guess he took pity on me when he saw me walking down the road with only one shoe on. I must have looked a mess. But the Amish boy in town said this farm was 'down yonder a spell.' Uh, it was considerably farther than I thought."

"Samuel Stoltzfus is a *gut* man," her grandma said. "He was a fine husband. His son works here in the afternoon on most days. Now that school is out, he's able to put in a few more hours. He chops wood, mows . . . the things Jonas and I can't get to anymore."

"That's a shame about his wife." Lillian took a sip of her lemonade.

"You talked about Rachel?" Grandma seemed surprised.

"Not much."

"It was God's will," her grandfather said softly.

"I guess." Lillian said and got questioning looks from both her grandparents. It didn't seem like God's will to take a man's wife at such a young age. "She must have been young. How'd she die?"

"The cancer got her, just like it's gonna get me," Grandpa said matter-of-factly and seemingly with no bitterness.

"Maybe not," Lillian said, not looking at him. She knew her grandfather had bone cancer and that it was a painful way to go. Grandma had mentioned the cancer in her last letter to Mom. The thought of anyone going through that kind of agony bothered her immensely.

"God has blessed me with a *gut* woman in Irma Rose. It's God's will that she will have to bury me first."

"Now, Jonas, you don't know that."

"She's right, Grandpa. They come out with new treatments all the time for cancer patients." Surely her grandpa would be open to every available option.

It felt strange to call her grandfather "Grandpa," but what else should she call him? That's what she'd called him when she was ten. The look on his face told her that he picked up on it and was pleased.

It seemed even stranger to call her grandmother "Grandma." Lillian felt sure Grandma had some strong reservations about her being here. And that was fair. Lillian had her own strong reservations about being here. Her worldly ways were as foreign to them as the lantern dangling above the table was to her.

It was a tiny bedroom, and Lillian slept like a rock. She probably would have kept sleeping if her cell phone hadn't started ringing. She peeled back the quilt on her bed and reached for the phone atop the nightstand.

"Hello."

"Are you okay? I didn't hear from you." The connection was a bit crackly, but adequate.

"Hi, Mom. I didn't know I was supposed to check in."

"How is your grandpa?" Mom went on, ignoring Lillian's irritated tone.

"He seems okay. He looks a lot older than Grandma, who by the way seems okay too."

"Well, I still can't imagine why you would want to go and live there, Lillian. You will never make it in their world. I'm staying with Paul, and he said you're welcome to come stay here."

"Mom! Why would you do that? Paul treated you like dirt when you were dating him before!" Lillian sat up and pushed back tangled strands of hair. "Why do you keep choosing the wrong men?" Wondering if this wasn't the pot calling the kettle black, she was determined to learn from her mistake with Rickie.

"Lillian, things are different now."

"They're always *different*, Mom."

"Just come home."

"I don't have a home, Mom."

"I will get you back all the money I borrowed, Lillian. I promise. Then you can start fresh somewhere. Although I think it was a mistake leaving Rickie. He took such good care of you."

Lillian threw herself across the bed in disgust. *If you only knew.* "Why don't you just come here, Mom? Spend some time with your parents and find some peace." She knew it was a safe request. Her mother would never come, nor did she want her to.

"Is that what you're doing, Lillian? Looking for *peace*?"

Lillian bristled. "I don't know what I'm looking for, Mom. I just needed to get away, and I'm broke."

"Well, I hope you find what you're looking for."

"I wish you meant that."

"You're my daughter. Of course I mean that. But just remember that you have options. You can always come and stay with Paul and me and—"

"Good-bye, Mother. I'll talk to you later." Hanging up on her was better than enduring a full-blown fight. It was too early in the morning. She pulled the quilt over her head and buried her face in the pillow.

"Shame on you, Irma Rose," Jonas whispered with a chuckle as he passed her in the hallway outside Lillian's room. "That looks like eavesdropping to me."

"I was just wondering if the child was still alive. It's nearly seven o'clock. She missed breakfast hours ago. And she's either talkin' to herself or she's on a portable telephone." She continued to press her ear against the door.

"I'm going to hope it's a mobile telephone," Jonas said jokingly, then paused. "Give her some time, Irma Rose. I think our Lilly has had a hard life. God sent her to us for a reason. You can't expect her to give up all her worldly possessions overnight."

"*Ya*, I know. I really do, Jonas. But she said in her letter that she wanted to find peace in her life. If she meant that, I'd think she might try to live our ways while she's here. You're probably right, though. It's going to take her some time."

As Jonah kissed her on the cheek and headed down the hallway toward the bathroom, Irma Rose stood there trying to shift doubt to hope. Just because Sarah Jane wasn't happy here didn't mean Lillian couldn't be.

"Is that Samuel's son outside?" Lillian asked her grandma as she sat at the kitchen table eating a bowl of oatmeal. The blinds were open, and she could see the boy chopping wood off to the side of the barn. She wished her grandfather would join them. Felt like less tension when he was around.

"*Ya.* He's been a huge help ever since Jonas got down." Her grandma walked to the window and watched the boy. "He's a fine lad."

"His father seems like a nice man too."

"*Ya.* He's been a good father to the boy since his *mamm* died."

Lillian saw her grandma taking note of her attire. Blue jeans and a white T-shirt. She'd purposely not packed any of her flashier clothes and had thought her attire plain enough, but Grandma seemed to have her nose turned up a tad.

"I hung some dresses on the peg in your room. I thought they might be more appropriate for our community."

Lillian had seen the dresses the night before. She couldn't help but cringe at the thought of having to wear them and wondered if Grandma intended her to do so. Evidently. Plain dark-colored dresses that would hit her about mid-calf. *Ugh.* She was more comfortable in her own traditional attire. Plus, blue jeans seemed much more practical for farm life. Although maybe Grandma would be embarrassed to introduce her to the community dressed in blue jeans? Might bring forth questions Grandma didn't want to field. She'd think about it, but for now she decided it best to change the subject.

"I'm sorry I slept so late this morning. I know you get up early and we have lots of chores to do. I don't want you to think I'll do this every morning—sleep late. I was just really tired from the trip. But I'm a pretty good cook if you'd like for me to cook supper tonight."

Grandma straightened the black apron atop her dark-brown dress and turned to face Lillian. Her sheer exhaustion was apparent, along with doubt Lillian could do the job. "Well, I wouldn't know how to act if I was given a break in the kitchen." She paused and considered the idea. Then shook her head. "It's a mite challenging to cook on a wood-burning stove. And Jonas likes to have things a certain way. I don't know . . ."

"I'll be glad to give it a shot, Grandma. Cooking is the one thing Mom did really well, and I learned early on how to prepare a meal. You said you and Grandpa eat at four thirty. I can have it ready."

"Your *mamm* is a *gut* cook?"

Lillian sensed her need for a *yes*. "She is. She said she learned from you."

Grandma's face flooded with emotion. "And she taught you to cook . . . like *we* do?"

"I suppose I didn't know it at the time, but yes. I made my first shoofly pie when I was nine. And I know how to make apple butter." Lillian was about to tell her grandma those types of delicacies were few and far between, but when she saw the elated look on her grandmother's face, she held her tongue.

"There are a few meats in the freezer above the refrigerator. We keep the bulk of our meats in a freezer at Kauffman's Market in town. And there's plenty of canned goods in the basement. You'll see them long 'bout the far side on some shelves. If you need anything extra, I—"

"I'm sure I can find everything. I just might need you to show me a little bit about cooking on this woodstove." Lillian studied the ancient piece of equipment. "Take a break, Grandma. Let me help you some while I'm here."

Lillian washed her cereal bowl, thinking how worn out her grandma looked. Twice she'd heard her up during the night with her grandpa. It sounded like he was vomiting. She'd thought about going to see if she could help, but her grandpa seemed like such a proud man, and she didn't want to embarrass him.

"I think I'll go introduce myself to David," Lillian said as she dried her hands on the dish towel. She headed toward the door, then impulsively turned around. "Grandma, is Grandpa okay this morning?"

"Your *daadi* had a bad night. He ate a little breakfast and went back to bed."

"What about chemotherapy? Would that help him?"

"He's chosen not to have any such thing."

"If it's an option, did he consider it?"

"He's on medications for the pain. Jonas says it's God's will and that he will ride it out at home, as best he can."

"Oh," Lillian said. She wanted to argue that God—if there was a God—would want him to fight. But it seemed she and her grandmother might be moving in a positive direction amid very different worlds. Offering to prepare supper earned her some points. She hated to rock the boat, especially about God.

"You start work early," Lillian said when she walked up behind the boy busily chopping wood. The sun was still working its way upward, and dewy droplets speckled Lillian's tennis shoes as she walked across the freshly cut yard. "I'm Lillian."

David removed the oversized glove on his right hand and extended it. "Nice to meet you. I'm David."

As he removed his straw hat with his other hand in a polite gesture, David's traditional bangs fell forward and his bobbed haircut came into view, a lighter shade of brown than his father's. He had inherited Samuel's handsome square jaw and natural good looks.

"I'm Jonas and Irma Rose's granddaughter." Lillian moved toward the boy and shook his hand.

"*Ya*, I know," he said, smiling. He put his glove back on and motioned for her to step aside as he drew the axe back and swung at the log centered before him.

"Oh, they told you about me?"

"No, my *daed* did." He placed another log on the pile and prepared for another split.

Lillian waited for him to swing the axe before she spoke. "Really? So, your dad mentioned me?"

"*Ya.*"

David looked about eleven or twelve years old. Old enough to interpret any interest she might have in his father. She'd have to be careful. "Did he tell you I came here all the way from Texas?"

His expression shifted to contemplative, and his tone took on a hint of mischief. "He said you were real pretty, like my *mamm*." Grinning, he heaved another log on the pile.

The compliment made her stomach flip. "I'm sorry about your mother," she said softly.

"It was God's will."

She grimaced, thankful the boy's back was to her. How could they all accept tragedy as simply being *anyone's* will? His mother must have been in her twenties when she died of cancer. How horrible to be taken from your husband and child at such a young age, whatever the motivation of a suspected Higher Being.

Knowing it was best to leave it alone, she said, "Well, I just wanted to come and introduce myself. I'm sure I'll be seeing you around."

David nodded and tipped his hat in her direction.

Samuel finished plowing for the day and headed to the house to clean up before picking up David. He wondered if his son had met Irma Rose and Jonas's granddaughter. He wondered how her first day had gone without the modern conveniences she was used to.

As he bathed, thoughts of the *Englisch* woman filled his mind. Reaching for the bar of soap, he pondered what would bring an outsider into their world. To be *Amish for a while*, she'd said. Interesting. Maybe trouble had found her. The *Englisch* Samuel knew always seemed to seek out Amish ways when they were in trouble. Although her spirited laugh led him to believe the woman didn't have nearly a care in the world.

It had been a long time since he'd laughed.

Samuel knew it was always best to keep a comfortable distance from the *Englischers*. And practicing separation from the rest of the world came easy to him . . . most of the time.

Lillian was glad she'd offered to prepare supper that evening, but she was exhausted from the daily chores that Grandma evidently struggled with every day. Normally a night owl, Lillian felt sure she'd hit the bed by sunset. Otherwise, she'd never make it up by four-thirty to start all over again. Her face twisted in disbelief that she hadn't thought out more carefully her choice to come here. And this was only day one.

But given the day's events, preparing supper was the right thing to do. She had watched her grandma take numerous trips up and down the stairs to take care of her grandfather, patiently instructing Lillian as to the daily chores in between. The dark circles under her grandmother's eyes were testimonial to her exhaustion, but she never complained.

Grandma obviously enjoyed the hard work, taking pride as she instructed Lillian on how to use the treadle machine for sewing, how to fire up the gas-powered washing machine, the proper procedure for hanging clothes on the line, and which strawberries were ripe for picking in the garden. Grandma had also managed to knock out three loaves of homemade bread and bake a rhubarb pie while Lillian watched.

She'd said she didn't want to overwhelm Lillian with too much work on her first day. Surely she was kidding.

"I'm on a light load," her grandma had said earlier that afternoon. "I thank the Good Lord for sending us David to help with the outside chores. And we gave up our milk cows when Jonas got too sick for us to milk twice a day. And goes without sayin' that we don't harvest the fields anymore. We have a small garden and plenty of meat in the freezer. And the *gut* people in our district never let us go without."

Lillian was worrying what the next day would bring when Grandma offered up the information. "Tomorrow, we'll add some canning to the other chores, and we'll see 'bout picking some peas," she'd said merrily. "We'll start out slowly."

Forcing an enthusiastic smile to match her grandma's eagerness, Lillian wondered if she'd even make it to sunset this evening.

After locating a rump roast in the freezer, along with some potatoes and carrots, Lillian was now topping off the meal by preparing a salad, along with laying out some applesauce and jellies, which Grandma said was a necessary part of every meal. In between one of her many trips upstairs, Grandma had laid out one of the loaves of homemade bread on the table.

As the roast and vegetables simmered atop the wooden stove, Lillian wondered if coming here had been a bad idea—for several reasons. Evidently her grandfather was sicker than she suspected. Sickness made her uncomfortable. Cancer made her even more uncomfortable. People with cancer died. And death . . . well, death was something she hadn't come to terms with.

"Lillian, it sure does smell *gut* in here." Grandma had returned from another trip upstairs. Her hair was in the traditional bun beneath her white prayer *Kapp*, and several strands of gray had fallen forward.

"I hope you like it." She took a break from chopping the tomatoes for the salad and checked on the roast. "Grandpa's having a bad day, isn't he?"

Her grandma took a seat on the wooden bench and rested her

head in her hands. As if sensing Lillian's fears, she said, "*Ya*, he is. But they're not all bad days. Some days he does real *gut*. Then he gets down for a spell. Maybe tomorrow he'll be better."

Lillian didn't say anything. She was at a loss for words.

"Ah, there is Samuel to pick up the boy." Grandma nodded toward the window. The blind was open, and Lillian looked past the blooming begonias along the windowsill above the sink. She heard the clippity-clop of hooves and then Samuel directing Pete with a "Whoa, boy."

Foregoing her preparation of the salad, Lillian bolted toward the screen door, then turned back to face her grandma. "I thought maybe I'd invite Samuel and David for supper. Is that okay?"

Grandma's face scrolled into a questionable expression and Lillian feared she might be going to nix the idea, so she added, "Or, maybe, since Grandpa isn't feeling well today, it might not be a good day for . . ."

"I think that's a nice idea," her grandma interrupted. "I'll finish the salad. You go talk to Samuel and the boy."

"Great!" She flew out the door to catch Samuel before he carted David away.

Irma Rose dragged her tired body off the bench and started slicing the tomatoes. She peered out the window as Lillian jetted off toward Samuel and David. The glow in the girl's eyes had been unmistakable at the mention of Samuel's name. Now, her brow furrowing, Irma Rose watched her granddaughter near Samuel. Widowers Samuel's age were rare in their Old Order district. Choosing not to remarry by now was even rarer. It had been almost two years since Rachel's passing. Samuel should have already found a good Amish woman and remarried. That's the way it was done—to move on as quickly as possible. She'd hate to see a good man like Samuel get distracted.

Tending to a farm and raising a child was more than a full-time job. Samuel needed a good woman. An *Amish* woman. But as she watched her *Englisch* granddaughter through the window, laughing with Samuel and David, pangs of worry gnawed at her insides.

Samuel looked distracted indeed.

3

SAMUEL HEARD THE SCREEN DOOR OF THE FARMHOUSE slam and looked up to see Lillian darting across the yard toward them. He helped David stack the last of the chopped firewood, but his eyes remained on the *Englisch* woman.

"She's real pretty, Pop. Just like you said."

Samuel glanced over at his son, who was also watching the approaching woman. "And *she's* very different from us, David."

"And *we're* different from her," David said shrugging. "So?"

Samuel didn't say anything but waved at Lillian as she drew nearer.

"Hello!" she called out, catching her breath as she came to a stop before them. "I thought you both might like to stay for supper. I cooked a roast."

The woman was clearly proud of her work in the kitchen, and her bubbly spirit made the offer tempting. He and the boy hadn't eaten roast in a long time.

"Roast sounds real *gut*," he said. He put a hand on David's shoulder. "Are Jonas and Irma Rose up for it?"

"Grandma said you are both welcome."

"What do you think, David?" Samuel asked.

"Are you kidding me? That'd be a real treat. *Danki*, Ms. Lillian!"

"Go get cleaned up, David." Samuel motioned David toward the watering pump near the barn.

"How old is David?" she asked.

"He'll be twelve come August." Samuel started toward the farmhouse.

Lillian's face registered a variety of questioning expressions, and he assumed she must be curious about the Amish ways.

"I suppose he has a few years, then, before his *rumschpringe*," she said confidently, as if to impress him with her Pennsylvania Deitsch. Although . . . she was looking a bit too smug . . .

"What's a *rumschpringe*?" he asked.

Her face went blank. "Oh, I'm sorry. Maybe I pronounced it wrong or got it confused with something else. I thought it was when an Amish person turned sixteen and ventured out to explore the world, leading up to courtship."

She looked so confused, but he was having fun. He nodded thoughtfully. "Hmm, never heard of it."

As they neared the front porch, she turned toward him and planted her hands firmly on her hips. "Well, I could have sworn that's what *rumschpringe* was and—"

She caught sight of his face. "Are you messing with me, Samuel Stoltzfus?"

At her expression, he couldn't help but laugh.

"Shame on you," she fussed. But her eyes twinkled.

"I might be Plain, Lillian, but I do have a sense of humor, no?" He opened the door and motioned her inside ahead of him, grinning all the while.

Lillian placed the platter of roast surrounded by potatoes and carrots on the table. Grandma brought the salad and some chowchow.
Once they were all seated—all but Grandpa—Lillian enthusiastically motioned toward the food, "Dig in!" She was anxious to see
how everyone liked the meal.

All three of them stared blankly at her.

"Did I forget something?" She didn't think so.

With a significant look, her grandmother bowed her head,
followed by Samuel and David. *Ouch.* Chagrined, she lowered her
own head as Grandma blessed the food.

Following the prayer, Samuel seemed to sense her embarrassment and gallantly began a conversation. "David, it's been a while
since we've had such a fine meal laid before us." He winked at
Lillian. *Or did he?* It was quick, but she sure thought it was a
wink. Her stomach flipped again. She could feel a blush building
in her cheeks.

"*Ya*, Ms. Lillian, this is a fine meal," David said, stuffing a bite
of potatoes in his mouth.

"Thank you, David. I wish my grandpa was well enough to
join us, but he—"

They all heard a loud, gruff voice at the bottom of the stairs.
"The smell of *gut* food and the promise of *gut* company ain't
gonna keep me away."

"Jonas, I declare," Grandma reprimanded. "You should have
let me help you down those stairs."

Giving her an incredulous look, he asked, "What for?" When
he reached the kitchen, he rubbed his forehead and looked hard
at Lillian and then at Samuel. "What have we here?"

Feeling the need to defend her invitation, Lillian began rambling like a crazy person. "I, uh, invited Samuel and David for supper. David has been working so hard, and I figured Samuel probably worked hard all day too. And . . . and . . . maybe a good meal would be good for both of them. And I haven't had anyone to cook for in such a long time. And, uh, Grandma looked tired. And, by gosh . . . I don't know much about sewing, working in a garden, or much of the Amish ways . . . but I can cook!"

Lillian drew in a breath and held it. She wanted to crawl in a hole. Forks halted midway to mouths. No one was moving or talking. They were all just staring at her as if she was nuts. Maybe she was.

Grandpa's tired face rolled into the biggest smile Lillian had ever seen. "I *meant* . . . what have we *here*? What's for supper?"

Samuel and David sat motionless. Lillian glanced at her grandma, pleading for assistance.

"Lillian prepared supper, Jonas. She cooked a roast with potatoes and carrots."

"Our Lilly can cook?" Grandpa took a seat at the chair on the other end of the oblong table, across from Grandma.

"She's a *gut* cook too," Samuel said.

"*Danki*," Lillian said sheepishly.

"*Gut*! You're learning the *Deitsch wege*," Grandpa said. He helped himself to a slice of roast. "I told you, Irma Rose. The girl will come around to our ways in no time."

Lillian suspected her grandma doubted any type of transformation was in the works.

A distant trill sounded. *Oh, crud!* There couldn't have been a worse time for her cell phone to start ringing. Maybe no one had noticed.

"Is that a telephone I hear?" David asked, glancing toward the stairway.

"It's probably Mom." Lillian said sheepishly as the phone continued to ring. She hoped it was Mom and not Rickie. Mom being the lesser of the two evils. "I'll get it later."

Her grandmother looked up at her and started to say something, then hesitated. Lillian assumed Grandma was about to reprimand her for having the phone in the house, but evidently that wasn't what was on Grandma's mind.

"How is . . . um . . . how is your *mamm*?" Grandma looked back at her plate and shuffled her food around a bit.

"Same as always," Lillian said, knowing it was an undignified response. "I mean, she's fine."

Grandma nodded. An awkward silence followed. Everyone ate.

It wasn't long, though, before Grandpa spoke up. "So how was your first day, Lilly?"

"Well, I slept too late. But otherwise I tried to help out the best I could."

"Lillian had a *gut* first day. Cooking supper was a mighty big help too." Grandma smiled in her direction as she took a bite of carrots. "And the meal is delicious."

"*Appeditlich* it is!" Grandpa said. "But tomorrow maybe you should go to the neighboring town of Intercourse. There is lots to see in town, and you can pick me up some of that special root beer I like."

"Sure, that'd be great."

Lillian looked up to catch Samuel gazing in her direction. Then felt another set of eyes on both of them. She shot a look in

Grandpa's direction. He was grinning like a fat cat.

"Maybe Samuel can show you around? It's a far piece to town and I don't think you'd better be headin' off in the buggy so soon." He lifted his chin slightly, putting the question to Samuel.

It was hard to miss the look Grandma fired in her husband's direction. But before she could say anything, Samuel stepped up to the plate.

"I'd be happy to show Lillian around."

Irma Rose began clearing the dishes, watching Samuel and David thank Lillian for the meal and say their good-byes. She feared trouble was brewing—a concern that intensified as she watched Lillian head out the door with them toward Samuel's buggy.

While the thought of Samuel and their granddaughter developing a courtship was a farfetched notion, stranger things had happened in their district over the years. And now, thanks to her husband, a date was set for the following afternoon. She couldn't help but think of what the Good Book said: "Be ye not unequally yoked together with unbelievers: for what fellowship hath righteousness with unrighteousness? and what communion hath light with darkness?"

Someone would have to be pretty thick to miss the looks going on between Lillian and Samuel. They'd taken a bit of a fancy to each other. She would like nothing better than to see Samuel settle down with a good woman and for Lillian to settle down with a good Amish man and become part of their community. But such things just didn't happen. As much as she'd like the chance to make up for her failures with Sarah Jane, she knew anything more than a friendship between Samuel and Lillian was wrong. They were just too different. She'd need to keep a close eye on this and pray about it.

———◆———

Lillian watched Samuel and David climb into the box-shaped gray buggy, which was unlike the topless two-seater she'd ridden in with Samuel the day before. What was it about Samuel that piqued her interest so? The fact that he was Amish and mysterious to her way of life, or the fact that she was wildly attracted to him?

Not that it mattered much either way. She planned to be Amish to some extent—to avoid the use of modern conveniences, work hard, and find some sort of peace in her mixed-up mind. A quiet lifestyle far away from Rickie and her mother, void of the complications of the city, would bring her peace. She'd just wait for it to come. In the meantime, having a new Amish friend would be nice. But nothing more than that.

"See you at four-thirty tomorrow?" Lillian asked, reaffirming their plans for Samuel to pick her up the following day.

"What about me?"

"You can come too," Lillian said quickly, thinking it would seem less like a *date* with David along. She glanced at Samuel.

"David, you have evening chores to do." Samuel settled into his seat and prepared to give Pete a flick of the reins.

"I promise I'll get them all done." The boy glanced at Lillian, his eyes coaxing her to come to his defense.

"We don't have to stay too long, Samuel, if David needs to get home to do his chores."

Looking defeated by the two of them, Samuel nodded. "Then I will pick you and David up at four-thirty when he finishes his chores here. Since it's suppertime 'bout then, we can eat at the Family Cupboard Restaurant between Bird-In-Hand and Intercourse, if you want. Me and David treat ourselves every couple of weeks anyway. They sell the homemade root beer Jonas talked about near there. "

"Sounds great."

"*Danki* again for supper!" David yelled as Samuel turned the buggy around and headed down the dirt drive.

"I like Lillian, Pop," David told his father as they both walked up the stairs to bed.

Samuel started to tell his son he was sure Lillian was a fine woman but not to get any ideas.

David caught his hesitation. He nudged his father in the arm and snickered. "You like her, too, no?"

Samuel knew where his son was heading. "Of course I like her. She seems like a fine woman."

"No. I mean you *like* her," David said as he reached the door to his bedroom.

Might as well nip this right now, Samuel thought. "David, listen to me. The *Englisch* woman seems nice enough, but don't be gettin' any ideas. It's not like that. We're just gonna show her around town. She's Jonas and Irma Rose's *kinskind*, and it's a favor to them."

He could tell by the grin on David's face that he wasn't buying it. "She's funny. She's got lots of energy. And she sure is pretty."

"David, I already told you . . . Lillian is not like us. So get any crazy notions out of your head, boy." He tried to keep his tone firm. Last thing he needed was for his son to take a fancy to an *Englisch* woman. No question, the boy needed a mother. But while Levina and Sadie might not fit the bill, Lillian was certainly no better for him and his son. Maybe agreeing to show Lillian around town tomorrow was a mistake.

In an attempt to practice the Amish lifestyle and help Grandma more, Lillian got up and headed downstairs for breakfast at four-thirty. She cheated, though, setting the alarm on her cell phone. That was the one modern convenience she wasn't ready to give up—it was her only connection to the outside world. But the phone was slowly losing the charge.

She didn't hear Grandma get up with her grandpa during the night, and she was glad to see him joining them for breakfast.

"*Guder mariye,* Lilly," he belted. His jolliness so early in the morning warmed her heart. But then she saw Grandma's disappointment at her choice of attire. What was the problem with blue jeans and a T-shirt? *Scowl away,* she thought. *I'm not wearing one of those frumpy dresses on the peg upstairs.*

"Why doesn't my bread look as pretty as yours?" Lillian asked that afternoon. She and her grandma stood in the kitchen making bread.

"Maybe you didn't knead it enough."

"I sure *thought* I did. I pounded on that dough till my elbows couldn't take it anymore."

Grandma smiled. "I've had years of experience, Lillian. You'll get it with time. It's only your second day here and the first time to make bread, no?"

"Yeah, but I've always thought of myself as a pretty good cook." She glared down at the lopsided mound before her and frowned. "I'm sure disappointed in this bread. Might have to feed mine to the birds or something."

Grandma laughed. "The bread is fine, Lillian. I'm sure it tastes mighty *gut*." She patted Lillian on the arm.

"Where's Grandpa?"

"He's resting."

"Did he have a better night last night?"

"*Ya*, he did." Grandma popped another loaf into the wooden stove. "As I said, he has *gut* days and bad days."

"Grandpa's funny. He makes me laugh."

Her grandma closed the door on the stove and turned to face her. "You're a lot like him, Lillian. You have the fire in your belly, a zest for life."

Hmm. A compliment from the woman who seemed more than a little apprehensive she was there . . . with her blue jeans and cell phone in tow.

"Why did my mom leave, Grandma?"

Lillian wished immediately that she hadn't brought up the subject. The pain registered instantly on her grandma's face.

"Your mother was of age to choose whether or not to seek baptism into church membership. She chose to seek out the world." The tone in her voice indicated she'd rather not elaborate.

"But isn't that pretty rare?"

"'Train up a child in the way he should go: and when he is old, he will not depart from it,'" her grandma said softly. "I suppose we failed."

"It was her choice, Grandma. That doesn't mean you failed." Lillian took a seat at the kitchen bench, hoping her grandma would take a break and do the same. But she stayed occupied at the kitchen counter, rinsing dishes and avoiding Lillian's gaze.

"Your mother wasn't shunned, Lillian. She could have come to visit any time." She paused. "But we saw very little of her over the years. I wrote letters to her, but . . ."

"Mom made a lot of bad choices over the years, Grandma. It's just hard for me to understand how she grew up in such a faithful home and then turned from it. She never even took me to church."

Her grandma bent slightly over the sink, shook her head, and reached for her chest as if Lillian had stabbed her in the heart.

"I mean, I went to church with friends when I was growing up. I just didn't have any formal religious education."

This wasn't going well. The woman remained hunched over the sink, and Lillian was afraid she might be crying. "Grandma?" she said softly. "I didn't mean to upset you. I just have a lot of questions where my mother is concerned."

Her grandma slowly turned to face her. "As do I," she said softly, forcing a half smile before changing the subject. "Now, let's get this next loaf of bread into the oven."

———

Lillian headed to the woodpile where David was diligently splitting wood.

"Your dad should be here soon." She walked up behind David, who was stacking the chopped logs.

The boy spun around. "Hi, Lillian." Breaking from the chore at hand, his eyes were dancing with curiosity.

"What is it?" she asked as he stared a hole through her.

The boy hesitated, tilting his head to one side, pushing back his straw hat. "What's it like out there?"

Oh, boy. This was probably an area she shouldn't be delving into. How much had his father told him? She didn't want to speak out of place.

She said the first thing that came to mind. "Complicated."

"Huh?"

"It's complicated *out there*." Lillian said, letting out an absent-minded sigh, briefly reflecting on her own life. "And people just aren't always nice to each other."

"Why?"

"That's a good question."

She could tell David's young mind was awhirl. But his next question caught her completely off guard. "Do you have a boyfriend?"

"No," she answered, thinking about Rickie and surprised he hadn't called her by now. Knowing her brief good-bye letter had probably left him reeling, it was a welcome relief he hadn't contacted her.

"Why aren't you married? You seem kinda old."

"I'm twenty-seven. Is that *old*?"

David chuckled. "I guess not too much. Do you want to get married?"

"I don't know." Lillian frowned. She had watched her mother survive two bitter divorces, and the whole marriage thing had left a bad taste in her mouth. "Maybe."

David cocked his head to one side. His amazing blue eyes—just like his father's—squinted thoughtfully as he pondered a question he quite obviously wanted to ask her.

"What?" she asked, while wondering where Samuel was. It was after four-thirty by now.

"If Irma Rose and Jonas are Amish, why aren't you?"

"I'm *kinda* Amish," she said sheepishly. "I mean, my mother was raised Amish, and my grandparents are Amish." What a dumb answer, even in response to an eleven-year-old boy.

"I don't think you can be *kinda* Amish."

"I'm living on an Amish farm with my Amish grandparents. I gave up modern conveniences, and I even made bread today." No response from her young friend, who clearly needed more. "And I want to feel peace in my mind and in my heart."

He stared blankly at her. "Oh."

As he continued to study her, Lillian could tell there was more coming. "Why do you wear those boy breeches?"

Lillian glanced down at her blue jeans. "Well," she began, "I guess that's why I said I'm *kinda* Amish. I'm working on it . . . slowly."

"Oh."

Hoping that had satisfied him, she glanced down the dirt drive toward the road and looked at her watch. "Wonder where your dad is? It's almost five o'clock."

"I better get cleaned up." She watched while David stowed the axe near the woodpile and headed toward the water pump by the barn. As he splashed water on his face, she thought about what his life must be like. So Plain. So uncomplicated. How she wanted that for herself.

"My *daed* is never late," David said, drying his hands against his trousers as he met her near the farmhouse.

"He's late today." She smiled and took a seat in one of the wooden rockers on the porch. David sat down on the porch step.

"Hum," he said after a while. "Hope nothin's wrong."

"Probably just running late."

The sound of a running horse carried across the field. Lillian and David moved toward the yard. As Samuel's buggy peeled around the corner and onto the driveway, she figured he was rushing because he was late. But as clods of dirt flew from the speed of the horse's hooves and Samuel's face came into focus, Lillian knew this was more than trying to make up for lost time. Something was wrong.

4

SAMUEL SLOWED PETE TO A STOP. "WE HAVE TO HURRY, David," he yelled without addressing Lillian. "Ivan said Lilly's birthin's gone breech."

"Huh?" Lillian asked David. Instinctively she followed him to the buggy.

"Lilly's our cow!" The boy picked up his pace. Lillian continued right behind him.

"I'm sorry, Lillian," Samuel said as she reached his side of the buggy. "We'll have to schedule our trip to town for another day."

"Your cow is delivering breech?" She leaned in toward him, scoping out how she was going to crawl into the backseat. "I've never seen a cow giving birth. Can I come? And who is Ivan?" She paused. "And your cow's name is *Lilly*?"

Samuel's mouth twitched to one side and his brows drew inward. He was either irritated or amused. She wasn't sure. When he finally did open his mouth to speak, she was fairly certain he was going to deny her request to go see Lilly the Cow have her baby. But luckily, David had other plans.

Hurriedly, he jumped out of the passenger seat of the buggy and motioned for Lillian to crawl into the backseat, requiring Samuel to exit the buggy in order to fold the front seat forward.

Samuel moved with hesitancy, so she wasted no time crawling in the back. She didn't want him to change his mind.

David was barely back in the front seat when Samuel motioned Pete to make a U-turn and head down the dirt drive. Once they reached the road, it was full-speed ahead.

"Wow," she said, more to herself than anything. She had no idea the buggy could move so fast.

Samuel wondered what Ivan would say when he showed up at his farm with an *Englisch* woman. A chatty *Englisch* woman, at that.

"Where are we going? To your farm? Is Lilly your cow or Ivan's cow? Now, who's Ivan? She'll be okay, right?" Lillian paused and drew in a breath as she grabbed on to the back of the seat to steady herself from the increasing speed. "*Lilly.* Lilly will be okay, right? And her calf too?"

"I don't know about Lilly yet," Samuel responded.

David started giggling before Samuel could attempt to answer the rest of her questions. Samuel feared what the boy might say. Rightfully so.

"You have the same name as our *cow.* Jonas calls you *Lilly.*" His son turned around to face her, snorting with delight, and Samuel wondered if the boy was offending her. But then Lillian laughed.

"Yep! I certainly do," she said. "And the first time you make a *mooing* sound toward me, we're gonna have a problem." She playfully poked David's arm, and he grinned. "Now, who is Ivan?"

"Ivan is my older brother, and we're going to his place," Samuel answered, pleased to see his son enjoying her company but a little worried just the same. "Some of our cattle graze on his land." He glanced briefly over his shoulder. Her face was aglow with anticipation.

"I've never seen a cow give birth before," she said. "I hope everything goes okay for Lilly. Thank you for letting me tag along."

Letting you? Samuel didn't know he had a say-so. He hadn't had the time to waste arguing with either of them. He had a cow in distress.

"There's Ivan's place." He pointed to his brother's farm toward the left.

"This will be a first for me," she repeated.

Samuel didn't see what all the fuss was about.

Lillian wondered why she rambled on like a silly teenager every time she was with Samuel. She made a mental note not to do that any more, then concentrated on her surroundings.

Ivan's farmhouse looked a lot like her grandparents' farmhouse—white with a large porch. Although amongst the greenery were flowering blooms, unlike at her grandparents' place. She'd assumed Grandma had given up gardening when Grandpa got so sick. Maybe planting some flowers would be a good project for her to undertake at their own farm—to brighten the place up. She'd heard that gardening brought peacefulness.

As they pulled up the dirt driveway, Lillian honed in on a man in a straw hat hovering over a cow out in the pasture. Standing beside him was a woman dressed in a brown dress and black apron. The traditional white *Kapp* held her dark hair in a bun underneath. They waved as Samuel's buggy drew near.

"Poor Lilly," David said, suddenly realizing the gravity of the situation. "Bet she's in a bad way 'bout now."

"She's hurtin' for sure." Samuel hopped out of the buggy and folded the seat up. He extended his arm to help Lillian step down. She noticed his strong hands.

She must have misgauged how far down the ground was because falling into his arms was an unplanned action that caught them both off guard. His arms around her waist . . . her head burrowed against his firm chest . . .

However, Samuel moved fast, freeing himself of any contact with her like she had a contagious disease he didn't want to contract.

"I'm sorry," she sheepishly said. "I guess I lost my footing."

"No harm done," he replied nonchalantly. But Lillian caught his eyes veering in his brother's direction. He cleared his throat. "Better go tend to Lilly."

She followed him to the pasture, where David was already leaning down beside the ailing animal. The cow made an agonizing sound. Maybe witnessing the birth of a calf was a bad idea—especially one that was having this much trouble entering the world.

"Calf is backwards, hind end first with both hind legs bent," Ivan said as he leaned down beside David. "Gonna have to turn it around and pull it out. I got some baling twine right here that we can tie around the limbs once we get it where it needs to be. It's gonna take both of us, Samuel, to pull."

Ivan looked up as if just noticing Lillian.

She smiled. "Hi. I'm Lillian." She offered him her hand. He rose slightly to reciprocate but didn't follow through. Instead he eyed his hands, which were clearly not fit for shaking, and shrugged. He glanced at Samuel and then at the woman standing nearby.

"I'm Ivan. This is *mei fraa*, Katie Ann." The woman nodded politely but didn't move from her spot a few feet away.

"This is Jonas and Irma Rose's *kinskind*," Samuel said, looking slightly uncomfortable.

Both Ivan and Katie Ann looked surprised. "I didn't know Jonas and Irma Rose had a granddaughter," Katie Ann said. "How long will you be visitin'?"

"I'm not sure. I'd like to find out more about the Amish lifestyle since I am Amish," Lillian answered. "Amish by birth," she added, noticing the confused looks on their faces.

Ivan and Katie Ann turned to Samuel, apparently waiting for further clarification from him.

David spoke up before anyone could gather their thoughts. "She wants to feel peace in her mind and heart." He nodded his head up and down as if to tell the others that it was a fact and didn't warrant further discussion. But when they all looked like they might have a thing or two to throw into the conversation just the same, poor Lilly let out a wail of a *moo*.

"You goin' in or me?" Ivan asked his brother. "This ol' girl ain't gonna be able to take much more."

"I'll go in, turn the calf, and get it right," Samuel said. "Then we'll tie on with the twine and pull. Lilly won't have the strength."

Go in . . . ? Lillian watched as Samuel rolled up his sleeve and soaped up. *No way.*

She cringed as she watched him go to work. Poor Lilly had been in distress before, but this new sound escaping from her was indicative that his arm was in a place it didn't need to be. It was a gut-wrenching, agonizing, horrible, mooing sound. And she could swear the cow's eyes were rolling back in her head.

"Stop!" she finally said. "Stop! She can't take any more."

They all looked at her with sympathy, but it was Katie Ann who walked to her side and spoke up. "They gotta do this, Lillian. Otherwise, the calf will die."

Death. She was suddenly very uncomfortable. This was a bad idea. "No, no . . . of course," she said. "I know they have to do this. But can't you give her something for the pain?"

Ivan and Katie Ann looked at each other.

"I mean, don't they have drugs for this type of thing?" she asked, when no one commented.

Samuel continued working. Now he called out. "Ready. Give me the twine."

Lillian looked at Katie Ann. This couldn't be right.

"They gotta hurry and get that calf out, and it would take poor Lilly too long at this point," Katie Ann said. "It's the only way to try to save them both."

Lillian watched as David stroked the cow's head. "It's okay, girl. Everything is gonna be just fine."

"Ivan, I'm ready," Samuel said, standing up with a double strand of twine in his hand.

Ivan grabbed the twine with his brother. Lillian couldn't believe she'd opted for this type of adventure.

It seemed like an eternity of pulling and tugging. And all the while poor Lilly voiced her objections. But when two front legs emerged, followed by a tiny little calf's head, it was a sight to see. And Lillian was thrilled.

Ivan brushed past her and briefly inspected the calf. After he nodded to Samuel that all was well, Lillian dropped to the ground to welcome the new baby.

"Hello," she said softly as she stroked the slithery, wet skin. "Look at you." What an amazing event. She had just arrived in Lancaster County and already she had witnessed the miracle of birth. Fabulous. Just fabulous. "You are so beautiful," she said, leaning in closer to the new baby. "Welcome!" Ah. It was a good feeling. A peaceful feeling.

"Look, guys!" When no one responded, she looked toward them all, huddled near Lilly's head. She knew immediately what was wrong. "No," she said softly. "No."

"Poor girl just couldn't take it," Ivan said, patting David on the shoulder.

"No," Lillian repeated softly. "What about her calf?"

Samuel sat down beside her. "The baby is *gut*," he said with a tenderness in his tone she hadn't expected.

She looked at the mother cow. Someone should close her gaping eyes. She'd never gotten to see her calf.

"Some things are just His way and not meant to be," Samuel said, still in a soothing tone.

"*Whose* way?" Lillian blurted, tired of them writing off everything as God's will around here. *Don't say it*, she thought.

"God's," Samuel said as he gave her a questioning look.

That was enough. She'd had enough about God's will. First it was God's will that Samuel's wife died so young. Next it was Grandpa's cancer. She would tell them exactly what she thought about God's *will*.

She was prepared to do just that when she glanced at David.

His face registered a pain far greater than her own. He was struggling to fight back tears, and his eyes were pleading with her. Pleading for what, she wasn't sure. She walked to where he was sitting near Lilly's head and sat down beside him.

"Where there's life, there's death," he said softly with a maturity beyond his years. He tried to choke back any sign he might possibly cry.

"Yes," Lillian replied as she looked into his young eyes, unhardened by worldly ways.

It was a quiet ride back to Irma Rose and Jonas's farm. Samuel's heart hurt for David and their friend. Understandably, David was taking it pretty hard. He'd had Lilly for four years. He'd been there when she was born. When she'd grown, Samuel had wanted to take her to auction, but David wouldn't hear of it. He was attached to the old girl, so Samuel didn't push it.

His new *Englisch* friend, on the other hand, didn't even know Lilly. But she was taking it hard too.

"Here we are," he said as he pulled in front of Jonas and Irma Rose's farmhouse.

"I'm so sorry," she said, shaking her head.

"Sorry for what?" Her voice was the saddest thing Samuel had ever heard.

"About Lilly." She shook her head again. "I know it was just a cow. And I didn't *know* the cow. But it made me incredibly sad just the same."

"There's no need to be apologizin', Lillian," he said, finding it a bit odd she'd react this strongly. "With so many farms in

Texas, I'm surprised you've never seen a calf birthed. And this
happens sometimes. The momma dying."

"I live in the *city*," she said with a hint of irritation.

Samuel shrugged.

As he stepped out of the buggy, their eyes met before she
hopped down. How beautiful she looked, he thought, even with
her sad eyes. She looked lost on a whole bunch of levels.

"I promise I won't fall this time," she said, forcing a smile as
she stepped out of the buggy with ease. "Thank you for allowing
me to come with you."

Samuel nodded and watched her walk to David's side of the
buggy.

"I'm sorry about your cow, David."

David nodded his head. "*Danki*, Lillian." Then to Samuel's
surprise, David hugged his new *Englisch* friend. Alarms began going
off in Samuel's head.

Lillian avoided David and Samuel for the next two days. She
was embarrassed about her reaction to Lilly's death. It was
understandable for David to be so upset. It was *his* cow, and he
was a child. But she was unsure what Samuel must think of her
at this point. He definitely gave her funny looks sometimes. Still,
after busying herself in the kitchen with Grandma for two days,
she was ready to venture out. She needed a break.

As Grandma had warned, they had incorporated more activities into their daily routine. Lillian felt like a professional canner
at this point. They'd made red-beet jelly, rhubarb jam, apple-
cider jelly, and apricot preserves. It was somewhat tedious at first

and she had to learn which recipes required hot packing and which ones required cold packing, but she had to admit, she was enjoying it. And to her surprise, she enjoyed the lengthy conversations with Grandma.

She especially enjoyed hearing how her grandparents met and about their wedding—an all-day affair that sounded incredible.

"Your *daadi* Jonas was a handsome man," Grandma said proudly. "And he still is in my eyes." Her eyes twinkled when she spoke of their younger years. Although Lillian noticed her grandma avoided any conversations having to do with her mother, even when Lillian tried to nudge the conversation in that direction.

The canning came easy. And she was getting the hang of the bread making. The sewing was another story. Getting the treadle machine to function at the right speed while trying to sew a straight line—or worse, a curved line—was a challenge. She felt relieved when Grandma said that might be a chore she'd keep for herself.

"Grandma, I think I'll go to town today." She held up a loaf of bread ready for the stove. "Hey! This one looks much better."

"*Ya*, much better. I told you that you'd get the feel of it." Grandma accepted the bread and headed for the stove. "It's a long walk to Intercourse and Bird-In-Hand. It would take you half a day on foot. You and Samuel didn't plan another trip?"

"Uh, I haven't actually talked to them since Lilly died."

Grandma closed the door of the wooden stove and turned to face her. "I would take you myself, but it wonders me if Jonas would be doin' well unattended."

"How far is it?"

"It's a good piece. You go up Black Horse Road, cross over Lincoln Highway into Beiler's Bed and Breakfast drive. Use it as a throughway to get to Leacock Road. Just keep goin'. When Jonas is havin' one of his better days, we'll saddle up Jessie and you can practice driving the buggy."

"Really? That would be great! Jessie is a beautiful animal." Lillian went to the barn every afternoon and lavished attention on the horse. And how fun it would be to drive the buggy to town.

Grandma's face twisted. Lillian knew exactly what was causing her displeasure.

"Maybe you ought not ride the buggy dressed that way, Lillian."

She watched as her grandma scanned her attire from head to toe. It was the same as it was every day—blue jeans and a T-shirt. Today, a red T-shirt. And Lillian still didn't see a problem.

Oh, I see. You'll let me drive the buggy if I wear one of the frumpy dresses on the peg upstairs. No deal.

"Well, I'll be walking today, anyway," she said, turning away from the woman before she told her exactly what she thought of those dresses. All the Amish women wore them. There was no sense of style, little choice of color. And they hung halfway to the floor! It was the one Amish custom she was not going to partake in. Wasn't the fact that she didn't wear makeup or jewelry enough? *The blue jeans stay.*

"Glad to see you have some better walking shoes." She pointed to Lillian's tennis shoes. "We can talk about learnin' you how to handle Jessie on another day when Jonas is feeling better." Her

brows jutted upward as if wanting a commitment that Lillian
would indeed wear the dress at some point in the future.

Time for a change of subject. "I thought maybe I might plant some
flowers in the flowerbeds and around the trees in the yard," she
said. "Is that okay with you?"

Grandma lit up. "I think that would be *gut*. I've been telling
myself to make time for tending to the yard. But with Jonas and
all . . ." She shrugged and glanced upstairs. "We have accounts in
town. You can charge the flowers, and there's a scooter in the barn
you better use. It was your *mamm's*. The towns of Paradise, Bird-In-
Hand, and Intercourse are close enough together to use a scooter.
Lots of Amish use them. It's much too far for walkin' on foot." Her
tone indicated she was willing to forget the blue jeans for now.

"That'll be fun. I'll use the scooter and get some flowery
plants in town."

"You won't be able to tote much back. There's a basket on
the front of the scooter, though, that you can use for carryin'
your buys."

"Maybe I'll get a ride back from some nice Amish person, like
I did on my way here." She thought of Samuel, starting to regret
avoiding him for the past couple of days.

Grandma rubbed her hands on her apron, her mouth pursing
in obvious indecision.

"What, Grandma?"

"Samuel came callin' for you yesterday."

"Came calling? When?" *And why didn't you tell me?*

"He came to the door yesterday. Him and David both," she
said, sounding fearful she'd made a mistake by not telling Lillian.
"You were resting upstairs."

"I was reading a book." Her tone was indicative of her frustration at not being told she had a visitor.

Grandma began to pace across the wooden slatted kitchen floor. "I was worried that you might have taken a fancy to him." She shrugged. "I don't want to see you get hurt."

Lillian chuckled. "Grandma, I can take care of myself. And, I assure you, if Samuel 'came callin', he was only being friendly. Maybe he wanted to apologize for not being able to take me to town," she speculated. "Did you think he might have taken a fancy—so to speak—to *me*?"

"Oh, *ya!*" Grandma belted. "Yes, I did. And it worried me too. The both of you are very different." She shook her head.

"It's okay, Grandma," she said smugly, feeling a newfound sense of pleasure that Samuel had come looking for her. "It will be fine."

"*Ach*, I know that *now*. Katie Ann came by earlier to bring me some vegetables from her and Ivan's garden. She explained to me that Samuel was courting Levina Esh. She saw them having lunch today." She waved her hand. "It just feared me for a minute that he might be thinking of courting you. I saw you both laughing together the other day and my mind ran amuck about it. But now I know it was just silly thinkin' on my part."

"Oh," Lillian said softly. "That's wonderful for him . . . and *Levina*." She whipped around and headed toward the screen door. "I'm off to town."

As the door slammed, she bolted down the porch steps, feeling anything but wonderful.

5

SAMUEL WAS ADMIRING THE CRAFTSMANSHIP ON A FINE Amish table he hoped to purchase someday. Someday when he had a wife and more children. The shop was his favorite in Bird-In-Hand, and his friend Big Jake was a mighty fine woodworker. But the table was too big for just him and David. Maybe someday he would see fit to make the purchase.

"Why don't you just buy that table, Samuel?" Sadie Fisher asked as she approached Samuel. "You've been eyeing that thing for months."

"Hello, Sadie," he said, not feeling up to making small talk. He'd done enough of that with Levina earlier in the day when she pinned him down for lunch. No more going shopping on Thursdays for him.

"How've you been, Samuel?"

"*Gut*, Sadie. And you?"

"*Gut, gut*," she said, taking a step backward and eyeing him up and down. "Samuel Stoltzfus! You are thinning up. Do I need to come over and fix you and David some of my special meatloaf? And maybe a lemon meringue pie for dessert?"

"No need, Sadie," he said, forcing a smile. "Me and the boy do just fine."

Looking only a tad defeated, she said, "Oh, I think my cookin' would plump you right up. It's just what you and David need." She leaned closer to him and grinned.

There couldn't have been a better time for Lillian Miller to pull up on a scooter.

"Hello, Samuel," Lillian said, out of breath as she approached him and Sadie. He was glad to see her happy. Last time he'd seen her, she was a mess. "I don't know what Grandma was thinking. It was a long way to get here, even on a scooter." She curled her bottom lip, blew upward, and cleared a strand of wayward hair dangling across her face.

He glanced at Sadie and then back at Lillian. The two women seemed to be waiting for an introduction. There was a tension in the air he couldn't quite put his finger on. He should have never hesitated. He should have introduced them right off. Lillian beat him to the punch, though.

"And you must be Levina?" Lillian asked. "I'm Lillian Miller." She extended her hand to Sadie.

Samuel cringed when he saw the fire blazing in Sadie's eyes. He opened his mouth to make the correction, but Lillian wasn't through. "My grandma told me how the two of you were a couple—or 'courting' I believe is what she said. And she also said—"

"This is Sadie!" he quickly interrupted when he saw Sadie's mouth draw up and her hands land on her hips.

Lillian dropped her extended hand. "Oh . . ."

What she was smiling about, Samuel would never know.

"My grandma said you came to see me yesterday. I'm sorry I missed you. I was upstairs reading." Lillian's smile broadened. "Maybe you could come by later?"

Sadie ripped him to shreds with her piercing eyes. And yet, for the first time since he'd known her, Sadie Fisher was speechless.

Once again, his *Englisch* friend was not. "I just want to apologize again about the other night, the way I carried on when the cow died. How's the little calf, though?" Her eyes lit up, and Samuel couldn't help but smile.

But venom was spewing from Sadie's direction. Ignoring Lillian, she turned to Samuel. "Samuel Stoltzfus, exactly who *are* you courting these days?"

"I'm not courting *anyone*," he said cautiously, glancing back and forth between the two women. Although he kept his focus pretty much on Sadie. She was mad as fire and a mite scary looking.

Lillian spoke up first. "Uh, I'm sorry if I caused a problem. I just—"

"I best be gettin' on," Sadie interrupted, making sure her voice drowned out Lillian. She straightened her apron and held her chin high as she allowed herself a long hard look at Lillian. "Nice to meet you, Lillian," she finally said and walked off. No, *stomped* off was more like it.

"Sorry," Lillian mumbled when Sadie was out of earshot.

"For what?"

"Uh, for messing things up with your lady friend."

"Sadie and Levina are both widows in our district. And I am a widower. Need I say more?"

Of course he needed to say more.

"So, which one is it? Sadie or Levina?"

"Neither," he answered. "Why does it interest you so much?"

He reached up and stroked his beard, sporting a curious smile. He was dallying with her. Her insides flipped, and her cheeks took on a tingly sensation, which she knew meant they were red as her T-shirt. "It doesn't," she snapped in a much too defensive tone.

"Coulda fooled me."

"Well, aren't you a little full of yourself, Samuel! I believe you are the one who came to see me yesterday." She shot him a catty smile.

"David wanted to make sure you were doin' okay. You were so upset when Lilly died." His expression shifted to a look of concern, and he leaned down toward her as if to see if she really was all right.

"I'm fine. And, as I said, I'm sorry for my emotional display."

"No apology necessary." He tipped his hat. "Well, we're in town. Want me to show you around?"

"I guess," she said, unsure what she wanted from the handsome Samuel Stoltzfus. "I actually want to buy some flowers. Grandma said she didn't have time to do much gardening with Grandpa so sick. I thought it might be nice to brighten the place up."

"Do you know anything about planting flowers?"

"How hard can it be? Dig a hole and put them in."

He shook his head. "It's May. Do you know what *kind* of flowers to plant this time of year?"

"Uh . . . I guess not."

"Come on. I'll help you."

Two hours later, Samuel helped Lillian load flats of colorful fo-
liage into his buggy.

"How exactly were you going to get all this home, since you
scooted all the way here?" He lifted the scooter up and placed it
in the backseat.

"I knew you'd come around and give me a ride," she said in a
playful tone. Her eyes flashed alongside her smile.

Something twisted in Samuel's gut. He shook his head as she
handed him a flat of flowers to store in the back of the buggy.

"What?" she asked.

"Nothing," he mumbled, suddenly reticent.

"Oh, come on," she said, poking him lightly on the arm. "Must
be *something* on your mind."

He shook his head. "No, nothing." After loading the last of the
flowers, he walked around and opened the buggy door on her side.

"*Danki!*" she said as she hopped in. There was that childlike
enthusiasm again—a quality he found mighty attractive.

Which was the whole problem. Lillian Miller stirred things
in him better left alone. She was beautiful. She was interesting.
And she was off limits.

It was almost four-thirty. He better pick up the pace to get
her home and pick up David.

───

"Jonas, the three of them are *still* sittin' out by the barn," Irma
Rose said as she peeped out the window. "They've been out there
almost three hours. Since right after supper. For goodness sakes,
what could they have to talk about for so long?"

"Irma Rose, you might be gettin' thick around the midsection, but I didn't think you were gettin' thick in your head too." He chuckled. "Our young *kinskind* is being courted by Samuel. Now quit your spying."

She was glad Jonas was having a good day, but his sharp tongue was about to get him in a mess of trouble.

"Ouch, Irma Rose." Jonas snickered. "You're hurtin' me with that look you be givin' me."

"This is serious, Jonas. Samuel is courting Levina Esh. Katie Ann saw them having lunch today. It isn't proper for him to be spending so much time with Lillian." Their *Englisch* granddaughter didn't even go to church. And she couldn't see fit to wear a more appropriate outfit either. Lillian was a high-spirited, lovely child. Irma Rose wanted nothing more than for her to be happy. But she had seen Samuel and the boy suffer. This just had trouble written all over it.

"Are you sure Samuel is courting Levina? Both those widows—Levina and Sadie— have been chasin' that Samuel for a long time." Jonas chuckled. "He don't seem to want to be caught by neither of 'em."

"Katie Ann sure saw fit to tell me about their lunch today."

"That don't mean they're courtin'." Jonas shook his head.

"It just scares me, Jonas. I don't want to see our Lillian or Samuel and the boy get hurt." She took another peek out the window.

"Irma Rose," Jonas said in a softer tone. "It ain't up to you."

"I know." She walked away from the window. "But I'm still going to worry."

Lillian was impressed with how little it seemed to take for Samuel and David to be happy. Their Plain, uncomplicated lifestyle provided them with everything they needed. Despite her worldly ways, she'd never been able to achieve the one thing they seemed to possess in abundance: peace.

The one thing both father and son talked about with pride was their love of the land and sense of stewardship to care for God's creation.

"Tilling God's earth and providing plentiful crops is an important part of our lives," Samuel said now. "With more of our farmers having to venture out into the *Englisch* workplace, some of us are still blessed to harvest our land and enjoy the fruits of our labor."

Lillian thought hard about what he was saying. "Tomorrow, I'm going to plant all those flowers I got in town today," she said.

"It'll be nice to see some flowers here again."

"What are we going to do tomorrow, Pop?" David enthusiastically asked, as if assuming the three of them would spend time together.

Evidently, that was *not* Samuel's plan. "David, you've already missed today's chores. I think it'd be best if we headed home tomorrow after your work is finished here." Samuel lifted himself from the tree stump he was sitting on. "As a matter of fact, maybe we can salvage some chores tonight."

"But, Pop—" David protested, only to have Samuel interrupt him.

"Lillian, please thank Irma Rose again for that fine meal."

She stood up from the wooden chair she had placed in the

front yard earlier. "I will," she said softly, trying to mask her disappointment.

Hot and cold. One minute Samuel was warm and kind and seemed pleased by her presence. The next minute, he was formal and withdrawn. Just like earlier today, in town. Yet despite his quiet demeanor on the ride home, they'd had a good evening, laughing and talking about all sorts of things. She felt like after tonight she knew him and David much better.

And yet . . . hot and cold. Samuel could turn on a dime.

"*Ya*, we best be on our way, David," he said as he extended his hand to Lillian. "Bye, Lillian."

His tone was curt, as if forcing distance between them. But as she latched onto his hand, she thought she felt him hold it longer than normal. Maybe she was just imagining that.

———

Samuel could sense that something was on David's mind. He hadn't said a word since they left Lillian. He pulled back on the reins and slowed Pete to a trot. "It was a mighty fine meal, *ya?*" he asked.

The boy nodded but kept staring ahead.

"Something on your mind?" He slowed Pete even more, to allow a chance for the two of them to talk. Once at home, they'd need to work on the chores they had let go to spend time at the Millers' farm.

David shrugged. "Nothing, I guess."

Samuel wasn't convinced. "You like Lillian, don't you?" He suspected whatever was on David's mind had to do with her.

"You like her too!" The boy's tone was defensive and bordering on angry.

"Of course I like her. She's a very nice person, and—"

"No, I mean you *like* her, and you don't want to admit it!"

"Whoa, boy," Samuel instructed Pete as they pulled into the yard. He turned to David, surprised at his son's tone of voice. "Boy, what is goin' on in that head of yours?"

Children start getting rebellious at this age—he remembered his own temperament at that period. But David had never taken such a sharp tone with him before.

"I think you should court Lillian." He turned and faced Samuel with a look that almost demanded he consider the notion.

Samuel opened his mouth to reprimand the boy for thinking *he* could choose a courting partner for his pop. But seeing the look in David's glassy eyes stopped him short. Clearly the boy had taken a hard fancy to Lillian.

Another reason they should stop spending time with the woman.

"David," he began slowly, "it wouldn't be proper. She's from a worldly place, and it just wouldn't be right." He shook his head.

The boy instantly cheered up, obviously sensing Samuel's defenses were down. "She's gonna come around, Pop. You'll see. It's just gonna take her some time to learn about our ways. She wants to make a change. Maybe we can help her."

"It's not that easy, David."

David crawled out of the buggy and turned to face Samuel, who was still sitting and pondering his son's words. He seemed to be waiting for his dad to go on, to give him a better reason not to pursue a courtship with this woman who was so different from them.

His son knew to reject pride, arrogance, and haughtiness. The boy had been studying the *Ordnung*. How could he explain to the boy that submitting to the will of God does not come easily to an outsider? It wasn't always easy for an insider.

"'Come out from among them, and be ye separate, saith the Lord,'" Samuel said, hoping to remind the boy of their need to resist influences from the outside world.

David smiled. "'And be not conformed to this world: but be ye transformed by the renewing of your mind, that ye may prove what is that good, and acceptable, and perfect, will of God,'" he responded proudly. "Lillian just needs our help to find her way. That's all. We're not conforming to *her* world, we're just giving her a hand to renew her spirit and find that peace of heart and mind she wants."

Samuel stared at his son with a combination of admiration and fear. Where had the boy learned of such things at such a young age? It was a maturity way past his years. But leave it to a boy his age to find a loophole in the Scriptures. "It's not that easy." Samuel repeated softly. But David was already on his way into the farmhouse.

It was nearing eight o'clock when Lillian headed upstairs. She knew Grandma and Grandpa were already in bed. As she plopped down across her quilted counterpane, she looked around her small room. "Sure would be nice to watch some TV," she whispered. Glancing at the dark-colored dresses on the peg, she frowned. Sadie had sported one of the Plain dresses—a dark green one—while she was goggling all over Samuel earlier.

Lillian realized she'd certainly messed things up for any potential courtship between Samuel and Sadie. She wasn't having much regret about it. The more time she spent around Samuel, the more time she wanted to spend with him. She just wasn't sure if the feeling was mutual.

A familiar trill. She grabbed her cell phone on the first ring, hoping she hadn't wakened her grandparents. She was glad she'd thought to borrow a shopkeeper's electricity to charge up the phone while she browsed in the market today—awkward, to be sure, but he hadn't seemed to mind. And she just wasn't ready to part with this last modern convenience.

"Hi, Mom."

"Lillian, how are you?"

Something was wrong. Lillian could tell by her mother's tone. She'd heard it before, way too many times. "What's wrong, Mom?"

"What makes you think something is *wrong*? I just called to check on you . . . and your grandpa."

"I'm fine, and Grandpa had a pretty good day today." She waited for her mother to get to the point.

"Good, good."

When her mother didn't offer up the reason for the call, Lillian decided to step up to the plate. "Mom, I want to know why you left the Amish faith and chose to go out on your own." She knew her tone was demanding, but she needed an answer.

"Lillian, I have too much going on to get into this with you right now." Mom's tone was equally as sharp.

"You've *always* had too much going on to talk to me about it, Mom. And Grandma doesn't seem to want to talk about it either."

"You asked your grandma about it? Don't do that, Lillian," Mom exclaimed.

Realizing she struck a nerve with her mother, she went on. "I will ask her again if you don't tell me what happened. Because I know *something* happened, Mom."

"I chose to leave, Lillian. That's all. It was my choice to choose baptism into the church or to leave the Old Order district."

"Then why do I get the impression there's more to it than either you or Grandma are telling me?"

"I have no idea." Her tone was still sharp, and once again Lillian could tell they were heading down a bad road. "Now, tell me about your grandfather. Is he in a lot of pain?"

"Why don't you come see for yourself, Mom? He's *your* father." It was a mean thing to say, especially since she knew her mother wouldn't come. And even more so, if she was honest with herself, because she didn't want her mom there.

"Did I raise such a hateful child?"

"*Raise?* Is that what you're calling it these days?"

"Lillian, let's don't do this. Why does everything have to be a fight with you?" She could hear her mother's voice crack, but she wasn't sure if it was for effect. There was another reason for her mom's call. She just hadn't gotten to the point yet.

"I don't want to fight with you, Mom."

"Sweetie, I don't want to fight with you either. The reason for my call was to check on you and your grandparents, and also to tell you that I'm mailing you a thousand dollars. I know I owe you much more, but I have sent you what I could for now, to help you while you're there."

Lillian silently hung her head.

"It might be a couple more weeks before I can send you some more," her mother went on when Lillian didn't respond. "My new job at the employment agency pays commission for every placement. It turns out I match up employees with employers quite well."

"Thanks, Mom," Lillian said. Guilt rose to the surface. Why couldn't she just once give her mom the benefit of the doubt? Probably because history had a way of repeating itself. Sarah Jane Miller had filled her life with promises and disappointments. She was certain the phone call was because her mom needed something from her.

"Now, I have to go get ready for dinner. Paul is taking me to the new Italian restaurant in town. Things are going fabulously well with us." Her mother paused. Lillian closed her eyes, shook her head, and sighed. "Anyway, the offer still stands for you to come and stay with us, sweetie."

"I like it here, Mom."

"What about all the things you've had to do without? Television, for starters."

"I miss TV sometimes, but I stay busy. I've learned how to make homemade bread and jellies, and I even sew a little. There's tons to do around here. Tomorrow I'm going to plant some flowers. And Grandpa is a hoot." She laughed, thinking about some of the things her grandfather said sometimes.

"You're a lot like your grandfather," her mother said lovingly.

"That's what Grandma says." *Odd.* Was this turning into a

normal conversation? Maybe this would be the new norm. That would be a welcome change.

"Your grandma? She's well?" Her mother's tone resonated with the same sense of hesitation Lillian heard when her grandmother asked about her daughter.

"She's tired a lot from taking care of Grandpa."

"Are you wearing the Amish dresses?" Her mother chuckled, which hit Lillian the wrong way. She might not want to wear the frumpy dresses, but she didn't want her mother making fun of them either.

"No. But Grandma sure wants me to." She glanced at the three dresses on the pegs—dark blue, dark green, and a deep purple. "It's hard to picture *you* wearing them."

"I didn't know any different. They are a far cry from the black pants outfit I will be wearing to dinner. Which reminds me, I need to go get ready."

The conversation was going so well. It felt good to have a normal one with her mother. Maybe she would go out on a limb. "Mom, I met a man here."

"Really? So soon?" Lillian could hear shower water turn on in the background. She knew her time was limited.

"His name is Samuel. Samuel Stoltzfus."

Lillian heard the shower water shut off. "Lillian, listen to me," her mother said, pausing. "That is an Amish name. Please tell me you don't have a crush on an Amish man."

Oh, how quickly her mother's tone changed. "Yes, he's Amish," she said firmly.

"Oh, Lillian! That will *never* work."

"First of all, we're just friends, Mother." She was twenty-seven years old. And, based on the choices her mother had made, she shouldn't have to defend her own.

"Well, keep it that way."

It appeared Lillian was going to defend her own choices after all. "I might. I might not. I really like him. And his son, David."

"Oh, great. There's a child involved too?"

"He's eleven. He's a great kid, and—"

"Lillian, I have to run. Paul is calling from downstairs for me to hurry. I'll talk to you soon."

Her mouth was still open, midsentence, when she heard the line go dead. The false pretense of a normal conversation with her mother was nice while it lasted, but she could have predicted the final outcome.

———

The next morning Lillian swore she smelled smoke as she headed downstairs for breakfast. She looked at her watch. "Oops," she whispered. It was almost six o'clock. She'd probably missed breakfast. Cereal would have to do. Grandma was already headed to town by now.

That is smoke I smell.

Reaching the kitchen, she came to a sudden halt when she saw Grandpa casually puffing away on a cigar at the kitchen table.

"Grandpa! What are you doing?"

"Nothing like a fine cigar after breakfast." He flicked ash into a nearby coffee cup, his eyes twinkling with mischief.

"You can't do that . . . can you?" Amish people didn't smoke.

He chuckled. "We grow tobacco, my little Lilly. And some of us older folk partake in a cigar from time to time."

"Oh." She watched him take another puff. "But that's not good for you. I mean, you're sick. Maybe you shouldn't be smoking." She walked closer to him and frowned. "Does Grandma know about this?"

He sat up straighter on the wooden bench. As he held the cigar in one hand, he blew smoke and stroked his beard with the other hand. "Might be best not to mention it to her." He smiled with the sneaky satisfaction of a child.

"She's going to smell it." Lillian crossed her arms and shook her head.

"*Ya!* You'd think so! But every time she goes to town, I have me a smoke. Been smokin' me a cigar like this for months when she's afar. I open the windows and the doors." He pointed to the three open windows in the kitchen and the open screen door.

"Well, I could smell it coming down the stairs. Why don't you go on the porch?" Lillian knew she shouldn't be encouraging him.

"It's more comfortable in here, and near the coffee. Besides, I think Irma Rose has a bad nose. She don't smell good. I passed some gas the other day that would have knocked over a large cow. She didn't even give a flinch." He laughed as he took another drag.

Lilly blushed. "But, Grandpa, it's not good for you. You're sick and shouldn't be smoking."

"Lilly, I'm going to the Good Lord—soon. Ain't nothin's gonna change that." He grinned. "Just hope I go on a day when Irma Rose is in town, so I can go with a cigar in my hand."

"Grandpa, you might live many more years." She could only hope. The thought of him not there put her stomach in knots.

"Not gonna happen, my Lilly. I'm on my way out the door."

"Don't say that!"

He lifted his hairy chin, pushed back his straw hat, and gave her a hard look. With the cigar dangling from one side of his mouth, he said, "So, tell me about Samuel."

He clearly wanted to change the subject. And she supposed if it was going to get changed, she was glad it was to Samuel.

"He's nice. I like David too." She reflected on the hours of talking and laughing the three of them had shared the night before. It was nice. Although, based on Samuel's reaction, it might not be happening again.

"He's a fine man. The boy is a hard worker." He winked at her, the cigar still dangling to one side.

She wasn't sure how much to say. "Yes, he seems like a good father too."

"Gonna be spending more time with him?"

"Uh, I don't know. I'm sure I'll see him around." It was a vague answer but a truthful one.

"Well, it appears you'll be seeing him tomorrow."

"What? When?"

"It's his turn to have church service at his farm. You will be goin' to church?" His tone was an assumption she would be in attendance.

One thing at a time, though. "You have church service at a *home*? How did I miss that? I knew service was held every other week, but I must have missed the fact that it was at home."

"'God that made the world and all things therein, seeing that he is Lord of heaven and earth, dwelleth not in temples made with hands,'" he said. "*Ya,* we have church service in folks' homes. We each take a turn 'bout every ten months."

"Oh." She thought for a minute about the opportunity to see Samuel and where he and David lived. "I guess I can go."

Grandpa eyed her up and down. "Don't make a lick o' difference to me, but your Grandma sure would be pleased if you'd wear one of them dresses upstairs."

She frowned. "They're just not for me, Grandpa."

He sat quietly for a few seconds. "Maybe just give it some thought," he suggested.

Suddenly his face took on a fearful expression and he stuffed the cigar into the coffee cup. "Quick! Start fanning the room! Dump this out!" He handed her the coffee cup. "My hearing must be off too! I usually hear Jessie's hooves before he hits the dirt drive. Look at that! They're already in the yard!"

She grabbed the coffee cup and dumped the contents as instructed. Grandpa moved faster than she'd seen him since she arrived, waving his arms about, pushing the smoke toward the open windows. She watched with amusement at his wholehearted effort to keep his secret. Then, shaking her head, she said, "I'll go outside and try to stall Grandma. I'll show her the flowers I'm going to plant today."

With her grandpa still flailing his arms wildly around the room, she moved toward the open screen door. "I still think you shouldn't smoke," she whispered before she walked onto the porch.

"Hurry, child! Or Irma Rose will have my hide!"

6

LILLIAN HAD BEEN STARING AT THE DRESSES ON THE PEGS for nearly ten minutes. She needed to make a decision soon. She glanced toward the bed, where she'd laid out the only dress she brought with her: a blue one, but much shorter and *way* more stylish than the ones on the peg. All the other women would be wearing dresses similar to those Grandma had put in her room. Maybe it would be best not to stand out.

She pulled the dark blue dress from the peg.

"Grandma's already in the buggy, Lilly!" Grandpa yelled upstairs. "You comin'?"

Changing quickly, she ran down the stairs to see her grandfather sporting a wide-brimmed straw hat and a pair of suspenders she didn't remember seeing before. His eyes lit up when he saw her.

"You'll make your *mammi* very happy, Lilly."

"Feeling good today, Grandpa?" she asked. He seemed to be walking a bit taller this morning.

"It's a good day to go to church," he said, pushing back his hat and taking another look at her. "What a fine Amish woman you make."

"Thanks, Grandpa."

He made his way slowly down the porch steps and across the

front yard. A little wobbly, but all in all Grandpa seemed to be doing well. She stayed close by, occasionally offering her elbow for support. Grunting a little, he heaved himself into the driver's seat of the buggy while she went to go lavish a little attention on Jessie before they took to the road. "Hello, boy," she whispered as she stroked the horse's snout.

"Look at our Lilly. How 'bout that?"

Lillian poked her head around Jessie's. Grandma was sitting in the buggy and had her hands to her mouth as if overwhelmed by what she saw. After a moment's pause, she took a shaky breath. "I think you should drive us to worship this fine morning," she said, scooting off the seat. "I'll sit in the back. Jonas get up and push that seat forward so I can crawl in."

"Bossy, bossy," he snickered.

Thrilled, Lillian joined her grandpa in the front seat. With Grandma settled in the backseat, Grandpa handed over the reins. Lillian glanced over her shoulder. Grandma's hazel eyes shone with vivacity. If that's all it took for her to gleam like that, Lillian knew she should have worn the Plain dresses way before now. After all, they were just dresses.

Before she catapulted Jessie into action, Lillian reached into her apron pocket and pulled out the little white prayer covering she had stuffed inside. Hurriedly she wrapped her long brown hair into a tight bun and secured it with a hair band from her wrist. It was a last minute choice to bring along the hat, but she was glad she had. Her *Kapp* wasn't properly ironed, but she might as well wear the entire get-up.

She twisted in her seat and gave her grandma an "All set?" look. It warmed her heart to see the smile that stretched across the older woman's tired face.

"*Danki*, Lillian," she whispered.

Lillian smiled as she gave Jessie a giddyup. Why hadn't she just worn the silly dresses sooner?

As if sensing the women were having a moment, Grandpa lightened the mood. "Let's kick up some dirt, Lilly! Let ol' Jessie stretch his legs. Give a gentle flick with the reins. Jessie will do the rest."

Doing as her grandpa suggested, Lillian carefully maneuvered the buggy down the dirt lane to the main road. Then she looked at Grandpa again. He grinned and nodded.

"*Ya!*" she yelled, which thrust Jessie forward so fast Grandma fell backward against the seat.

"Thata girl, Lilly! A *wunderbaar* day to feel the wind in our face," Grandpa said as Jessie got comfortable in a quick gallop.

"Jonas, the Good Lord will still be there when we arrive!" Grandma yelled, regaining her composure as she adjusted her *Kapp*. "This is Lillian's first time to drive the buggy. She might not feel comfortable moving along so fast."

"Sure she does. Pick it up, Lilly! Another gentle flick of the reins."

Lillian glanced at her grandma, who was preparing herself for another increase in speed. But when she smiled in Lillian's direction, Lillian took that as the go-ahead and did indeed pick up the pace.

"Yee-ha!" Grandpa wailed.

Samuel's mother and two sisters, along with Katie Ann, had been busy readying the farmhouse for church service since the early-morning hours. Samuel, Ivan, and David were setting up tables and benches inside and out to prepare for the meal after worship.

"How did you meet the *Englisch* woman?" Ivan asked Samuel as they carried a bench from the barn.

"She was tryin' to find her way to Jonas and Irma Rose's farmhouse. She was walking along the road with only one shoe." He chuckled at the memory. "I gave her a ride."

"Is she planning to study the *Ordnung* in preparation of baptism? She is, after all, Amish by birth." Ivan placed the bench beside the long wooden table.

"I don't know. She says she wants to live a peaceful, quiet life for a while."

"Hmm, I see. The worldly ways of the *Englisch* are so different." Ivan shook his head.

"*Ya.*" Samuel wasn't clear about Lillian's plans, but he knew her heart was filled with compassion and kindness. That much was evident in the way she interacted with David, the way she reacted when the cow died, and her overall desire to lead a good life free of complications. Although misdirected in her attempts at finding such peace, Samuel knew her motivations were of God. She just didn't know it yet.

"Isn't that Jonas and Irma Rose coming up the drive?" Ivan pointed toward the dirt road leading to Samuel's farmhouse.

Samuel looked up. "That's Lillian driving," he said to his brother. "And . . ."—his heart did a somersault—"she's dressed in Plain clothes."

"It's a far cry from the boy breeches she wore when I saw her last." Ivan tipped back his straw hat and strained to have a better look at the approaching buggy.

"*Ya*," Samuel whispered, too stunned to say much else. He was pretty sure he'd heard her say she'd never wear one of the traditional Amish dresses.

As the buggy came to a halt, Samuel stifled a grin. Irma Rose's hair looked like she'd been through a tornado. Loose gray strands fell forward from beneath her *Kapp*, and she looked a tad pale. Lillian was sporting the same messy hairdo, but seemed to be bursting with pride.

"*Guder mariye!*" she yelled as they pulled up. "I drove the buggy!" Her contagious laugh even prompted a smile from Ivan.

"Good morning to you too," Samuel said as he walked toward the buggy. "How was the ride?" he asked Irma Rose.

"Lillian did a fine job," she said, stabbing strands of hair back under her *Kapp*, housed underneath a black bonnet. She drew in a deep breath, an obvious attempt to gather her composure.

Jonas popped out of the buggy. "I don't think I've been that fast in a buggy since my *rumschpringe!*" He paused and drew in a cleansing breath. "What a ride. And what a glorious day for worship." He shook Samuel's hand and made his way to one of the benches to take a seat.

Lillian slid off her seat and pushed it forward so Irma Rose could crawl out of the back. Samuel helped her out of the buggy. "Thank you, Samuel," she said, offering him a half smile. She headed toward Jonas, presumably to also take a rest after their adventurous ride.

Lillian couldn't have looked more beautiful. The crisp morning air tinged her cheeks a rosy pink, and her eyes were aglow with a passion for life. Her heavenly smile enhanced her dimples. In spite of his earlier resolve to keep things simple between them, he had to admit he felt strangely weak in the knees. He couldn't have been happier she'd chosen to attend worship service at his house on this fine Sunday morning. It was going to be a good day indeed.

As he had welcomed the others, Samuel extended his hand to her. "You look . . . lovely," he said. Surprised he'd verbalized the thought, he searched her eyes for a reaction. Her gaze met his, and she gave his hand a gentle squeeze.

"Why, *danki*, Samuel."

Samuel could hear faint rumblings and voices in the background, but he couldn't seem to decipher anything. The feel of Lillian's hand in his, the way her eyes connected with his . . . He was lost in her world.

"I dressed Amish," she whispered as she let go of his hand.

"And a mighty fine Amish woman you look." He couldn't seem to walk away from her, even though he heard someone calling his name.

"I think your brother is calling you," she said, obviously pleased she was diverting his attention.

He turned to see Ivan waiting for his help to carry another bench. "*Ya, ya.* Make yourself at home," he said to her and reluctantly made his way toward Ivan.

Samuel certainly seemed smitten with her this morning, and Lillian couldn't shake the smile he'd brought to her face. The way he held her hand and the look in his eyes left no question in her mind: he was glad she was here. She headed to where her grandparents were sitting. Grandma stood up right away.

"Let's head in with the other womenfolk, Lillian, and give a hand with the meal preparations." She grabbed Lillian's hand and continued holding it all the way into Samuel's kitchen.

"Hello," Lillian said softly when she entered the room. In addition to Katie Ann, there were two other younger women, and another woman about Grandma's age. They all paused at their respective chores and waited for an introduction. She was under the spotlight, no doubt.

"This is Lillian, *mei kinskind.*" Grandma's tone was proud. It touched Lillian's heart. Grandma gave her hand a squeeze. "And, Lillian, this is Mary Ellen, Samuel's sister." She pointed toward a woman about Lillian's age, who nodded in her direction. "This is Rebecca, another of Samuel's sisters." The slightly older woman also nodded and smiled. "And, this is their *mamm,* Esther."

"Lillian and I have met," Katie Ann spoke up. "Welcome to our worship service."

Lillian nodded. "Thank you for having me." She glanced around the kitchen, which mirrored her grandparents' kitchen, with the same white walls, table and bench, and wood-burning stove. Samuel's mother continued to study her as the other women returned to peeling potatoes, buttering loaves of bread, and arranging pickles on a tray.

"What church district do you come from?" Esther Stoltzfus finally asked.

"Uh, I don't come from any church district," Lillian said, unsure how Grandma would like for her to answer.

Grandma held her chin high. "Lillian comes to our district from the city—from Houston."

Esther looked confused.

"Lillian, maybe you could help me get the butter bread ready?" Katie Ann asked.

Grandma seemed relieved with the change of subject.

———

It was a church service unlike any church service Lillian had ever attended. Not that she had attended very many. The men and boys sat by themselves in one room, and the women and girls sat in another room. There was a central room in between where the preaching took place. Since it was almost completely in German, Lillian understood very little of the two-hour service.

Her back ached from the backless bench. There was no organ or music, just songs that were sung unusually slow. When the service was over, the men left first, then the young women, and lastly the older women. Lillian tried to follow tradition as best she could.

Despite the awkwardness of the whole event, she came away from the service feeling a sense of fellowship and calm. While some of those in attendance gave her questioning looks, everyone was friendly. Sadie Fisher, however, didn't acknowledge her presence. She'd noticed the young woman sitting on the same row, at the far end from her. As they exited the service and moved toward the kitchen, Lillian caught Sadie watching her, but the woman quickly turned away when their eyes met.

Samuel, on the other hand, locked eyes with her several times. Each time, a smile swept across his face.

The men began to seat themselves at the benches outside while the women started to carry out trays of food. It seemed incredibly old-fashioned to her the way the women waited on

the men. She had never seen Grandpa so much as serve himself a
cup of coffee at home. And Grandma never seemed to mind tending to his every need, on good days or bad. Nor did these women
seem to mind that the men were eating first. So she followed suit
and helped carry out food trays and pitchers of sweet tea.

"Hi, Lillian."

After placing a pitcher of tea on the table, she gave David a
hug. "Hi, David. How's it going?"

"*Gut*," he said.

Frowning, she pointed to a large bowl on a nearby table. "I
canned some of those, but I have to tell you, I don't care for
them."

"Those are *riewe*. Red beets. They're *gut*."

"Yuck. I don't think I'll be having any of those. But I'm going
to have lots of that pie." She nodded her head toward one of the
many desserts lining the table.

"That's *schnitzboi*. Snitz pie," he said grinning.

"Well, I'm going to be sure and have some. Where's your Pop?"
she asked, looking around for Samuel. "Eating with the other
men?"

David didn't say anything.

"What are you snickering about?" she asked playfully.

"Oh, nothing." He nervously kicked at the grass.

"It's my Amish outfit, isn't it?" Maybe it just didn't work for
her, like she suspected. Although his father had sure seemed
happy to see her wearing the traditional dress.

"No, that's not it. I think you look Plain."

"Well, *Plain* is good, right?"

Ignoring her plea for acceptance, he said, "Pop's in the barn.

He asked me to take him some sweet tea. But *you* can take it to him if you want." He reached for a glass of tea on the table and pushed it in her direction, still grinning.

She accepted the tea and winked at him. "I think I will." She walked toward the barn. "Save me a piece of that pie!"

"I will."

———

Samuel filled Pete's trough with oats. "There's a mighty crowd takin' over the house, ol' boy. Maybe I'll sit a spell with you." Knowing he should get back to the group with the extra chairs he'd been sent to retrieve, he took advantage of the opportunity to sit quietly for a minute. Taking a seat behind his woodworking bench, he eyed the many uncompleted projects. So much to do and so little time. Between caring for the boy, farming the land, and the many other chores necessary to keep the farm running, his favorite pastime was quickly becoming a thing of the past.

He picked up a birdhouse modeled after a plan his pop gave him before he died. It would be a fine home for the redbirds, if he could ever finish it.

He didn't hear Lillian walk into the barn. When he looked up, she was there.

"David said you wanted some tea," she said, handing him the glass.

"*Danki.* David could have brought it out here."

She remained quiet as he took several big gulps. He set the glass down, fearing he'd hurt her feelings with his comment. "I mean, I hate for you to have to get away from the other folks to bring me tea."

"I don't mind."

"What did you think about the church service?"

"Long." She sighed. "And my back's a little sore."

"The benches take some gettin' used to."

"But it was nice. I didn't understand most of it, but there was a certain something in the air. I don't know. I guess maybe a fellowship. It was like one giant family. I didn't really have a family growing up. It was just me and Mom."

"I reckon we're like one big family in most ways. Do you plan to study the *Ordnung* while you're here?"

"That's like the order of conduct, right?" She pressed her lips together and thought for a minute. "I guess if I'm really going to live the Amish life while I'm here, I should."

"It's not easy, Lillian. Especially since you come from worldly ways. Don't you miss television, electricity, and all the other modern conveniences?"

"Of course I do. But I don't miss living by myself and being afraid to go home alone at night. I don't miss my mother's reckless behavior and always needing something from me. I don't miss the busyness, the constant fast pace. I don't miss—" She caught her breath as vivid and painful memories of Rickie stabbed at her insides. "I don't miss a lot of things. All my life, I've sensed there was something else for me. I just didn't know what."

"Is this the something else you've been looking for?"

"I hope so. I don't know. I just know that I've felt lost for a long time, and something about being here, living with Grandma and Grandpa"—she paused—"and meeting you makes me believe maybe it is."

Alarms began to ring in Samuel's head. His fascination with

her aside, he knew it would be best to get things right in *both* their minds if they were going to stay friends.

"Lillian," he began.

"Yes?"

"I hope you find what you're lookin' for." She nodded and seemed to be waiting for more. "I mean, truly living our ways would mean a lot of studying and acceptance of God's will. It's not just about wearing the clothes, gardening, making bread, getting up early, or making quilts."

"Hey! I haven't thought about quilts. I want to learn that too."

She was missing his point. "Our way of life is *here*, Lillian." He held his hand to his heart. "It's a faith we carry without doubt and a way of life we practice with humility and selflessness."

"I know," she said as if trying to convince him.

He shook his head, realizing any feelings he had today at seeing Lillian in her Plain clothes were best put aside. No matter her intentions, they lived in two different worlds.

"Why are you shaking your head?"

It was time to clear the air. "I like you, Lillian. And I would like to be a friend to you." He hesitated; she seemed to hang on his words. "But for it to be anything more between us isn't possible. David seems to have taken a fancy to you, and I don't want to see the boy get hurt by an *Englisch* woman with no sense of our ways."

A little presumptuous of him, Lillian thought, as she weighed her options. There were two ways to play this. One, she could save face and say she completely agreed and then change the subject. Or two, step out on a huge limb and see if Samuel could practice what he was preaching.

Choosing option two, she said, "I think maybe *you* have taken a fancy to me, also, Samuel Stoltzfus." She lifted her chin and shot him a curious grin.

His eyes widened.

Sensing his shock at her comment, she decided not to back him into a corner where he might choose to not even remain friends. "But . . . okay," she said.

"Okay, what?" He pushed back the rim of his straw hat as though trying to see her better.

"We'll be friends. Nothing more. And we'll make that clear to David as well."

"I think that's a fine idea. I'll talk to David, so the boy doesn't get any misconceptions 'bout us spending time together."

"That's perfect. You and David are the only friends I have here, and I'd hate to lose that." She leaned forward a bit. "So . . . *friend*. Wanna come have another talk by the barn tonight?"

"There's chores to do and I think—" He stopped midsentence when his eyes met with her pleading gaze. "I reckon it would be all right. David and I will come over after suppertime, though. I don't want us to wear out our supper welcome with Irma Rose. Plus, that will give us time to catch up on some chores around here."

"Sounds good. I better head back. I'll see you and David later."

It was nearing six o'clock when Samuel walked downstairs that evening. David was at the kitchen table generously helping himself to leftover butter bread and pickles.

"David, Lillian asked us to come by this evening to talk for a while."

The boy grinned. "You're courting her."

"No, David. Lillian is a friend. Anything else wouldn't be right. I want you to understand that."

With the same maturity beyond his years that Samuel had noticed before, his son said, "I know our ways are different from hers, Pop. But she's here, and she's learnin' our ways. Whose to say God won't work a miracle? Maybe she'll realize she'd like to become Amish."

"David, you know that doesn't happen very often—an *Englisch* man or woman converting. And even if they choose our ways, most can't stick to it. I've told you before: don't be gettin' any silly notions in your head about Lillian. Now go get cleaned up, and we'll just go visit for a while."

Mischievously, David said, "Ivan is picking me up any minute. I told him after church service I would spend the night with him and Katie Ann so I can help him paint the fence starting early in the morning. Didn't he tell you?"

Samuel felt a slight pang of panic. Most of the time he'd spent with Lillian had been with David in tow. Safer that way. "Uh, no. No one told me."

The boy choked down a piece of bread and jumped up from the table. He reached the window and stared into the sunset. "Here comes Ivan now."

Samuel followed his son to the window and saw Ivan's buggy

coming up the driveway. "What am I going to tell Lillian? I told her we'd come for a visit. I didn't know you were going with Ivan."

David spun around on his way to the door. "Guess you'll have to go visit her all by yourself, Pop."

It wasn't right. Going to see Lillian by himself would seem like he was courting her. But if he *wasn't* courting her, then why was he worried about it? It was just a friendly visit, after all.

So why couldn't he control the buzz of activity in his belly at the thought of being alone with her?

7

LILLIAN CONSIDERED CHANGING OUT OF HER AMISH DRESS and back into her blue jeans, but she didn't. As she roamed the yard inspecting her gardening efforts from the previous day, she heard the screen door slam. Grandma took a seat in one of the wooden rockers on the front porch.

"The yard looks *gut*, Lillian."

"*Danki*, Grandma. It was fun planting all these." She waved her arm around, motioning toward her work.

She thought back to Samuel's comments about nurturing the land and how work could be healthy and enjoyable. Planting the flowers didn't seem like work, and it certainly brought her a sense of calm. She noticed she felt the same way after a successful day of baking, or when she mastered a particular sewing task. It was a sense of accomplishment, but there was something else too.

"How's Grandpa feeling?"

"He's resting. I'm thankful he was able to attend worship this morning, but I think he's paying the price about now." She shook her head. Lillian could see the worry in her tired eyes, magnified by dark circles underneath. "The *Englisch* doctors in town changed his medication. Seems to give him a boost of energy, but then he's down and out in the evening hours." She shook her head again.

"I'm sorry I didn't finish my other chores in time to help you with supper." She paused. Grandma was shaking her head as if it didn't matter. But Lillian knew she was going to have to start taking on more chores around the house and try to complete them in a more timely manner. Otherwise, Grandma was going to end up sick right alongside Grandpa.

"Grandma, I think maybe I should just make it a point to cook the meals. That includes breakfast. I've been getting up early, and I've seen what Grandpa likes to eat for breakfast. Why don't you start sleeping in a little bit, and let me handle the cooking?"

As if she didn't hear a word Lillian was saying, Grandma said, "Child, what are you watchin' for down that driveway?" She strained to see down the dirt drive.

"Huh?" Lillian was anxious for Samuel and David to arrive, but she didn't think she was that obvious.

"Are you waiting for Samuel and David?" Grandma wrinkled her nose.

"Oh . . . They're just coming by. For a quick visit." She shrugged her shoulders to signify it was no big deal.

Grandma's lips pursed together and she gave her granddaughter a stern look. "Now, Lillian," she began slowly. "You'd have to be thick as pea soup not to see that you and Samuel have taken a fancy to each other. But you need to be very careful. There's a child involved here, and it seems to me that the boy has taken a fancy to you as well."

So, it wasn't just her imagination. Samuel *did* like her a little more than he was willing to let on. Even Grandma had picked up on it. "We're just friends, Grandma. That's it."

In a tone indicative she wasn't buying it, her grandmother said, "*Ya.*"

"Really. We've talked about it." Lillian took a seat in the other rocker. "We're just going to be friends, and Samuel said he'd talk to David about it."

In spite of her obvious concern, Grandma chuckled.

"What?" She watched her grandma shaking her head.

"You've talked about it?" Grandma's face grew serious. "Lillian, if you've *talked* about it, then the notion for courting must be in both your heads. And you need to know it would be devastating to the community, and to Samuel and David, if he fell *in lieb* with you. You *aren't* Amish and it could cause a world of trouble for Samuel." Her mouth twisted as if biting on a sour grape.

"What?" Lillian couldn't believe what she was hearing. "Grandma, first of all, we barely know each other. No one is *in love*. We're just friends. And I would never allow Samuel to get into any kind of trouble."

"You say that now, dear. When two people are attracted to each other, reckless decisions can be made."

"I know all about reckless decisions, Grandma. I watched Mom make a whole slew of them over the years." She looked away, trying to avoid certain memories that crept into her dreams at night. Her own reckless decisions had stemmed from her attraction to Rickie. But unlike her mother, she refused to allow herself to keep making the same mistakes. She blinked her eyes, shook her head, and turned back toward her grandma. "I like it here. So I don't see why Samuel and I can't be friends."

A worried look still scrolled across the older woman's face. "I didn't say you couldn't be friends, Lillian. I'm sayin' you are both treading into dangerous territory. I'm pleased as punch you like it here and want to stay on for a while, but to live among us is to learn our ways and to give up many things you're used to having. Most people come here looking for something they don't find."

Lillian's chest grew heavy. "Don't you want me here?" She realized just how much she wanted to be here.

"Your *daadi* and I want you here very much." Grandma smiled, but the worry quickly returned. "But running away from something isn't always the answer either."

Lillian thought for a minute and tried to ignore the lump forming in her throat. Maybe Grandma was having second thoughts about bringing her into their community. "Grandma, I'm not running away *from* something—I'm running *to* something. There's been something terribly amiss in my life."

"Do you think you've found that something in Lancaster County?"

"I do, Grandma. Or at least . . . I might have. These last few days have been wonderful. But if you don't want me here, I would understand. I know I have a lot to learn." Tears were building, and she didn't want Grandma to see her cry. Then she'd feel obligated to say she wanted Lillian there.

Grandma reached over and cupped her hand over Lillian's. "Lillian, there is nothing I want more than for you to live with us—for as long as you like." She paused. "But the *something* you are running to won't be found through gardening, cooking, or making bread." She looked at Lillian's blue dress and black apron. "Or by wearing our Plain clothing."

"That's what Samuel said."

Grandma looked shocked at first that she and Samuel had

such conversations. But then she softened. "Well, Samuel's right. Find God, Lillian. The rest will follow."

Find God? And exactly where had He been hiding all her life? She'd tried praying, waiting to see if an all-powerful Being really existed, but her prayers had gone unheard. When she and her mother slept in the car when she was twelve, where was God then? Where was God when her mother begged the landlord for just one more day to pay the rent? When Rickie strode into her life and trapped her in a twisted maze of good and evil, why didn't this Supreme Being show her a path to safety sooner?

Find God. She had looked for God. And while she hadn't ruled out the possibility Someone had helped her through some tough spots, she hadn't ruled out the possibility it was all just coincidence either.

As if reading her mind, Grandma said, "Try to find *not* what the Lord has done for you, but what *you* have done for the Lord."

Lillian pondered her statement for a minute. What could she have possibly done for God when she wasn't even sure He existed?

But if He did exist . . .

Suddenly, it was as if every bad thing she'd ever done was rising to the surface and demanding to be heard. There was an inner conflict going on inside her head she didn't understand. It was confusing.

"Grandma, I want so badly to feel a calmness inside. I want so badly to live a good life." Her heart was heavy. "It's just hard for me to understand why sometimes things happen the way they do." She brushed away a tear.

"There, there, child," Grandma said, again reaching over and placing her hand atop Lillian's. "Some things are just God's will."

There it was again: God's will. That was the part she had the biggest problem with. "But I have doubts, Grandma. I have doubts, and I know that's not right. How can I find God with all these doubts in my mixed-up mind?"

Grandma lifted Lillian's chin up. "I think this is a very good start."

As Samuel turned onto the dirt driveway leading up to Jonas and Irma Rose's place, he'd made up his mind to stay only a few minutes. He'd say *hello*, talk briefly about church service, admire the flowers he knew she'd planted the day before, then be on his way. But all that changed when she met him at his buggy in the front yard. He didn't think he'd ever seen a more fragile-looking creature. Tears stained her rosy cheeks, and her eyes glazed over with emotion. Towering over his *Englisch* friend, he softly asked, "Lillian, what is it?"

She shook her head.

Idle chitchat wasn't on her agenda. Something had her all awhirl. "Lillian?" he asked again.

"I'm sorry, Samuel," she said, dabbing at her eyes.

"Did something happen?" Maybe Jonas had a bad spell. "Is it Jonas?"

"No, no." She took another swipe at her eyes. "Just ignore me. I was having a talk with Grandma . . . a talk about God. I just got kind of emotional and a little upset."

Wondering if this territory was best left alone, he asked, "What got you upset?"

"I have so many doubts about God, and I don't have a relationship with Him. And I want to, Samuel. I really do. But I
don't know how to go about it."

She was clearly waiting for answers. And he didn't have any.
It wasn't his job to show Lillian the way to God. *Unequally yoked.*
The phrase pounded away in his head. Missionary work was not
part of the Amish way. Steering clear of nonbelievers in an intimate way—friendly or otherwise—was.

When he didn't respond, she turned her back toward him.

"Lillian?" he asked, unsure what to say or do.

After a few seconds, she turned back around. "Let's don't do
this," she said after taking a deep breath. "I had a conversation
with Grandma that got me thinking about things. About God.
And then you got here. You just caught me during an emotional
moment. Let's talk about something else."

"*Ya,*" he said relieved. They'd talk about something else for a
short while, and then he was hightailing it home. He shouldn't
be there in the first place. The *Englisch* woman was mixed up, all
right. She was a downright mess.

But a beautiful mess.

What a whiny baby. Lillian hardly knew the man and yet she had
gotten teary in front of him twice. Once over a cow and now
about her lack of faith. She frowned as he followed her to their
spot on the side of the barn. From now on, cheery conversation
was in order.

"Sadie didn't acknowledge me at church service today," she
said without thinking first. Not exactly cheery conversation.

"She was jealous." Samuel seemed to regret the comment the minute he said it. He glanced away when she met his eyes with a look of surprise.

"Really? Why would she be jealous? You and I aren't courting." She should have avoided emphasizing the word *courting*. He looked uncomfortable.

As silence formed a barrier between them, Samuel changed the subject. "The other evening we spent most of our time talking about life here. Tell me about yourself, Lillian. Tell me about your life before Lancaster County."

She watched him place his straw hat on the stump nearby. His flattened hat hair did nothing to take away from his stunning looks. As she watched him stroking his beard, she tried to envision the face underneath. "What do you want to know?"

"Whatever you're comfortable telling me." He shrugged.

"Hmm, let's see." She'd made so many mistakes. Surely he didn't want to hear about her failures. Better to focus on the positives in her life. "I was a teacher in Houston. I wanted to make a difference in the lives of children, help them see their potential and feel good about themselves. I love kids."

"Well, David sure likes you."

"He's a great kid. You've done a good job with him."

"*Ya*, he's a *gut* boy. But, I can really only take credit for the past couple of years. Before that, I give credit to his *mamm*. After Rachel died, I've done the best I know how."

She wanted to know more about Rachel. But before she could say anything, he said, "So tell me more."

"I guess saying I'm a lost soul trying to find my way would sound a little dramatic." She cringed and forced a half smile.

"Less dramatic would be to say I needed to get away from my mother for a while, and I had a bad breakup with my boyfriend." She paused and looked up to see him hanging on her words. "So I'm trying something new."

"What happened with your boyfriend?" he asked.

This was veering away from the cheery conversation she'd hoped for earlier. She shrugged, unsure how much to tell Samuel.

"Did you love him?"

"I thought I did."

He was waiting for more. There was so much more. She hesitated, but the look on his face was kind and encouraging. "Rickie was great in the beginning. Very loving and kind."

His eyes were intently focused on her, and she wished she could finagle her way out of this conversation. She'd make it brief so they could move on to something else. "Then he just changed."

"What do you mean?"

Closing her eyes, she pushed the vivid details of her and Rickie's last confrontation out of her mind. She was far, far away from him and didn't want to dredge up the memories. "He just changed," she repeated as she shook her head. "I should have never moved in with him."

"You lived with him? And you weren't married?"

"It was a horrible mistake. I should have never moved in with him," she repeated. She meant it, but why all of a sudden did she feel like Samuel thought less of her with this confession?

She prepared herself for a turn in his attitude toward her, but he surprised her. "All of us make mistakes. God forgives us for those mistakes." His tone was gentle and kind.

Lillian shook her head. "He wouldn't forgive me, Samuel. I've made too many mistakes. I try to be a good person and live a good life, but I keep falling down. I've tried so hard not to make the mistakes my mother made. And yet, somehow, I let Rickie creep into my life. He wasn't good for me."

Samuel tilted his head to one side; she felt as though he was staring right through her. "Of course God would forgive you, Lillian. All you have to do is ask Him. The important thing is to get up when you fall down, and it sounds like you have."

"You make it sound so easy, Samuel."

In an unexpected gesture, he reached over and briefly patted her hand. "Maybe you should try it."

Something was going on inside her. Something she couldn't get a grasp on. All this talk about God and forgiveness stirred emotions inside that she wasn't familiar with. Grandma and Samuel—both so solid in their faith . . . Maybe there was something to it all.

Suddenly she felt cheated out of whatever insight they both seemed to have.

"I can't help but wonder how different my life might have been if Mom had just stayed and raised me here." Would she be privy to the same strong faith Samuel and Grandma had? She cringed at the thought of some of the situations she and her mother had endured over the years.

"Do you know why your *mamm* left?"

"No, I don't. Mom won't talk about it, and I don't think Grandma and Grandpa really know. I guess I'm looking for answers in several areas."

"Where's your father?" He balanced both elbows on his knees and leaned forward. Facing him, she did the same—putting their faces about a foot away from each other. As darkness closed in around them, she could see Samuel's features illuminated with interest.

"I don't know." This was another painful subject. Somehow they'd gone offtrack in an effort to keep things upbeat.

"We don't have to talk about this," he said softly, as if sensing it caused her discomfort.

"It's okay. I don't know where my father is because I don't know *who* my father is. Mom said she doesn't know. But she's lying. She does this thing with her eyes and nose when she's lying." She blinked repeatedly and crinkled her nose, to show him. "Like that."

He smiled broadly, amused by her imitation, which lightened the mood.

"I know. It looks funny. But I'm telling you, that's how I can tell she's lying. I can recognize a lie immediately. I've heard plenty over the years."

"It sounds like you had a hard childhood."

"Let's just say my mother wouldn't have received the Mother-of-the-Year award."

His bewildered gaze made her wonder if talking so intimately with him was a mistake. She'd probably shared too much about Rickie. And she'd barely touched on that painful part of her past. He probably had the perfect childhood. Great parents. A wonderful family. She, on the other hand, didn't know who her father was, had duplicated her mother's legacy by living with a man she wasn't married to, and wasn't even sure she believed in God.

"Parenting is a hard job." He pushed back his windblown

bangs and wiped his forehead. "So, if you weren't really *in lieb* with Rickie, have you ever been truly *in lieb*?"

Samuel had a way of changing the subject when he felt it was time to move on. Where was he going with all this? And if they were just going to be friends . . . why was he so interested? "No, I don't think I have," she said, realizing it was heartbreakingly true. She looked at the ground.

"It's a *wunderbaar* thing to be *in lieb*," he said.

She looked up at him. He looked as if he were a million miles away, presumably with thoughts of Rachel. She couldn't imagine losing someone so dear. Placing her hand atop his just felt very natural.

Samuel knew he was in dangerous territory. Somehow his plan to keep the visit brief and be on his way hadn't panned out the way he intended. But the feel of her soft hand resting on his gave him comfort. Her touch ignited senses in him that he had buried along with Rachel. His blossoming friendship with Lillian was confusing. Wonderfully confusing.

Underneath the moonlit sky her face was radiantly aglow, as if the clouds parted solely for her benefit and bathed her in the magic of the night. He tried to put his apprehension at ease and just enjoy the moment. It had been a mighty long time since he'd felt this good. But as he attempted to bask in the present, visions of Rachel began to flash through his mind. How he'd loved her and missed her. The feel of her soft skin. Her passion for life.

Lillian had that same passion.

Scolding himself for comparing the women, he gently pulled

his hand from underneath Lillian's and sat up a little straighter, leaning away from her. Surely God would help him steer clear of such temptation. To hold hands, no matter how calming the effect, wasn't right.

———

As Samuel pulled his hand away, Lillian worried if perhaps she'd crossed a line she shouldn't have. Cupping her hand over his had been an unplanned expression of mild affection that just happened. She didn't mean anything by it. But she didn't recognize the emotion she was experiencing. It wasn't a physical longing, but a yearning of the heart. Her need to be close to Samuel was overwhelming.

"What are you thinking about?" she asked, fearful her small gesture might have caused him to withdraw. There was so much she wanted to know about him.

He shrugged. "I reckon I was just thinking about a lot of things."

"Rachel?" she asked softly, hoping he would open up to her.

But he shook his head. "Not so much."

His expression said otherwise, but Lillian wasn't going to push it. She decided to change the subject this time. "Are you curious about the outside world? I mean, have you ever been tempted to walk away from all this?"

"I know all about the outside world. During my *rumschpringe* I was allowed to experience the *Englisch* world. I watched television, went to movies, rode in cars with *Englisch* friends, drank beer, and kicked my heels up at the local dance hall." He paused. "You look speechless. And one thing I have learned about you is that you're usually not without somethin' to say."

She looked away, feeling a little embarrassed. "Yes, I tend to talk a lot."

"That's a good thing, though. You have a bubbly spirit."

"Which means I talk a lot."

Samuel reached beside him and retrieved his hat. Placing it atop his head, he stared intently at her. He gave her the strangest look, and Lillian couldn't decipher it.

"Just because I choose this life doesn't mean I don't know what's out there." He swung his arm toward the highway. "I hope you find what you're looking for, Lillian."

Jonas stumbled around the kitchen until he found some leftover butter bread. A slice of bread and some lemonade was in order. Irma Rose would be fit to be tied if she knew he'd made his way down the stairs by himself so soon after taking his pills. But he was hungry, and the poor woman was snoring so loud he didn't have the heart to wake her. The Good Lord had seen fit to give him the cancer, but he knew his wife was plumb worn-out from tending to him all during the night. She shouldn't have to be caring for him during the sleeping hours. Some things he could do for himself. A man should be able to walk down the stairs and get a slice of bread and some lemonade if he wanted them.

As he filled his glass up, he thought he heard voices. The wooden door in the kitchen was open, and he hobbled to the screen door. "Well, well," he whispered as he spotted Lilly and

Samuel out by the barn. "Looking mighty cozy." Jonas sighed. Irma Rose would have a fit about now.

Feeling a little light on his feet, Jonas headed back toward the lemonade pitcher he had left on the table. He topped off his glass and took a big gulp. Having another look outside, he couldn't help but share some of his wife's worry about Samuel and Lilly. They'd have a hard road ahead of them should they start courting. Straining to get a better look, he chuckled. If they thought they *weren't* courting, they were fooling themselves.

Knowing Irma Rose might stir and be all wound up he was gone, he finished off the butter bread and put the lemonade back in the refrigerator. Taking a step into the den, he looked up at the stairs. Going up was a mite more challenging than coming down. And it sounded like he had bees in his head. *Buzz, buzz, buzz.* A bothersome noise, getting louder by the second.

He reached for the back of the wooden rocker to steady himself. Seemed like his legs were turning to jelly, and the bee noise was getting louder and louder. He took another couple of steps. *Just need to get back in bed, that's all.*

As everything went dark, he never felt his lanky body slam onto the wood floor. Nor did he feel it when his head caught the corner of the rocker. And he couldn't feel the rush of blood spilling into a pool beneath him.

8

LILLIAN RESPONDED TO SAMUEL'S COMMENT ABOUT FINDING what she was looking for by simply nodding. The tone of his voice indicated he might not be interested in playing much of a role in that process.

As he stood up, presumably to leave, Lillian tried to think of something to say, something that might make him stay. She wasn't sure, but Samuel seemed hesitant to go.

Say something. Anything. He appeared to be waiting for her to come up with a reason for him to linger. But maybe she was reading him wrong.

Before she could come up with anything, a loud noise from inside the house caused them both to redirect their attention.

"What was that?" she asked, turning toward the porch.

Samuel began to move toward the house. Lillian was right behind him. Sensing something was wrong, they both burst into a run, taking two steps at a time up the porch steps. As they moved through the kitchen, Lillian heard her grandma calling her name repeatedly.

"Grandma!" she answered, never slowing her pace behind Samuel as they entered the den.

Grandma was hurriedly making her way down the stairs toward her husband. "Lillian!" she yelled. "Lillian, help!"

The three of them rushed to Grandpa's crumpled figure on the wood floor. Grandma gently lifted his head. Tenderly cradling it in her lap, she brushed back his blood-soaked hair. "Jonas, wake up," she cried. "Oh, Jonas. Oh, Jonas, wake up." She looked up at Lillian and Samuel. "Lillian, he won't wake up. My Jonas won't wake up. Oh, Lillian . . . *do* something."

Lillian was frozen, legs glued to the floor. So much blood. Grandma's agonizing cries echoed through the old house, and Lillian felt like she might pass out. One thought consumed her. *Is Grandpa dead?*

Samuel ripped his shirt from his body before Lillian had time to gather her thoughts. Applying pressure to Grandpa's head, he turned to face her. With a calmness Lillian found incredible, he firmly said, "Lillian, bring me some wet towels and then go get your portable telephone."

"Jonas," Grandma cried. "Please, Jonas. Wake up, my love."

"Now, Lillian!" Samuel yelled, bolting her into action. She retrieved a wad of towels from the kitchen drawer and soaked them with water from the sink. Dropping the towels into Samuel's hands, she looked down at Grandpa. His mouth hung open, and his face was pasty white. He was dead. She just knew it. This couldn't be happening. She was just getting to know him.

"Not yet, God. Not yet," she silently prayed.

"Go get your telephone, Lillian," Samuel said, holding the wet towels against the gaping gash in Grandpa's head. "Hurry."

She bolted up the stairs, continuing to pray. Aloud she repeated, "Please, God, don't let him die. Please, God, don't let him die."

She repeated the prayer all the way back down the stairs, whispering as she neared the threesome. Samuel was holding his hand out for the phone. He grabbed it, fiddled with it, and handed it right back to her.

"I don't know how this works," he said, frustrated. Then he rattled off a number and instructed Lillian to dial it. When it started ringing, she handed it to him.

"Mr. Pierson, this is Samuel Stoltzfus. I'm out at Irma Rose and Jonas's place, and we need some help. Can you bring your car out here? Jonas is hurt, and we need to get to a hospital." He nodded and set the phone down as he turned his attention to Irma Rose. "He's on his way."

Lillian watched the way Samuel calmly handled a crisis. She, on the other hand, was fighting waves of panic, and she still worried she might faint. She sat down on the floor beside Grandma and put her arm around her. The woman's cries softened. But as she rocked back and forth stroking her husband's face with hands covered in blood, Grandma's lips moved in prayer. If ever there was a time to pray, it was now.

Lillian closed her eyes and pleaded with God for her grandfather's life. If there was a God, he wouldn't let her grandpa die.

———

"What's all the fuss about? Irma Rose, why in the world are you crying?" Jonas reached up and touched his head. Samuel sighed, feeling the relief wash over him. Lillian let go with sobs she must have been stifling the whole time, and Irma Rose looked toward the heavens and whispered softly, "Thank you, Lord."

"I think you gave the ladies a scare, Jonas," Samuel said,

continuing to apply pressure to Jonas's head with the wet towels.
"Mr. Pierson is on the way with his car, and we'll get you to the
hospital."

Jonas looked around at the three of them before honing in on
Irma Rose. "You know I *hate* hospitals, Irma Rose. I'd rather you
just fix me up here."

"You silly old man," she blasted. "I can't fix you. You need a
doctor." She shook her head in exasperation. "What in the name
of the Good Lord made you come down here by yourself?"

Samuel glanced at Lillian, who was still crying. Discreetly he
reached for her hand and gave it a quick squeeze.

Jonas was glaring at Irma Rose as if he'd like to rip her head
off. "I was hungry!"

"Why didn't you get me from my sleep then?" Irma Rose
demanded, patting her eyes.

Ignoring his wife, Jonas looked over at Lillian. "Lilly, why are
you crying?"

Lillian wiped her eyes. "You scared us, Grandpa."

Jonas patted her hand. "Thought I was dead, didn't ya?" Then
he chuckled.

"That's not funny, Grandpa!" Lillian's tone of voice made it
clear she was not amused.

"You scared us all, Jonas," Irma Rose belted out. "From now
on, if you get a hankering for a late-night snack, you get me or
Lillian."

"*Ya*, I'd have starved to death waiting on one of you."

Samuel tried not to laugh. He glanced at Lillian, who was
also fighting a trembly grin. He was glad she'd stopped crying.
Always a joker, Jonas was turning a bad situation around, with
everyone laughing to keep from crying.

"You were snoring so loud, Irma Rose, the house could've fallen down and you wouldn't have taken a notice." Jonas turned his attention to Lillian. "And our *kinskind* here was busying herself with other things." He looked at Samuel and grinned.

Lillian picked up on the curious stares all around them at the hospital. True, they were all covered in blood, but she heard the occasional whispered, "Oh, look, they're Amish." She supposed it would have been worse if they were somewhere other than Lancaster County, where so many Amish lived.

"Thank you, Mr. Pierson," Samuel said, shaking the man's hand.

Lillian could tell right away the men shared a friendship. So Samuel had friends who weren't Amish. And a good thing too. Mr. Pierson had arrived within minutes of Samuel's phone call, and without his help it would have been difficult to get Grandpa up off the floor.

"I'm glad you called, Samuel. Any time I can help you folks, you let me know." The gray-headed man smiled. "I'm going to go call Mrs. Pierson and let her know everything is all right."

As they waited for Grandpa to get his head stitched up, Lillian looked at Grandma seated nearby. Her head was tilted back, and she appeared to be sleeping. Samuel leaned against the wall, looking as haggard as she felt.

"Thank God he only needs a few stitches and that he's okay otherwise," Lillian said to Samuel as she stood beside him. *Yes, thank God.* She had prayed, and Grandpa had lived. It worked.

When Samuel didn't respond, she asked, "Are you okay?" He didn't look okay.

He took a deep breath and blew it out slowly. "I haven't been here since Rachel died."

Instinctively, she reached for his hand. And as her fingers brushed against the top of his hand . . . he pulled away. And it stung.

Samuel recognized Ms. Morgan behind the desk. The nurse had stayed with him and Rachel right up until the end. For weeks, the woman had tended to Rachel's every need. Samuel hoped she wouldn't recognize him.

He scooted slightly away from Lillian. He should have never squeezed her hand when they were on the floor tending to Jonas. She had just looked so sad and scared at the time, and it was nothing more than a comforting gesture. But he needn't have her thinking his action was an open invitation for affection—particularly *public* affection.

Glancing at Lillian, he feared his deliberate action had hurt her feelings. She'd been through enough on this night. He didn't want to add to her upset, but this touching of the hands needed to stop. It wasn't proper, and it roused feelings in Samuel he shouldn't be having. Especially right now, only a little ways from where he'd said good-bye to his beloved Rachel in a small room down the hall.

"Samuel?" The tenderness in her voice warmed his heart and frightened him just the same. "I know it must be hard for you to be here. If you need to leave . . ."

He wasted no time accepting an excuse to leave before he said or did something he'd regret.

"I'm glad Jonas is going to be okay," he said abruptly. "Tell

Mr. Pierson I needed to head on home. I'll take a taxi cab. He'll wait for you all and take you home." His emotions were flailing and he needed out of there.

"Okay," she said. "I don't know what we would have done if you hadn't been there, Samuel. Thank you so much."

Samuel nodded and took a step away from her and toward the exit door. He'd almost made a clean getaway when he heard her call his name.

"*Ya*," he answered, turning reluctantly.

"Maybe you'd like to come over for supper tomorrow night? You and David." She paused when he didn't answer. "As a repayment of sorts for all you did tonight." She smiled as warmly as he'd ever seen.

He looked at her a moment, then shook his head sharply. "*Danki*, Lillian, but I can't." The woman was frustrating him, confusing him, and he was irritated with himself for allowing her to do so.

Her pleading green eyes made it mighty hard to walk away. But he did.

Irma Rose might close her eyes from time to time but seldom her ears. As Lillian plopped down beside her in the waiting room, she opened her eyes and looked at her granddaughter. She had heard the sharpness in Samuel's tone when he declined the supper invitation, and it saddened her to see her granddaughter unhappy. But it was bound to happen. Samuel was content with his world, willingly locked into his life among the Plain folk, and he was a smart enough man to recognize what was happening between the two of them. Probably best he put an end to anything before it got started. It would be more painful for both of them down the road if he didn't.

"It takes a strong man to walk away from something he might want but knows isn't right by God."

Lillian tucked her head in embarrassment, "You heard?"

Irma Rose patted her leg. "I did."

"It was just an invitation for a meal. But the way he spoke to me was rather harsh."

As Irma Rose suspected, her granddaughter was hurt. "Be true to yourself, Lillian. There's a spark between you and that Samuel, and it has nowhere to turn but into flames. And if it had continued, you'd both have been burned far worse than you are now."

"It's not what you're thinking, Grandma. We talked about it. We were just going to be friends."

"*Ya*, so you say. But I saw him squeeze your hand at home when we were tending to Jonas. And I saw you reach for his hand a few minutes ago." Wondering if she'd already said too much, she went on. "Has he kissed you yet?"

"Grandma! Of course not."

Lillian's incredulous look screamed guilt. If they hadn't kissed, she imagined it wasn't for lack of wanting on Lillian's part.

"Lillian, we might be Plain and not know much about worldly things, but we love and we have desires, just like the rest of the world." She could only assume her granddaughter was no longer pure. Living out in the world, she was bound to have succumbed to things that would be unheard of in their Amish community. There was no judgment. It was just a fact.

"Samuel isn't wise about worldly ways, nor are your *daadi* and me. Temptation to step astray is unheard of in our community. We live by the *Ordnung*."

Lillian's face took on a flush, and her eyes filled with tears. Irma Rose regretted instantly that she'd clearly said something to hurt the girl's feelings. "Lillian, I just meant—"

But her granddaughter interrupted her. "You think I'm *seducing* Samuel. You think I'm filled with impure thoughts and tempting him to go against his beliefs!"

"That is not what I said, Lillian. What I meant was—"

"Grandma, you really don't know me at all. I'm nothing like my mother." And with that the child stormed off, leaving Irma Rose with a heavy heart.

Irma Rose knew Lillian spoke the truth. She *had* been fearful Lillian would pull Samuel into her world, in every way. Apparently she'd been wrong.

After four days of not seeing Samuel and barely speaking to her grandma, Lillian decided it was time to make amends with everyone. Grandma had tried repeatedly to apologize for anything she might have said to hurt her feelings, but Lillian had made little effort to recognize her attempts. She and Grandma had continued on with their daily chores, often side by side, but the tension was thick. Samuel had come to the door asking about her the day before, and she refused to come downstairs.

Today was a new day, and she was going to start fresh.

"Grandma," she said as she walked into the kitchen early that

morning. "I told you I'd make breakfast. Sit down and I'll do it."
She gently pried the spoon from Grandma's hand and began to
stir the eggs.

"You haven't had much to say to me, Lillian. I'm feeling badly
about things," Grandma said. She sat down on the bench at the
kitchen table.

"I'm sorry. I got my feelings hurt, and I should have talked
things out with you."

"I am sorry, Lillian. For me to presume that by living out in
the world you had not made good choices was wrong of me."
Lillian turned around to see her grandma shaking her head.

"Oh, I've made bad choices, Grandma. Make no mistake. But
I've tried to avoid some of the same blunders I watched my
mother make over the years." She had to accept responsibility for
her bad judgment when it came to Rickie. But she planned to
better her life by learning from the experience, as opposed to
reliving the pattern via a repetitious string of men who were
wrongly suited for her—as Mom did.

Grandma seemed to be in deep thought, a place she retreated
to anytime there was mention of her mother.

"I want to study the *Ordnung*. I want to learn everything about
living Amish. Maybe it would help me to get my mind right."

"Lillian," her grandma began, then paused. "Nothing would
please me more. Please don't take offense by what I am about to
say . . ." She hesitated again.

"What, Grandma?" Lillian stopped stirring the eggs and
turned completely around.

"Just do it for the right reasons."

"You mean not for Samuel, but for myself?"

"*Ya.*"

"I am. And I'm going to talk to Samuel and set things right with him as well. I want him to know I'm not interested in anything more than friendship with him and that there is no reason why we can't get back on track with that." And she meant it. She'd had a few days to realize that she needed to realign her proiorities. Lancaster County represented a new beginning. She wanted to get back to making the right choices.

———

"Well, hello there," she said to David later that afternoon. "Hey, where've you been?" he asked. His tone indicated his feelings might be hurt.

"I've just been thinking about things," she said as she followed him to the barn. "Whatcha doin'?"

He was carrying a cardboard box with a lid on it. "These are old newspapers I found in the other barn. They were getting wet, though, so I was moving 'em in here."

"Are there any more? Want some help?" She eyed the box, thinking maybe she'd catch up on the history of Lancaster County when she had some spare time.

"That was the last box. There were three of them." He pointed at two other boxes stacked nearby. "This barn stays dry. The other one has a few leaks. Pop says we'll fix those one day for Jonas and Irma Rose."

"Speaking of your pop, here he comes." She watched as Samuel maneuvered Pete onto the dirt driveway. "David," she said hesitantly. "Do you think it would be all right if I talked to your pop alone for a minute?"

"I think if it will make him stop being so sad, then *ya*." David shrugged and turned to walk off.

"David, wait," she said, realizing things didn't seem the same between them. He turned around and faced her, and the look on his face confirmed her suspicions. "Things are just complicated sometimes, you know?"

He seemed to be thinking as he glanced up to see his pop getting nearer. "I reckon sometimes grown-ups make things complicated that needn't be."

"*Ya*," she whispered as he walked off. "You're probably right."

Samuel was glad to see Lillian waiting for him in the front yard. He smiled with newfound confidence as he approached her. He had done a lot of soul-searching and prayed for answers over the past four days. He was creating problems that need not be there and worrying about things he shouldn't. They'd discussed the terms of their friendship, and there was no reason they had to stray from that. Being attracted to Lillian didn't mean he had to act on it.

"Hello, Samuel," she said as he walked to where she was sitting in the grass.

"I tried to talk to you yesterday. I feel badly about speaking so harshly to you when I left the hospital." He sat down in the grass beside her.

"I think I understand, and there are some things I want to clear up." She paused, then started to wave her hand in front of her nose.

"What?" he asked as she edged away from him.

"You smell like you've been rolling in manure, Samuel

Stoltzfus." She crinkled her nose as he sniffed at himself, feeling highly embarrassed.

"I came straight from the fields spreading manure, and the wheels from the plow probably slung some my way." He went to stand up, but she put a hand on his arm.

"No, sit down. I can take it." She giggled, but quickly removed her hand. "I just wanted to tell you that I think maybe you have the wrong impression about something, and I want you to understand that—"

"No, Lillian. Me first," he interrupted. "My chores aren't the whole truth as to why I said I couldn't come to supper. I've been worried that maybe you and me were moving in a direction that might not be right in God's eyes. But I've prayed hard about it, and I think maybe it's still His will for us to be friends." There. He'd said it. Now, with the Good Lord's help, he'd live the life God meant him to live and be the man he knew he should be.

"That's exactly what I wanted to tell you."

Samuel sighed with relief.

"Only, I have one more thing to tell you. I'm going to be studying the *Ordnung*. Grandma is planning to teach me everything about the Amish faith. And I just want to make it clear to you that I'm doing this for *me*, no other reason. I seem to have gotten sidetracked from my original plan when I came to Lancaster County: to find a sense of who I am and my role on this earth. I don't understand about God, or having a relationship with Him. But I *want* to understand. And I prayed to God to let Grandpa live. And it worked."

It worked? She wasn't exactly fully on the road to becoming Amish, but she at least had a foot on the path. So instead of arguing that her motivation for prayer was still misdirected, he said, "I think that's a fine idea." Studying the *Ordnung* would be good for Lillian. And they seemed to be clearing the air about some things.

"What's your pop and my Lilly have their heads together about?" Jonas asked David as he took a seat in the other rocker on the front porch.

"Not sure," David said.

Jonas strained to have a better look. Lilly had been moping around ever since they came home from the hospital. He didn't know what had happened, but he was hoping they'd fix whatever it was.

"I brought you boys some sweet tea," Irma Rose said, walking onto the porch toting two glasses. She looked out toward Lillian and Samuel. "Nice to see them talking again," she said as David attempted to get up and give her his seat. "Keep your seat," she said, smiling. "I can see better standing up."

"Pop's seemed kinda down lately," David said.

"Well, our Lilly has been in a *baremlich* mood too." Jonas shook his head.

"Definitely not herself lately." Irma Rose sat down on the porch step.

"They'll both be better now," David said. "They just have to get things uncomplicated."

"What do you mean, David?" Jonas asked him, curious where the boy's mind was.

"Lillian said her world was complicated. And by coming here, she's complicated my pop's world. She didn't mean to. It just happened." The boy shook his head and frowned. "They're both just making things complicated for themselves, and they needn't be. It's all real clear to me."

"What's clear?" Irma Rose asked.

The boy took a sip of his tea and said proudly, "She's my new *mamm*. Her and Pop just haven't figured it out yet."

Jonas knew his eyes were bugging out of his head. But he also knew a person wouldn't have to look far to find eyes gaping even larger than his own. You could've mistaken Irma Rose for an owl. She sat motionless, eyes bulging, speechless.

"Take a deep breath, Irma Rose," Jonas said, hoping his wife wouldn't say too much to the boy. He had to agree with David. Samuel and Lilly were making things too complicated. One day at a time. Once Lilly completed her studies of the *Ordnung*, there was no telling what the Good Lord might have in mind for them. But if they took to courting, it would be a long road to travel. He hoped they both survived the trip in one piece. He hoped Irma Rose would survive it. The woman was looking a tad pale.

"Well, David, stranger things have happened. I'm sure God will guide both your pop and our Lilly in the right direction," Jonas said as he reached over and patted poor Irma Rose on the hand.

David smiled. "He already has."

9

"WHAT DO YOU MEAN THERE IS NO EQUALITY OF THE sexes?" Lillian asked Grandma the next morning as they began to tackle the *Ordnung*.

"It's very clear in the Bible, Lillian." Grandma dried another plate and handed it to Lillian to put in the cabinet.

"It actually says in the Bible that women are to be subservient to men?"

Grandma looked confused, and Lillian realized she didn't understand the question. "The women serve the men, so to speak?" she translated.

"'He is the image and glory of God: but the woman is the glory of the man,'" Grandma said with pride. "'For the man is not of the woman: but the woman of the man. Neither was the man created for the woman; but the woman for the man.'"

Lillian sat down at the kitchen table, pondering the biblical reference. "I might have some trouble with this one, Grandma. Relationships should be an equal partnership." She shook her head. "I've noticed the way the Amish women always sit in the back, eat last, and wait on the men hand and foot."

"We are proud to do so. We don't question the Bible." Grandma placed another plate in the cabinet and took a seat at the kitchen table across from Lillian. "It is our job to care for our husbands, the children, and the home."

"I understand that, and that part is fine. But to say there is no equality just doesn't seem right."

"The man is the ruler of the home."

Lillian chuckled. "Now Grandma, you seem to have a pretty strong thumb on Grandpa."

Playfully Grandma said, "*Ya*, but Grandpa doesn't know that." She paused. "But in our early years, things were different. And I'm still proud to do for your Grandpa, even in his silliness."

"When I get married, my husband is going to have a clear understanding that we are entering into a union as *equals*."

"*Ya*, as long as you don't marry an Amish man," Grandma said, tilting her chin upward. "To marry an Amish man, you would say in your vows that the man is the head of the household and that you are his helpmate."

"Who made this rule?"

Grandma seemed taken aback. "Why, God, of course. We don't question the Bible, Lillian. Let's move along."

Lillian was still wrestling with the literal interpretation of this particular Bible reference when Grandma continued, "The two most important things to understand are our rejection of *hochmut*, which is pride and arrogance, and that we are not forward, self-promoting, or assertive. We let things be."

Grandma folded her hands together and sat up a little straighter. "For example," she pressed on. "It is perfectly fine for us to ride in automobiles. But to own such a means of transportation would be arrogant and prideful. There are so many different kinds of cars. All the choices of price, color, and accessories could cause us to be competitive—which would be a breeding ground for arrogance and pride. We have to watch our young folks when they go through their *rumschpringe*. Many times they add radios in the buggies or opt to install flashy trinkets, which distinguishes one from the other. That is not acceptable in our way of life."

"Okay," Lillian answered softly, realizing Grandma was enjoying her role as teacher. However, this topic was clearly non-negotiable.

"And when I say we let things be," she added, "that means we accept all things as being God's will. The *Englisch* often mistake our passiveness as not caring. That's not true. We do care. But we believe God will resolve a situation in a way that's best for all concerned."

As if checking items off on a mental list of things to teach Lillian, Grandma continued. "Our children become adults when they are baptized and make a lifetime vow of obedience to the *Ordnung*."

"How is the *Ordnung* different from the Bible?" Lillian didn't know a lot about the Bible. But at least the Bible was a book that could be studied. So much of the *Ordnung* was unwritten.

"Let me see how I can explain this so you will understand," Grandma pondered, pausing. "You really can't compare the *Ordnung* to the Bible, Lillian. We believe in literal interpretation of the Bible. Meaning we don't question it. That belief is part of the *Ordnung*, which is our governing system. The *Ordnung* is a means of making sure we all live by the Scriptures in the Bible."

"Shouldn't all the rules be written down for people to study and to prevent misinterpretations?" *You'd think over the many years someone would have done that.*

"The *Ordnung* varies from district to district. Governance is local."

"So why aren't the rules for the *Ordnung* in this district written down and studied?" Lillian had spent the better part of her life studying written texts, all the way through college. She'd made a career out of teaching others to do the same.

"We just know them," Grandma answered. "We begin learning the order of conduct in the *Ordnung* at a young age. It's passed down from generation to generation."

Seeing there was no hope for a written study guide, a practical question popped into Lillian's head. She knew the rule but hoped it could be bent. "Grandma, I don't understand why we can't cut our hair. It seems to me that as busy as we are, it would be a lot easier to manage, and—"

Grandma vigorously shook her head; it appeared that there was no questioning this rule. "No, no, no, Lillian. 'But if a woman have long hair, it is a glory to her: for her hair is given her for a covering.' This is in Corinthians, Lillian. We do not cut our hair."

Grandma abruptly jumped up. "I have something for you, Lillian. Wait here."

It was a couple of minutes before she returned from upstairs. Rejoining Lillian at the table, she handed her a black book. "Is this for me to keep?" Lillian asked. She'd never owned a Bible.

"It is. And you'll notice an inscription inside from me and your grandpa." Bouncing back in time, she said, "I bought it when you were born."

Lillian read the inscription: *This Holy Bible presented to Lillian Miller by Mammi and Daadi.*

"I've dreamed about this day." Grandma's eyes grew moist. "I'd hoped that maybe someday you'd come callin' for the Lord. I'd meant to give it to you when you were here last. You were young, but I meant to send it after you left." She shook her head. "And I forgot."

"Thank you, Grandma." Holding the book gave Lillian an unfamiliar sense of hope.

"You seem to need words to study," Grandma offered. "Study the Bible, Lillian. It is the contents of this book that we live by. To understand the *Ordnung*, you must first understand God's Word."

"I will, Grandma." She blinked back her own emotions.

The lesson continued for the rest of the morning while they baked extra loaves of bread for a sick friend of Grandma's. With a full plate of her own, Grandma never complained and always volunteered to help those around her.

For the next several weeks, Samuel and David ate supper once a week with Lillian, Irma Rose, and sometimes Jonas, when he was well enough. Lillian always cooked, and much of the menu came from Samuel's garden. It was the highlight of Lillian's week. Finally, she had a family. A *real* family. David and Samuel had become as much a part of her little group as Jonas and Irma Rose.

"How are your studies of the *Ordnung* coming along?" Samuel asked one evening after supper.

Lillian handed him and David each a piece of shoofly pie. "It's a lot to learn, but I'm getting there. It's hard because so much of the *Ordnung* isn't written down. Everyone here starts learning at such a young age and I guess it just sticks. I'm trying to absorb and store all the information as best I can."

She thought it best not to mention her constant questioning of their ways. Grandma spent much of their morning sessions exasperated by Lillian's inability to just accept complete obedience to God's will without all the questions. But with strained patience, Grandma continued to instruct her daily about the code of conduct they all lived by. She realized how hopeful Grandma was that she'd choose their ways.

"She's a fast learner," Grandma said, placing a piece of pie on a plate. "I'm going to take this upstairs to Jonas."

After waiting until Grandma was out of earshot, Samuel asked, "How is Jonas? I noticed he hasn't been at supper the past two weeks."

"I don't think he's doing so well," she said, taking a seat on the bench beside David and across from Samuel. "He's been in bed a lot during the day too. It's hard on Grandma. I've offered to help her with Grandpa, but she insists on taking care of him all by herself."

"Men are funny about things. Maybe Jonas wouldn't be comfortable with you tending to him," Samuel said.

"Well, he's going to have to get over that, or I'm afraid Grandma's going to just wear herself out."

"*Ya*, it's hard when you're a caregiver."

"You took real good care of my *mamm*," David said to Samuel.

"I did the best I could."

Samuel often looked uncomfortable at the mention of Rachel. Lillian sure wanted to know what the woman looked like and more about her. But she'd never know. Samuel offered up little

information about Rachel and she'd learned the second commandment forbid photos: *Thou shalt not make unto thee any graven
image, or any likeness of any thing that is in heaven above, or that is in the
earth beneath, or that is in the water under the earth.*

She had been studying. And putting on her Amish attire had
become as natural as brushing her teeth in the morning. But to
go without *any* pictures the rest of your life . . . That particular
rule, like several others, seemed to take things too literally. But
literal interpretation of the Bible was the Amish way. There was
no picking and choosing of the rules.

"It must be hard not to have any pictures to remember her
by," she said, resting her chin in her hands. She glanced back and
forth between Samuel and David. "I don't like that rule."

"I remember exactly what she looked like," Samuel said softly
and in a tone she seldom heard him use. He seemed a million
miles away with thoughts of Rachel.

Lillian's stomach twisted. For all her honest efforts to keep a
healthy distance from Samuel, the thought of him having loved
someone *that* much bothered her immensely.

"*Ya*, me too," David said, lost in the same world as Samuel.

"But wouldn't it be nice to have a picture of her?"

Both of them looked at her like she was crazy.

"We have a picture of her," Samuel said. He pointed to his
head.

"It's not the same." She shook her head and paused. "When I
have children, I want to have pictures of them growing up."

"It's not our way, Lillian," Samuel said, as if there was no room
for further discussion.

"Do you want *kinner*?" David asked with a keen interest.

"Lots of them." She loved children. "And I'm going to be a much better mother than my mother." The mention of children caused her to reflect on her students at Northbrook High. She'd regretted having to leave her teaching job.

"I don't think she did such a *baremlich* job," David said.

Lillian nudged her shoulder against his and smiled. "*Danki*, David."

"I think you'll make a fine *mamm*." David glanced at Samuel. "Don't you, Pop?"

Samuel looked uncomfortable. "I'm sure she will," he said.

Lillian found the awkward way he made the remark touching.

———

She is so good with David.

There was no doubt in Samuel's mind Lillian would be a good mother someday. It was hard for him not to occasionally fantasize about a life with her. With each passing day, he found her more beautiful and more interesting. He'd allowed the occasional fantasy to float around in his head, but he always followed it up with a dose of hard reality. Lillian usually did or said something to remind him of their many differences or brought up one of the Amish "rules" she didn't agree with. She seemed to be going through all the motions by learning the *Ordnung*, attending worship, studying the language, reading the Bible, and following community traditions. It was just a mighty big change for her, and he had serious doubts she'd choose a life in their world. Her ideas about pictures were a good example.

"Why did your *mamm* leave here?" David asked.

"David!" Samuel said, reprimanding the boy. "That's *schnup-pich.*" He knew it was a painful subject for Lillian.

"No, it's not snoopy," she said, pausing. "I don't know why she left. I think something happened, though. Something *big* that no one wants to talk about."

"Like what?" David pushed.

"David," Samuel warned. The boy should have no interest in such things. Plus, the look on Lillian's face told him that her bubbly spirit was taking a nosedive.

"I don't know." Her lips folded into a frown. But, in a forced effort, she sat up a little straighter and smiled. "And I'm starting not to care. She made her choices, and I'm making mine."

Her statement was strong, but Samuel knew it wasn't true. She cared a lot.

Lillian walked Samuel and David to the buggy, as had become the norm each time they came for supper. David always needed to go back into the house for something—either to go to the bathroom or because he'd forgotten his hat or needed a drink of water. It was always something, and he wasn't fooling anyone. Lillian could see right through his forgetfulness and last-minute potty breaks. His intent was for her and Samuel to spend a few minutes alone. And she had to admit: it was a welcomed gesture on young David's part.

This night in particular, David stayed gone longer than usual. Maybe it was the full moon, or maybe it was the way Samuel was looking at her, but Lillian's heart was bursting with emotion.

Despite their initial attraction, they'd pushed impure thoughts aside and a special friendship was blossoming. She was just about to tell him how much she enjoyed their weekly suppers when he hit her with a piece of news.

"I know staying for supper has become a regular thing on Wednesdays," he said, sounding hesitant to continue. "But next week David and I will be eating supper elsewhere." His gaze shifted from her to David, who was slowly making his way back to the buggy.

She was disappointed, but tried not to sound as let down as she felt. "All right," she said, and then added, "But you know you're always welcome to change your mind."

"Change his mind about what?" David asked as he walked into earshot.

Samuel crawled in the buggy and shut the door, motioning for David to do the same thing. "I was just telling Lillian how we wouldn't be havin' supper here next week."

David let out a big sigh. "*Ya*, we have to have supper with Sadie Fisher." He shook his head in obvious disappointment, but Lillian doubted his unhappiness equaled her own sense of displeasure.

No wonder Samuel hurried into the safe haven of his buggy; probably afraid of her reaction. The thought of him having supper with anyone other than her—much less Sadie Fisher— was a hard blow. But she kept her thoughts to herself. She and Samuel weren't courting. How could she justify such jealous thoughts?

"It's even worse we have to go on a picnic with her the next Saturday," David said as he frowned and continued to shake his head.

"What? A picnic?" she asked, foregoing her plan to keep her thoughts to herself. "How cozy," she added sarcastically, shooting a look of disapproval at Samuel.

"She kept asking to cook for me and the boy," Samuel said defensively, "so I finally accepted her kindness." He shrugged, signifying he owed her no further explanation.

Kindness? There was nothing *kind* about it. She bit her tongue so hard it hurt. When she didn't respond, Samuel added fuel to the fire.

"The elders think I should at least give courtin' Sadie a try. So she's cooking supper for me and David next week. And we're going on a picnic the following Saturday."

"*Courting?* You're going to court her?" Her tone was demanding and laced with angry bewilderment.

"I don't know, I just . . ." He paused briefly, but his tone firmed up. "*Ya,* I am." As he sat up a little straighter, his look challenged her to argue.

Trying to stare him down, she was having a much harder time controlling her emotions. She knew what that meant: tears were not far behind. "Fine," she said. She turned her back and walked briskly toward the house. "Just *fine.*"

"I told you she'd be real mad, Pop," David said as they headed toward home.

"No need for her to be. We're only friends." Samuel really didn't want to have this conversation with his son. He knew exactly how the boy felt about Lillian. And how David felt about Sadie.

Maybe Sadie wasn't the one for him and David, but Samuel knew he needed to go through the motions, at least.

Whatever it took to keep Lillian from creeping into his dreams at night.

But Lillian's reaction to his news only made him want to be with her that much more. She was as jealous as she could be, and it warmed his heart. And to have such notions made him wonder if he was doing right by Sadie. His intentions were mostly in the right place. But was he really being fair to her? Agreeing to give it a try because the elders thought it was a good match didn't seem the best way to approach a courtship. If he was true to his heart, he'd have to admit that courting Sadie would distract him from the person he really wanted to be with but couldn't have.

Samuel refused to set himself and his boy up for heartbreak if Lillian chose to leave the district.

"I'd rather be havin' supper with Lillian next week," David snapped. "And I sure don't want to go on a picnic with Sadie either!"

Samuel stopped the buggy with a sharp pull on the reins. He turned to face his son, whose face was shriveled into a scowl. "I did not raise you to speak to me in that tone, David." He'd never heard his son use such an angry voice. Yet another reason he needed to put some distance between not only him and Lillian, but *David* and Lillian. The boy was way too attached to her.

Samuel prepared to reprimand the boy even more, but stopped when he saw David's scowl shifting into a look of hopelessness. As his son's eyes clouded with tears, he hadn't the heart to scold him further.

"I miss my *mamm*," he said softly, turning to face Samuel.

"I know."

"And if you court Sadie, I'll miss Lillian." His tone pleaded for Samuel to reconsider his plan.

He gave Pete a flick of the reins and bolted back into a trot down the dark dirt road. How could he tell his son how much he'd miss Lillian, too, and still make him understand that it was best to put some distance between them? He didn't want to send the boy mixed messages.

"Please don't court Sadie, Pop. Please!"

In a tone harsher than Samuel had ever used with the boy, he said, "This talk is over!"

Lillian was glad her grandparents were upstairs asleep. She lit the propane lantern above the kitchen table and rummaged around for a snack. Grabbing some butter bread and a glass of tea, she plopped down on the bench and stuffed herself silly. It was misery eating, she knew. And she didn't care. "I'll just be a big fat Amish woman," she whispered angrily, stuffing another piece of bread in her mouth. It was a flippant statement, and she was glad no one was around to hear it. One thing she'd learned since her arrival was that all the hard work allowed for extra calories. It was a healthy balance.

How could Samuel even think about courting Sadie? She shook her head. It was fine being friends with him as long as it was an exclusive arrangement. Sharing him with the likes of Sadie Fisher was another thing. And this was worse than just breaking their friendship bond. He was actually going to pursue a romantic involvement with Sadie. Courting to the Amish meant a prerequisite to marriage. Surely Samuel was not considering marrying this woman? She shoved another piece of bread in her mouth.

"How's my Lilly?"

She hadn't heard Grandpa come down the stairs. "Grandpa!" she scolded. "You're supposed to get me or Grandma before you come down the stairs by yourself."

He waved her off and took a seat across from her at the kitchen table. "I was hungry."

"Well, you should have gotten Grandma up."

Frowning, he whispered, "She's cranky, Lilly, when she gets woke up." He leaned in and helped himself to a piece of the bread she had piled on a plate. "Hungry?" he asked sarcastically, eyeing the mound before her.

"I'm eating my misery away," she said, stuffing in another piece of the moist buttery bread.

"And what does my Lilly have to be miserable about this fine evening?"

"Samuel is going to court Sadie Fisher," she said around a mouthful.

"*Ya*, I heard there's a rumor about that going 'round town." He shook his head. "And this makes my Lilly feel like she has to eat a loaf of bread?" He shot her a questioning grin.

"I know how things stand with Samuel and me, Grandpa. Really, I do."

"Do you now? Because it sounds to me like you're jealous." His grin transformed into a look of disapproval. "And jealousy is a sin, Lilly."

"I'm not jealous, Grandpa. There's no reason to be. Samuel can certainly court whoever he wants. We share a friendship. Nothing more."

"Who you tryin' to convince, Lilly, me or you?"

"Well, of course I know we're just friends. It's just . . . well, if he's courting Sadie, I won't get to see him and David as much. We're buddies. That's all. Samuel and I agreed it was best to keep it that way."

Grandpa smiled broadly. "My silly little *kinskind*. I may be a Plain man who's been married longer than I remember, but the only two people who don't know you and Samuel are *in lieb* are you and Samuel."

"We're not in love, Grandpa! But we have a special relationship."

Grandpa frowned, as if he knew she was lying. "A courtship with Samuel would be filled with challenges," he said. "But the Lord sometimes makes the good things worth the struggle."

"Well, there's no courtship going on with me. He's courting Sadie."

"Maybe that's for the best, then," he said softly.

"How can it be for the best when—" Stopping abruptly, she knew what she'd almost done.

"When *what*, Lilly?"

She looked down at the half-eaten loaf of bread and sighed. Was she fooling herself by thinking she could remain friends with him? If the thought of him courting Sadie sent her into this much of a tailspin—well, perhaps she *did* have feelings. But no one had to know. "I just got used to having them around. They've become like family."

"*Ya*," her grandpa said as he sat up a little taller and stroked his beard. "They surely have."

It took a couple of days for Lillian to adopt a more mature attitude about the prospect of Samuel and Sadie courting. After a good cry, she concluded that at this point in her life she wasn't worthy of Samuel's affections. It was only right he should seek someone better suited for him and David. So after keeping her nose in the air and ignoring Samuel those first two days, she spent the rest of the week making polite small talk when he arrived to pick up David—if she happened to be outside when he showed up. Funny thing, she always seemed to be outside when he arrived.

But she made it a point to stay in the house when she heard Samuel coming up the drive to pick up David the following Wednesday. As she peeked out the window, her heart was breaking. The thought of Samuel and David spending an evening with Sadie was almost enough to make her run outside and beg them not to go.

The temptation was mounting when she heard her cell phone ringing upstairs. Knowing Grandpa was sleeping, she jetted up the stairs two at a time. Grandma met her at the top of the stairs with a frown. "Sorry," she whispered, offering her grandma a sheepish smile. She'd meant to turn it off and just check messages to save her battery. Charging her battery in town was a hassle, and she knew it irritated Grandma to hear it ringing in the house. Although her mother hadn't called her in weeks—not since she'd called and said she was sending Lillian money. Money that never arrived.

"Hello," she said breathlessly into the phone.

"I miss you."

She sat down on the bed and pushed back her hair. She recognized the voice immediately. "Hi, Rickie."

"Did you hear me, Lillian? I miss you." His humble tone filled her with memories. In the beginning, things had been so good between them. It took a while for him to show his true colors. But he did. More than once.

As if reading her mind, he went on. "There's nothing we can't fix, Lillian. I want you in my life, and I'm willing to do whatever it takes to make things right between us." He paused, then continued when she didn't respond. "It's been weeks, Lillian. I've left you alone like you asked in your letter. And that was really hard. I wanted to call you so much, but I thought if I gave you some time, you'd come around. Come home, Lillian. Please. I promise—"

"Rickie," she interrupted before his tone tempted her to believe him. She knew better. "I've started over in a new place. I have a new life."

"I know," he said. "And I think that's great. Putting some distance between us has made me realize how much I love you. Please, Lillian, come home."

"I *am* home, Rickie." And she realized she meant it. Her feet were firmly planted, and she wasn't going anywhere.

"Then I'll come to you. I'll get on a plane tomorrow. Your mom said you're in Lancaster County with your grandparents."

She'd specifically told her mother she didn't want Rickie to know where she was going. *How could she do that?* "No, Rickie!"

"Just for a short visit," he pushed on. "We just need some time together to sort this out."

Rickie was a born salesman. He might sell expensive cars for a living, but he wasn't about to sell her his story that he was a changed man. "No," she repeated.

An uncomfortable silence brewed, and Lillian said, "Rickie, I need to go."

"Is there someone else?"

She didn't say anything.

"Oh, I see," he said after a while.

"There's no one else, Rickie. But I've changed my life."

"I heard. Your mom said you're living with the Amish. Surely you haven't become one of them?"

She would have flown through the phone line if she could have. How dare he say *them* as if they were from another planet? "As a matter of fact, I have," she said firmly. She wasn't sure if this was true, but she hoped it would deter Rickie.

"So you're all into God now?" He sounded disgusted.

Her first instinct was to yell at him, to defend her actions. But . . . *That isn't the Amish way.* As soon as the thought registered in her mind, she realized it stemmed from the hours of time she'd spent with Grandma studying the *Ordnung.* She had a long way to go, but some of it was sinking in. The way she might have handled Rickie in the past no longer seemed appropriate.

"I'm learning to live a different life, a better life. I think the way to do that might be through God."

She could hear him yelling at her choice of lifestyle, but it became fainter and fainter as she realized the implications of what she just said, and the fact that she *meant* it. She *was* giving God a shot . . . for the first time in her life. Trusting that He was there.

"Good-bye, Rickie," she said softly, and she hung up the phone.

When she returned downstairs, she gazed out the window in the den. Samuel and David were gone, and Sadie would be cooking for *her* family tonight. A combination of bitterness and despair crept through her like a virus, targeting her heart and landing in the pit of her stomach. She'd grown to love Samuel and David, and with that love came a new sense of unselfishness unfamiliar to her. How could she deny Samuel and David a life with someone who might be better for them?

"I'm trying, God. I'm trying to have faith. I'm trying to live a good life. Please help me to trust that You will provide what's best for me," she whispered, "and for Samuel and David."

She felt a hand on her shoulder.

"Grandma, I didn't hear you come downstairs. Is everything okay?" She was embarrassed that Grandma might have heard her praying. She wasn't entirely comfortable with her evolving relationship with God.

"*Ya*, Jonas is sleeping soundly," Grandma said, sighing. "He isn't feeling well."

Her gray hair was bound tightly in a bun on her head. Deep wrinkles spiderwebbed from the corners of her eyes and trailed downward, burrowing into sunken pale cheeks. The circles under her eyes were more prevalent than usual, and her stance indicated sheer exhaustion might cause her to surrender to gravity at any minute.

"Grandma, you can't go on like this. You have to let me help you with Grandpa." She grabbed her grandmother's elbow and walked her to the nearby rocker. All the while Grandma was shaking her head.

"Why not?" Lillian asked.

"Your *daadi* is a proud man, Lillian. Sometimes he gets down in a bad way. He wouldn't want his Lilly to see him like that." She kept shaking her head.

"Irma Rose!"

Grandma jumped when she heard him calling, but Lillian gently grabbed her shoulders. "Grandma, let me go to him. I can handle it. You have got to get some rest."

She watched her Grandma eyeing the staircase as if it were Mount Everest. "But he might need—"

"Whatever it is, I will handle it. Go have a snack or something. I'll take care of Grandpa."

Before Grandma could refuse, she headed for the staircase. Halfway up the stairs he cried out again. But it wasn't Grandma's name or Lillian's name he was calling. Lillian froze in her tracks on the staircase, her legs trembling.

10

FORCING HER FEET TO MANEUVER UP THE STAIRS, LILLIAN eased into her grandparents' bedroom, dimly illuminated by one small lantern on a nightstand by the bed. On a wooden hutch across the room there were at least a dozen pill bottles, a pitcher of water, a glass, and a Bible. Grandpa was tucked under a brown-and-red quilt, his eyes closed. His thinning gray hair was tousled and flattened against a feather pillow, and his breathing was labored, his mouth opened wide.

Taking a seat on the wooden chair beside the bed, she said, "Hi, Grandpa." She reached over and touched his arm.

Twitching his pale face, he slowly opened his eyes and smiled. "Sarah Jane," he said softly. She'd hoped maybe she heard him wrong when she was walking up the staircase.

"Grandpa, it's Lilly," she said. She gently squeezed his arm and leaned in closer to make sure he could see her clearly.

"I've missed you," he said tenderly.

"I saw you at breakfast this morning, Grandpa."

"*Ya, ya,*" he whispered. "Is the pond frozen up? Reckon we'll have to shine your skates up."

"Grandpa, it's summertime," she said hesitantly, resisting the urge to cry. *What is wrong with him?* He'd been frail since she arrived, but his mind was always sharp as a tack.

146

He laughed. "I'm a silly old man. I know you're a might too old to be skatin' on the pond." He leaned in close and his eyebrows lowered as he reached over and gently clutched her arm. Gazing hard into her eyes, he said, "You'll be breakin' your *mamm's* heart if you leave us, Sarah Jane. I know something's goin' on with you. Talk to your Pop."

"Grandpa," she whispered, "it's Lilly."

He was looking right through her with a glassy expression. "It's the *Englisch* man, ain't it?"

"What?"

"*Ya.* Your *mamm* ought not know 'bout this, Sarah Jane. But I reckon' I've seen the newspapers you've been stashing in the barn. The *Englisch* man writes of worldly ways, Sarah Jane, things best not learned. And you ought to stay away from him."

Her mind was awhirl, thinking about the boxes David moved into the barn. "What *Englisch* man?" she asked.

Grandpa released his grasp on her arm and pushed back gray bangs that were too long and had fallen forward. Swiping his brow, he frowned and shook his head.

"Grandpa, what *Englisch* man?" she asked again. But, he closed his eyes.

"Grandpa?"

Within seconds, the labored breathing returned, and she realized he was fast asleep. Lillian sat quietly for a few minutes, until she heard footsteps coming up the stairs. She turned to see Grandma entering the room.

"What did he need?" she asked.

"I don't know." Lillian paused. "He thought I was my mother."

Grandma patted her shoulder. "It happens. I reckon it's those pills the doctor gives him." She waved her arm toward the hutch. "Sometimes he thinks I'm *his* mother."

"Does he just snap out of it?" She hoped so.

"*Ya.* He mostly acts up like this right after he takes the pills."

"Oh," she said softly, contemplating whether or not to share the conversation with her grandma. Deciding she wasn't up for such a discussion, she excused herself.

She barely choked down her breakfast the next morning. After cleaning up the kitchen, she told Grandma she was going to the barn to brush Jessie and lavish a little attention on him for a while. Giving her loose strands of hair a final tuck under her white *Kapp*, she asked, "Need me for anything else right now?"

"You go on," Grandma said. "I'm going to take these *dippy eggs* on up to Jonas." She poured a glass of orange juice and toted everything up the stairs.

On the way to the barn, Lillian pondered on what Grandpa had said the night before. Between that and thoughts of Sadie cooking for Samuel and David, she hadn't gotten much sleep.

"Hello, Jessie," she said, prying the barn door open. Giving the horse a quick stroke on the snout, she made her way to the stacked boxes in the corner and heaved the top box down to the dirt floor. In the dim light of early morning, she saw *The Intelligencer Journal, November 2, 1980* folded neatly on top. Lifting the newspaper up, she could see the box was filled with past issues.

Why did Mom save all these? And what Englisch man was Grandpa referring to?

The Intelligencer Journal was a daily publication. But upon further inspection, she noticed they were all thick Sunday editions. *Why only Sunday papers,* she wondered.

The Budget was the choice of newspaper for the Amish in Lancaster County—the national Amish publication coedited by both the Amish and English. Grandma read *The Budget* every Wednesday. Grandma also read *Die Botschaft*—strictly for Old Order Amish—every week. But she'd never seen *The Intelligencer Journal* in the house.

Placing one of Jessie's saddle pads on the dirt floor, she took a seat with the November 2 issue of *The Intelligencer.* She scanned the headline. "U.S. President Jimmy Carter and Ronald Reagan Debate in Cleveland, Ohio."

"Wow," she whispered as she flipped through the pages to the entertainment section. *Star Wars: The Empire Strikes Back* and *Friday the 13th* were movies featured at the theatres. Both movies were made before she was even born. "Sailing" by Christopher Cross was the top record. And everyone wanted to know who shot J. R., evidently from some TV show named *Dallas.* The headline said the November 21 conclusion was expected to draw more viewers than any other show in TV history.

She set the paper aside and retrieved the next issue in the box. *November 9, 1980.* Ronald Reagan won the presidential election in a landslide victory. The NASA space probe Voyager I made its closest approach to Saturn and sent the first high-resolution images of the world back to Earth. And people were still talking about who'd shot J.R.

While all this was fascinating, why did her mother save all these papers? Clearly, it had something to do with an *Englisch* man who wrote about worldly events, as Grandpa put it. Continuing to flip through each Sunday edition, she looked for something each issue had in common.

After an hour, she was starting to doubt the newspapers had anything to do with anything. But July 27, 1980, offered up a clue. As she had been doing, she scanned the front page headlines. "Former Turkish Prime Minister Nihat Erim Killed by Two Gunmen in Istanbul, Turkey." And "Pope John Paul II Visits Brazil—Seven People Crushed to Death in Crowd."

No wonder the Amish didn't read the daily papers and stuck with *The Budget* and *Die Botschaft*. Bad news was everywhere.

The most interesting items to her were what movies were showing and the top albums. She scanned the entertainment section and almost closed the paper when something in the columns section caught her eye. Actually, not the column itself, but the inscription beside it. She couldn't be sure, but it looked like her mother's handwriting. *Daniel and Sarah Jane forever.*

She pulled the newspaper closer to her face to get a better look. Daniel Foster looked to be in his late twenties. Maybe thirty. Although it was hard to tell from the black-and-white photo above his column, he looked to be a handsome guy. Sporting clean-cut short hair and a pair of large, gold-rimmed glasses, he smiled above his column, entitled "Outside the Box." She read:

The road to happiness is filled with paths of self-discovery. One slip, and you can end up going down the wrong path with no map to guide you back to the main road. How do we as individuals choose which road will fulfill our destiny with the least amount of challenges? Are we born into a predetermined plan? Is it fate? Or do the choices we make render us capable of creating our own destiny?

These are questions I have pondered. In the end, I believe we create our own destiny. But notwithstanding an occasional trip down the wrong path. The key is realizing when it's the wrong path and having the courage to do a little backtracking until you are back on the road to the life you were meant to live.

Were all his columns this *heavy*? She grabbed the next paper and read:

Dreams are the manifestations of our daily thoughts. Although some dreams might seem like they came out of nowhere, that's not true. We have but one mind, and the thought processes—whether in waking hours or asleep—belong to us exclusively. So the next time you have a bizarre dream that makes no sense, take the time to dissect it. There might be a message in there somewhere.

Lillian tossed the paper aside and went on to the next issue, thinking about her mom reading the columns twenty-eight years ago. Clearly, his message had intrigued Mom.

Religion and spirituality—are they one and the same? I think not. I know people who are religious and who lack a shred of spirituality. Then there are those who never attend church but possess more spirituality than most . . .

She read at least ten more columns. Two of the ten had hearts drawn around them. All thought-provoking in some way, she could see why her mother would have a crush on the guy. But she wasn't naïve and she'd done the math. Her mother would have been eighteen in 1980. Mom left the Amish community in 1981. Lillian was born in 1981. Could this guy be her father?

Her heart was pounding against her chest. Maybe, just maybe, she'd be able to find her father. He was handsome, a good writer, deep, and apparently spiritual.

Her heart raced faster. Finally, after all these years . . . just maybe.

There was only one way to find out.

―――

"Hi, Mom," Lillian said. She'd retrieved her cell phone and headed back to the barn without Grandma's knowledge.

"Lillian, what a surprise. Is everything okay?"

"Yeah, everything is fine."

"I know you're probably wondering about the money, Lillian. I had it all ready to put in the mail to you, and I—"

"It doesn't matter, Mom," she interrupted. "I want to talk to you about something else."

"What's that?"

"Who's Daniel Foster?"

The line was silent so long, Lillian wondered if her mother was still on the other end. "Mom?"

"Yes, I'm here."

"I found the newspapers in the barn. I read his columns, and I saw where you wrote—"

"Lillian!" her mother interrupted hastily. "I don't know where you're going with this, but just leave it alone."

Her mom's voice was quivering, and Lillian knew she'd hit the nail on the head. "He's my father, isn't he?" She knew her tone was demanding, but she'd been denied any knowledge about her father because her mother had refused to discuss it, always saying she just didn't know who he was. Lies. All lies. She knew exactly who he was.

"Is *he* why you left Lancaster County? Is he, Mom? I have a right to know who my own father is. It's him, isn't it?" She realized her voice rose to a near yell.

"Lillian. Please let this go." Her mom was crying, but Lillian pushed on. She felt it was her right to know.

"Mother," she said sharply. "You said you never knew who my father was. If you covered this up for all these years . . . That is *so* wrong. You owe me this."

"I was young, Lillian. I was just so young." She was crying full force now.

Lillian softened her tone. "Mom, please. Please tell me. I'm trying so hard to start a new life. I'm trying so hard to find answers and fill the voids. This is part of the process for me. You have wonderful parents. You can't deny me the right to even know who my father is." Her own tears began to flow as she realized she needed to know, but at the same time was afraid to know.

"DNA does not make a person a parent, Lillian."

Confirmation. "Oh, Mom. So Daniel Foster is my father."

"Yes."

Lillian grabbed her chest, sure that her heart was going to leap through her skin. "Why didn't you ever tell me?"

When her mother didn't answer, Lillian went on. "Is that why you left Lancaster County? You were pregnant with me? Why didn't you tell someone? It would have been hard, but I don't think Grandma and Grandpa would have—"

"Shunned me?" her mother interjected with a sharp tone. "No, Lillian. They would not have shunned me in the traditional sense because I wasn't baptized. But I was eighteen years old, and I had premarital sex with an *Englisch* man. Reprimanding by the community would have been equally as harsh as a shunning. I couldn't have stayed. The embarrassment for your grandparents . . . I just couldn't stay. It was best to leave and never say anything."

"All these years, Grandma and Grandpa never understood why you chose to leave the district." She paused. "And what about me, Mom? You let me believe that you didn't know who my father was. How could you do that? How?"

"Lillian," Mom cried, "you don't understand."

"Then explain it to me!"

"I made a horrible mistake and I didn't know what to do. Daniel gave me some money, and I left to start a new life."

"Why couldn't you have started a life with him?"

Mom wept harder. "He wouldn't have me, Lillian. He wanted nothing to do with me or having a baby. Daniel said he would deny the entire thing, that I would be an outcast in my community, and that it would be best for me to leave town."

"And you never saw him again? Did he ever see me? Did he know you had a girl?"

"I never heard from him or saw him again. Please, Lillian. Now you know. Let it go."

"I'm going to find him. He'll want to meet me after all these years. I'll find him, Mom, with or without your help."

Sobs were vibrating through the phone lines. "No, Lillian. It was a long time ago. Please don't do this. I doubt he even still lives near Paradise."

"Mom!" she cried. "That's three miles down the road. I could have bumped into him on the streets in town. How could you not have told me?"

"Lillian, leave it alone."

"Good-bye, Mom."

She hung up the phone, nervous anticipation flooding over her, commingled with fury and sympathy for her mother. As angry as she was with Sarah Jane Miller, hearing her mother relive that painful part of her past pulled at her heartstrings in an unfamiliar way.

Samuel eyeballed a big wooden table outside a shop in Paradise. It wasn't as nice as the one in Intercourse—the one he would buy someday. He wondered if that day would ever come. Lately his visions of the table in his kitchen came with a detailed picture of him and David sitting at the table with several other children—and Lillian cooking supper. It was a notion he couldn't seem to shake.

Telling Sadie the night before that a courtship wasn't going to work had been hard. Extra hard when she started to cry. But carrying on with her when he couldn't shake his feelings for Lillian wasn't fair. Not even the elders could push him into a courtship with someone he didn't think he could ever love. And it wasn't fair to the boy either.

He'd rather hold out hope that maybe Lillian could find her way to the peaceful way of life she was longing for. That maybe she'd find God in her heart. She'd so lovingly accepted him and David into her heart. Why was it so hard for her to accept God's will in her life? It wasn't his way, but maybe he should help her more. After all, she'd had no upbringing that would teach her such things.

It was a difficult situation—compounded by the fact he could list all the reasons Lillian wasn't right for him and David. But the bottom line was she brought out feelings in him he'd only ever had for Rachel. And allowing himself to indulge usually resulted in guilt. Guilt that he shouldn't have such thoughts when Rachel was the love of his life. He still dreamed of her. Only now, not as often. It was both comforting and worrisome when Lillian showed up in his dreams more often than Rachel these days.

As he continued to fantasize about a life with Lillian, he caught a glimpse of her out of the corner of his eye. Was she looking for him? She was sure looking for something. He headed toward her.

She appeared frazzled. Her hair looked like she'd been on another high-speed buggy ride, tousled and dangling about her beautiful face. But something was wrong. Her eyes were swollen and registered an uncharacteristic seriousness.

"Hello," he said as he walked up to her.

"Hi, Samuel," she said with little emotion. He was being punished, which he probably deserved. He'd need to set her straight about Sadie right away.

"What are you looking for?"

She shot him a look that confirmed what he suspected, and didn't answer. Yeah, she was mad all right.

"Are you not speaking to me?" he asked, leaning down.

"Where's Sadie?" she blurted out. "I figured the two of you would be planning your picnic for Saturday."

He grinned. He couldn't help it. She was jealous. And it felt so good. "*Ya,* the picnic," he teased.

"What are you grinning about?" She put her hands on her hips and attempted to stare him down with her big green eyes. Swollen eyes.

"What's wrong?" he said, changing the subject. "I can tell you've been crying."

"Don't worry about it," she said harshly. "I'm fine."

"You don't look fine."

"Well, I am."

"What do you think would be good to take on a picnic?" He was toying with her, and in light of her current mood, he knew he was stepping on thin ice.

"Samuel Stoltzfus, what you and Sadie decide to take on your picnic is of no concern to me." She leaned in and cut him down to the bone with her look.

"You like tuna salad, don't you?"

"Who cares what I like. Go ask Sadie what she likes!" Her tone was getting really mean. Better tell her.

"Why would I ask Sadie what she likes when it's you I'm taking on a picnic on Saturday?" He shot her a wide smile, hoping to cheer her up.

"What?"

"I told Sadie last night after supper that I just wasn't going to be able to court her. It just wasn't right to even try."

Her hands dropped to her side and her look softened, but he still had a sense something was wrong. "Oh," she said softly. "And why's that?"

A loose strand of hair was sweeping across her face. Wanting desperately to push it back into place, wanting an excuse to touch her . . . he did nothing.

"It just didn't feel right."

"But I thought that's what the elders wanted?" she asked, backing away from him somewhat.

"In the end, the elders want me to be happy. I have to make choices that are best for me and David."

She smiled, but not the fullface smile he was used to seeing from her. "Are you asking me to go on a picnic with you and David on Saturday?"

"Nope," he said, playing with her again.

Those hands landed right back on her hips, and she opened her mouth to say something . . . but stopped, straightened her apron, and took a deep breath instead. Samuel thought he better tell her the truth. "I'm asking you to go on a picnic with me. Alone. David will be helping Ivan do some work out at his place."

"Oh," she said softly.

"And me and the boy have more vegetables than we can ever eat. I thought we might bring some for supper tonight, if you think that would be all right."

"That's fine."

She lacked the enthusiasm Samuel hoped for. Not that he expected her to run into his arms for changing his mind about Sadie. But . . . something more than this.

"Lillian, what's wrong?"

She motioned for him to follow her. Away from a group of tourists chatting in the street, she sat down on a wooden bench outside a small Dutch bakery. He took a seat beside her.

"I just found out who my father is," she said, fighting tears.

"And I'm going to find him and meet him. I'm sure he's wondered about me all these years, like I've wondered about him. I think it will help me to put some things behind me, so I can have the life I'm looking for." She paused and looked him hard in the eyes. "And, Samuel, yes, I'm trying to find a place for God in my heart. I have a lot to learn, but I'm working very hard to find my way. Finding my father will fill a void I have in my life."

It was music to his ears that Lillian was working to accept God into her life. And if it would help her to make peace with her father, well he was all for that.

"He lived right here in Paradise. Evidently, he and my mother had a love affair. She became pregnant with me and knew people in the district would look down on her, so she left. I don't know why she couldn't have told me sooner." A tear rolled down her cheek as she shook her head.

His need to comfort her was overwhelming. But he didn't move. Fantasizing about Lillian was a safe secret he could live out in his dreams. The reality of actually touching her, even as innocent as that might be, would imply intentions he was still unsure of.

"That was twenty-eight years ago. He was a young writer who worked for *The Intelligencer Journal.* Who knows where he might be now."

"*Ya,* that's true," he said as he continued to fight the urge to put his arm around her, offer her hand a squeeze . . . something. "So, what's his name?"

She sighed. "I'm still in shock that I have his actual name. And I can sort of put a face to the name, from the picture in his column. It's just all very surreal."

"Do you want me to help you find him?" It wasn't his way to pursue anyone or anything outside the district, but if it would fill the void in Lillian's life and help her to move forward, then he was going to help her.

She sighed, looking down at her hands in her lap. "His name is Daniel Foster."

Samuel tried not to react, but he was stunned. Grimacing, he shifted his position on the bench. How in the world would he tell her that she wasn't going to have to look very far for her father? Not farther than about twenty yards. Samuel could see Daniel Foster's shop from where they were sitting.

11

LILLIAN WAS THINKING ABOUT THE SUPPER THEY'D HAVE later, about their picnic on Saturday, about finding her father, and what her future might hold. Hopeful thoughts were flying around in her head. It seemed odd when Samuel jumped up and began to pace in front of her.

"What's wrong?" she asked. He was nervous as a cat.

"I don't exactly know how to tell you this, Lillian." He paused and sat down beside her again. But the words didn't come.

"Samuel, you're scaring me. What is it?"

"Daniel Foster," he said softly.

"My father. What about him?"

Samuel removed his straw hat and ran his hand through his hair. Placing it back on his head, he began to stroke his beard as if in serious thought. Lillian couldn't help but notice his huge arms underneath the blue shirt and the way his suspenders draped across his solid chest.

"What?" she asked again. "Samuel, what is it?"

"Lillian, stay calm."

"Samuel, you better just tell me whatever's on your mind because you are *really* scaring me!"

"Daniel Foster is standing right over there." He pointed toward their right.

Lillian jumped up and peered in the direction he was pointing. "What?" She sounded confused.

"He owns that shop," he said hesitantly, knowing it would be a blow to her to find she'd walked past her father's shop dozens of times in the past couple of months.

"What?" she asked again, staring down Lincoln Highway.

Samuel stood up and reached for her arm, fearful she might take off running in that direction. That probably wasn't the best plan. He watched Daniel arranging a table full of wares right outside his antique store. "He's the owner of Outside the Box," he told her.

"The name of his column," she whispered. "I've been in that shop." She pulled away and headed toward her father. The closer they got, the faster she moved.

"Wait, Lillian." He grabbed her arm and brought her to a halt. "Have you thought this through?"

She turned briefly to face him. "No, I haven't thought it through. But I've imagined a million times what it would be like to meet my father. I can't wait another minute." She picked up her pace again.

Samuel knew very little about Daniel. Besides exchanging friendly greetings over the years, the only thing he knew about the man was he'd been married for a while but later divorced. As they neared the store, he couldn't help but wonder if Lillian was entering a hornet's nest.

Lillian was bursting with anticipation. Part of her wanted to run into her father's arms and tell him how long she'd waited for this moment. However, about ten feet from the store she stopped. Her mother's words flooded her like a rushing river. *"He wouldn't have me, Lillian. He wanted nothing to do with me or having a baby. Daniel said he would deny the entire thing, that I would be an outcast in my community, and that it would be best for me to leave town."*

That was a long time ago though. Surely he had wondered over the years if he had a daughter or a son. So many times she'd wondered if she had brothers and sisters. So many questions.

"Lillian, this might not be the best time—"

"I'm not waiting. I've waited my whole life." But her feet weren't moving. What would she say? She scanned the table full of antique trinkets and household items on the display table outside the shop. A FOR SALE sign hung in the window. Maybe he was retiring. People bustled by her, seemingly in slow motion.

"Are you sure about this, Lillian?" As Samuel shook his head, clearly indicating *he* wasn't sure about it, she wondered how this moment had crept up on her so quickly. Years of imagining, dreaming. And now, all in one day, she'd discovered who he was and where he was. Swallowing hard, she stood stiffly in place watching the man arrange items on the table outside his shop.

Her father. Standing not ten feet away from her.

It wasn't just her life that would be changing forever, but his too.

Placing her hand on her chest, she took a deep breath. Her heart was beating much too fast. She could faintly hear Samuel—

"Lillian, are you okay?"—but she couldn't peel her eyes from Daniel Foster. Maybe Samuel was right. Maybe she needed to think things through and plan things out.

But she knew she wouldn't. She was going to meet her father. Today. Now. Her lifelong vision would be a reality in a matter of minutes.

Gradually, she uprooted her feet and eased her way forward. She'd only taken a couple of steps when she stopped. Realizing this was the most important moment in her life to date, she sidestepped to the wall of the shop next to Daniel Foster's, leaned against it, and closed her eyes. She could feel Samuel next to her as she attempted to block out the noise of passersby, cars, the clippity-clap of horse hooves, and the conflicting voices rambling around in her head. *Stay. Go.*

God, she prayed silently, pressing her eyes closed even tighter, *I don't know You very well. And it might be wrong of me to ask for Your help right now. But this is so incredibly important to me. Please help me to say the right things and to accept whatever it is that's Your will.*

Her plea for help and guidance sent a flood of emotion running through her. Fighting tears, she went on. *I'm so sorry. I'm just so very sorry for all the things I've messed up in my life. Please help me to do this right.*

It seemed wrong to ask for His help when she'd been absent from Him her entire life. Was it a selfish request? Did He even hear her?

No sooner than the thought registered did she feel a sweeping wave of courage. More profound was an unfamiliar sense of guardianship surrounding her, as if Someone wrapped her in a blanket of protection and love. *Is this You?* she silently asked.

As a tear trickled down her cheek, she allowed herself to feel the glory of prayer. "Thank You," she said as she opened her eyes and wiped the tear from her cheek.

She looked over at Samuel standing by the wall next to her. His eyes were closed. Was he praying for her? She watched him intently, presumably offering up prayers on her behalf. This moment on the busy sidewalk of Lincoln Highway would be with her a long time.

"Are you ready?" he asked, opening his eyes.

"I am."

Side by side, they eased their way toward Daniel Foster.

"Good afternoon," the man she now knew to be her father said. "Can I show you anything in particular?"

"We're just having a look," Samuel said when she didn't respond.

Lillian could see he still resembled the picture. He was a handsome man. His dark hair was now salt and pepper and receding, and he had replaced his gold-rimmed glasses with smaller ones that hung low on his nose. Considerably shorter than Samuel, he still towered over her. He had a friendly smile, and Lillian knew right away that everything was going to be fine.

"I'm Lillian Miller," she said, wondering if the name Miller would ring any bells. Maybe she should have planned this conversation out. Too late. She was there and waiting for any recognition from him.

"I'm Daniel Foster." He extended his hand to her as though she was any new customer wandering up to his shop. "Welcome to Outside the Box."

It had been twenty-seven years and there were tons of Millers. She'd have to be more clear. "My mother is Sarah Jane Miller."

Instantly Daniel took a step backward. His smile faded, and he gave her an odd look she couldn't decipher.

"I, uh . . ." She stumbled. "I . . . think you're my father."

Samuel was stroking his beard and pacing slightly. Daniel just stared at her.

"I'm so happy to finally meet you," she went on. "I've waited my whole life for this moment, and I didn't think I'd ever find you. And, here you are, three miles from where I'm living with my grandparents. It's just so good to meet you." She instinctively stepped toward him.

"What do you want?" His tone was more than abrasive and sent chills up her spine, halting her in her tracks.

"I, uh, don't want anything. Just to know you." She felt Samuel gently touch her arm. It gave her little strength; her knees were buckling with the weight of the moment. "You still look a lot like your picture from the column you wrote years ago. I see you named your store after it." She was rambling. "Maybe we can have a cup of coffee and get to know each other when you have time and—"

"I don't know you. I don't want to know you. Whatever your mother told you is a lie. Sarah Jane Miller has lied to you." He took a step back.

"So you do know my mother, then?" she asked, resisting the urge to cry. "Are you my father?" It was a simple question that she felt deserved an answer.

"I just sold my shop; I'll be moving from here in two weeks. If you try to find me, I'll call the law on you." His face drew into a raging scowl, and his posture became aggressive. He leaned forward as if he might dive for her.

Every wonderful fantasy she'd had about meeting her father was stolen from her in less than a minute. On instinct, she stepped back from him. She wanted to run. To go back. To start over. Resisting the urge to flee, she spoke again.

"Sir, I'm not here to cause you any trouble at all."

"Is it money you want?" His fists were clinched at his sides and he stared her down as if she were threatening his life.

"No!" she said emphatically. "Of course not."

"Lillian, let's go," Samuel gently took her elbow and attempted to guide her away from him.

"Yes, I think you better go," the man said. The man who couldn't *possibly* be her father.

"But, I just . . ." The words weren't coming. The fantasy was over. She now understood why her mother had chosen to avoid even an informal community shunning. She'd never felt more abandoned in her life. A bastard baby, with a father who didn't care if she was alive or dead.

"Lillian, let's go," Samuel said again, pulling her farther away from Daniel.

She yanked free of Samuel's hold. As a tear rolled down her cheek, she walked toward her father. He didn't step back this time. She couldn't read his expression, but she was not going to leave without letting him know how she felt.

"I dreamed about meeting you my entire life. I dreamed about this moment since I was a little girl. In a few short minutes, you have not only denied me my dream of what it would be like to meet you, but you've discarded me as if I were dirt." She stepped closer to him, and this time he did step back. "Well, I'm not dirt. I am a wonderful, vivacious woman. I'm smart. I graduated from high school at the top of my class, and I went to college and became a teacher. I am a fabulous cook. I care deeply about other people." By now she was sobbing almost uncontrollably, and she struggled to form the words so he could understand her. "I'm sorry that you won't have the opportunity to know me."

She paused. His expression softened, and the water forming in the corners of his eyes pushed her to go on. "So go ahead and toss me aside. It's certainly your choice. But I am a good person, and it will be your loss."

And with that, she spun around and ran down the sidewalk.

Samuel kept up with her until she was away from the crowds. When she crossed the highway and headed down Black Horse Road, it appeared she might keep running all the way home. He grabbed her arm. "Lillian, stop," he said. "Did you come in the buggy?"

She pulled free, shook her head and kept on walking until she was a good piece down the road. "Well, I brought my buggy. I have to go back," he yelled. She waved him on and didn't stop. "I'll be back to pick you up."

Fast as he could run, he headed to where he'd parked his buggy and got on his way. A few minutes later, knowing he was going a bit too fast through town, he still gave Pete an extra flick of the reins. It didn't take long to catch up with her.

"Get in," he said, guiding Pete to a stop.

She wouldn't look at him as she crawled into the buggy. It didn't seem like she was going to stop crying any time soon. Maybe he needed to just let her get it all out.

"I'm sorry," he said softly.

She didn't say anything and continued to stare off into the pasture. When he passed Irma Rose and Jonas's farm, she spoke up.

"Where are we going?" She swiped at her eyes.

"To my favorite place."

Samuel hadn't been to the overlook since Rachel died. He used to go there when he wanted to be by himself—just him and God. He'd never taken anyone there. Not even David. Today he was going to take Lillian. She needed all the spiritual guidance she could get right now, and Samuel knew God would be waiting there for her with open arms to comfort her in her time of need. Aside from the incredible view of the valley below, it was where Samuel felt most connected to God.

She'd stopped crying by the time they reached the overlook. He helped her out of the buggy and toward the edge of the cliff. "Don't get too close to the edge," he said as he pulled her to the ground with him. "Let's sit here a while."

For a split second, a hint of happiness swept across her face. "This is the most beautiful place I have ever seen," she said before placing her hands over her face. She started to cry again.

"I'm so sorry, Samuel."

"What do you have to be sorry about?" he asked, turning to face her.

"That I cry a lot."

"I think I heard you say earlier that you care deeply about others," he said. "That's nothing to be sorry about."

"Thank you for being here with me."

As he watched her staring at the ground, fiddling with a

blade of grass, he worried how she was going to handle all this. But one thing he knew for sure. He wouldn't let her handle it alone.

"There's nowhere else I'd rather be," he said.

Samuel's words warmed Lillian's heart, and his presence eased her pain somewhat. The meeting with her father had been a setback. A painful, heart-wrenching setback. But now she knew. She'd put it behind her and move forward.

"There's something about this place, Samuel. It's very . . . I don't know. I mean, it's beautiful here, but there's something else. It's very calming. Serene. It's like I feel . . . I feel . . ."

"God?" He asked.

She speculated for a moment. "Yes, I suppose that might be it." She recalled the feeling she'd had while she prayed before meeting her father. She'd had the same feeling then.

"And that's only the beginning. I have my strongest sense of Him here too. But one day you'll take that feeling with you everywhere you go. When that happens, it will become easier for you to accept things as God's will."

"It's hard for me to accept what happened earlier as God's will. I would think God would have preferred things to go differently." She cringed and shook her head as the memory of her father's look and words came flying to the forefront of her mind.

"We don't question God's will."

"That part is hard for me. And I want to, Samuel. I want to accept all things as God's will." She paused. "And I'm working on it."

"I can see that. It'll come, Lillian. Talk to Him. But more important, listen to Him."

"What do you mean? I've said my prayers, but I've never heard a response."

"Are you sure?"

"I've never heard God talking to me." She shook her head, quite sure of that one.

"Ever have a thought or feeling and wonder where it came from? A thought that just seems to come out of nowhere, or a comforting feeling?"

"Sometimes." She recalled again how she'd felt when she prayed before she met her father. Leaning against the storefront wall, she'd felt an overwhelming sense of calm. "Is that God?"

"I believe it is. I think some people are so busy talking to God that they forget to listen too." He bumped his shoulder gently against hers. "I'm sorry about what happened today, Lillian."

He'd changed the subject again, as she had gotten used to. "I'm sorry too," she said. "Sorry for me. Sorry for you. And sorry for my mother."

Wow. It was the first time she'd thought about her mother since all this had happened. For the first time, she saw her mother in a whole new light—as a young Amish woman who got involved with an *Englisch* man, got pregnant, was afraid of becoming an outcast in her community, and decided to venture out into a world she knew nothing about. Maybe there was enough compassion in Lillian's heart to forgive her mother for her childhood.

"Are you gonna be all right?" he asked.

"It's not the storybook reunion I'd hoped for by any stretch of the imagination. But I'll have to put it behind me. Now, at least, I know. I'm not completely sure how I feel about all of it, but . . ."

As she and Samuel sat together at the overlook, Lillian trailed off, trying to push the events with her father out of her mind. While she knew it would take a long time for her to completely heal, a new sense of calm and peacefulness seemed to be slowly seeping into her heart. It was a welcomed feeling. For the next hour they sat at the overlook. Mostly they were quiet.

"I'm sorry that Sadie cried when you told her you wouldn't be courting her," David told Samuel on the way to Lillian's that evening.

"How'd you know she cried?"

"I heard her from upstairs."

"I thought you were sleeping."

"Nope. But Pop, she just wasn't the one. You know that, *ya*?"

Samuel nodded, unclear exactly what he thought these days. But he knew it wouldn't be right to court Sadie.

"Well I'm glad we're going to Lillian's house for supper. I like being around Irma Rose and Jonas too."

Nodding again, Samuel wondered if Lillian was feeling any better. Time healed so many things. Time and God. But it had only been a few hours. A blow like this would take a long time for her to get over. He knew all about pain, healing, and the time it took.

As his thoughts drifted to Rachel, David came out of the clear blue with a direct question not suitable for a boy to ask his pop.

"Are you going to marry her?" David's eyes grew wider and wider as he waited for a response.

"Not right for you to be asking me that, boy."

"But it could happen?"

Samuel could handle his own feelings, even if they were all mixed-up. His thoughts about a life with Lillian were his secret. But, he knew what was right and wrong. "No, David. I've been tellin' you for weeks that Lillian and I are friends. Just like she's a friend to you."

"But she's studying the *Ordnung*."

"So do a lot of people who come from worldly ways. And I think the *Ordnung*—and God—will help Lillian to find her way. But outsiders don't stay, David. It's rare. So you need not be thinking about things that may not happen."

This was exactly what Samuel feared—David getting too close to Lillian. And he sure couldn't be telling his son that he had allowed himself to get too close to her.

"But it *does* happen sometimes. Besides, aren't people good friends before they get married?"

Samuel glanced at his son. The boy's youthful optimism caused him to briefly contemplate the possibility. "I guess, David. It does happen sometimes. And, *ya, gut* marriages start out with friendship first."

Nonetheless. He shook his head as doubt resurfaced.

Lillian was glad to see Grandpa down for supper. She'd prepared one of his favorites: roast with potatoes and carrots. The events of earlier that afternoon weighed heavily in her heart, but her family was all together. It was cause for happiness and she refused to let Daniel Foster take that away from her.

"Boy, what are you *rutschich* about?" Grandpa asked David when they all sat down to eat. Unless there was a problem with his meds, Grandpa never missed a beat.

"Jonas, leave the boy alone. He's not squirming," Grandma said.

"*Ya*, he's *rutschich*. And grinning like he's got some business for sharing. What's on your mind, son?" Grandpa leaned an ear inward, waiting for an answer.

"David, why don't you give the blessing," Grandma said as she shushed Grandpa.

They all bowed in prayer.

"Dear Lord, thank You for this food before us and the many blessings You have given to us. Thank You for the land that provides us with this fine food, and we know all things are God's will. *Aemen*."

"*Ya*, God's will. *Aemen*. Thank you for that offering, David," Grandma said.

"And one more thing!" David said, bowing his head again. As everyone else hastily lowered their heads, he added, "*Danki* for bringing Lillian to Lancaster County and for Pop deciding not to court Sadie. *Aemen*."

All eyes shot to Samuel, whose embarrassment—and anger—were apparent. Planting clenched fists slowly on the wooden table, he scolded his son with his eyes to the point Lillian feared a trip to the woodshed for David when they got home. That wasn't fair, though. It was such a sweet thing for him to say—about *her*, anyway.

Grandpa chuckled, but quickly stopped when Grandma fired him a look like she might take *him* out to the woodshed for a lashing. As Grandpa pursed his lips together and frowned, Lillian tried to lighten the mood.

"I'm glad God brought me here, too, David." She reached across the table and patted his hand. "That was a very sweet thing to say."

Maybe that would keep him out of trouble with Samuel. But by throwing out the fact that Samuel wasn't courting Sadie in the same breath as his comments about her . . . Well, it *was* cause for speculation by all of them.

It took him a few seconds, but Samuel's scowling look softened and his fists unclenched. *Whew.* Maybe David was in the clear.

Grandma still had a visual hold on Grandpa, warning him not to speak. But as was Grandpa's nature, he spoke anyway. He was looking down when he said it, almost in a whisper, as if a tiny bit afraid of Grandma. But everyone heard him loud and clear.

"Don't know why you kids keep hee-hawing around and don't just take to courtin'." He shrugged.

"Jonas Miller!" Grandma snapped. "This is not your place to talk of such things!" She turned to Samuel. "It's his medications, Samuel. Makes him all cuckoo."

Samuel nodded and opened his mouth to say something, but Grandpa beat him to it, turning toward Grandma. "Irma Rose, if you don't quit blaming them pills for everything I say, I'm gonna stop takin' 'em!"

"Don't take that tone with me, Jonas Miller!"

David's eyes widened in amusement. Glancing at Samuel, Lillian was glad to see him suppressing a grin. He winked at her.

Everything was going to be just fine. And she wondered if maybe, just maybe, Samuel might be toying with the idea of them actually courting. It was always hard to tell with him.

"Irma Rose—" Grandpa prepared to fire back, but stopped and cupped his hand to his ear. "Somebody's here," he said, leaning back to see out the window.

"Jonas, watch yourself. You're gonna fall right over," Grandma said.

"We expecting company? It's the supper hour," Grandpa growled as he shoveled another load of roast onto his plate, seemingly fearful he might not get his share.

"Jonas, I declare. There's nothing wrong with your appetite, 'tis for sure." Grandma wiped her mouth with a napkin, indicating she'd get the door.

"I'll get it, Grandma," Lillian said as she stood from her place on the bench, which was next to Samuel. She smiled in his direction, glad to see he wasn't going to take offense at Grandpa's comment.

Smile still on her face, she contemplated the evening's excitement as she pulled on the wooden door and peered through the screen door. What she saw turned her legs to rubber. Suddenly she was struggling not to suffocate on the air around her. Air poisoned by the past that now found her.

"*Rickie*, what are you doing here?"

12

"ARE YOU GOING TO LET ME IN?" RICKIE ASKED, GRINNING as he studied her from head to toe.

Lillian opened the screen door onto the porch and closed both doors behind her. She couldn't believe Rickie was actually here. Always perfectly groomed, his neatly clipped blond hair accentuated his golden tan. Deceptively charming deep blue eyes scanned his surroundings. Dressed in khaki pants and a yellow golf shirt, he appeared to be the epitome of the perfect man. His looks were undoubtedly what had attracted her to him in the first place. Oh, how he had fooled her, though.

"What are you doing here?" she asked him again between clenched teeth, not wanting anyone to see him.

"That is not your best look, baby," he said, shaking his head and taking in her Amish attire. Him calling her *baby* turned her stomach. "I know you said you've started a new life, and I can see that—but it's hard for me to understand how you could just leave without even talking to me first. That's cold, Lillian. I provided you with a home. I've taken care of you. How could you do this?"

"Taken care of me?" she asked in a loud whisper. "Go home, Rickie. You should have never come here."

Ignoring her, his eyes darted over her shoulder. "Going to let me come in and meet your grandparents?"

"No. We have company tonight. You just need to leave!" Panic was starting to set in. She didn't want any of them to see the kind of person she used to be with. It was hard for her to believe she ever dated Rickie, much less lived with him.

"Lillian, I came a long way to talk to you," he said. "You owe me that much. I love you, and you just took off."

"You know why I left, Rickie." She glanced over her shoulder. The faint voices coming from inside crippled her thought process. Somehow she needed to get rid of him, at least for now. "We can talk tomorrow," she said as she backed up toward the porch door, hoping he would venture back to his rental car.

"Lillian, please," he begged, standing steadfast. "I know I made mistakes, but do you realize what a mistake you've made by coming here? You can't possibly want to live this life. When you get this God thing out of your head, I'll be waiting for you to come home." Walking toward her, he added, "But I won't wait forever, Lillian."

She took a step backward. "I don't want you to wait for me at all, Rickie. It's over. You should have never come here!"

She heard the rustling of feet inside. She dreaded introducing Rickie to anyone.

"I don't believe you, baby," he said, closing the gap between them.

"Don't call me that! I'm not your 'baby.' Please, Rickie, just . . . go home. I don't love you." She held her arm out to keep him at a safe distance.

"What's wrong with you?" His voice spiked up a notch. "And

what's with the freaky clothes? Have they brainwashed you or something?"

How dare you. But fighting with him would only heighten the risk of someone coming out on the front porch. She needed him to just go. "If you'll leave now, I promise we will talk tomorrow. Where are you staying? I'll call you in the morning."

"Lillian, it's only five o'clock in the afternoon. I'm *not* going to wait until morning to talk to you."

"Then let me at least finish supper with my family. I'll call you when I'm done. I can meet you in town or something."

"Fine," he said as he turned to head down the porch steps. He'd almost hit the grass when he called over his shoulder. "Change your clothes too. You look ridiculous."

Her pulse quickened. Thoughts of tackling him to the ground raced through her mind. But he was leaving, and that's all that mattered. She made an about-face and opened the screen door about the same time Grandpa opened the wooden door.

"Who's our company?" he belted out, causing Rickie to spin around and head back up the porch steps.

"Hello, sir, I'm Rickie." He extended his hand, and Lillian's panic settled in even further when Grandpa eased past her and shook his hand. "I'm a friend of Lillian's," Rickie added.

"It's suppertime. Come in and fix yourself a plate." Grandpa turned to go back in the house, obviously anxious to get back to his roast more than anything else.

"Thank you, sir," Rickie said, making his way past Lillian. She flinched as his arm brushed against hers.

"Lilly, come make the proper introductions," Grandpa said over his shoulder.

A sense of dread accompanied her as she followed Grandpa and Rickie into the house.

"This is a friend of Lilly's," Grandpa said, resuming his place at the table. "David, maybe you could scoot that rocker from the den over here to the table for this man."

"No, thank you, sir. Actually, I ate on the plane. I just came to see Lillian." An arrogant smile swept across his face—the same smile that had won her over in the beginning but now was making her stomach turn. "I need to make her realize how much I've missed her." He paused. "I don't want to interrupt your Amish dinner."

Lillian wanted to gag. The look on Samuel's face was one of confusion mixed with irritation.

"I imagine it's about the same as an *Englisch* dinner," Grandpa said sarcastically, still stuffing roast in his mouth. "Lillian, best you introduce everyone to your friend."

Grandma's facial expression resonated with sympathy. David seemed oblivious, or was just as preoccupied with the meal as Grandpa.

"Uh, Rickie, these are my grandparents, Irma Rose and Jonas." She pointed to each respectively. "And this is Samuel and David."

Samuel stood first and shook Rickie's hand, followed by David.

"Nice to meet all of you. I see you really don't use any electricity, just like in the movie *Witness*."

Lillian wondered if anyone saw her cut her eyes in Rickie's direction. Could this day get any worse?

"Well, we don't shoot at people like I hear they done in that movie," Grandpa said. "Or protect shot-up detectives. Right silly, if you ask me."

Lillian was still standing near the doorway, hoping she could coax Rickie back out the door—and then out of her life forever. Mom was going to hear about this.

"David, I reckon we better be on our way," Samuel said, standing up. He walked directly to the hat rack and retrieved his hat without even looking in Lillian's direction.

"No!" she blurted out. "We haven't had dessert."

"Me and the boy have chores to do. *Danki* for supper," he said, still barely making eye contact. "We'll let you and your friend catch up." The way he said "friend" revealed more than just a slight irritation.

"Nice to meet you both," Rickie said, nodding at Samuel and David as they headed toward the door.

"Likewise," Samuel responded, almost pushing David through the doorway.

"I'll be right back," Lillian said in a frenzy, leaving her grandparents with Rickie. That in itself was probably a mistake. No telling what Rickie might say. Or Grandpa, for that matter.

"Samuel, wait," she said, scurrying down the porch steps.

"David, tell Lillian thank you for supper and go wait for me by the buggy."

"*Danki*, Lillian," David said hesitantly, as if he knew something was wrong.

"Don't go," she said, touching Samuel's arm. "I thought you and David might stay for a while."

"Your company came a long way to see you."

"He should have never come here," she said firmly. She wanted to throw herself into Samuel's arms, a place she knew would be safe.

"*Ya* . . . but he *is* here." He raised his brows as if asking her what she would do about it.

"Not for long. As soon as I go back inside, I'm going to make sure he gets on the next flight home."

"I have to get David home, Lillian."

She could hear the remorse in his voice, and she worried to what extent he was feeling it. Did he regret leaving so early? Did he regret ever befriending her in the first place?

As he turned to walk toward the buggy, Lillian followed him. "Samuel."

He turned around to face her. "*Ya.*"

"Thank you again for being with me today."

Samuel shook his head and then gazed intently into her eyes. "Lillian." He paused. "I'm glad I was there for you today."

She definitely sensed there was a "But" coming.

"But, you have . . ." He hesitated.

"I have what, Samuel? Just say it." Although she wasn't sure she wanted to hear it.

"A lot of things going on that I don't understand. All this with your father, the problems with your mother, and now this. These are all worldly conflicts I'm just not used to." He shook his head again.

The regret was still evident in his tone. In a defensive explosion, she tried to redeem herself. "What my mother did is *not* my fault. What my selfish father did is *not* my fault. And Rickie showing up here this way is *not* my fault. Are you going to punish me for these things I have no control over?"

He gently grabbed her shoulders and leaned down. "Lillian, I'm not punishing you for anything. I'm just being honest and telling you I'm not used to all this."

She didn't know what to say. It seemed no matter how far she traveled, drama was determined to follow her.

"Make peace with all the confusion, Lillian," he said softly. "It's the only way you'll find the happiness you're looking for."

"I'm trying! I found my father, which answers a lot of questions. I understand a little better about why my mother left here, and I broke up with a boyfriend who is a jerk! He should not be here."

Samuel didn't say anything, instead looking over her shoulder. She clenched her teeth as she slowly turned around.

"A *jerk*?" Rickie was standing on the porch step and had clearly heard her last remark.

Lillian glanced back and forth between the men. Samuel dropped his arms to his side. Rickie folded his arms across his chest.

"Exactly what's going on here?" Rickie went on. "Are you involved with this Amish guy or something?" His voice deepened to a growl as he spoke—a sound she'd grown to recognize and fear.

"He is my friend, Rickie."

She clasped her hands together and momentarily closed her eyes. *Please God, don't let Rickie hurt the people I love*, she silently prayed.

"Are you *praying*?" Rickie asked, a disgusted look sweeping across his face. "Give me a break!" As he came flying down the porch steps, Lillian instinctively backed up. His eyes were ablaze. "Get in the car, Lillian. I'm taking you home," he said softly as he forcefully grabbed her arm above the elbow and began dragging her toward the car. "We will get all this straightened out at home, sweetie."

Lillian glanced over her shoulder at Samuel, who hadn't moved. His feet were firmly planted in the grass a few feet from the porch steps as he watched Lillian's life unraveling. She looked around for David. To her horror, he was standing by the buggy as Samuel instructed, taking it all in with a look on his face Lillian would carry with her for a long time.

"I'm not going with you, Rickie," Lillian said as she tried to wiggle out of his grasp.

"Oh, but you will. Did you really think I wouldn't come get you?" He spun her around to face him, tightening his grip on her arm. "I just wanted to enjoy my freedom for a little while." He chuckled.

"You'll never get me on a plane, Rickie," she said.

"Oh, I know that. But I'm going to get you back to my hotel room. I don't know who you think you are! Leaving me a cheesy little note and walking out of my life without so much as a warning! This is something we need to talk about."

"I've had one too many talks with you, Rickie."

"Well, you've got one more talk coming," he threatened, opening the car door. "And quit looking over your shoulder. Do you really think that Amish guy is going to come to the rescue?" He snickered. "His kind would let someone shoot up the place, rape his wife, and kill his dog without doing anything. They're *passive*." He paused and glanced briefly at Samuel as if to confirm he was indeed still in the same spot. "Now, get in the car, Lillian," he growled. "We are going to talk."

"No, Rickie. I'm not going." She struggled to pull away, looking toward Samuel. She knew Rickie was right. No matter how strong her friendship with Samuel was, she knew he would remain non-assertive. She was not going to make it any harder on him by begging him to help her. Plus, she couldn't bear the thought of Rickie going after Samuel—and David having to witness such a horrible event.

Rickie swore. "I left my cell phone in the house. Get in the car, Lillian, if you don't want any trouble for your new friend. I'll be right back."

She crawled into the front seat. The car door slammed shut, along with her hope. Facing forward, she couldn't look back at Samuel. She just couldn't. Resting her head in her hands, her body trembled with the realization of what was happening. She'd just take it, one more time. Then she'd come home. She'd be humiliated, but she'd survive. Somehow she always survived.

"God, give me the strength," she said aloud, "and please get Rickie out of my life forever."

After a while, she wondered what was taking Rickie so long. She slowly turned around, still unsure if she could bear to look at Samuel. No one was in sight.

Sitting up a little straighter, her eyes darted across the yard toward the house, then to her right, her left. Where was he?

David was nowhere in sight either. Where was Rickie? Her heart raced, fearing a confrontation between Samuel and Rickie. She opened the car door and bolted out.

She was running toward the house when the screen door swung open. Grandpa walked out on the porch holding a glass of tea as if he had not a care in the world. At the same time, she heard the clippity-clop of Pete's hooves and watched as the buggy spun around. David was driving.

"Grandpa! Where's Samuel?" She scrambled up the porch steps in time to catch the strained look on Grandma's face before Grandpa closed the door behind him. She turned to watch David galloping down the dirt driveway. "Grandpa!"

"Samuel thought it best for David to run over to Ivan's for a bit. Katie Ann has a shoofly pie she made 'specially for them. He'll be right back."

Confusion. Panic. Where was Samuel? She saw Grandma peek out the window. Her face resonated with pity. Lillian wondered if Grandpa was utilizing his authority as head of the household, instructing her to stay in the house—for her own safety.

"Grandpa," she said frantically, gently grabbing his arm. "Where is Samuel?"

"Why, he's in the woodshed right here beside the house." Grandpa took another sip of tea.

"What?" She turned to venture in that direction, but Grandpa stepped forward.

"Lilly, I think it best if you come sit with your ol' Grandpa on the porch." His expression turned solemn. "Do what your *daadi* says."

"But, I—"

"On the porch, Lilly." Grandpa pointed to one of the rockers, taking a seat in the other one himself.

She reluctantly sat down. "Grandpa, listen to me. Rickie is not a very good person. Samuel could be in trouble. I have to go to him." She looked toward the woodshed.

Grandpa tilted his head back and stared into the yard. "Lilly, you will have to trust your grandpa and do as I say," he said firmly, before cutting his eyes in her direction. "And we will not speak of this again."

A rustling to her right drew her eyes. There came Samuel, walking side by side with Rickie. As they reached the front of the house, Samuel headed toward the porch and Rickie walked to his car. Rickie never looked her way. Samuel said nothing as he walked up and took a seat on the porch step.

"I'll have Irma Rose bring you something to drink," Grandpa said to Samuel. "We'll have us a nice glass of tea. David should be back shortly."

"Samuel, what—" Lillian started ask.

"Maybe you'd like something cold to drink, Lillian?" Grandpa interrupted as the three of them watched Rickie's car ramble down the dirt drive. Rickie looked none the worse for wear, but something had happened to make him tuck his tail and run.

Lillian turned back to look at Samuel. His face was as solemn as Grandpa's.

"Samuel, are you all right?"

Before he could say anything, Grandpa spoke up one more time. "He looks mighty fine to me." His look left no question in Lillian's mind that there were to be no more questions. Now . . . or ever.

"Who was that man, Pop?" David asked Samuel when they pulled into the driveway.

"You heard Jonas," he said. "An old friend of Lillian's."

"Pop, I'm almost twelve. I know what's going on."

"Do you, now?" Samuel brought Pete to a halt and hopped out of the buggy. David followed him into the house.

"It's her old boyfriend," David said, watching Samuel light the lantern above the kitchen table.

Samuel eyed the kitchen, again picturing the table at his favorite shop. As was the case recently, the image in his mind included Lillian. But it was hard not to have doubts that such a notion was ever going to happen. The thought of Lillian being involved with the likes of that Rickie fellow brought on a rage that was not in line with his upbringing.

As Samuel poured him and the boy each a glass of cold milk, David said, "I didn't like him. I saw the way he tried to drag Lillian to the car. He's not a *gut* man."

"Only the Good Lord can pass judgment, David."

Samuel reflected on the judgment he himself had just passed on the man out in the woodshed.

"*Ya*, I know."

Samuel regretted the boy saw as much as he did. Especially Rickie pulling Lillian to the car like a rag doll. Sending David to Ivan's was a good move. The boy needn't ever know why Rickie hightailed it back to the city. For that matter, no one ever had to know. But Samuel would know, and he'd have to live with it.

It was hard for him to imagine what life must have been like for Lillian, living with a man like that. He imagined things must have been even worse behind closed doors. No one to see him doing her harm. Cringing, he recalled her fearful expression when Rickie dragged her off—a look that shifted from dread to compliance to embarrassment, all in a split second. Her face had revealed a painful past not fit for any human being. Lillian would never cause harm to another person. It sickened him to envision anyone hurting her. That Rickie fellow sickened him for sure.

He couldn't help but worry how many more skeletons from Lillian's closet might show up in Lancaster County.

Grandma and Grandpa were sitting at the kitchen table when Lillian walked back into the house.

"Mighty fine mess we had here, Lilly," Grandpa said, uncharacteristically somber. "I don't think we'll be seeing that pretty *Englischer* again."

"I hope not, Grandpa." Lillian hands trembled as she poured herself a cup of hot tea and took a seat beside her grandma at the kitchen table. "I'm sorry about all this."

"*Ya,*" Grandpa said. "We will put this behind us. No talk of it again."

Grandpa spoke with a conviction Lillian hadn't heard before. Grandma had temporarily taken her place as a traditional Old Order Amish woman, allowing Grandpa to rule the roost. Her expression was distant and staid.

"I hope Samuel will still want to be friends after all this," Lillian said, fighting tears.

Her grandparents didn't answer, as if they were harboring the same thought.

"I think I'll head upstairs," she said finally, feeling defeated by the events of the day. She barely heard her grandparents wishing her a good night's sleep as she headed up the wooden steps. She was almost to the top of the stairs when Grandpa called to her. "Lillian."

"Yes, Grandpa?" She turned around, not sure if she wanted to hear what he had to say. His voice still resonated with the same somberness.

"God does not judge us by the actions of others," he bellowed. "And me and your Grandma don't either."

Lillian tried to muster up a smile. She nodded, turned back around, and headed upstairs feeling embarrassment and regret. Everything she'd been working to attain seemed to be teetering toward failure. Feeling herself curl up into the place she often went after an encounter with Rickie, she realized she could either allow herself to revert back to the person she used to be—or fight for the peaceful life within her grasp.

"Guess who showed up on the doorstep this evening, Mom?" Lillian asked her mother when she answered the phone.

"Lillian, I think Rickie deserves another chance, and that's the reason I told him—"

"Mother! I decide who I am going to be with. You made a terrible mistake sending Rickie all this way!"

"Rickie is a very nice-looking, well-mannered man with a good job, Lillian."

"He has you so fooled, Mom."

"Is this about the Amish man?" Her mother's tone resounded with disapproval. "Are you not giving Rickie another chance because of this other man?"

"It has nothing to do with Samuel."

"You should give him another chance."

Sensing her mom's complete and utter disappointment in her, she considered setting her straight about Rickie. But her mom had introduced her to Rickie, and she knew her mother would blame herself. Yet again, Lillian found herself in a role reversal, feeling the need to protect her mother. But she wondered when her mom was ever going to be a mother to *her*.

Still, she and her mother had sufficiently hurt each other enough over the years, and she wasn't going to rub this in her face. Besides, she felt humiliated that she'd let it go on for as long as she did.

She recalled the parting of ways between Samuel and Rickie, wondering what exactly had happened out in the woodshed.

"Samuel and I are just friends, but Rickie could never be the man Samuel is."

"Oh, Lillian! I can hear it in your voice. You've fallen for this Amish man." She heard her mother's sigh.

Lillian took a deep breath and decided to change the subject. "I met my father today."

No response. "Well, Mom?"

"I'm trying to imagine what that must have been like," her mother replied.

Lillian thought back to her meeting with Daniel Foster. Shattered dreams. Suddenly, she didn't want to talk anymore.

After a while, her mother said, "I'm sorry, Lillian. I really am."

Again she didn't respond.

"I was hypnotized by Daniel's writing. He was wise about the world. He was forbidden. Just like Eve, I bit the apple. When he found out I was pregnant with you, I saw his true colors. Sweetie, I tried to warn you about him. Did you tell him who you were? Was he horrible?"

"Yes, I told him who I was. And yes, the whole thing was horrible." She paused, trying to imagine what it must have been like for her mother. "I suppose it was horrible for you, too, Mom. But you should have told me much sooner who my father was."

"I just wanted to protect you. How did you find out about the newspapers? I can't believe they're still in the barn after all these years."

"Grandpa thought I was you one night. He said he knew you were saving newspapers, and it would be best to stay away from the *Englisch* man. I had already seen the boxes of newspapers, so I looked through them. You made little notes beside some of his columns."

She heard a sniffle on the other end of the line.

"Mom?" she asked when there was no reply.

"How is Grandpa?" Now Mom was changing the subject, but she was also crying.

"He's okay, most of the time. I think his medicines cause him to get confused at night sometimes."

And, then, as if it had been building for years, Sarah Jane Miller wept uncontrollably. Lillian had never heard her like this. Thank goodness she hadn't told her about Rickie. "Mom? Are you okay?" Her own tears began to build. "Mom?"

"I'm so, so sorry, Lillian. I'm sorry I've been a bad mother. I'm sorry I didn't tell you about Daniel." She wept harder. "I miss my *mamm* and *daed* so much."

It was the first time Lillian had ever heard her mother speak any *Pennsylvania Deitsch*. It was the first time she remembered her mother apologizing for the way she had raised her.

"I miss them so much, Lillian," she went on. "And I'm so sorry for everything I've put you through."

Lillian tried to gain a level of composure before she said anything. The whole day had been an emotional disaster. Now she just felt sick about everything. She needed a hug. Oddly, she needed her mother.

"Mom," she said softly, choking back sobs. "You're not a bad mother. You made mistakes. We all do. I'm sorry for everything you went through."

"You don't have to try to make me feel better, Lillian. I know what kind of life I've led and how it affected you."

But I want to make you feel better, a little voice screamed. *I really do.* "It's okay, Mom." She sniffled and attempted a smile. "Besides, I think I turned out pretty good. And you get some credit for that."

"Oh, I don't know about that."

"Well, I do. Remember when I was in first grade and all the kids were going to the roller skating rink? We didn't have any money, and I knew that, but I wanted to go so badly. It was Cheryl Henston's birthday party. Remember?"

"Yes, I remember," her mother responded softly.

"I knew you pawned something important to get me a new outfit and a present to take to the party." She paused. "And Mom, I remember you singing to me when I was little. I remember you hugging me, bandaging scrapes, brushing my hair—" She stopped when she heard her mother sobbing again.

As Lillian's own cries of forgiveness leaped forward, she realized she'd been so busy thinking about the ways her mother had wrecked her life, she hadn't stopped to realize all the good things her mother had done. It wasn't as if she forgot the good things. She just had allowed the bad things to dominate her memories.

"I love you, Lillian. I'm sorry about telling Rickie where you are."

"I love you, too, Mom. I really do."

"Give your grandpa an extra big hug from me."

Both of them still crying, Lillian hesitated before saying, "Mom, why don't you come give him a hug yourself?"

"Oh, I can't face them, Lillian. I just can't. Do they know about Daniel? Did you tell them? They knew who he was back then. He lived in Paradise. Do they know?"

"No, no, Mom. They don't know. It's up to you to tell them if you want to. But either way, come to Lancaster County. Come see your parents."

She pleaded several more times with her mother, and her mother's response was consistent: "I just can't, Lillian. I can't."

The next morning, Lillian awoke with puffy eyes. It had taken effort to talk to God before she fell asleep. She couldn't help but feel like He had let her down. And she could feel doubt about His existence creeping in. But she had prayed just the same, like she had been doing each night.

She'd prayed for her mother: "Please God, help me and Mom to both make good decisions and heal from the bad ones. And help us to be close, the way mothers and daughters should be. Please help Mom to find the peace she is looking for and keep her safe."

She'd prayed about Samuel and David: "I pray that maybe there is a place for me in Samuel and David's life, God. Please keep them both safe."

Next were Grandma and Grandpa: "I'm so thankful for my grandparents and the relationship You've given me with them. So very thankful. Please keep Grandpa in my life. I pray his medications will keep him from being in pain and that he'll be able to live many more years. I pray that Grandma will get more rest, and that we will continue to grow closer. I've learned a lot from her."

Those were the easy ones. Much harder was to pray for Rickie: "I pray that Rickie will find his way to You and make the changes necessary for him to live a good life." That was all she could muster up on Rickie's behalf.

Her father was the toughest of all and she kept it simple: "Please let me forgive him."

She had put all her worries in one big bubble and blown it up to heaven for God to handle. Her last words before falling asleep were, "I'm putting it all in your hands, God."

This morning, as she forced herself out of bed and dressed, she wasn't sure if Samuel would show up for their planned picnic around noon. She wouldn't blame him if he didn't.

As Samuel guided Pete down the dirt driveway a few minutes before noon, he still worried if Lillian would be able to shed her worldly ways and past boyfriends. He had spent several long, sleepless hours last night raging with bitterness at the thought of that Rickie fellow. And several more questioning his feelings for Lillian. Now those concerns resurfaced.

But as he neared the farmhouse, he saw Lillian sitting on the front porch. And he realized one thing was for sure: despite everything, no matter her past, he couldn't stay away from Lillian.

She ran to meet him. As he stepped out of the buggy, she stopped right in front of him. "I was afraid you might not come."

"I invited you on a picnic. Why wouldn't I come?" he said, feeling a little guilty that he considered not showing up.

"Because of yesterday, I thought you—" she blurted out.

He forcibly shook his head, hoping they could put things behind them. "Let's forget about it." He paused. "You look different."

It was true. She glowed with a radiance that made her more beautiful than she already was. How was that so? He'd expected she'd still be a mess.

"I look just the same as I always do," she said beaming. She scanned her outfit and pointed toward her feet. "Right down to my black leather shoes!"

Seeing her so lighthearted set Samuel's heart and mind to rest. It was going to be a good day after all. Something was different, all right. He wasn't sure what. But he need not pay it any more mind. His heavy heart from the prior night, along with his worries, were beginning to wash clean.

"The picnic basket!" she said. "How can we have a picnic without any food?" She ran back into the house, returning with a large basket in one hand and a small knapsack in the other.

"I invited you on the picnic. I should have brought the food," he said, thinking back to when Lillian had offered to pack the basket. "What's that?" He pointed to the knapsack.

She smiled. "It's a surprise." She handed him the basket but kept hold of the knapsack.

"What kind of surprise?" he asked, intrigued.

She winked at him. "You'll see."

13

LILLIAN FELT LIGHT AND CAREFREE AS SHE AND SAMUEL exited the buggy and walked toward the lake. It was a beautiful summer day without a cloud in the sky, and the clouds in her mixed-up mind were slowly clearing as well. And Samuel was with her. Despite the horrors of the previous day, she wanted to face her future with hope and determination. She'd come too far to let Rickie or Daniel Foster deter her efforts.

"What are you thinkin' about?" Samuel asked, walking alongside her.

"What a beautiful day it is." Her eyes twinkled. "And how lucky I am to have you for a friend. Plus, I'm clearing the baggage in my heart that I've carried around for such a long time. I'm breathing in the blessing of this new day."

"We can talk about yesterday if you want," he offered, apparently regretful he'd avoided the subject earlier.

"No. I think I've figured out a way to put it all behind me."

Obviously curious, he nodded. As they moved closer to the lake, he asked, "What'd you think? Is this a good spot?"

"Perfect," she was quick to say. "It's beautiful here." And it was. The "lake" looked more like a large Texas pond. Tall pines surrounded them and a small pier edged across the water.

"It's quiet here most of the time. The tourists don't know it's here."

"Well, this is a great spot. Let's go get the blanket and picnic basket."

"And you can tell me what's in that bag," he said as they returned to the buggy. His eyes widened hopefully.

"I told you it's a surprise," she teased. "First we dine on this fine meal I have prepared—tuna-salad sandwiches, potato salad, some nasty beets, and funnel cakes for dessert. And, *ya*, I made the funnel cakes."

Samuel spread the blue and gray quilt on the ground. Lillian set the picnic basket on the quilt but kept guard over the knapsack, giving him a grin.

He was glad to see it. It had been a rough couple of days, especially for her. The sight and sound of her carrying on the way she was today reminded him of the first time he'd met her, toting the red suitcase and laughing up a storm. What a beautiful mess she'd been.

Now, as he watched her dishing out their lunch onto paper plates, he thought about how far she'd come. She looked Amish, and she sounded Amish. And she had gone a long way toward learning the *Ordnung* and some *Pennsylvania Deitsch*. She just might make it if she didn't let her old life get in the way.

They settled down to eat, chatting about nothing in particular, each of them careful not to bring up unpleasant topics. Lillian frowned when all of the food was gone. "I don't think I made enough. I should know by now how much you eat."

"I'm plenty full. It was the perfect amount. And tasted mighty fine too."

Shining with delight, she stowed food containers, plates, and the like back in the picnic basket.

"Now, let's have a look at the surprise in that bag." He rolled his eyes toward the heavily guarded knapsack.

Looking a bit embarrassed, she explained, "It's not really that big of a deal. Just something I wanted us to do . . . together."

"You've got all my attention."

"You might think it's kind of silly, but it's something I want to do." She reached for the bag and opened it. First thing she pulled out was a gardening spade.

"Are we digging a hole?"

"Yep. We sure are."

"Hmm . . . Mind if I ask what for?"

Leaning her head to one side, she shot him a serious look. "To bury this." She held up the knapsack.

Samuel sat up a little straighter. "Do I even dare ask what you've got in there? It's not like a dead critter or something, is it?"

"Yes, it's a dead animal, and I'm going to perform a pagan ritual."

He couldn't believe his ears.

She slapped him playfully on the arm. "Samuel! I'm kidding." She was eager to press on. "But we have to dig a hole."

"How big a hole? And more important, what are we burying?"

"Stop looking so scared," she said, letting out another round of giggles. "I have a few things I want gone, that's all. It's symbolic of a new beginning for me. No dead animals, I promise."

"What's in there?" He reached over and attempted to have a peek.

She quickly snatched the bag and pulled it to her chest. "You'll see," she said, once again embarrassed. Whatever the girl had the notion to get rid of, it sure seemed important to her.

"What about over there for your hole, where there isn't any grass?" He pointed to a nearby patch of ground.

"Perfect!"

He heaved himself up and offered her a hand. Once on their feet, he shook his head. "I sure am wondering what you're up to."

"You'll see," she said, heading toward the grassless spot a few yards away.

She watched Samuel digging her hole, his muscles bulging beneath his blue cotton shirt. His physical strength was evident, but it was his emotional strength she found most attractive. In addition to his unquestionable faith in God, his faith in her seemed to be growing. And his extreme sense of discipline did not overshadow his ability to enjoy life. He was able to play and have fun, but he took his responsibilities as seriously as his faith. Hard work was part of the Amish lifestyle, and Samuel worked harder than most. His role as David's father only added to his attributes.

A few inches down, the ground was moist, and it wasn't long before Samuel had a hole in the dirt about two feet deep and a foot wide. "Big enough?" he asked, wiping his brow.

"*Ya.*" Still toting the knapsack, she went to retrieve the quilt from where they had eaten. She spread it beside the hole and motioned for Samuel to take a seat, then joined him. As she reached into the knapsack, she glanced his way and smiled. "As I said, this might seem silly to you. But it will help me to move forward."

"If it's important to you, then it's not silly at all."

She reached into the bag and pulled out the first item she planned to discard. Retrieving the small diary, her thoughts traveled back to a time when she was fourteen—a mixed-up teenager harboring hateful thoughts about the life she was forced to live because of her mother's decisions. With no extras and living in a run-down shack, she'd saved her occasional lunch money to buy the diary. Absent of hopes and dreams, woeful accounts of her daily challenges filled the small book. Her plan: to show it to her mother someday and say, "Read this, Mother, and don't shed a tear because I have shed enough for both of us."

Samuel sat patiently as she scanned the pages. February 3, 1995—a particularly painful day. She silently read:

Dear Diary, today is possibly the worst day of my life. I haven't seen Mom in two days. She has a new boyfriend. There's no food in this place we call a house. And Mitzi died. I buried her in the backyard. I don't know what happened. I found my precious kitty lifeless on the front porch. She was skinny, but I'd been feeding her whatever we had in the house. I don't think that's why she died. Her eyes were open and her white and black fur was wet. She wasn't breathing, though. I brought her in the house and cried for almost two hours. I loved her. When Mom never showed up, I just dug a hole in the backyard and put her in it. I don't know much about God, so I didn't really say any prayers or anything. Then, it started to rain, so I went back in the house. This was a very bad day.

She jumped forward to July 23:

Dear Diary, something is wrong with Mom. I don't think she's drunk, but something else is wrong. She's slurring her words. I'm not sure if it's drugs or something. I told her I was hungry, but she just cried and mumbled something I didn't understand.

September 12:

Dear Diary, I'm feeling very sad because I want to go to the dance at school. Henry Webster will be there, and I really like him. I think he likes me too. But Mom says I can't go. It costs five dollars to get in. I don't have anything to wear anyway. I hate my life. I hate my mom.

Lillian cringed, recalling the events of that year. Hard to believe it was thirteen years ago. So much had changed. She had changed. And her mother had changed as well. Continuing to allow the bad memories to override the good memories was only hurting her. After her recent conversation with her mother, she knew the only way to continue along in her quest for peace was to replace resentment with forgiveness. She tossed the book into the hole.

"I forgive you, Mom," she said softly.

Samuel's expression was solemn, but he offered her a comforting smile and nodded his head. She reached into the knapsack for the next item. Opening the envelope, she pulled out the newspaper clipping she had cut out the day before. Studying the young face of her father, she read his column—such heartfelt insights on the page. Why couldn't he have made a place for her in his life?

She glanced at Samuel, who was studying her actions intently. He acknowledged that he saw the clipping, and she tossed it in the hole.

"I forgive you, Daniel Foster."

She blinked away tears, determined not to cry. If she continued to weigh herself down with the years behind her, she would never be free to experience the life before her with joy and happiness. The peaceful life she longed for—a life where she didn't harbor any resentments—was within her grasp. Releasing the burdens of her heart, forgiving those who hurt her, and turning her life to God would free her soul to be the person she wanted to be.

She reached into the bag.

"Are you sure about this, Lillian?" Samuel asked when he saw her retrieve the next few items. His forehead creased with worry.

"*Ya*, I am. This represents all my worldly clothes, along with a few other things." She folded the blue jeans and placed them in the hole, followed by a bag of makeup, several pieces of costume jewelry, a small battery-operated radio, and two books she no longer felt were suitable reading material. Some of the jewelry was from Rickie. She didn't see the need to mention that.

There was one thing left in the bag—her last tie to the outside world. As she pulled out her cell phone, Samuel said, "What about talking to your *mamm*?"

"I'll do what everyone else here does. I'll go to town and use the pay phone, or the shanty at the Lapp farm."

Samuel seemed leery about the cell phone, her final separation from the outside world. The lines in his forehead became more evident.

"It's fine," she replied as she tossed the phone atop the pile. "Grandma hates that thing. She winces every time it rings."

Samuel knew that giving up her worldly items and forgiving those who hurt her was all part of Lillian's plan to move forward in her new life. But he also knew it wasn't easy for her. Just like it wasn't going to be easy for him to add his own piece of the past to the pile.

"Okay, that's it." She twisted her hands together in a nervous sort of way. He reckoned he'd feel nervous in her shoes too.

"Wait," he said when she reached for the spade, preparing to refill the hole. He reached into his pocket. "I have something to add."

He'd been thinking about it the whole time he watched her giving up her worldly possessions and letting go of the things that haunted her. The item in his pocket didn't haunt him, but it would be equally as hard to give up.

He pulled out the wallet-sized picture of Rachel and handed it to Lillian. The edges were worn, but her face as beautiful as ever.

"Samuel," she whispered, as if she couldn't believe her eyes. "But I thought . . ." She paused, looking at the photo. ". . . pictures aren't allowed."

"I'm not perfect, Lillian." He thought back to the day his

Englisch friend Carl Johanson from the supermarket gave him the picture a few days after Rachel died. "We don't have to tell anyone about this," Carl had said as he slipped him the picture of Rachel. Carl adored Rachel and evidently had sneaked in a picture when she wasn't looking, knowing she had the cancer real bad and that someday Samuel might want it. He'd carried it in his pocket ever since. No one knew he had the picture, not even David.

"She's beautiful, Samuel," she said, taking note of the woman's exquisite facial features. Her eyes were a warm hazel color, and her tightly wound hair a honey-brown shade. "Wow." She handed the picture back to him.

He took one last look at the woman from his past, then looked at Lillian. Her face was as serious as he'd ever seen her. And she'd never looked prettier.

Slowly, his hand made its way toward the hole. But Lillian's hand was quickly on his arm. "No, Samuel," she said, shaking her head. "No."

"She's part of my past." His arm wavered over the hole in the dirt. "And pictures aren't allowed."

Lillian disagreed. "It's not the same, Samuel. Rachel is a wonderful part of your past, someone to remember. You loved her, and she's David's mother. I don't want you to ever forget her. I would never allow you to mix her picture with these things I want to bury forever." She continued shaking her head in a very determined way.

Samuel froze. He wasn't sure what to do. His hand held fast to the picture, still hovering over the hole. The whole while he watched Lillian make peace with things from her past, he'd thought burying the picture would be the right thing to do. He wanted to be able to move forward too.

"Put the picture back in your pocket, Samuel," Lillian instructed, guiding his arm away from the hole. "We won't tell anyone. But I think you need to keep the picture."

"I reckon it's not right, though."

"It'll be our little secret." Her eyes sparkled with warm sincerity.

As he placed the picture back in his pocket, his gaze locked with hers in mutual understanding.

———

That night at supper, with her entire family assembled at the table, David offered the blessing, and everyone dug into the feast Lillian had prepared. She'd mastered *Yummasetti*, a traditional Pennsylvania German dish—ground beef, Amish noodles, bread, butter, onion, peas, chicken soup, mushroom soup, sour cream, and lots of cheese. Her city life would have sent the high-calorie meal straight to her thighs, but there was always enough work here to keep a nice sense of balance when it came to worrying about weight gain.

Everyone loved the meal, and she'd even made rhubarb pie for dessert.

"Our Lilly has turned into a fine Amish cook," Grandpa announced. "*Appeditlich!*"

"It's real *gut*, Lillian," David said. Although Lillian noticed he'd been awfully quiet since he came in from his chores outside. Maybe he felt left out, knowing she and Samuel had spent the day together.

"Are you ready to start school soon?" she asked. "Let's see, you have two more years left, right?"

"I reckon," David said softly, barely looking up. Lillian

glanced at Samuel, who shrugged slightly, also sensing David's solemn mood.

Lillian knew Amish children only attended school through the eighth grade. Weeks ago, Samuel had shown her David's school. The one-room, red schoolhouse was within walking distance of every child who attended. There were rows of wooden desks facing a long blackboard. There were no televisions, computers, or any other type of electronic equipment. It was like stepping back into another time period. Samuel explained that Amish teachers taught lessons in English.

Reflecting on her trip to the schoolhouse with Samuel, she thought about her twelve years in public school, plus her four years in college. In her mixed-up world, teaching had been the one goal that had remained constant. Once again, she recalled her regret at having to give up her teaching job.

"What are we gonna do when young David returns to school?" Grandpa asked. "We've become mighty dependent on him 'round here."

"David will still come around after school," Samuel said. "And Jonas, I'll do whatever I can to help too."

Grandpa sat up a little straighter. "*Ya*, well, I've been feelin' downright well here lately. Whatever medical concoctions those *Englisch* doctors are given' me tend to make me wanna tackle that yard with the push mower."

"Jonas, you will do no such thing!" Grandma snapped.

"Irma Rose, don't go bossin' me." His tone was equally firm. "I know yard work is for the womenfolk, but I'm gonna do it since I ain't been able to do much else."

"If I catch you mowing that yard, I'll do more than boss you,

Jonas Miller." She shot him a look that would've had everyone
else at the table cowering, but Grandpa just sat up even taller.

"After I be done mowing the yard with the push mower, then
I'm gonna go after the repairs to that hog pen. Thinkin' about
takin' on a few hogs this next year."

"Jonas! We have more than we can say grace over to take care
of 'round here. I'm pleased as punch you are feelin' better, but
you can get those crazy notions out of your head."

Lillian glanced at Samuel, who was trying not to laugh. Even
David was stifling a grin. When Grandma and Grandpa got going,
it was always an amusing display of misdirected affection.

"I'll do whatever I want," Grandpa muttered, diving into some
rhubarb pie.

Grandma rattled off a bunch of *Pennsylvania Deitsch* Lillian
didn't understand, but Samuel and David looked shocked. And
Grandpa didn't say another word.

As the men ate their rhubarb pie and began their own conversation, Lillian and her grandma cleaned the supper dishes.

"I think I smelled cigar smoke in here this morning when I
returned from the supermarket," Grandma whispered. "Do you
think that grandpa of yours would be silly enough to be smokin'
with his bad health?"

Lillian figured Grandpa was in enough trouble for one day.
She shrugged.

Whispering again, Grandma said, "Those medications have
his mind all amuck. Do you know what he told me last night?"

Whatever it was, Grandma looked appalled. Her lips pursed
together as she leaned in close to Lillian's ear. "He said he wants to
have more *kinner*," she groaned in exasperation. "Now, is that not the

silliest notion you've ever heard of in your life? First of all, Jonas
knows the Good Lord was only able to bless us with one child. I
couldn't have any more. Secondly, has that silly ol' man looked in
the mirror lately?"

Lillian tried not to smile. Grandma was clearly upset.

"He's just been saying and doin' the craziest of things. It's
those pills." She glanced over at her husband and frowned.
Swiping a plate dry with the cup towel, she placed it in the
cupboard.

Grandpa didn't notice. He was well into his second piece of
rhubarb pie, as were Samuel and David.

"Well, at least he's feeling better," Lillian said, trying to cheer
up Grandma.

"And I praise God for that. I just wish it wouldn't make his
mind so cluttered, where he's not thinkin' like he should be."

As they whispered to themselves in the corner of the kitchen,
Grandpa interrupted them. "Oh, Irma Rose and Lilly!"

"What, Jonas?" Grandma asked with a sigh. She glanced
his way.

"I almost forgot to tell you both somethin'."

"What, Grandpa?" Lillian asked.

"No tellin'," Grandma whispered under her breath. She turned
her back to dry another dish and place it in the cupboard.

Lillian watched while Grandpa swallowed his last bit of rhubarb pie. A big smile stretched across his wrinkled jowls. "Sarah
Jane will be here on Wednesday."

Grandma spun around, sending the plate in her hand crashing to the floor.

14

LILLIAN PULLED THE BROOM FROM THE PANTRY AND BEGAN sweeping up the pieces of the broken plate. She'd begged her mother over the phone to come to Lancaster County. Had she finally decided to make peace with her parents?

"While you were out tending to your pretty flowers in the yard, Lilly, that noisy portable phone kept ringin' this morning," Grandpa bellowed. "It took me a few tries, but I finally was able to talk into it." He paused. "I told Sarah Jane she needed to come for a visit. She'll be here on Wednesday."

He made the statement as nonchalantly as if he saw his daughter all the time. When no one said anything, he went on. "Lilly, I say you prepare a special supper for your *mamm*. Show her what a fine Amish cook we've turned out 'round here. Said she'd be here by suppertime."

"Jonas, are you sure about this?" Grandma asked in a skeptical tone.

"Irma Rose, our Sarah Jane will be here on Wednesday." His announcement left no room for argument.

It was quiet for a bit before Samuel stood up to retrieve his hat from the rack. "That's great news, Jonas," he said, placing the hat on his head.

"*Ya, gut* news! Isn't it, Irma Rose?"

"Of course," Grandma said. Emotion flooded her face. "That's *wunderbaar* news."

"I'm going to walk Samuel and David out," Lillian said, not wanting to voice her concerns in front of her grandparents.

Once they were outside, Lillian told Samuel and David, "I begged my mother to come see her parents. She was adamant about not coming. I wonder what Grandpa said to change her mind?"

"Whatever he said, I think it's great she's coming," Samuel remarked.

Lillian shook her head. "You don't know my mother. She probably just *said* she would come. Grandpa is so excited about her coming, and she'll probably never show up. That will break his heart."

"People change their minds," Samuel said. As they headed to the buggy, he continued. "Think positive. It'll mean the world to Jonas if your *mamm* comes for a visit."

"It'll mean *everything* to Grandpa. And that's what worries me." She paused. "And another thing: Grandma said Grandpa has been saying all kinds of crazy things lately, mostly due to his medication. What if he didn't even talk to her? I'd better go into town tomorrow and use a pay phone." A guilty feeling swept over her; she was beginning to regret disposal of that one worldly item. How much easier it would be to walk inside and call her mother from the comfort of her bedroom.

"Pop, did you tell her about next weekend?" David asked, changing the subject.

"I was gettin' around to it." He turned toward Lillian. "I

know you've been around my *mamm* and the rest of my family at church services, but they want to have a big shindig next Saturday and have you, Irma Rose, and Jonas to the house for supper. They know me and the boy eat supper here a lot, and I think they'd like to do something for your family."

Lillian got along well enough with Samuel's family, but she knew they still regarded her as the *Englisch* outsider. Conversation was always polite, but limited. Neither his two sisters, nor sister-in-law had allowed her into their inner circle. Several times after church service she'd tried to make conversation with them. They were cordial, but guarded. His mother barely acknowledged her.

"And, of course, your *mamm* is welcome too," Samuel added.

"I wouldn't count on her being here."

"You never know," Samuel said optimistically. "People change."

She started to say, "Not my mother." But that would be the old Lillian talking. She had to admit: people could change. She had changed. And she had buried any bad thoughts she'd harbored about her mother in a hole by the lake. Plus, she'd had some hard but good conversations with her mom lately that helped her see her mom in a new light.

Her eyes glistened with hope. "I pray she does come." And she meant it. She just doubted it.

The next day, she set out to go talk to David. She sensed something was bothering him. It was a beautiful day for a walk and it was an off Sunday. Alternating Sunday worship services was one of the "rules" she wasn't about to argue with. While the service always left her with a sense of fellowship and heightened spirituality, it was incredibly long.

Walking down the dirt road toward Samuel's farm, she reflected on the events of the past few days. Deep in thought about her mother, she heard a buggy approaching from behind. She spun around and watched the buggy slowing down.

Of all people . . .

Sadie Fisher let out a "Whoa, boy" that any man would have been proud of. As she coaxed her horse to a stop, she yelled, "Need a ride?"

She didn't really. However, Sadie's expression was nonconfrontational and it seemed safe enough.

"Heading to Samuel's?" she asked, guiding her horse back into motion after Lillian crawled in.

"*Ya.*"

"I heard you were learning the *Ordnung* and some *Pennsylvania Deitsch.*" Her tone was neither sarcastic nor condescending.

"Yes, I am."

"Are you thinking of converting and staying in our community?" Again, her tone wasn't bitter.

"I'm learning as much as I can so I can make a good decision." *Why does this seem like dangerous territory?*

"That sounds like a *gut* plan." Sadie issued a pop of the leathery strap and picked up the pace.

Lillian didn't know what to say. The woman was being nice. She just nodded.

"It's no secret I was hoping to marry Samuel someday."

Uh oh. Here we go. "Maybe you still will," she replied.

Sadie shrugged. "*Ach*, don't be silly. He took a fancy to you, and I'm happy for the both of you."

"What?" She didn't mean her response to sound as surprised as she was. "No, no," she added. "We're only friends."

"Sure you are."

The woman didn't seem the least bit jealous or upset. Maybe it was a trick.

"I'm actually on my way to Samuel's as well."

Ah ha! She knew it.

"Levi Zook's barn burned down and a barn raising is planned for Saturday. I was going to let Samuel know, so he wouldn't make any plans."

"Oh," Lillian responded, wondering how that would affect the family shindig planned for both their families on the same day. She had heard about the Amish barn raisings. The whole community participated and framed and roofed-in a barn all in one day.

"And I know Jonas isn't well, but it'd be nice if you were able to come help tend to the menfolk."

Sadie's tone was sincere. She didn't seem to harbor an ounce of resentment that Samuel and Lillian had become friends. "I'd be glad to help," Lillian replied.

As they pulled onto Samuel's driveway, Sadie asked, "Can I tell you a secret?"

"Sure." What kind of secret could she have to tell her?

Lillian took in Sadie with fresh eyes. Sadie was a feisty red-head with ivory skin and sky-blue eyes. Tiny creases in the corner of each eye hinted she might be a few years older than Lillian. She was tall and thin. Her striking appearance was unique to the

Old Order district. Lillian had noticed almost all the women had dark hair and olive complexions.

"I've been writing letters to a man in Texas."

The look on Lillian's face must have revealed her shock.

"Not to worry—he's an Amish man. I'm going to travel there to meet him!"

"Really? Is that allowed?" Lillian wasn't sure. "I'm from Texas," she added.

Skipping past her latter comment, Sadie said, "*Ya*. My husband died three years ago and Samuel was my only prospect for marriage here. My biological clock is ticking, as the *Englisch* would say." She glanced at Lillian and smiled for the first time. "I have no bad feelings about it, Lillian. Once I found out that Samuel carried no interest, I rested my efforts."

Lillian doubted Sadie's biological clock was ticking too much ahead of her own. She knew the Amish started their families early. She couldn't help but wonder why Sadie had no children. It wasn't proper to ask.

"How did you meet him?" Lillian knew there were scattered, small Amish districts in Texas.

"His family traveled here for my cousin's wedding. That's how I found out 'bout him. His wife also died about three years ago. But he wasn't able to attend the wedding. So I haven't actually met him. We've just been exchanging letters. No one knows, either, except for my cousin."

They were now parked in front of Samuel's farmhouse. Lillian could see David on the front porch. "Sadie, I have to say I'm a little surprised that you're telling me your secret."

Sadie shrugged again. "I guess I wanted to show you I wasn't going to stand in your way." She kept going over Lillian's protests. "But I'll ask that you keep it to yourself for now, if you don't mind."

"Sure. I won't tell anyone."

Sadie nodded. "Listen. I don't reckon I need to come in. Can you just let Samuel know about the barn raising?"

"I will. And I'll come help."

"That would be *gut*." Sadie guided her horse in the other direction. Before she pulled out, she yelled out the window. "Lillian?"

"*Ya?*"

"Come for a visit anytime. I'd love to hear all about Texas." She smiled and headed down the road.

Lillian decided she liked Sadie. Who would have ever thought? An unlikely friendship, but one Lillian felt she would pursue.

By the time Lillian reached the front porch, Samuel was outside with David. "And to what do we owe the pleasure?" Samuel asked as he walked toward her.

"Actually, I came to see David."

"*Ya?*" David asked, sounding alarmed.

"I wanted to talk to you. How about taking a walk with me?" she asked.

"Can I, Pop? I did most of my chores."

"You can do the rest when you get back," Samuel said, firing a questioning look in Lillian's direction.

Offering no explanation, she smiled at Samuel and motioned for David to walk beside her. Halfway down the driveway, she said, "Something was bothering you at supper last night. Anything to do with me?"

"No," he said. Although he didn't deny something was wrong.

Lillian thought for a minute and decided honesty would be best. "I thought maybe you were upset that your Pop and I spent the day together without you. Most of the time, it's the three of us together."

David shrugged, but didn't say anything.

"*Ya*, that's it, isn't it?"

"No. That would sound like I was a kid."

"You are a kid."

Once on the main road, she said, "I think me and your pop are just trying to get to know each other better. Is that okay with you?"

"*Ya*, I reckon so."

"Sometimes me and your *daed* might want to spend some time alone, getting to know each other." She paused. "But it doesn't mean that I don't still want to do things with you. Like this—our walk. This is our time to talk. So there will probably be times when it's just me and your *daed*, or just you and your *daed*, or just me and you. See what I mean?"

"*Ya*, I know."

He seemed to understand. Maybe he just needed to hear it from her. "So, everything is okay?"

Before David had time to answer, they both heard a blaring noise coming from down the road. As the buggy drew closer, Lillian was surprised to hear music blasting from within it. That certainly wasn't allowed. As the speeding buggy came frighteningly close to running them over, a frantic boy inside struggled to turn down the music. His blond bangs were slicked back and he was wearing blue jeans and a black T-shirt.

"Did he steal that buggy?" Lillian asked alarmed. "And what was that he was drinking?"

David didn't seem worried. As they watched the boy disappearing down the road, he said, in an envious tone, "That's Milo Yoder. It's his *rumschpringe*."

During *rumschpringe*, the community expected a certain amount of misbehavior from a teenager. But all this? Loud music, blue jeans, and whatever the boy was drinking in the brown bottle?

"Wonder where he's going in such a hurry and dressed like that?" she asked, frowning. She thought it tainted the Amish reputation for him to be acting like that.

"I can't wait until my *rumschpringe!*" David said as Milo Yoder's buggy disappeared completely, leaving only a dusty cloud behind him. "I'm gonna go to the movies, wear *Englisch* clothes, watch television in town, listen to loud music . . ." He paused. "And smoke cigarettes."

"Oh, David, I hope you won't smoke." She realized right away that it wasn't her place to speak to him in such a harsh tone, but the thought of David smoking bothered her. Turning to face him, she asked, "Why would you want to do all those things anyway?"

"Because you can do all those things during your *rumschpringe*," he said sheepishly, as if her tone surprised him. He looked down at the ground and kicked the dirt. "Besides, I bet you've done all those things."

Ouch. She certainly had. But that was different. David hadn't been exposed to any of those things, and she didn't want him to be. She wanted him to stay exactly as he was—free of complications and worldly ways. The outside world could snatch his innocence away before he realized what happened.

"Yes, I have done all those things," she answered. "And, it's not all it's cracked up to be either."

Standing on the side of the road, David pushed back his hat and gave her an inquisitive look.

"If there's something you want to ask me, go ahead." She folded her hands in front of her. "I'll tell you whatever you want to know."

"Have you ever drunk beer or smoked cigarettes?" His tone was almost demanding, but she'd started it.

"*Ya,* I have." *And please, don't do either one.*

"And I reckon you've seen lots of movies," he hesitated before he went on. "With all kinds of stuff in them."

"*Ya,* I have."

"Gone to a shopping mall and hung out with your friends?"

"Yep."

"Played an instrument?"

Lillian thought back to her short stint as a flute player while in middle school. Even though she had to give it up when Mom couldn't afford to buy her a flute of her own, she had loved making music. However, she knew the Old Order Amish community forbid instruments. Music was worldly and contrary to the Amish ways and was said to stir up emotions.

"I played the flute for a while," she finally said.

"Drove a car?" He crossed his arms, his tone still demanding. She should have never instigated this conversation.

"Yes," she answered. "But, David . . ." She wanted to tell him what a horrific childhood she'd had and how she wished she could have grown up right here. He wasn't done, though.

"Danced to band music?"

"*Ya.* I've done all those things, David. They may all sound fun and exciting to you, but you don't understand that—"

He was quick to interrupt her. "I'm going to do all those things during my *rumschpringe!*"

"Well, maybe just be choosy and make wise decisions when you go through your *rumschpringe.*" Fearing his exposure to the outside world, her emotions spilled out in an unplanned confession of sorts. "I'm sure all those things sound exciting, David. Driving a car, hanging out with your friends, drinking beer, smoking . . . but let me tell you what else can go along with all that fun-sounding stuff."

David was hanging on her words.

"Have you ever woken up and not had any food to eat? Ever slept in a car overnight because you didn't have a home to sleep in? Has anyone ever pushed you or threatened to beat you up at school? Anyone ever stolen from you? What about a terrible crime; ever witnessed anything like that? Been in a car accident that was so scary you didn't drive for six months?" She paused. "There is just a lot of bad stuff out there. That's all I'm saying. I wish I could have grown up here."

David wasn't saying anything. Maybe she'd said too much.

"I'm sorry. I should have never said all those things," she said with regret. She sat down on the side of the road in the grass. Slowly he followed her, his eyes begging for answers. "But living here seems to come with an invisible protective barrier that keeps you safe from everything out there." She waved her hand aimlessly to indicate a far-off place filled with worldly evils. "I told you before, it's complicated. And where there's all that stuff you think is so cool, there's a whole lot of ugliness too. I just don't want you to go through all that—*rumschpringe* or not."

They sat quietly for a few minutes.

"I won't do all those things, Lillian," he said softly. His big blue eyes were warm and tender, like Samuel's.

"Outside of this peaceful, tranquil, wonderful place is a world very different from yours. It might sound fun and intriguing, but trust me—it can steal from you, rob you of all the wonderful qualities that make you special. I just don't ever want to see that happen."

"It's all right, Lillian. I reckon I don't need to do all those things." It was quiet for a while before David said something Lillian felt sure she would remember for the rest of her life.

With a maturity way beyond his years, and possibly *her* years, he said, "Pop says when God closes doors, other doors will open. I had to think 'bout that for a while—like if I was in a big room with lots of doors." He paused. "I reckon sometimes we might not pick the door God woulda picked for us. But I think the door is like a two-way mirror. You best be happy with whatever ya see, no matter which side of the door you're on." He turned toward her and smiled. A smile she affectionately returned. "I reckon it'd be better to just try to pick the right door in the first place."

He couldn't have been more right.

⸺⸻⸺

Samuel noticed right away that the boy's frame of mind seemed much improved after his talk with Lillian. Neither one of them offered up any details, but that was all right. He reckoned they were forming their own special bond.

Lillian headed home after she filled him in about the barn raising on Saturday. He figured all his kin would be there, so maybe they'd find some time to visit with Lillian there, as opposed to the private shindig they had planned. A barn raising was a whole bunch of work, but a festive occasion just the same.

He found it a little worrisome that Lillian and Sadie might be pursuing a friendship, but he knew Lillian needed some womenfolk as friends. Sadie was a good girl; she'd just never been the one for him.

It was later that afternoon that his son shared some troublesome news. "Me and Lillian had a real *gut* talk today," David said. He settled into a rocker on the front porch next to Samuel.

"And what did you two have your heads together about?"

"She's done a whole bunch of stuff in her life. Sounds like she had a pretty hard time growing up."

"*Ya,*" Samuel said. "But I think she turned out real fine."

"Hard to believe she's smoked cigarettes, drunk beer, seen crimes and all kinds of bad stuff." David took a swallow of his lemonade, unaware of the can of worms he'd just opened up. "She's even slept in a car and seen people get beat up."

How could she? Had Lillian learned nothing through her studies of the Amish ways? *"Come out from among them, and be ye separate, saith the Lord."* In her studies of the *Ordnung,* did she bypass 2 Corinthians 6:17? Samuel wasn't naïve. He knew the boy would be entitled to a *rumschpringe* in a few years, just as he had been. Along with that would come some misbehaving as he took a peek at the outside world. It wasn't Lillian's place to encourage such behavior, though. Those kinds of things were best not talked about. And it sure wasn't her place to expose his son to behaviors Samuel wanted him to have no part of.

His blood was pumping and bubbling to a boil. David's

next comment sent it rushing through his veins like whitewater rapids.

"I'm real glad she told me all about her times in the *Englisch* world, about all the things she's done. Now I know what to do when my *rumschpringe* comes 'round." He placed his lemonade on the table between them. "I'm gonna go get washed up before we head to Lillian's for Sunday supper. She always makes something extra *gut* on Sunday."

Samuel nodded. They'd been having supper mostly twice a week with Lillian—Wednesdays and Sundays. Tonight, if it was up to him, they wouldn't be going anywhere for supper. He planned to tell Lillian exactly how he felt about exposing his son to her worldly past. It wasn't his way—to get all stirred up about things. It wasn't proper. But she'd crossed the line when she shared her colorful past with his son. Smoking cigarettes, drinking beer? What was she thinking?

15

"Answer the phone, Mom," Lillian whispered. Somehow she and Grandma had let the pantry run dry of flour, so this quick trip to town was a good opportunity to call her mother. She needed to hurry, though. Samuel and David would be heading over for supper soon.

"Hello."

"Hi, Mom."

"Lillian! How are things going?"

"Everything is fine. Did you tell Grandpa you were coming here on Wednesday?" Might as well get to the point.

"Yes, I did. And I'm really going to try, Lillian."

"Mom! What do you mean, you're going to *try*?"

"Well, Lillian, I do have a job. Hopefully it will work out where I can come."

"What made you change your mind? I thought you didn't want to come for a visit?"

"I just . . ." She paused. "I just need to see my parents. And when your grandpa asked me to come, well, it was just hearing his voice, I guess. I know he's sick, and I didn't want to disappoint him. He suggested Wednesday. Where are you calling me from? I've tried to call you on your cell phone several times."

"I don't have my cell phone any more. I'm calling you from a pay phone in town. Mom, Grandpa is counting on you coming. He will be very upset if you don't show up. You were so adamant with me on the phone the other day about not coming. Don't disappoint him, Mom."

"Don't take that tone with me, Lillian. I will do the best I can. I have to get someone to cover for me at work and see if I can get a flight."

"Mother, you should have thought about all that before you told Grandpa you're coming."

"I'm going to do the best I can, Lillian. That's all I can do."

"You're not coming." She wanted to reach through the phone line and—well, that wasn't the Amish way, so she tried to toss the thought.

"I don't know, Lillian. I'll try. I'd like to. Things with Paul aren't going very well either. I'm not sure if it's a good time to leave."

"I have to go, Mom."

"Wait, Lillian. Tell me about your Amish man. How are Grandma and Grandpa?"

"Come to Lancaster County and see for yourself." She slammed the phone down, knowing again that her behavior was not reflective of her newfound faith. Grandpa was going to be heartbroken.

Grandpa was sitting at the kitchen table when Lillian returned. Grandma was placing a loaf of homemade bread on the table. "Sorry it took so long," she said, checking on her beef stew she'd left simmering on the wood-burning oven. "I wanted to call Mom." She turned around and looked at her grandpa. "Grandpa, I'm not sure Mom's going to make it." She thought it best to prepare him.

"She'll be here," he said confidently. "Sarah Jane will be here on Wednesday."

"Jonas, did you hear Lillian?" Exasperated, Grandma evidently doubted the arrival of her daughter on Wednesday as well. "Sarah Jane might not make it."

Grandpa rattled off a round of *Pennsylvania Deitsch* Lillian didn't understand, but Grandma scowled, walked to him, and poked him in the arm.

"We don't talk like that in this *haus*, Jonas." She leaned down closer to him. "Sarah Jane has not been to this house in seventeen years. You needn't go gettin' your hopes up. That's all I'm saying."

Grandma was on the same page as Lillian.

"Lilly, what will you be cookin' for your *mamm* on Wednesday?" Grandpa questioned, obviously pretending he hadn't heard a word either of them said.

"I'll come up with something *gut*, Grandpa."

"Where's Samuel and the boy? I'm hungry," he belted out. Grandma rolled her eyes.

Samuel and David arrived about ten minutes late. Uncharacteristic. They were always on time. Samuel looked tired and bothered about something throughout the entire meal.

"Didn't you like the stew?" Lillian asked, noticing that although everyone else was about finished, Samuel still had quite a bit in his bowl.

"The stew was fine. Can I talk to you on the porch, Lillian?"

Something was wrong. Everyone at the table shot Samuel a questioning look.

"*Ya,*" she whispered softly. "Do you want some peach pie first?"

"No, *danki,*" he said, standing up.

This isn't good. Why was he so bothered? Everything was fine when she left his house earlier.

"You kids run along," Grandpa said. "David, I've been needin' me a chess partner for a long while. Your grandma won't play."

"Jonas, someone has to keep this house running," Grandma said. She stood up and began to clear the dishes.

"I'll help you in a minute." Lillian stood up to follow Samuel to the door.

"No, no. You go on. I've got it," Grandma replied.

"Let's be headin' into the den, David. A good game of chess will help settle our full bellies." Grandpa shuffled out of the kitchen.

Out on the porch, Samuel didn't waste any time. "I don't know what you were thinkin' when you told my boy all the things you did in your world. I don't want him to know anything about your world. Bad enough he witnessed that *baremlich* scene here with your friend, Rickie. I'm not sure I want you around him." He knew his eyes were ablaze and his tone sharp.

Instantly, her eyes glassed over. She looked shattered. Samuel realized right away he should have eased into the conversation, or at least toned it down a notch.

"What?" she asked. Her legs appeared wobbly before she folded into one of the rockers. Samuel took a seat in the other rocker.

"I don't want David exposed to your world, Lillian." He shook his head, but could hardly look at her.

"But this is my world." Her voice was cracking. This was harder than he'd reckoned it would be.

"But your worldly ways are spilling into our ways, Lillian. What were you thinkin' when you told David about drinking and smoking?" He paused. "And all that other stuff you told him about life in the city? The boy needn't be hearing any such things. It will be right hard enough when he has his *rumschpringe*. He doesn't need any encouragement from you to try all those things."

Her hands were on either side of her cheeks and her eyes were all watered up. His first instinct was to go wrap his arms around her, but that wasn't going to help things. Refocusing on what was best for David, Samuel knew he couldn't let her reaction muddle his thinking.

"But I don't want him to do *any* of those things. The reason I—" Her voice was still cracking, but he didn't want to hear her excuses.

"There is no reason for any of it, Lillian. And, I'm sorry to say, I just would rather you not spend so much time with David."

"Samuel, you don't mean that. You and David have become like my family."

He knew she was crying, so he just avoided looking at her.

Didn't she realize his heart was breaking too? But he had to do what was best for the boy.

"Don't you care about me?" She sounded pitiful. He wasn't sure he could respond without his own voice breaking up.

"*Ya*," he said softly, forcing himself to look down at the ground and not at her.

"Samuel," she reached for his hand, and it took every bit of his might to pull away from her.

"I'm gonna go, Lillian. And I think it's best if me and David stop comin' for supper." He stood up, but this time his eyes were drawn to hers like a magnet. He had trouble looking away, but he did. If he didn't go now, he'd never be able to.

She was all curled up in the rocker crying hard. Walking away from her would be difficult.

"Samuel, please . . ."

"I'm real sorry, Lillian, that you're hurtin'."

"Just let me explain."

He could barely understand her for the crying. He walked back into the kitchen. As the door slammed behind him, he worried how he'd keep his emotions inside. He just kept telling himself it was the best thing for David.

"David, we need to be goin'," he said as he walked into the den where Jonas and David looked like they'd barely gotten started on their chess game. Irma Rose wasn't around.

"We're just getting started," Jonas said, sounding disappointed.

"*Ya*, Pop. I figured you and Lillian would be talkin' for a while." David smiled, but it quickly faded when he saw the look on his pop's face.

"Come on, boy. We've got things to tend to. Sorry, Jonas." He grabbed his hat off the rack and headed for the door.

Lillian was still curled up in the rocker. It took everything he had to make his legs walk down the porch steps and leave her like that.

"Lillian, what's wrong?" David made his way onto the porch and was standing behind Samuel, his eyes dark with worry.

He turned around in time to see Lillian jump out of the rocker and run into the house.

David didn't move. "Pop, what's goin' on?"

Samuel motioned for David to come along. It was going to be a hard conversation to have with his son. But it was for the best.

———※ ※———

"But, Pop, she was just tryin' to tell me not to do all those things," David said later. "I think she was just tryin' to protect me."

He knew David was suffering right along with him and Lillian. "It's not right to talk about such things, David."

"But I want her to be *mei mamm* someday!"

Samuel had suspected the boy harbored the same hopeful image of the future he did: all of them as one big happy family. "Watch your tone, boy," Samuel said, careful not to scorn him too much. He was hurting for sure.

"But, Pop—"

It was tough to see his son's eyes welling up with tears. But someday he'd realize that this was the best thing for him. "On up to bed now," Samuel said, fighting his own emotions. Couldn't let the boy see him watering up.

David ran up the stairs without saying another word. Samuel put his head in his hands. He couldn't shake the image of Lillian crying.

"Lillian, can I come in?"

Lillian attempted to control her crying, to no avail. "*Ya*," she said to her grandma, through the bedroom door.

How could Samuel do this? Was his friendship so limited that there was no room for mistakes or forgiveness? She thought she was helping David see how bad choices could turn out. Samuel didn't even want to hear her explanation. Obviously, he didn't care about her the way she cared about him. If he could give up on their friendship so easily, then maybe it truly wasn't meant to be.

No. She just didn't believe that. It *was* meant to be. It had to be. He and David were in her life. And she'd prayed so hard about it. Wasn't God listening? How could this be happening?

"There, there," Grandma comforted, taking a seat on the bed.

Lillian wept in her arms. "He didn't even let me explain, Grandma," she said after telling her what happened. "I want David to make good choices when he has his *rumschpringe*. He'll be exposed to so many evils out in the world. I was just trying to prepare him so he'd know what to avoid. I would never encourage him to make any of the mistakes I made." She cried some more while her grandma held her.

"I know you wouldn't lead the boy astray, Lillian. Maybe just give Samuel some time to think things out."

"He was so cold, Grandma. He just left me there, in pieces. It was horrible—like he didn't care about me at all. How could he do that? I don't understand."

Grandma gently pushed her away and cradled her cheeks with

her hands. "Let me try to explain something to you in a way I reckon maybe you can understand. I know you love me and your grandpa. I know you love Samuel and David. But when you have *kinner* of your own, you'll understand a whole different kind of love. It's a love so powerful that you'll cause hurt to yourself if it means protecting a child."

"David doesn't need protection from me. I do love him. I would never, ever do anything to hurt him." She pulled away from her grandma and threw her head on the pillow.

"I know that, dear. I think when Samuel talks to David and thinks this through, in his mind he'll come to know that too." Stroking Lillian's hair, she went on. "Sometimes, we think we're doin' right by our young ones. Maybe sometimes we don't always do so."

———————

As Irma Rose tried her best to comfort Lillian, she couldn't help but wonder why her own daughter had left so abruptly—if it was something she did. There was no handbook for raising children, and she reckoned she'd done the best she could. Her heart went out to Lillian. And to Samuel. He was only trying to do what he thought was best for the boy. Hopefully he'd come to reason that Lillian only had David's best interest at heart.

"Did you call your *mamm*?" she asked when Lillian seemed to be a little better.

"*Ya*." She sat up on the bed and dabbed at her eyes. "She said she's going to try to come. But I know her, Grandma. She won't come and it will break Grandpa's heart."

And mine. As nervous as she was to see Sarah Jane, it was all

Irma Rose had thought about since Jonas shared the news of her visit.

~~~~

Three days since his conversation with Lillian, Samuel wasn't feeling any better. To worsen things, David was barely talking to him. Maybe he'd acted too harshly. If he did, it was out of love and fear for his son. He thought back to his own *rumschpringe* and cringed, doubtful he'd experienced hardly a tad of what Lillian must have experienced in the *Englisch* world. Should he fault her for that? No. But sharing her past with his son was strictly off-limits. She should have known that.

Lost in regret and confusion, Samuel realized it was nearing four o'clock. He'd need to stir up some supper for him and David. Normally they'd be heading to Lillian's on Wednesday. His heart was heavy as he thought about facing each day without Lillian in his life.

"Have you talked to Lillian?" he asked, sitting down at the kitchen table across from his son.

"*Ya.*" David bit into a cookie. It didn't appear he was going to say anything about it.

"Is she okay?"

The look David fired at him surely deserved a trip to the woodshed and some discipline, but he let it go.

"No, she's not *okay*. And she fears talking to me—afraid she'll get me and her in trouble."

Samuel hung his head. "I was just trying to protect you." *Maybe I made a mistake.*

"Pop, I'm gonna be seeing the *Englisch* world in a few years. She was just trying to tell me not to make some of the same mistakes she made."

"*Ya*. But such *Englisch* things are best unspoken." He shouldn't have to justify his actions to David.

"Why? If her blunders might help me to not walk a bad path, then why should they not be talked about?" David's tone was bordering on rude, and Samuel didn't like it. But he considered the possibility that maybe his son was right.

"Maybe I should talk to her." Samuel stroked his beard and thought about what he would say. He was having a world of trouble trying to figure out how he was going to reconcile this situation.

"I don't think she wants to talk to you, Pop. I think she's gone from being real upset to real mad." David paused and bit into another cookie. "Besides, she's got worry in her heart about Jonas. She's fearing he's going be real upset when her mother doesn't show up today."

Samuel had been so focused on how much he missed her he'd forgotten that Wednesday was the day Sarah Jane Miller was due to arrive. It was gonna break Jonas and Irma Rose's hearts if she didn't show. And Lillian's. He should be there to wait with her or comfort her if her *mamm* didn't show up. What a fine mess he'd made of things.

"Your grandpa hasn't moved from that rocker on the porch for the past two hours. It's nearin' six o'clock, way past the supper hour," Grandma said. "He needs to accept that Sarah Jane isn't coming."

Lillian could hear the regret in her grandma's voice. Honestly, she wasn't sure who was more upset, Grandma or Grandpa.

"I'm sorry, Grandma. Maybe I should go talk to Grandpa." She stood from the kitchen table and headed toward the door. Grandma just shrugged.

How could everything have fallen apart like this? She missed Samuel so bad it hurt, but she was equally angry at him for snatching away their friendship as if it meant nothing. And now this. She knew her mother wasn't going to show. Just history repeating itself.

She took a seat in the other rocker on the porch. "Grandpa," she said hesitantly. "How long are you going to sit out here?"

He stared down the dirt driveway. "Until Sarah Jane gets here."

Lillian started to ask him how long that would be, but he spoke first.

"So, when are you and Samuel going to mend your ways?"

"I don't know if we are." She didn't want to talk about this right now. There were enough emotional issues swirling in the air.

Grandpa winked. "Sure you are."

"I don't know, Grandpa. He walked away from me like I meant nothing to him."

"*Ach*, Lilly, he was just not thinkin' right at the time. Thought he was doin' the best thing for the boy. He's come to his senses by now, and I'm bettin' he's missing you up a storm about now. You two have spent a lot of time together these past few months."

"Well, I don't miss him." It was a big fat lie, which Grandpa saw right through.

"Sure you don't," he said, drawing out his words. "Might

take a little more time, but you kids will be seeing eye to eye again soon."

She hoped so, but it had been three days. Of course, she'd made her feelings pretty clear to David when she told him how mad she was. *Wonder if David told his dad?*

She didn't feel any better today than she did on Sunday. However, she was really worried about her grandparents.

Mom, this is so like you to do this.

The screen door slammed, and Grandma joined them on the porch. "Lillian, I've left some supper keepin' warm on the oven. You need to eat yourself something."

"She's waiting to eat with her *mamm*, Irma Rose," Jonas said with a forceful tone.

Grandma glanced at Lillian and then back at her husband. "Jonas, you can't stay out here all night."

When he continued to stare down the driveway and didn't respond, Grandma shrugged. "Suit yourself. I'm going in the den to read for a bit." She turned to head back in the kitchen.

Grandpa moved faster than she'd seen since her arrival. He sprang from the rocker so abruptly you'd have thought his behind was on fire. "There she is!" he yelled. "There's my Sarah Jane!"

Lillian could hardly believe her eyes as a car turned onto the driveway. She reached for her grandpa to steady him. He was so much better lately, but he was sure unsteady on his legs. She strained to see better.

"What?" Grandma asked, turning to rejoin them on the porch. Her voice crackled with disbelief. "Is it true? Is it Sarah Jane?" She put her hands to her mouth and Lillian could see her trembling.

As the car neared the house, Lillian strained even harder to see. She smiled.

"It's Mom," she said, running down the steps. "Thank You, God," she whispered on her way to the tan Ford pulling to a stop. She looked back at her grandparents and waved them to come closer.

The car door opened, and Mom stepped out. Lillian didn't think she had ever looked more beautiful. Her black slacks and conservative blue blouse framed her tall and slender figure. Perfectly groomed, as always, her blonde waves rested at her shoulders, teased for some height.

It warmed Lillian's heart the way her mom's face lit up when she saw her. There was no shock at Lillian's apparel, no snide comments. She just smiled.

"You look beautiful, Lillian," she said.

Lillian fell into her arms. "So do you, Mom. I'm so glad you came."

The embrace lasted a long time. Lillian felt like she could have stayed in her mother's arms forever. Memories of all the good things she experienced over the years came flooding over her. Yes, there had been hard times. But her mother deserved credit for the good times too. This being one of them.

Gently, her mother pulled away and eyed her up and down. "You really do look beautiful, Lillian. The Amish look works for you." She kissed her on the cheek before glancing up at her parents on the porch.

Sensing her nervousness, Lillian said, "It'll be fine, Mom. They are so excited." She grabbed her mother's hand and began pulling her toward them.

Grandpa stretched out his arms wide in front of him. Tears poured down his face. She glanced at her grandma, whose hands were folded over her mouth. The rise and fall of her shoulders indicated she was unable to control her sobs of joy.

"Sarah Jane," Grandpa said, weeping. He took her in his arms and held her tight. It was only seconds before Sarah Jane cried out, "Pop, I'm so sorry. Oh, Pop, I'm so sorry for everything. I'm so sorry . . ."

Grandma ran to them, throwing her arms around them both. "Sarah Jane," she cried.

"*Mamm*, I'm sorry. I'm sorry. I didn't know how to come back. I didn't know what to do. I'm sorry." She turned toward her mother and lovingly embraced her.

Lillian stood frozen, tears streaming down her face. It was a joyous moment. Only one thing would have made it perfect.

No sooner had she processed the thought when she turned to see a buggy pulling up the driveway.

"Samuel?" she whispered.

16

"I'LL BE BACK IN A MINUTE," LILLIAN TOLD HER GRANDparents and mother over her shoulder. Grandpa acknowledged hearing her, but she wasn't sure what he said. She was focused on the approaching buggy. Disappointment flooded over her when she realized it wasn't Samuel.

It was Samuel's brother, Ivan. Maybe he was here to deliver a message from Samuel.

"Hi, Ivan. What brings you out here?" Lillian watched him step out of the buggy.

"Everything all right?" he asked, approaching her.

She wasn't sure what he meant. Was he talking about Samuel?

"What?" she asked.

"I saw a car I didn't recognize pulling in. I worried maybe Jonas was down again. Just stopping to check on you all."

Not what she was hoping to hear. "Everything is fine," she said, forcing a smile. "Actually, my *mamm* is here, so my grandparents are very excited to see her."

"*Gut* news," he said, crawling back into the buggy. "Just checking."

"Ivan, I was wondering—" She stopped. She didn't know Ivan well at all. To question him about Samuel seemed inappropriate. "Thank you for checking on us." She waved.

Guiding his horse into motion, he tipped his hat and said, "Anytime," as he pulled back down the driveway.

———

For the next two hours, Lillian listened to her mother confessing to her parents more than was probably necessary. But it seemed to be a cleansing of her soul. She began with her affair with Daniel Foster and subsequent pregnancy and led into how shame and embarrassment kept her from returning to the Old Order district, with the exception of a few visits here and there. Much of what she said Lillian had never heard before or didn't remember. Grandma and Grandpa hung on her every word.

Lillian knew it was difficult for her mother to share her past, and she had never been more proud of her. As Mom released years of pent-up emotion, her face twisted in agony as she recalled certain events. In the dimly lit kitchen, Grandma never let go of Sarah Jane's hand, and Grandpa cried a lot. Lillian sat with her arm around her mother, giving her a gentle squeeze when she struggled to continue.

She concluded with Lillian's confrontation with Daniel.

"Oh, Lillian," Grandma said sadly, shaking her head, "I'm sorry we didn't know what you were goin' through."

"It's all right, Grandma. I have put it behind me. I just needed some answers to be able to move forward."

Not entirely true. It would take a while to recover from the sting of meeting her father.

As everyone attempted to gather themselves after the emotional conversation, her mother asked, "So, Lillian, where is your friend?"

Her heart sank with regrets about Samuel. As she opened her

mouth to try and communicate some sort of response, Grandpa interjected his own thoughts about it.

"Lillian and Samuel are like peanut butter and jelly. They ain't nothin' alike, but they're real good when they're together. They're both mixed-up over some silly nonsense they need to get worked out. My guess is they'll be workin' it out at the barn raising this Saturday." He smiled, which was a welcome sight after all the heartache the past couple of hours. "Nothing like a good barn raising to lift the spirits. Wish I was a younger man not all eaten up by the cancer. I'd be out there on Saturday lending a hand."

"I don't know how things will turn out," Lillian said, despair in her voice. "I miss him a lot, but he's made no attempt to come see me. I'm pretty sure he meant what he said."

"Hogwash! He'll be back here at suppertime every few days before you can shake a stick." Grandpa said. "Then the whole family will be back together again."

Lillian tried to perk up. "I hope so, Grandpa. I really do."

———

"Pop, maybe you ought to go talk to Lillian," David told his dad. Samuel dimmed the lantern in his bedroom. "And tell her you're sorry."

The boy was right. Plus, Samuel knew he'd been a hard man to live with lately. Hearing David's spirited talk of the *Englisch* ways had left him fearful about his son's future. But his reaction to everything Lillian had said to David was from the hip, without thinking about her intentions. He'd been preaching faith to her, yet his own faith in *her* had temporarily deserted him.

"I'm planning on talkin' to her at the barn raising Saturday.

Ivan stopped by and said he dropped by their place to check on things. Her *mamm* was there. I know they all have lots of catching up to do, so I'm going to let them all be for now."

"Maybe she won't be so mad by Saturday. You hurt her feelings real bad, Pop."

Samuel watched his son's eyebrows jutting inward and his lips scrunching. There was a time when he'd have never allowed David to speak to him in such a manner. But he reckoned he might have made a mistake and it had obviously had great effect on the boy.

"*Ya*, David. I know." He shook his head. "Saturday, I will talk to her."

As Sarah Jane loaded her suitcase into the car, Irma Rose stifled her tears. Jonas had said his good-byes to Sarah Jane upstairs. Irma Rose knew how badly her husband wanted to come downstairs, but he was having one of his bad days. Lillian walked with them to see her mother off, but the child was clearly in another world. Hopefully, she and Samuel would be getting things worked out real soon.

It had been a glorious two days, and Sarah Jane promised to be back for Christmas.

"I'm sorry I can't stay longer." She hugged Lillian first and then Irma Rose. "I would have liked to stick around and go to the barn raising tomorrow. It's been a long time since I've been to one." She looked at Lillian. "I hope that tomorrow you and Samuel will get things worked out. Tell him I'll look forward to meeting him when I'm here for Christmas."

"I don't know if we'll get things worked out or not, Mom."

Irma Rose sure hoped so. Lillian had been a miserable soul the past few days.

"Nothing like the festivities of a good barn raising to set everyone's sights in order," Irma Rose said.

As Sarah Jane gave her a final hug, Irma Rose wished the embrace could last forever. Her daughter's return was a dream come true and a prayer answered. So many issues put to rest. Now it was time to move forward with refreshed spirit and joy. The Lord's blessings were with them.

"I love you, *Mamm*," Sarah Jane whispered in her ear. "I never stopped loving you."

Irma Rose couldn't control her cries of happiness. "Oh, my blessed daughter," she began, "you were our gift from the Good Lord, and you still are. I love you so very much."

As her granddaughter stood watching, Irma Rose struggled to pry herself away from Sarah Jane. It had been so long—and two days just wasn't enough. She would count the days until Christmas when they'd all be together again.

———

Samuel woke up Saturday with high hopes he would get things fixed with Lillian. It had been a terrible six days since he had seen her. He should've explained his feelings about the situation and not reacted the way he did. She had come a long way since she arrived in Lancaster County, and he should have kept the faith she would never do anything to soil David's upbringing.

"*Guder mariye*, Pop," David said, rubbing his eyes as he walked into the kitchen.

"Good morning to you. I made us some red-beet eggs this morning. We'll need all our energy to help with the barn raising." He shoveled some eggs alongside a piece of toast for his son.

"We'll see Lillian today too."

"*Ya*, we will." And Samuel couldn't wait. He was going to make things right.

"I sure hope things go back to the way they were before you—" The boy clamped his mouth shut, seeming to force back comments that might get him in a heap of trouble.

"I'm sure everything will be *wunderbaar gut*. It'll be a grand day," Samuel said, taking a seat beside his son. "Now, eat your eggs. We need to be there at daybreak and that's sneaking up on us."

There were over fifty buggies parked up near the Zook farm when Samuel and David arrived. John Lapp, an Amish carpenter by profession, was already lining the men out and assigning areas of work. No time to waste. They would need to complete the framing by the noon meal, giving time to eat, and then they'd put on the roof in the afternoon. As long as that much got done, the closing in could be handled by family and friends the following day, if need be.

The last of the buggies pulled in. Samuel reckoned there were over a hundred and fifty people in attendance. The women were gathering in the kitchen to prepare the meal, and the smaller children were scurrying around and playing games. Without a cloud in the sky, it was a fine day for a barn raising. Although it neared the end of August, the summer heat was still upon them. Yes, it was warm. But a slow breeze eased the effects of the sun's brilliant rays.

Samuel watched his son accepting an assignment from John Lapp, then turned and scanned the work area. There was no sign of Lillian. A few of the women were scattered about, but most of them were inside busy with meal preparations. She would have to come outside sooner or later. He hoped it was sooner so he would have a chance to talk to her, explain his harsh reaction.

The men and older boys had been at work about two hours when the first offering of iced tea was made. Several of the women-folk began walking around handing glasses to the workers.

Samuel was ready for a cold glass of tea. More than that, he was ready to see Lillian. He was surprised he hadn't caught a glimpse of her yet. Surely she wouldn't forego the barn raising because of him.

"Why, Samuel, what in the world are you doing here?" Ellen Zook asked, handing him a glass of tea.

Sending her a questioning look, he asked, "Why wouldn't I be here? You know I wouldn't miss a barn raising. I'm mighty pleased to help."

Ellen looked confused. "Well, I guess I was figuring you to be at the Miller place this morning." She paused. "I mean I think the whole district knows you spend a lot of time out there with Irma Rose, Jonas—and their *kinskind*. Word is that you and Lillian might have taken a fancy to each other."

"Isn't Lillian here? I thought she'd be inside helping with the meal?" Maybe she'd decided not to come.

"Uh, Samuel," Ellen began, "I just assumed someone had gotten word to you."

"Word about what?" He didn't like her tone. "Word about what?" he asked again.

"Why, Samuel, I'm sorry to say . . . Irma Rose passed this morning. I just figured you'd be with the family. They said she just went in her sleep and—"

He didn't hear another word she said, as his legs mechanically carried him to the buggy. He yelled at Katie Ann to keep an eye on David while he quickly maneuvered the buggy onto the road. "Let's go, Pete!" he yelled, jolting the horse into a full run.

He and Lillian had talked about death on more than one occasion. One thing Samuel knew for sure: nothing scared her more than death. And as much as Lillian had grown to love Irma Rose and Jonas, he knew she must be over the edge with grief.

"Come on, boy!" he yelled, picking up even more speed.

Lillian was anxious to see Samuel at the barn raising. From the moment she opened her eyes Saturday morning, it was all she could think about. Despite the fact he hadn't come around, maybe, just maybe, he'd had time to reflect on his decision and had a change of heart. Maybe he missed her and realized she'd never, ever do anything to hurt David. She couldn't rewrite her past. Besides, she had changed so much. Didn't that matter?

"You're up earlier than usual," Grandpa commented when she served him some scrapple alongside his eggs. She wrinkled her nose. She had never acquired a taste for this popular Amish meal. She didn't want to eat anything made up of leftover parts of a hog. She was floored the first time she saw Grandma putting parts of hog heads, hearts, liver, and other scraps in the mushy mix of cornmeal and flour. But Grandpa loved it, so she cooked it for him on occasion.

"The barn raising is today," she said. "From what I under-stand, it all gets started at daybreak. So I don't want to be late. *You're* the one who's up early." She smiled.

"Food," he said. "The smell of food gets me movin' in the morning. Your Grandma, on the other hand, is out like a light."

"Well, I'm glad to see you're feeling better this morning." She knew the past two days had exhausted him both physically and mentally. In addition to the heart-wrenching conversations, they'd all stayed up much later than usual while her mother was there. Both her grandparents had looked worn-out the night before.

"Maybe you better go give your *mammi* a nudge. You know how much she likes scrapple, and she'll be all upset if she has to eat it cold." He dove into the soupy mush. "Um, um . . . mighty *gut*," he said.

Thinking how Grandma liked to get her day off to an early start, Lillian headed up the stairs. She knocked on the door twice, but there was no answer. "Grandma?"

Knocking again, she yelled a little louder, "Grandma, I made scrapple. Come get it while it's hot."

Nothing.

She walked down the upstairs hall to the small bathroom. Gently she pushed the door open. "Grandma?" The door swung wide, but no Grandma.

She headed back toward her grandparents' room, pondering whether or not Grandma would have gone outside. No, there wouldn't be any reason to.

An unfamiliar tingling rushed from her head to her toes, caus-ing her to feel light-headed as she turned the doorknob. Something wasn't right. Her heart rate increased, and she was suddenly afraid to enter the room. And yet, unable to turn back, she pushed the door open.

Well, thank the Lord. Grandma was curled up in bed asleep, facing the other way. She hadn't gone missing and wasn't lying in a pool of blood from a bad fall or anything.

"Grandma, wake up. You scared me." She walked toward the bed. "Wake up, sleepyhead. I made scrapple—that nasty mush you and Grandpa like."

As she neared the edge of the bed, the tingling rush shot through her veins again. She stopped. "Grandma?" she said softly. Her feet were rooted to the floor, and she couldn't move. Grandma snored. She always snored. Why was there no snoring?

"Grandma!" Still unable to move, she yelled again, "Grandma, wake up!"

She could hear footsteps coming up the stairs. *Oh God, no. Please, no.* She forced her feet to move and sat down on the edge of the bed. As she reached over and touched her grandma's arm, she knew instantly—Grandma was dead. Her cold, lifeless body was curled into a ball.

Lillian knew Grandpa would be in the room within seconds. Maybe she was wrong. She ran to the other side of the bed so she could see her grandmother's face. The older woman's eyes were closed; she looked peaceful. But clearly she wasn't breathing.

"Grandma." She pushed her gently. Nothing.

"What are ya hollering about up here, Lilly?"

She turned around to see Grandpa standing in the doorway. A tear rolled down her cheek. "Grandpa . . ."

He stood frozen in place. "No, Lilly. She's just sleeping. I'm going first. I got the cancer." Staring at her with a blank look, he asked, "Did you tell her you made scrapple? That'll get her moving."

"Grandpa," she said again, trying to control herself—for once. The man nearing the bed had been married to this woman for almost fifty years. She couldn't even imagine how he must feel. Her own heart was breaking.

His feet edged slowly toward the other side of the bed. "Irma Rose, get on up out of that bed and get you some scrapple."

Lillian couldn't hold it anymore. Crying softly, she attempted to swipe away the tears trailing down her cheeks, in an unsuccessful effort to stay strong for Grandpa. She stood up from the bed and walked to the window to make more room for Grandpa. As she gazed out the window, she heard his sobs from behind her.

"Oh, Irma Rose, not now. It's not time. Sarah Jane will be back for Christmas."

Lillian turned around to see her grandpa lifting the love of his life, limp and lifeless, into his arms. How could this have happened? She wasn't even sick. Grandpa was the one who was sick. Grandpa was the one she'd prayed for, every night, to get well. And he was so much better. Had this happened because she didn't pray enough for Grandma?

She began to go over her nightly prayers, reciting them in her head. Maybe she had given Grandpa more prayer time. But it was because he was sick. This was unfair of God. Had she known her grandma was at risk, she would have prayed harder for her.

First Samuel. Now this. God wasn't listening to her. Otherwise he would have never let this happen.

It was even more heartbreaking to watch Grandpa swaying back and forth, cradling Grandma in his arms.

"Oh, my Irma Rose, my darling beloved," he wept. "Don't leave me on this earth without you. Wake up, Irma Rose."

While her own heart ripped in two, she knew she would need to produce all her strength to see her grandpa through this. She walked to the bed and sat down beside him.

"Grandpa, I think we need to send for someone," she suggested. Tenderly, she stroked his arm.

"Call the Good Lord and tell him to send her back to me, Lilly. Get your cell phone and call heaven. Tell God to send her back to me for a bit longer."

"Grandpa, it was just her time. She's with God now." She wasn't sure where the words were coming from because it *wasn't* Grandma's time.

"*Ach*, no . . . Oh, no." He cried harder, and Lillian didn't think she'd ever seen a more frail creature. Like a lost child, he wept.

"Let her lie in peace," she said softly. "Come on, Grandpa." She tried to pull him away, but he clung tightly. "Grandpa, we are going to have to go into town and let someone know. I think there are, uh, things that we have to do."

She had no idea what they needed to do, and she had no idea where her strength was coming from. Perhaps it was knowing Grandpa's pain was far worse than her own. Seeing him like this was almost as heartbreaking as losing Grandma. She took a deep breath and tried as best she could to gather herself. She hated to leave him alone. Why hadn't she held onto that cell phone? Why hadn't she prayed harder? Why did this have to happen?

She started to cry again.

"Lilly, travel to town to the funeral home. They'll tell you our

252

ways. I want to be alone with my Irma Rose," Grandpa said as he gently laid her back down.

"Okay, Grandpa." She gazed upon the woman who had taught her so much, whom she had grown to love over the past months. Nothing would ever be the same.

Forcing herself to stand up and do as Grandpa asked, she turned to face him when she reached the bedroom door. Still cradling his beloved wife in his arms, his body trembled with grief. He'd cried out to Lillian to do something, to reverse the situation, to beg God for more time. She realized even a man with Grandpa's faith couldn't accept such a loss as merely God's will. It didn't make him any less faithful to God, only human.

As Samuel pulled up at the Miller farm, his heart was heavy. The timing of all this was terrible. *And Irma Rose?* It was shocking. He'd reckoned Jonas would go way before his wife.

He shook his head as he parked the buggy and walked toward the front door. Lillian was going to be a wreck. The girl was as emotional a person as he'd ever known, and he knew she would be falling apart. She should have come to him this morning. He should have been the one to help her with things, to comfort her.

Yet . . . he reckoned if the situation were reversed, he wouldn't have searched her out either. He'd said some pretty strong things to her.

"Hello, Samuel," Lillian said as she opened the screen door and motioned him to come inside. "It's very nice of you to come." Her tone was unusually curt.

"Lillian, you should have sought me out this morning when this happened. I'm so sorry, Lillian." He hugged her—a hug she did not return.

"Grandpa's in the den if you'd like to visit with him. The funeral home has already been here to pick up Grandma. They will be bringing her back on Monday. The funeral will be here on Tuesday. Mr. Jackson said they are familiar with Amish customs and will make sure everything is done accordingly."

She rattled on like a robot, with hardly a hint of expression on her face. But he knew better. Her red, swollen eyes told the tale.

"Lillian," he said softly, reaching for her. "You don't have to be strong for my benefit."

"I'm fine," she said, turning toward the den.

"Grandpa, Samuel is here to pay his respects." She sat down in a chair near her grandpa, and she wouldn't even look at Samuel.

He extended his hand to Jonas, who clasped it with both of his hands. "Thank you for coming, Samuel. The *Englisch* doctor said he thinks Irma Rose's heart just plumb gave out." He squeezed Samuel's hand before letting it go. Hanging his head, he said, "Probably my fault. She'd been working too hard to take care of me. But I reckon it was God's will. I sure will miss my Irma Rose."

Jonas didn't seem to notice, but Samuel caught on to Lillian's attitude right quick at the mention of God's will.

"It's nobody's fault, Jonas. Don't do that to yourself," Samuel said. He glanced at Lillian, trying to make some sort of connection, only to find her keeping a solemn look on her face. She wouldn't even look his way. "I reckon we don't always understand why things happen the way they do."

Jonas shoulders began to heave up and down, and Samuel could see he was trying to hold back tears. "Sarah Jane was here, Samuel. Irma Rose only had two days with her. She just left last night. She was comin' back for Christmas."

Samuel sat down in a chair on the other side of Jonas, which put him face-to-face with Lillian. "I'm so sorry, Jonas." He reached over and put his hand on his shoulder. "Do you want me to arrange for the coffin carriers?"

"That'd be mighty fine if you'd do that."

"And I'm sure Katie Ann and my sisters will pitch in with the meal, along with a lot of other folks 'round here."

Lillian still wouldn't look his way. "All that's not necessary," she said in an almost hateful tone. "I can arrange the food, and I can—"

"Lillian, let Samuel handle those things," Jonas said.

"Grandpa, we don't need Samuel to handle those things. I can do it," she insisted. She was dead set on hurting him. That was clear. She didn't want him involved in anything to do with her or her family.

"Lilly." Grandpa looked up at her and gave her a look that caused her to sit up straighter. "You know I love you, no?"

"Of course," she answered with questioning eyes.

"I'm gonna say this one time: you get that chip off your shoulder right now. Quit blaming God for this. And get outside and go get things straightened out with Samuel. It's been bad enough, you moping around this house. And now my Irma Rose is gone. I don't have an ounce of tolerance for that attitude of yours."

Before he finished his harsh reprimand, Lillian's eyes were

full of water and she wasted no time jumping up and running toward the kitchen. He heard the screen door slam.

"Don't let her fox you, Samuel. This is killin' her inside, and she's seeing fit to blame the Good Lord. I reckon she's acting the only way she knows how, to be able to help herself cope." He sighed. "And another thing—you know she'd never do a thing to hurt that boy of yours, no?"

Samuel didn't think he could feel any lower. "*Ya*, Jonas. I know that. I made a *baremlich* mistake."

"Then I reckon you need to go out there and tell her that. She's going to need a lot of help getting through this, and I don't have the strength, Samuel. Lilly's come a long way in admonishing her old ways and learning our ways. I don't want to see her fall backward because of this. I know you care about that girl."

"Very much."

"Then get out there and make sure she stays on course with her studies, so she will want to stay with us. Don't let this be settin' her back."

Samuel stood up and headed toward the kitchen. "I'll make things right, Jonas."

Making his way out the back door and onto the porch, Samuel found Lillian sitting in the rocker on the front porch—the same rocker she was curled up in when he left her crushed and heartbroken the previous Sunday. She looked mad as a hatter.

"Leave me alone," Lillian said as Samuel took a seat in the rocker beside her. Grandpa had never talked to her that way, and she didn't need a lecture from Samuel right now either. She would handle this situation as best she could.

"Lillian," he said softly, reaching for her hand. She jerked it away.

"I don't want to talk right now, Samuel." Being angry—at Samuel and at God—was the only thing working for her at the moment.

"We're going to have to talk, Lillian," he said, looking down at the ground. "Because I made a terrible mistake, and I'm here to apologize. I know you love David and that your tellin' him about worldly things was only your way of trying to keep him out of harm's way. I know that, Lillian. And I'm sorry. I should have let you explain . . . should have thought everything through before I said all those things."

It should have been music to her ears, but she couldn't get past everything that had happened. Not right now. Staying mad was all that was keeping her together.

When she didn't respond, he went on. "I know how sad you feel right now, Lillian. We'll get through this together." He reached for her hand again, and again she pulled away. "The pain gets better over time," he added.

A huge part of her wanted to run into his arms and allow him to comfort her. The pain felt like it was eating her from the inside out, nibbling at her heart, a tiny little bit at a time. To be able to function or maintain at all, she would not be able to succumb to his offer. She would handle this on her own.

"Samuel, I can get through this, and I will be just fine." She raised her chin slightly and pulled her lips tight, fearful he might see them quivering. She had never felt more on the edge in her life.

"Lillian, I want to help you. I want to be here for you. I'm so sorry . . . about everything."

In an irrational display of emotion, she bolted from the rocker and put her hands on her hips. "Help me what, Samuel?" She knew she was yelling, and that had not been part of the plan. The plan was to stay void of feeling, to stay angry, so she didn't have to feel the pain ripping at her insides. "Help me to forget that I came from another world? Well, I can't! It is part of my past, and I can't make that go away. Do you want to help me get over Grandma dying? Well, I can't. I loved her. Do you want me to accept this as God's will? Well, I can't do that either."

The tears were falling and she was losing control. Samuel was on his feet, his arms outstretched and waiting to make everything right. Problem was things could never be right again. "I can't accept things as God's will. I just can't." There, she'd said it. Now he wouldn't have a problem walking away from her. Her inability to accept God's will would surely be more than enough for him to not want her around him or his son.

"So, there—you can go now. I will get over this on my own." She took a step backward, only to have him take two steps forward.

"I'm not goin' anywhere, Lillian," he said in a tender but determined tone. He inched closer to her. With no room to continue backward, unless she wanted to fall off the porch, she held her position by trying to stare him down. Although she could feel the tears pouring down her cheeks and suspected she wasn't being very convincing. "I don't need you, Samuel," she cried. "You gave up on our friendship. You gave up on me." She put her hands over her face and wept.

"I made a mistake, Lillian," he said. She felt his hand pull her head to his chest. His other arm molded around her back and drew her closer. "And you can go ahead and be mad at me, mad at God, and mad at the world. I'm not going anywhere."

"But I can't accept this as God's will, Samuel. I can't. I don't know what I'm going to do every day. When I make bread, can fruits and vegetables, wash the clothes, cook, practice my *Pennsylvania Deitsch* . . . All those things Grandma and I did *together*. We spent hours talking." The pain in her heart seemed unbearable, and her stomach was burning. This is what she wanted to avoid. She didn't want to feel this way. It hurt too much. "And what about Grandpa?"

His hand still cradling her head, he held her tightly against him. "It's hard, Lillian, but this is something you have to go through to be able to move on."

"I can't," she cried. "It hurts, Samuel. It hurts too much. I can't."

"*Ya*, you can," he said. "And you will. I'm going to be right here beside you."

"I'm not strong like you are." She shook her head as her nose brushed against his shirt, now wet from her tears.

"You're stronger than you think. And we will get through this together . . . because that's what people who love each other do."

She heard him loud and clear. Her knees buckled.

"I'm tired of fighting it, Lillian." He pulled her closer. Wrapped in the security of his arms, she wept. Then, gently, he eased her away, cupped her cheeks with his hands, and gazed into her eyes. His own eyes were swimming. One blink and he would be shedding tears as well.

"I love you, Lillian."

"Samuel . . ." she whispered.

With slow tenderness, he gently kissed away her tears. The feel of his lips brushing against her cheeks as he continued to cradle her face with his strong hands caused her to cry harder. Samuel loved her. He'd said they would get through this together. Her heart hurt, and nothing was going to change that. But knowing Samuel would be with her softened her feelings about God's will.

When one door closes, another one opens . . . While it was God's will to take Grandma, it was also His will for Samuel to love her. It didn't lessen her grief about Grandma's death, but it gave her hope for the future. Right now, she needed hope to cling to. She needed Samuel.

"Do you love me, Lillian?" he asked, looking hard into her eyes as he tilted her head upward to face him.

"With all my heart, Samuel. I love you with all my heart."

As if knowing her trembling legs struggled to support her, in one swoop he whisked her into his arms. Resting her head in the nook of his shoulder, she'd never known such comfort. She was safe. She was home. And somehow Samuel would help her to make sense of all this.

"We will get through this together," he said again, kissing her on the forehead.

Samuel knew from personal experience that in a time of loss, even the most faithful could doubt God's reasoning for things happening the way they did.

"I know you feel real bad right now. But you're not always gonna feel like this." He paused, clutching her tightly within his arms. With watery eyes, he said, "Me and the boy need you every bit as much as I know you need us. I know it's been hard for you to accept God into your heart as openly as you've accepted me and David into your heart. But He is in there, Lillian . . . in your heart. And He will be there to help get you through your grief."

He gently set her down on the porch and coaxed her to sit on the steps beside him. Turning toward her, he reached for her hand. "When Rachel passed, I was angry at the Lord. I never told a soul about it. Just didn't make sense at the time. It seemed awfully unfair to leave me and the boy alone—no *fraa*, no *mamm*."

He paused and looked away from her, staring down the dirt road. "I even had thoughts about leaving here. Taking the boy and just headin' somewhere else. I felt like my faith wasn't strong enough to stay."

He turned to her and smiled. "But I'm glad I did stay. There's nowhere on God's earth I'd rather be than here, in this district, and now with you."

Samuel had envisioned it in his dreams a thousand times, but nothing could prepare him for the reality of when he leaned in and felt the touch of her lips against his. He could feel her love rush through him. Resting one hand behind her neck, he pulled her closer. One kiss turned into two.

"Everything is going to be fine, Lillian," he finally said, as he brushed a loose strand of hair from her face and kissed her gently one more time.

17

THE FUNERAL WAS ALMOST TWO HOURS LONG AND HELD AT the Miller homestead. As tradition dictated, Grandma wore her wedding dress and white apron for her burial. Her wooden coffin was plain and simple—no ornate carving or fine fabrics. The community offered expressions of respect for Grandma, although admonition for the living was plentiful.

Lillian wished there were flowers and a eulogy for her grandma. However, such *Englisch* traditions were not the Amish way. Instead of singing, they spoke the words of the hymn. Following the service, Grandma was laid to rest in the Amish church district cemetery, in a hand-dug grave. The modest tombstone was identical to the others in the cemetery. As was custom, members of the community gathered to share a meal afterward. Sadie Fisher offered her home for the occasion.

"Thank you, Sadie, for organizing the meal," Lillian told her, catching her away from the crowd of women in the kitchen.

Sadie hesitated, then gave her an unexpected but much needed hug. "You're quite welcome. The entire community thought the world of Irma Rose. And it's best if these things are handled by someone not in the immediate family. How is your *mamm* holdin' up?"

Lillian looked toward the den, where her mother was comforting her grandpa. Mom was barely back in Houston when she had to turn around and come back for Grandma's funeral. She was a mess when she arrived, rambling on to Lillian about what a mess she'd made of her life. For Grandma to die the day after Mom's visit was quite a blow, but Lillian wondered how much worse it would have been if they had not been blessed with the time they had together. Bittersweet for sure.

But Mom pulled herself together, for her dad's sake. He needed her, and she needed him. Looking at her mom now, it was clear to Lillian that her mother's utmost priority was taking care of Grandpa. She hadn't left his side since her arrival.

"My mom is tired. She was up with Grandpa most of the night. He was sick. I don't know how much of it is from grief about all this or from his medications. The medicines make him sick sometimes." She paused. "You know, Mom hadn't seen her parents in a long time. She had just seen them for two days, and Grandma died the day after she left, and . . ." She shook her head, finding it hard to go on.

"It was just a real shock about Irma Rose," Sadie comforted, gently rubbing Lillian's arm. "We were all just so sorry to hear."

"You're a nice person, Sadie."

She smiled. "*Ya*, I try."

"I mean, I didn't think you were going to like me—because of Samuel and all."

"*Ach*, I was a tad bitter at first. Samuel's a good catch for marrying. But he was smitten with you from the get-go." She offered her a pat on the shoulder. "Besides, my letter-writing with the Texas man is goin' real good."

Sadie wasn't the only one who had opened her heart during this difficult time. Both of Samuel's sisters and sister-in-law had bent over backward to help with arrangements. Samuel's mother, Esther, was warming up to Lillian as well.

Grandma had worked so hard to make sure Lillian had a clear understanding of the *Ordnung*. Despite her constant questioning of the Amish ways—sometimes defiantly—Grandma never gave up on her. With patience and love, she nurtured Lillian toward a way of life she had been searching for. Lillian would be lying to herself if she accepted where she was now as her final spiritual destination, though. She still had work to do. Her inability to accept everything that happened as God's will would require faith—in God and in herself.

Samuel was proud of Lillian. Those who didn't know her well wouldn't recognize the effort it was taking for her to stay strong. He reckoned the extra effort was due to the state her mother and Jonas were in. Samuel could tell the whole ordeal was taking its toll on Jonas. Sarah Jane was glued to her pop's side and was trying hard to take care of him. But she looked like *she* needed taking care of herself. Lillian was filling the job, even though he knew her own heart was hurting in a big way.

"Lillian sure is being strong today," David said, echoing Samuel's thoughts. He took a seat beside Samuel at a wooden picnic table in the yard.

"She's trying to be strong for her *mamm* and *Daadi Jonas*."

"I remember when you tried to be strong for me when *Mamm* died. I knew you were hurting, like I reckon Lillian is hurting too."

"Sometimes we bury our burdens to tend to the needs of others," Samuel responded, remembering back to Rachel's funeral. At that time, he wasn't sure how he would live his life without her. But time had a way of mending the heart. "God so built us to heal ourselves through our love and faith in Him."

Lillian's fingers entwined with Samuel's as they sat at the overlook. It had been three days since Grandma's funeral and her heart was still leaden, as she expected it would be for a long time to come. But as she and Samuel sat quietly at the edge of the overlook, she reflected on everything that had recently happened. Rickie was out of her life. She'd found her father, however painful. She and her mom were in a new place—a good place. She'd been fortunate enough to get to know her Grandma before she died. She still had her grandpa. And Samuel loved her.

Knowing God didn't keep score, she was trying not to either. But there was a certain balance to it all. Maybe she'd started out looking for proof there was a God—proof that she could reach out and touch. Her search was misdirected in the beginning. But when she asked to have a relationship with Him, to know Him, God showed Himself to her many times over.

Completely accepting Grandma's death as God's will was going to take her a little longer. Just accepting her as gone was a painful conclusion for her right now. But through her faith, she hoped to continue to grow toward a complete acceptance of all things.

"It takes time, Lillian," she recalled Grandma saying during one of their talks—one of the many when Lillian questioned such blind acceptance of certain events as being God's will. "First get to know God, put your trust in Him, and He will work miracles in your life. You will learn to accept His will, even if you can't see the reasoning behind it at the time," Grandma had said.

She'd always wished the *Ordnung* was a book she could memorize and just make herself live by. But so much of the *Ordnung* was unwritten, visible only in the minds of the faithful followers, like Grandma. And Grandma had been a good teacher.

Being at the overlook was the perfect place to tell Samuel her news.

"Samuel," she said softly, squeezing his hand. "I have something to tell you."

He squirmed uncomfortably. "Me first," he sputtered. "I have something to tell you first."

Lillian doubted it was as important as her decision to be baptized into the Amish faith, but her news could wait. Whatever was on Samuel's mind had him extremely nervous. He took off his hat, pushed back his hair, put his hat back on, stroked his beard, twisted around in the grass again. What in the world was wrong with him?

"What is it, Samuel?"

When he didn't answer, she rushed on. "Because my news is pretty important." Playfully, she nudged her shoulder against his.

"Maybe you should go first, then," he said hesitantly.

"No, you go ahead." She was curious to know what news had him so worked up.

Turning toward her, he grabbed both her hands in his. He gazed lovingly into her eyes and said, "I love you, Lillian. When Rachel died, I didn't think I would ever love another woman the way I loved her." Struggling with his words, he forced them out with determination. "I wasn't sure I ever wanted to move on. But you changed all that. I fought it and fought it. You are as challenging an *Englisch* person as I've ever met. But one thing is for sure: I love you. David loves you."

Taking a deep breath, he went on. "It took me a long time before I could give myself permission to move on. But I want to move on with you, Lillian. I've wanted to ask you something since we were on the porch the day Irma Rose passed, but the timing wasn't right."

Lillian felt her heart leap. Quite sure all her feelings were visible to him, she tried to contain herself. Was Samuel about to propose?

"I know you haven't made mention of staying here or getting baptized, but I'm asking you to stay here, with me. I want you to marry me, Lillian. Do you think you could be happy here, in our district, with me and David? I'm real confused because you aren't baptized, and I don't know how you feel about that. It'd be impossible for us to wed if you aren't baptized, but I felt the need to tell you what my hopes were."

Thank You, God. She had struggled with her decision to be baptized, prayed hard that she was doing the right thing and for the right reasons. She still had a lot to learn. But she knew that she wanted to learn it here, around those she loved. With confidence, she had spoken to the bishop about her decision. Although a proposal from Samuel was the last thing she expected so soon after he professed his love for her.

As if reading her mind, he said, "I know it might seem soon, Lillian. But once you know who you want to spend the rest of your life with . . . *Ach*, I just couldn't see wasting time. I know we couldn't marry until after your baptism, if that's what you choose to do, and—"

"How's November sound to you?" she asked, opening her eyes wide and blinking back the salty sting of emotion.

"What?" he asked, confused. "That's only three months away, and your baptism would have to be in October. That's in only a couple of months, and—"

"October 19 to be exact." She threw her arms around him. "Oh, Samuel! That was my news. I talked to the bishop about being baptized. I wanted to make the decision to stay for the right reasons. I had hoped you would want to marry me *someday*, but I was staying either way."

As his lips met with hers, he drew her closer. "Lillian, nothing would make me happier than to watch you receive baptism in October and marry you in November."

"Then that's the plan," she said, leaning in for another kiss.

Lillian was surprised her mother was still around after nearly two weeks. Grandpa had several good days following the funeral, and several bad days. Mom was there for the good and bad. She got up with him at night when he was throwing up, helped him bathe when he needed help, and played chess with him as often as he was able. Seeing them together warmed Lillian's heart. But often she had to walk away to hide her tears. How Grandma would have loved Mom being here.

Something about Mom was different too. While Grandma's death devastated them all, there was something in Mom's demeanor reflective of a significant change. There was a calmness about her Lillian didn't remember seeing—ever. She'd gotten used to having her around too. Surprisingly, she enjoyed having her here. After spending so much time trying to cut the cord from her mother and their turbulent relationship, it was refreshing to be in new territory with her. They were kind and loving to each other. They talked, often late into the night. They shared stories, worries, past mistakes, and hopes for the future. It was the way mothers and daughters should be. In the aftermath of something so sad, something wonderful had happened. And Mom was thrilled about the wedding plans and excited to be involved in the planning.

Samuel and David resumed their places at the supper table almost every night. Much of the food continued to come from Samuel's garden and butchered livestock. Grandpa was able to eat downstairs some of the time, and Mom sat on the bench next to him. Everyone was painfully aware of the empty chair at the end of the table. Mom refused to sit in it, even though Grandpa said he would have more elbow room if she did.

David's summer vacation from school ended, and he wasn't able to help as much with chores around their place. He and Samuel did what they could to help keep both farms manicured, but work was piling up at both farms. Lillian wasn't sure how much earlier they could all get up in the mornings to accomplish all they needed to do. Grandma had certainly made her share of the daily chores look easy. In her absence, Lillian and her mom struggled to match up to Grandma's way of keeping things neat and orderly.

The family talked of Lillian's impending baptism often. Soon she and Samuel would publish their wedding announcement for the first Tuesday in November. Weddings were usually held on Tuesday or Thursday, most commonly the slowest days of the week. November was the wedding month, following the busy fall harvest and before the risk of unfavorable winter weather.

They had avoided the specifics of how all this was going to work since the first time Lillian made mention to Grandpa that perhaps he could live with them at Samuel's place. His gruff response left no doubt he would leave his family farmstead feet first. "I was born here, and I'll die here," he groaned.

But Grandpa's grief was taking a toll on his health. He couldn't take care of himself, and Lillian was not about to leave him alone. She and Samuel had discussed it several times, and each time there was no resolution. As much as they wanted to be together as husband and wife, Grandpa was not capable of taking care of himself.

A few days later, Samuel and Lillian excused themselves from the supper table early. Jonas wasn't sitting as tall as usual, barely touching his ham and potato salad. As they walked hand in hand toward the barn, Samuel knew Lillian had the same thing on her mind that he did.

"Grandpa can't stay alone," she said. "There's no way, Samuel."

"I know." He turned to face her. The sun had yet to give in to the moon, and in the evening light her eyes were full of worry. "I reckon me and David can move here when we're married. I just want us to be a family, Lillian. Jonas is a part of this family."

She sighed. "You love that farm of yours, Samuel."

A lot of heartfelt labor had gone into making his farm a

place to be proud of. The house had been run down and the fields overgrown when Samuel purchased the old property, back before he married Rachel. Now it was as nice a place as any in their district.

But despite his attachment to the farm, his attachment to Lillian was greater. "I love you, and leaving Jonas is not an option."

She buried her head in his chest. "What are we going to do? I love you so much, Samuel. I'll live anywhere, as long as it's with you. I just hate for you to give up your home, and I hate for Grandpa to have to give up the only place he's ever lived. But the only way I see this working is for one of you to let go of your property. It needs to be Grandpa. He can't take care of this place. It's hard on you and David tending to both farms."

"Home is where you make it, Lillian. My home is with you, David, and Jonas."

Kissing her tenderly, he could not imagine his life without her. Despite their challenges, Lillian filled his heart with love in a way he didn't think possible again. David loved her too.

But love of the land, tilling of the soil, and producing—it was the Amish way, and he had done a fine job at it. Letting the land dissolve into a barren oasis of deeply planted dreams was hard to swallow.

As darkness neared, they turned their attention to headlights rounding the turn onto the driveway.

"Are you expecting anyone?"

"No," she said, surprised.

They waited as a large truck slowly made its way down the dirt driveway. By the time the driver parked the truck, Samuel noticed Sarah Jane and David making their way down the porch steps. It was a really large truck with a sign on the side that said *Leeway Moving*.

"What's going on?" Lillian asked.

"It's your farm." He joked. "I have no idea."

"Over there!" Samuel heard Sarah Jane yell. "Park over by the barn."

As Sarah Jane and David met up with them, Lillian asked, "Mom, what is this truck doing here?"

Sarah Jane smiled. "It's a few of my things I couldn't live without. You know, my four-poster bed that I finally purchased from that lovely shop at the Trader's Village in Houston, and some other things I really *need*."

Samuel wondered if an answer to their prayers had just arrived. But he wasn't quite sure.

"Mom, what are you saying?" Lillian's face glistened as the sun faded and the moonlight seemed to focus exclusively on her.

"You should know, Lillian, I will be taking over some of those dresses from upstairs when you leave to be Samuel's wife. So you need to start thinking about sewing yourself some more. Because, if you must know, those dresses you are wearing are *mine*."

She winked at her daughter and headed toward the truck. "I said, park by the barn!" She threw her hands in the air and pointed toward the barn, continuing to instruct the driver.

Lillian was quickly on her mother's heels. "Mom?"

"I'm staying, Lillian," she confirmed. "We'll figure out what to do with all these things later."

"But, Mom—"

Samuel watched as Sarah Jane faced her daughter. "He's my

pop, Lillian. I'm going to take care of him. You need to start your life with your husband in November. I plan to spend the second half of my life making amends for the mistakes I made during the first half."

"But, Mom . . ." Lillian said again.

"By the barn!" Sarah Jane yelled. "We are putting everything in the barn for now!"

The driver got as close to the barn as he could.

While the moving van distracted her Mom, Lillian latched on to Samuel's hand and gave it a squeeze. "Oh, Samuel," she said, gleaming. "Is my mother answering our prayers?"

It seemed an unlikely source, but one that was upon them. "I think so," he answered.

Once Sarah Jane had the movers unloading her necessary belongings in the correct manner into the barn, she walked toward David, who was standing a few feet from Samuel and Lillian.

"David, your pop and my daughter look speechless," she said, giving the boy a hug.

Samuel noticed David's eyes light up. He had a clear reckoning as to what was happening.

"You're going to stay here and live with Jonas while Lillian comes and lives with me and my *daed*?" he asked, seeming a little unsure.

"*Ya*," Sarah Jane answered. "But I'm hoping I'll still have you to help us in the afternoons after Lillian marries your *daed*."

Lillian's eyes were aglow and she seemed pleasantly surprised at her mother's use of the *Deitsch*.

"You bet," David said. "Jonas will be expecting me to play chess after my chores."

"Well you'll have to beat me first," Sarah Jane said.

"Mom, are you sure about this?" Lillian asked her mother. "What about Paul? What about your job? Are you sure?"

Sarah Jane grew solemn and faced her daughter. "I should have come back here, Lillian. I should have trusted the love of my parents." She paused. "And the love of God. Being here reminds me of what it's like to live a lifestyle void of complications. I want to live out the rest of my years this way."

"Mom," Lillian said, embracing her, "does Grandpa know?"

"I sure do."

Samuel followed the voice to see Jonas hobbling down the porch steps.

"You people are the loudest bunch I've ever known. What does a sick ol' man with cancer have to do to be gettin' some rest around here?" He continued to hobble toward Sarah Jane, a smile stretched across his face.

"Pop," she said lovingly, walking toward him, "and I want to stay together."

He tried to hide it, but Samuel could see Jonas's eyes welling up.

"There's nothin' I'd like more in this *wunderbaar* world the Good Lord created," Jonas said, hugging his daughter. "Irma Rose is smiling from heaven."

Samuel looked at Lillian, whose eyes glazed with emotion. "The Good Lord has a way of takin' care of things," he said.

"*Ya,* He does."

Samuel watched as Sarah Jane gently eased her father away and walked toward him and Lillian. "Will it be all right with the two of you if I boot you out in November, after you're married?

It would be too crowded in this house with Lillian." She kissed her daughter on the cheek.

"Oh, I guess I'll have to take her to my place after we're married," he said jokingly.

"Lillian?" her mother asked. "What about you? Think you can go live with this man in marital bliss while I take care of your grandpa?"

"Mom, *danki,*" Lillian said, wrapping her arms around her.

"No, Lillian, thank *you,*" her mother said softly, but still in earshot of Samuel. "This is where I belong. It's where I've always belonged. I just didn't know how to find my way home."

Sarah Jane turned to Samuel. "A hug for your future mother-in-law?"

Samuel welcomed the hug. Whatever it took to make his Lillian as happy as she was at this moment.

"Bunch of mushy stuff goin' on, I say." Jonas rejoined the three of them after sharing some time with David.

"Now, I have another surprise for all of you. It's a really big surprise," Sarah Jane announced.

Samuel watched as Lillian's mother lovingly wrapped her arms around her daughter again. "And, Lillian, I'm so sure that everything is going to be *gut!*"

Irma Rose would have been so proud, Samuel thought to himself. *But what in the world was Sarah Jane's surprise?*

18

EVIDENCE OF FALL WAS ABUNDANT. COLORFUL LEAVES swirled around in the crisp air as buggies lined the drive at the Miller farm. It was the perfect day for a baptism. Lillian greeted community members from the den. Most of them she knew, and several she had gotten to know well over the past couple months since Grandma died. Particularly Sadie. They'd become quite close. She took Lillian to a quilting party and introduced her to other women in the community. Lillian even asked her new friend to be a *waiter*—the Amish term for bridesmaid—at her upcoming wedding, along with her mother.

Only two more weeks until she would be Lillian Stoltzfus. She glanced at her husband-to-be across the room, also greeting guests. Being in love with Samuel filled her heart with a joy she didn't know possible. It had been hard to accept God into her heart and to accept His will, but with Samuel and David's help, she had put all doubts to rest. For the first time in her life, peacefulness consumed her. The peacefulness of knowing all things of this earth were in His hands.

She was thankful to Him that Grandpa was having one of his good days. Following a rough couple of weeks, he looked strong and handsome. Glancing upward, she whispered, *"Danki."*

Still, not a day went by that she didn't think about Grandma. She missed her in a terrible way and knew this would have been a proud moment for her.

As everyone took their respective places, as they did in worship service, Lillian prepared to leave all worldly things behind and accept her birthright with newfound faith and confidence. However, once everyone settled in, she turned to her left . . . to see her mother preparing for baptism alongside her. Mom had mentioned she had a surprise, but Lillian couldn't have imagined this. What a blessed moment and a wonderful surprise—to choose baptism after all these years. Mom could have just chosen to stay and take care of her father, without committing her life to the *Ordnung*. It was yet another reflection of God in both their lives.

Despite exhaustion from taking care of Grandpa, Mom spent countless hours making sure Lillian was comfortable with the *Ordnung* and helping her with her *Deitsch*. As she took up where Grandma left off, teaching Lillian the Amish ways, Lillian witnessed an incredible transformation, a profound renewal of faith in her mother. A woman injured by life—and with scars to show for it—she seemed to be exactly where she belonged.

Now she merely smiled and squeezed Lillian's hand before returning to her preparations.

With three females and four males seeking baptism, they each sat with one hand over their faces to represent their submission and humility to the church. The deacon ladled water from a bucket into the bishop's hand, and the bishop sprinkled each of their heads three times, in the name of the Father, Son, and Holy Ghost.

The bishop blessed each new male member with a holy kiss,

and his wife blessed each new female church member with a holy
kiss. They were then all welcomed as new church members. And
as was the Amish way, a bountiful meal followed.

Samuel took a stroll out to the barn. His Lillian was a church
member and now they would be married in a couple of weeks.
He wanted some time to be alone, to thank the Lord for all the
blessings bestowed upon him and David.

The old newspapers were still scattered on the dirt floor of the
barn. He gathered them up and placed them neatly back in the
box. What a long way they had come. It was a struggle, but Lillian
had put the past behind her and moved forward with hope and
determination. He smiled as he recalled her receiving baptism.
She had never looked more beautiful.

"I saw you sneaking out here," he heard her say when she
entered the barn. "Most of the kitchen is cleaned up, so I snuck
out too."

Samuel put the last newspaper in the box and stacked it atop
the other boxes. This was a special day, and he hoped seeing the
newspapers didn't bring back any painful memories for her. He
walked toward her, and she smiled. Pulling her close, he said,
"Have I mentioned how beautiful you look?" He kissed her on
the cheek.

"Several times," she said, her face nuzzled into his chest. "I
feel so good about everything, Samuel."

"Do you feel any different?" He remembered feeling wonderfully different after his baptism.

She gently pulled away and looked up at him, her eyes aglow

with joy. "I do feel different. In some ways, it's all very surreal. I mean, if anyone had told me a year ago that Mom and I would be as close as we are, or that both of us would be baptized into the Amish faith, I never would have believed it." She paused and twisted her mouth into a frown. "Bad things happen sometimes. It was hard for me to accept those things as God's will in the beginning." She smiled again. "But, *gut* things happen too. It's a balance, I suppose. I shouldn't question His will. I miss Grandma every day. But I'm so grateful for Mom, and I never thought I would be able to say that. I'm so thankful, Samuel. To you. To God." He watched as her eyes glazed over with tears of contentment. "I'm just very happy."

"And soon we'll be married." He pulled her close again.

"I am so ready to be your *fraa*, Samuel. I'm going to be a good wife and a good *mamm* to David."

"Not just a *gut mamm* to David, I hope. I reckon there will be a lot of little Stoltzfus *kinner* running around some day."

"There is nothing I want more."

Samuel kissed her tenderly on the mouth. "I guess we need to go back to the others," he said with regret. He wanted to hold her in his arms forever. Only two more weeks—and then they'd be together for the rest of their lives.

Sarah Jane fumbled with the letter that arrived in the mail. With only two days until Lillian's wedding, she tossed the envelope nervously from hand to hand. It was addressed to Lillian and opening it would be wrong. It would be equally as wrong to toss it into the trash bin, but she was tempted just the same. The return address was from Oklahoma, and she cringed as her eyes met with the name above the address. Daniel Foster. Hearing from him was the last thing either of them needed.

"I'm exhausted just thinking of all the things left to do before the wedding," she heard Lillian say while walking into the kitchen. "Maybe we should have waited until the end of November, since we just had the baptism here a couple of weeks ago." She plopped down on the bench at the kitchen table and brushed back a strand of hair dangling in her face.

"I don't think you or Samuel could have waited a couple more weeks." Crossing her arms, Sarah Jane tucked the letter out of sight.

"Mom, I just didn't know I could feel this happy." She smiled. "How's Grandpa this afternoon?"

"Actually, he's having a good day. He's napping right now. Be warned, though—the doctors changed his medicine again, and you know what that means. We just never know how he'll respond to the change."

"*Ya.* I'm glad he's doing so well today. I pray he will be having a good day on Tuesday."

"I'll pray too," Sarah Jane said, smiling, but with the letter still hidden from Lillian's view. She knew she would have to turn it over, but still she hesitated. Despite her exhaustion, her daughter had never looked happier, and she didn't want to ruin that.

"David is going to mow the yard after school," Lillian said. "I'll finish making the bread and apple butter, and then I know we need to—"

"Lillian," she interrupted.

"*Ya?*"

"This came in the mail today." With reluctance, she handed over the letter. As she feared, Lillian's bright eyes lost some of their glow. Her face was solemn and she just held the envelope and stared at it.

"You don't have to open it," Sarah Jane told her, wishing she wouldn't. "We can just throw it away and pretend it never came." She thought about all the letters from her mother she had tossed into the trash. Her heart ached.

Lillian tilted her head to one side and held the letter up toward the window, as if trying to catch the sun's rays to read through the envelope. "No," she said softly. "I have to open it. I'm not going to let whatever is in this letter upset me. I've put all that behind me."

Sarah Jane took a seat on the bench across from Lillian. "I still say we can just throw it away." She cupped her chin in her hands.

"Mom, we can't do that." Lillian's tone was a tad reprimanding, and Sarah Jane knew she was right.

Lillian's heart was racing. Peeling back the flap of the envelope, she slowly removed the two-page letter, handwritten in blue ink on lined white paper.

Dear Lillian,

What is often at the heart of a man's soul is lost or forgotten by the time you reach my age. Bitterness, divorce, and life have a way of doing that. I know it might seem like I'm feeling sorry for myself, but that is not my intention. Rather, I would like for you to know that at my core, I am not the evil person that my actions have certainly dictated. Since you share my genes, I do not want you to fear the passing down of poisonous heritage. It is my hope that by breaking down the iron walls surrounding my heart, you will see a small glimpse as to who your father is—or once was.

Sarah Jane was a beautiful, vibrant woman. She probably still is. I have no excuse for the way I handled her pregnancy. To say I was young, at the height of my career, and afraid seems like a lame excuse. When you arrived at my shop, I assumed you were there to cause trouble for me somehow. Looking back, I know you just wanted to know who your father is. You remind me so much of your mother. Despite her unworldly ways, she had a zest for life she obviously passed on to you. It's unfortunate that as a young man I took advantage of her spirited nature and robbed her of the life she was intended to live. She had no real understanding of life outside of her community. I suppose all that changed when she fled the only life she had ever known to raise a child on her own.

If you sense remorse in this letter, you are right. Not many days went by when I did not wonder about you. When my wife and I married many years later, we were unable to bear children. I often suspected it was my punishment for abandoning you and your mother.

I understand from friends in Paradise that you were baptized into the Amish faith and will be married soon (not to worry—they do not know you are my daughter). There is no wedding gift I can give you to make up for my behavior years ago, or my behavior most recently. I can only hope that, in some small way, this letter will suffice as my gift to you, for it comes with a heartfelt and sincere apology.

May your new life bring you happiness always.

Regards,
Daniel Foster

Lillian handed her mother the letter. "Maybe this will give you some closure too," she said. With no memories of those hard times Daniel referred to, Lillian assumed perhaps her mother had more to gain from the letter than she did. Based on Mom's expression as she was reading, Lillian was right.

"He really wasn't a bad man," Mom muttered, fighting tears. "But I have struggled these past couple of months to forgive him. This helps." She handed the letter back to Lillian.

"I forgave him a while back, but this helps me too." There was comfort in knowing that her father had wondered about her and that he regretted his actions years ago, as well as his more recent ones. The tone of his letter saddened her, though. He sounded like a lonely man. She would say an extra prayer for him tonight. Maybe she would write him back someday.

Tuesday took forever to arrive. As Samuel and David hurried to get ready, Samuel feared he was going to be late for his own wedding. He had heard rumors that over two hundred people would be attending. What a mighty noon feast they would have after the ceremony and another grand meal in the evening. It was going be right crowded in the Miller house.

He couldn't wait to make Lillian his wife. "David, it's time, boy!" he yelled upstairs. "Are you 'bout done?"

Samuel was as nervous as a man could be. From the moment he laid eyes on Lillian, he'd connected with her in a way that made him fearful—fearful they could never be together. Now she had become a church member and today they would marry. And tonight . . . Well, Samuel couldn't help but think about tonight, their wedding night. The passionate kisses they shared were only a prelude to what he knew would be a *wunderbaar* night.

Sharing their love as husband and wife was a vision he couldn't shake. Nor did he want to. The thought of his beautiful Lillian, held close in his arms . . .

He hollered for David to hurry.

It was customary for the bride and groom to stay with her parents on the wedding night, so as to help with the cleanup the next morning. He packed a small duffel bag for him and one for David, since David would be heading to Ivan's place later in the evening.

"We ain't got time to waste, David," he bellowed up the stairs. "Come on with yourself."

"Oh, Lillian," her mom said when she walked downstairs. "You look beautiful."

Dressed in traditional Amish wedding attire, Lillian felt beautiful in her new blue linen dress, black *Kapp*, white kerchief, and apron. She knew this would be the only time she would wear the outfit, until they buried her in it. Sadie had made the dress for her and it fit perfectly.

"*Danki*, Mom." She was nervous, and she didn't think much was going to change that. "Samuel said there are going to be about two hundred people in attendance. That's more than when we held the baptisms here."

"The joining of two hearts for eternity is a blessed event," her mother said. "I'm so proud of you, Lillian. Against so many hardships, you prevailed and turned into a beautiful young woman. And an Amish woman at that." Mom pulled her in for a hug.

"Mom," she said warmly. "I'm proud of you too. I'm proud you're my *mamm*."

Gently her mother eased Lillian away from her. "I have something to give you."

She darted upstairs. When she returned, she handed Lillian an envelope. "It's the money I borrowed from you, Lillian. I had Claire, my friend back in Houston, sell the rest of my things."

"Mom, no," Lillian said, handing the envelope back. "I don't care about this money. I don't need it."

"What am I going to do with it, Lillian? I have everything I have ever wanted or needed." She pushed the envelope back toward Lillian. "Go and buy a wedding present for you and Samuel."

"This would buy a *really* nice wedding present, Mom," she said, counting the money.

"*Ya*, and that's what I want you to do with it."

"Do you miss Paul or your life, Mom?"

"Where did that come from?"

"I don't know. I just wondered." She hesitated. "It's just . . . you've always . . ."

"Had a man in my life?" Mom questioned. "I used to think that completed me, Lillian. I know that's not true. Having God in my life completes me. Besides, I imagine you and Samuel will give me lots of *kinner* to keep me busy. Plus, I have Pop."

"Did I say how proud I am of you, Mom?" She threw her arms around her mother again.

"I think you did. And I am very proud of you. Now, let's get you married. A crowd is gathering outside. Where's the groom?"

It was nearing eight o'clock in the morning when the crowd moved into the house. Lillian glanced around until she finally

saw Samuel. Her heart took on a fearful pulse when she realized
the time for the ceremony was upon them and Samuel had not
appeared. She smiled at him from across the room.

As everyone prepared for the four-hour ceremony, she twisted
her hands together. There was no wedding ring and no flowers
to carry or flowers in the house. Instead, they placed celery in
simple white glasses throughout the house—one of the symbolic
foods at Amish weddings. She suddenly had an urge to steal one
of the cut stalks and take a nibble. She should have eaten breakfast, but an early-morning bout of nerves had prevented her from
indulging in her mother's *dippy eggs* this morning.

Lillian knew the ceremony would be void of the traditional
kiss at the end. Of course, there would be no photographers or
fancy catering. It was not the wedding she'd dreamed of since she
was a child. It was better. The overabundance of love in the room
more than made up for any preconceived ideas about what her
wedding would be like.

Preparing to take her vows with the man she loved, she
looked around the room. As was customary, the women were
on one side and the men on the other side. Samuel had never
looked more handsome. Grandpa and David stood side by side,
each of them with a twinkle in his eye. Mom was beautiful. She
had tossed out her makeup and other worldly goods prior to
her baptism, and the lines of time and her hardships were evident. However, the radiance in her heart manifested itself across
her smiling face, lending her a beauty that makeup could have
never matched.

Lillian beamed at several women she had grown fond of over
the past couple of months. Struggling to keep her emotions

intact, she knew without a doubt that everything was perfect. She was ready to take her place as a daughter of the promise. Her journey of faith, hope, and love guided her to this moment. Now she would begin her life as Samuel's *fraa*.

They sang several songs in German at the beginning of the ceremony. The worship service was in German with a mix of *Pennsylvania Deitsch*. She was surprised how much of the language she now understood. After the preacher presented stories of the Old Testament, he offered marriage advice to her and Samuel.

"The Bible teaches us to treat each other with respect, not to raise our voices at each other, and to always show love," he recited. "Work hard, remember the man is the head of the home, and, Lillian, you are his helpmate."

Fondly, she recalled her learning session with Grandma concerning the preacher's statement. Not so long ago, his words would have caused Lillian to gasp. Instead, she was more than ready to allow Samuel to take his role as head of the home. By his side, she knew their partnership would be one of mutual respect.

Several other pastors spoke to the congregation, and specifically to Samuel and Lillian. It was near eleven o'clock when she and Samuel took their vows in front of their family and friends. With unwavering faith in herself, Samuel, and God, Lillian proclaimed her love to the only man she'd ever loved. "I, Lillian, take you Samuel . . ."

She managed to stifle tears of joy until Samuel professed his love for her. But upon hearing his solemn vow to love her forever, through good times and bad, a tear trickled down her cheek. He gently brushed it away. Had she looked around, she would have noticed there was hardly a dry eye in the house. But all Lillian saw was Samuel.

The wedding dinner was bountiful, consisting of the traditional *roasht*, along with mashed potatoes, gravy, creamed celery, buttered noodles, steamed peas with butter, and homemade bread and jam. There were side dishes of applesauce, chowchow, and pepper cabbage, and more pies, cookies, puddings, and dessert than Lillian had ever seen. Plus she was told no wedding would be complete without Amish *wedding nothings*, a deep-fried traditional wedding pastry. It was an amazing display, and on this day she planned to partake of all of it.

"We sit here, at the *eck*," Samuel whispered in her ear as he guided her to the corner of the wedding table.

They had placed tables together in the den to form a large hollow square with one side open. Samuel and Lillian sat at one of the outer corners, known as the bride's corner, or *eck*. Lillian's waiters sat to her left, along with other young unmarried women. Samuel's waiters sat to his right, along with more unmarried women. Young unmarried men sat on the remaining side of the formation.

Much preparation went into rearranging furniture in an attempt to accommodate the guests during the ceremony. However, they served the meal in shifts. Lillian and Samuel were served first, along with their wedding party.

Lillian realized she had worked up an appetite. A fabulous wedding cake sat before her and Samuel. As she waited for the ladies to serve the meal, the temptation to swipe the white icing with her finger was overwhelming. She felt Samuel's hand inter-twine with hers beneath the table.

"I love you, Lillian Stoltzfus," he whispered, oblivious to the people scurrying around the room.

"I love you too, Samuel Stoltzfus."

It was a glorious day, and Lillian bowed her head in prayer to thank God for the many blessings He had bestowed upon her and her family.

They sang traditional Amish hymns after the noon meal, fol-lowed by folk games in the barn for the children and unmarried young adults. As everyone socialized, mothers put babies down for naps upstairs, men gathered in the barn to smoke cigars and tell jokes. It was an all-day affair filled with fellowship, prayer, and a sense of belonging for Lillian.

"There you are," she said to Samuel, finding him on the porch later that afternoon. "I didn't see you for a while. I missed you."

"Hello, Mrs. Stoltzfus," he said smiling.

"I like the sound of that." She placed her hands on her full stomach. "I can't believe we have to eat again. I'm still full from the noon meal."

"I reckon the ladies are already preparing supper. But before we eat, we get to go play matchmaker for the young people out in the barn."

"Sadie told me about that. We actually get to pick out a boy and a girl and send them in the house holding hands?" She grinned at her husband. It sounded like great fun.

"*Ya*, the matched up boy and girl will go in the house, holding hands, and sit together at suppertime." Samuel arched his eyebrows and whispered, "The married ladies will all be gossiping about who is sitting together, who their parents are, and remarking about what a nice couple they will make."

"What if the kids don't like who we match them up with?"

"Then I guess a wedding won't be in their future," he said, snickering.

"No, I guess not."

She watched as Samuel's face took on a serious expression. "I love you so much, Lillian. I can't wait to show you how much I love you tonight."

After matching up the teenagers in the barn for supper, more socializing went on for several more hours. Lillian wasn't sure how she'd managed to eat another meal. It had been a long, exhausting, wonderful day. It was almost nine o'clock when their guests began to leave. Grandpa had a fabulously good day but had been in bed for hours. Mom had been a trooper all day, making sure everything was perfect.

As she sat next to Samuel at the wedding table, Lillian hated for it all to end. But, she reminded herself, it was only the beginning. And she was ready to begin her life as Samuel's wife.

"It's time, Lillian," her mother said as she leaned down and kissed Lillian on the cheek. "Time to start your life as Samuel's *fraa*."

Samuel and Lillian stood up. Hand in hand, they bade farewell to those guests standing nearby. Lillian knew the next morning would start early and members of the district would be

on hand to help with the cleanup. The next few weeks would be
spent visiting members of the community, as was customary.
These post-marriage visits were when she and Samuel would
receive a lot of their wedding gifts.

It was to be a busy time after the wedding. But, for tonight,
it would just be her and Samuel, his loving arms wrapped
around her.

19

THE MID-FEBRUARY TEMPERATURES CAME WITH A BLAST OF artic air that was keeping most of the community huddled inside with the comfort of woodburning stoves and fireplaces. Luckily, David's trek to school was a short distance from home. After tending to the cows, Samuel had gone to the farmer's market to pick up a few things. Normally, it was a task Lillian handled, but the weather was hardly fit to get out and Samuel insisted on making the trip for her.

Lillian was thrilled to see the delivery truck make it up the drive, and even more excited that her surprise would be in place before Samuel returned. She knew her husband had been goggling over the beautiful handmade table in town since before they were married.

She glanced around her Plain kitchen, void of all the gadgets she was once dependent on. It was amazing how she didn't think about or miss all the modern conveniences she'd grown up with. Everything she needed, she had right here.

With the weather at its worst, Samuel still made a trip to check on Mom and Grandpa daily. His latest report was that Grandpa's medication was continuing to help him tremendously. The two of them were making regular trips to town and playing lots of chess.

Although she had not had an opportunity to talk with Mom, rumor had it that a widower or two in the district were vying for her mother's attention. Sadly, Lillian knew Grandpa wouldn't always be around. Mom said she didn't need a man in her life. But Lillian still hoped that perhaps the right man might come along for her mother, giving her someone to share the second half of her life with.

———

Lillian was bursting at the seams by the time Samuel's buggy pulled up the drive. He was going to be so surprised—in more ways than one. She pulled a loaf of bread out of the oven and placed it on a cooling rack on the kitchen counter, near a platter of cookies she'd made earlier. She and David feasted on cookies and milk every day when he returned from school. It had become their special time to talk about the day.

Her heart raced as Samuel pushed open the screen door.

"I reckon my toes are never gonna thaw," he said, snow still clinging to his long black coat and speckling his black felt hat. "But it sure smells *gut* in here." He hung his coat and hat on the rack and entered the kitchen.

Lillian clasped her hands together and smiled as she watched her husband's face light up.

"Lillian," he said in awe, his hand skimming the surface of the large table he had been eyeing in town for over a year. He grabbed her in his arms and kissed her tenderly. "But, how—"

"It's a wedding present, from my *mamm.*"

He shook his head in disbelief. "I reckon I've been wanting this table for as long as I can remember." His eyes twinkled with boyish appreciation. "This is the best present I've ever received. Someday we will fill it up with little ones."

Lillian smiled. "Samuel," she said softly, with a hint of playfulness in her tone.

"*Ya?*" He was still enamored with the new table and matching benches.

"Someday has arrived."

All the cold weather in the world couldn't have taken away the warmth in Lillian's heart when she saw the look on her husband's face. "You mean . . . ," he asked, unsure.

She placed his hand on her stomach and smiled. "*Ya.*"

"Oh, Lillian. I love you so much."

"And I love you, Samuel."

Samuel came over to Lillian and held her, then took a seat on one of the benches. Lillian slid in beside him and reached for his hand. "I imagine our family will eat a lot of meals at this table."

Giving her hand a squeeze, Samuel nodded. "*Ya,* our family."

They sat quietly for a while. As the peacefulness and calm she'd so desperately searched for swept over Lillian, she bowed her head and closed her eyes.

Thank You.

Acknowledgments

THANK YOU TO MY FAMILY AND FRIENDS FOR YOUR SUPPORT and encouragement.

To Patrick, for sharing your life with me and believing in me every step of the way. You become more dear to me with each passing day. To my sons, Eric and Cory, you are my most precious gifts from God who inspire me daily. You three are the loves of my life.

Mother, how blessed I am to be your daughter. And what a bonus it is that you are a super, speed-reading, typo-catching queen! And to Daddy, may you rest in peace knowing I write happy endings . . . the way you always thought it should be. Thank you to my Mama, for your unwavering faith in God and me. I know you are smiling from Heaven. To my sister Laurie, who found her true love late in life. May you be blessed with all the happiness you deserve.

To my best friend and lifelong editor, Reneé Bissmeyer. You've read more manuscripts than I care to count, and your unwavering support always keeps me going past chapter six. Thank you for believing in me when I had doubts. We both know there aren't enough pages for me to express what our friendship means to me.

You are my "life editor," as well as my manuscript editor. It is a privilege to dedicate the book to you.

Thank you to Rene Simpson, my dear, dear friend who stepped up to the plate at the very last minute and spent four days at my house editing nonstop until the last revision was complete. And you did it all for "Happy Eggs" and guacamole. You are my hero! Your Samuel awaits. Don't give up.

To my second family at *The Schulenburg Sticker* newspaper, your flexibility with my job during my son's illness, and throughout the publication of this book, far surpasses the employer/employee relationship. Saying thank you hardly seems enough. A special thank you to my editor at *The Sticker*, Darrell Vyvjala, for teaching me about the wonderful world of editing. You are my mentor and my friend.

Sue and Darrell Buttrey, the miles may seperate us, but you are forever in my heart. Thank you for your dear friendship and support.

Thank you to my good friend and critique partner, Carol Voelkel, for finding time to overhaul the manuscript amidst a challenging job, family, and writing projects of her own. Never stop writing!

Thank you to Mary Sue Seymour for recognizing the potential of the manuscript from the first three chapters. It is a pleasure to work with you and call you my friend. Miracles *do* happen to those who believe.

Many thanks to Barbie Beiler and Anna B. King, who jumped in at the eleventh hour and critiqued the manuscript for accuracy. Your Mennonite and Amish backgrounds provided a wealth of information about the Plain people of Lancaster County.

To the Amish families in Lancaster County who opened their homes and hearts, allowing my endless stream of questions . . . blessings to you all.

A special thank you to Leslie Peterson for her encouragement during the revision process. Your suggestions and edits were delivered with kindness and patience. It was a pleasure to work with you on this project.

A huge thank you to Natalie Hanemann for believing in the book . . . and in me. You alleviated much of my "first-novel fear" by walking me through the process and explaining things as we went along. You, along with the rest of the staff at Thomas Nelson, made this a wonderful experience for me.

And, most of all, to God, for offering me the opportunity to fulfill my dream of writing through words I pray will glorify Him, and for the many other blessings He has bestowed on me.

Amish Recipes

Shoofly Pie

CRUMBS:

- 1½ cups flour
- 1 cup brown sugar
- ⅔ cup lard or shortening

Combine all ingredients. Mix well. Reserve 1½ cups crumbs to mix with liquid mixture.

LIQUID:

- 1 cup molasses
- ½ cup brown sugar
- 2 eggs
- 1 tsp. soda dissolved in 1 cup hot water

Combine molasses, brown sugar, eggs and soda water. Add reserved crumbs and mix well. Pour into 3 unbaked regular sized pie shells or 2 deep dish pie shells. Top with remaining crumbs. Bake at 350° for 60 minutes.

Rhubarb Pie

I	egg
I	tsp. vanilla
2	Tblsp. flour
I	cup sugar
I	cup diced rhubarb

Mix together and pour in regular sized unbaked pie shell.
Sprinkle with topping and bake at 425° for 15 min. Then turn
oven down to 350° and put pie on middle rack for 10 min.
Next, remove pie and cover edges with foil. Bake 20 more
minutes at 350°.

TOPPING:

3/4	cup flour
1/2	cup brown sugar
1/3	cup butter

Garden Chow-chow

1	gallon cubed unpeeled zucchini (about 4.5 lbs.)
1	qt. sliced onions (one a half large onions)
3	cups carrots (shredded)
2	head cauliflower (chopped)
4	red peppers (chopped)
¼	cup salt

Mix chopped vegetables in large container with salt and let stand 2-3 hours. Drain and put in sterilized jars. Cook syrup.

SYRUP:

1½	qt. water
½	qt. vinegar
½	qt. sugar
1	tsp. turmeric
1	tsp. celery seed
¾	tsp. garlic powder

Heat until boiling. Fill jars with syrup, leaving ¼ inch. Then cold pack* for 10 minutes. Makes 12 pints.

* Cold Pack: Put jars of food in water (up to the neck) and boil for a required amount of time. Lids need to be put on tightly before putting in water.

Cooked Celery

Always served at Amish wedding dinners with turkey roast.

1½	qt. cubed celery (about 2 bundles)
½	cup water
½	cup brown sugar
1½	tsp. butter
½	tsp. salt

Cook together on stovetop until celery is soft (about 15 min. on high heat). Then mix together the following:

½ tsp. flour

1 ½ tsp. vinegar

1/8 cup brown sugar

¼ cup cream

Pour into hot celery mixture and stir until thick. Do not boil.

Reading Group Guide

1. At the beginning of the story, Samuel had some serious qualms about being "unequally yoked" with Lillian, who was an unbeliever. Do you think that Samuel's worries are justified? Have you ever been in a relationship where you felt unequally yoked? Where did you draw the line between sharing the love and Word of God to unbelievers and being yoked or pulled down by an unbeliever?

2. What are some of the ways the Amish community gathers to help one another in *Plain Perfect*? Have you experienced similar support in your own community? What can we take away from the Amish example of community and fellowship? Are there any disadvantages to this close-knit community?

3. Why do you imagine Samuel feels guilt that thoughts of Lillian intermingle with his thoughts of Rachel? If you were in his place, do you think you could love again?

4. Do you think Sarah Jane made the right decision to leave the Amish community when she became pregnant with Lillian? What do you think the repercussions would have been had she stayed? Why do you think Sarah Jane never told Lillian who her father was?

5. Why does Lillian have such a hard time accepting everything as God's will? Are you able to accept the hard times in your life as God's will? What about the blessings and successes in your life—are you able to credit those to God's will as well?

6. David always believed that his pop and Lillian would end up together. How does that relate to what Christ teaches us about the faith of children? Compare his eager faithfulness to Irma Rose's hesitancy. Why do some adults seem to lose that faith?

7. What do you think Sarah Jane was trying to find in all of the men in her life? Is there someone you know that is guilty of the same misdirection—that is, filling up the emptiness in his or her heart with bad relationships or material things such as nicer cars and homes? Would you ever broach this subject with him or her?

8. Is admitting your past mistakes helpful or harmful in the raising of children? Was Samuel out of line in his reaction to hearing that Lillian told David all about her worldly past? Should Lillian have denied her past?

What do you think would have happened if she hadn't told David all about her past and just forbidden him from those worldly temptations? Is there a benefit to letting children make their own mistakes?

9. Food is an important theme throughout the novel—the preparation, the sharing, the eating. Is the Amish approach to food and meals different than an "outsider" view? Are there similarities?

10. Why do you think Lillian chose to bury her worldly things in that hole by the lake? Is there anything you wish you could bury in a hole, eliminating from your past and present? What's stopping you?

11. Why do you think Sarah Jane decided to come back to Lancaster County to visit her parents? What made her stay? Why do you think it took her so long to return?

12. Are there parts of the Amish life you would like to incorporate into your own way of life?

An Excerpt for

Plain Pursuit

1

LUNCH WITH HER EDITOR USUALLY MEANT ONE THING. Trouble.

Carley couldn't think of anything she'd done to warrant the meeting. Granted, she hadn't written any award-winning stories for the newspaper lately, but she'd held her own. Every deadline had been met. The stories had been newsworthy. But something was clearly on Matt's mind. His forehead creased with concern as they took their seats at a small deli near the office.

"They have good burgers here," Matt said, scanning the menu. He was stalling.

"I'm just going to have a salad." Closing the menu, she folded her hands and waited. It was straight-up noon, and the harried waitress was taking orders several tables over. Carley was glad to see her favorite sandwich shop back in business and full of hungry patrons. It had taken months for Houston to recover from the devastating effects of the hurricane, but life had obviously returned to normal.

Normal. Such a loose term, she thought, waiting for Matt to drop whatever news had prompted the lunch.

Matt finally closed his menu and sighed. "Carley, you're a good reporter . . ." The lines above his bushy brows became more prominent. She waited for the *but*. He cleared his throat instead, and she took the opportunity to remind him of her tenure.

"I've been with the paper four years. I'd like to think I've done a good job." He nodded his agreement, although his expression remained solemn. "What's wrong, Matt?"

She searched his face, her heart rate kicking up. Matt had been her editor at the paper since she started, and they'd been to lunch only twice. Once as a celebration of sorts when she won a prestigious award, and once when Matt felt an article she wrote had crossed the journalistic line.

She hadn't won any awards lately.

"Carley, you've got plenty of unused vacation. Why haven't you taken any?" His eyes cut to the jagged scar spanning three inches across her left forearm. Instinctively, her right hand covered the evidence of the event that had forever altered her life.

"I took two weeks off when Mom died." *Where is he going with this? It's been six months since the accident.*

"Carley," he grumbled, "that wasn't a vacation, and part of that time you were in the hospital yourself." He shook his head as the waitress approached.

"I'll have the grilled chicken salad," Carley said after Matt ordered his burger and fries. She immediately regretted her decision. What was the point? You couldn't live forever. She bet her mother would have loaded up with an extra helping of pie on Christmas Day if she'd known it was her last day on earth.

"No, wait. I change my mind. I'll have a burger and fries too."

"Good girl," Matt said after the waitress scurried away. "You're too thin as it is."

"Now what were you saying, Matt?" She'd rather get this over with and salvage her appetite.

"I want you to take some vacation time."

Although his tone left little room for argument, she quickly countered. "I don't need a vacation."

"If you don't see it, then I'll just come out and say it: you aren't at the top of your game. You're a far cry from it, Carley. Your stories lack the zing they used to have. The facts are there, but they're lacking . . . What's the word I'm looking for?"

"I have no idea." She folded her arms across her chest.

"Emotional capacity," he continued. "You used to weave emotion into your stories—just enough to spruce up the article." He shrugged, and she saw the pity in his eyes as they locked with hers. "The intensity of your writing just isn't there anymore."

"I—I didn't realize that." She fought the sudden tremor in her voice. "I'll work harder."

When it appeared Matt was going to argue, she dug deep for the truth. "I need to work, Matt. It's all I have."

She dropped her gaze, hating the vulnerability she knew her expression revealed. *Matt has to understand. I can't take any time off. What would I do?* Until six months ago, her leisure time had been divided among her mother, her boyfriend, and her friends. Now her mom was gone, and Dalton had broken off their three-year relationship. And after one too many declines, her few girlfriends quit asking her to participate in their activities.

She had nothing but work.

"That's what I mean, Carley," Matt urged. "You are a beautiful woman with no relationships or interests outside of work.

You're slowly withdrawing from life, and it's noticeable in your writing." He leaned over the table. "Carley, on a personal note, we're worried about you."

"Who is *we*?" She knew the answer. "Katrina?"

Her reporting rival had bumped up a notch to assistant editor awhile back and now latched onto every opportunity to remind Carley of her position.

"Yes, Katrina and I discussed it, Carley, but—"

"She doesn't like me, Matt."

Right away she realized the comment sounded childish.

"Not true." Matt shook his head and pushed an envelope in Carley's direction. "This is a month's vacation pay. You've accumulated a lot more than that. Take a month off, Carley. Come back refreshed. You should have taken more time off after the accident."

Carley peered at the envelope on the table as the waitress returned with their lunches and offers of ketchup and extra napkins. "I'm not taking a vacation, Matt. Why should I be forced to use my time right now?"

"Because you wouldn't like the alternative." He wrapped his mouth around his burger.

Carley wasn't hungry for anything except Katrina Peighton's hide. This was her doing, not Matt's.

"So let me get this straight. Either I go on vacation or I'm fired?"

"Don't look at it that way, Carley," Matt said between bites. "Take advantage of this. I would."

Her thoughts churned. *What will I do? Sit around my big empty house?*

No. Too much time to think.

She bargained. "I'll take a week off."

"A month, Carley. We will welcome you back with open arms in one month."

By the end of the meal, she'd reluctantly accepted the envelope. Not that she had any choice in the matter. Matt made it quite clear her vacation started directly after lunch.

$$2$$

CARLEY TRIED TO KEEP HER EYES ON THE ROAD AS SHE studied the map laid out beside her on the car seat. She'd never been to Lancaster County, Pennsylvania, but a sign flashed by, indicating twenty-six miles to the town of Paradise. Good. She was on the right track.

She watched the farmland scrolling by and thought about seeing Lillian. Her friend had fled the craziness of Houston a year and a half ago, moved in with her Amish grandparents, married an Amish man, and now happily resided in the town of Paradise with her new family. Carley couldn't help but wonder how much her friend might have changed. From her initial letters Carley knew Lillian's grandparents' farm in Paradise had provided Lillian with a safe haven where she could get her life together. But when Lillian wrote to say she had converted and was staying—that was a lot to swallow. Carley couldn't get past the lack of electricity, much less the fact that Lillian had married Amish widower Samuel Stoltzfus, become a stepmother to his thirteen-year-old son, and now had a baby of her own.

Of course, Carley knew she had changed too. Everything had changed last Christmas Day . . .

According to Lillian's letters, she had been baptized in the

Amish faith—a required step toward marrying an Amish man. Her friend also adhered to all their Plain customs, including the wardrobe. It was an unbelievable transformation. No television, makeup, jewelry. No computer.

Hmm. Carley eyed her laptop on the floorboard of the rental car. How was she going to charge the battery?

One thing shone through in all Lillian's letters: she was happy. As a writer, Carley excelled at reading between the lines. She had looked for clues that perhaps Lillian wasn't as content as she let on. She couldn't find one. Lillian's destination seemed to have brought her the peace Carley knew Lillian longed for.

Carley felt like she was still wandering, her own destination unknown.

Which brought her to her current situation. In her last letter to Lillian, Carley had asked her friend if she might come for a visit and do an article about the Amish ways. Lillian quickly responded with an invitation—which Carley accepted the day her forced vacation began. She would put her leave to good use. Even better, she would incorporate work into her trip.

Work would keep her sane.

Lillian popped a loaf of bread into the gas oven. Carley would be hungry when she arrived. Hopefully her friend would like the meatloaf and baked corn casserole she had prepared, along with the chocolate shoofly pie for dessert. If she hurried, she could have the meal ready before Anna woke up for her feeding.

She scanned the wooden table in the middle of the kitchen. It was covered with a variety of jellies and applesauce and some pickled red beets. For a moment she pondered whether she should have tackled the sauerbraten recipe instead. But the meatloaf was a lot less work, and Anna had been fussy all afternoon. She'd fallen behind on the household chores.

Maybe she should have baked a peach pie instead of the rich shoofly with its filling of molasses and brown sugar.

Or *maybe* she should stop worrying so much about Carley's arrival. But she couldn't help it. Their last time together, Lillian had sported blue jeans, a name-brand blouse, stilettos, full makeup and silver jewelry, and a designer handbag.

She tucked a loose strand of hair beneath her white *Kapp*, glancing down at her blue linen dress covered by a black apron. Her plain black leather shoes were a far cry from the spiked heels of her past.

The screen door slammed shut behind her. Samuel.

"It smells *gut* in here," he said, kissing her smile before tossing his hat onto the rack in the den.

"*Danki.* I hope it's *gut.*" She breathed in the aroma of baking bread while she mixed the sauce that would go on top of the meatloaf. "I hope Carley likes it."

"Your friend will be here soon, no?"

Lillian knew Samuel worried about her *Englisch* friend coming to visit. They had discussed it, and although Samuel assured her it was fine for Carley to stay with them for the month of May, Lillian also knew Carley's visit was an exception to an unspoken rule: *no outsiders allowed.* But it wasn't that long ago *she'd* been the outsider in the Old Order Amish district. How quickly a year and a half had gone by.

"She should be here any minute," Lillian informed Samuel.

"It's almost four thirty, and I know you must be hungry. David should be home soon too. He's at *Mamm's* doing some yard work." She stirred the sauce atop the gas range. "I think you'll like Carley, Samuel. And she promised me the story she writes for her newspaper will include only things we're comfortable with."

She caught the uncertainty on Samuel's face, which he quickly hid with a half smile. "*Ya*, I know," he replied.

"You said there are a lot of misconceptions written about the way we live. Wouldn't it be nice for someone to get it right in print?" She challenged his skepticism with a playful wink, hoping to alleviate some of his fear.

"*Ya*, it's just that . . ." He hesitated, grimacing.

"What?" She turned the fire down under the sauce and slid in beside him at the kitchen table.

"I'm sure everything will be fine, Lillian. I just don't trust those who print words about our lives, and I don't know this *Englisch* woman."

Lillian grasped his hand. "But I do. And I trust her, Samuel."

"Then I will trust her too." He gave her hand a squeeze. "Now where's my little *boppli*?"

"Anna should be waking up hungry any minute. I was just trying to finish supper before Carley gets here." She returned to the sauce, and Samuel stood. "Carley is a *gut* person, Samuel. Try not to worry."

As his arms wrapped tightly around her waist, Samuel nuzzled the back of her neck. "*You* are a *gut* person, Lillian. Besides, worry is a sin."

"*Ya*, it is," she whispered as she tried to push aside her own worries over Carley's arrival.

Writing has always been a part of best-selling novelist Beth Wiseman's life—whether writing books, articles, or a weekly column. When Beth was introduced to the Amish, she gained an appreciation for their simpler way of life and began writing love stories featuring this fascinating and endearing group of people. She and her family live in Texas.

QUAKER SUMMER

For Erin Healy,
my partner in crime.

He has showed you, O man, what is good.
And what does the LORD require of you?
To act justly and to love mercy and to walk humbly with your God.

—MICAH 6:8

Part One

The Fool on the Hill

ONE

Five months ago I raised Gary and Mary Andrews from the dead. I took a wrong turn trying to find a Pampered Chef party to benefit Will's eighth grade trip to New York City, and there it stood as close to the road as ever, their old house. Superimposed over the improvements of the recent owners, a small bungalow with cracked siding, smeared windowpanes, and a rusted oil tank figured into my vision. The mat of green grass dissolved into an unkempt lot of dirt and weeds supporting a display of junk: an old couch, a defunct Chevy, and rusted entities the purpose of which I never could say.

What happened inside that house remains there. All I know for sure is that Gary and Mary Andrews climbed onto our school bus every morning and never waved good-bye to anybody. We'd pull forward in a throaty puff of diesel, away from that little frame house, its once-white paint as gray as the dirt that always outlined Gary's hands and shaded behind his ears. As a sixth grader, I didn't realize children weren't responsible for their own cleanliness, that Mary's hair never glinted in the sunshine or smelled like baby shampoo because nobody helped her wash it; nobody thrust their fingers into her curls and scrubbed away the dust of a tumble in the yard with the dog; nobody applied a nice dollop of cream rinse to untangle knots from windy hours outside. I never stopped to think nobody in that house cared about them.

God help me.

So I sit now in the anonymity of my car, praying somebody steps out. Perhaps they'll look around, notice me sitting here, walk forward and ask if there's a problem.

No. No problem. I just knew the people who used to live here. Might you know where they live now?

No movement, no fluttering of the drapes, no shadows behind the blinds. Always quiet here. It always was.

I pull off the side of the road, the heavy tires eating the gravel. I turn for home. I'll find myself back here again soon. It's become the way of it.

I'm sorry. I'm so sorry.

I fell asleep last night to the eerie strains of "Blackbird," my last conscious thoughts of broken wings and sunken eyes. Waiting for moments to arrive when broken wings fly and sunken eyes see, waiting for that moment of freedom, flying into the light.

If I had to listen to one musical artist or band or composer for the rest of my life, I'd choose the Beatles. Their music encompasses all the emotions, all the moods, and all the tempos I'll ever need, taking me back to my childhood when my father would slip an album on the stereo, set the speed to thirty-three, and push the lever up to automatic. The fact that my father was younger and definitely cooler than the other dads around only helped the Fab Four become *the thing* to an elementary school girl who should have been listening to Bobby Sherman or the Osmond Brothers. I never really did go for the teen sensations.

Lying on my stomach, I would watch from eye level, chin resting on the back of my hands, and stare, gaze stuttering in and out of focus as the record fell to the turntable on the floor by the couch, the arm lifted, swung backward then forward, diamond-tipped needle poised with promise over the smooth outer rim of the vinyl disc. As it dropped with slow precision, I held my breath wondering if it would really make contact with the disc this time. Those old hi-fi systems didn't miss the mark often, but they did enough to glue your eyes to the entire process and make your heart skip a few beats until the needle found its groove.

And then, after the static and scratch, Paul sang about his mother, Mary, comforting him, telling him to "Let It Be."

I was a daddy's girl, my mother having left him when I was two and then died not long after in a motorcycle accident with one of her precursor-hippie boyfriends. Nevertheless, I closed my eyes for the duration of the song, wishing she still existed and could lift her hand and rest it on my shoulder. She must have done that long ago.

Or maybe not.

During the strains of "Blackbird," I dreamt of my father for the first time in many months, his dark, winged hair breezing back from his wide forehead. Snuggled in the comforter freshly snapped down off the line yesterday afternoon, I wallowed in the numbness of slumber as he returned anew. Nobody told me how precious dreams of the dead become, how our own subconscious somehow gifts us with the time and space to once again be with those who have left us behind.

And so I lay basking in my father's presence, wishing so much for more time. But isn't that always the way? There he was, living in that little house in Towson, and I only saw him once a week. How differently I'd do things if I'd known he was slated for an autumn death. An accident at work. He was a plumber, a fact that used to embarrass me, an expert at redoing historical houses during his last decade. Nobody knew that wall was ready to fall down. They were just doing the initial walk-through. He was only fifty-five.

The cool morning air spirals the window curtains, and I inhale the breeze off Loch Raven to the bottom of my lungs. At the crest of the hill beside our home, earth—turned over and ready for planting by the farmer who lives next door—casts its loamy smell over the yard. As yet, the sun rests below a horizon unadorned but for the crabbed Dutch elm standing long past its expiration date. I hate

that bleached thing. Why my neighbor, a sweet widower nicknamed
Jolly, doesn't pull it down is as much a mystery as his very name. As
far as I know, nobody knows Jolly's real name, and Jace and I wonder
if Jolly even remembers. Maybe it actually is Jolly. Jolly Lester. I
always figured it was John or Jacob or maybe James.

Jolly tries to live up to the name. Lord knows the man tries. But
some days, especially when the rain falls in a light slick from a plat-
inum sky, his sepia eyes tell me he misses his Helen with the longing
of someone who loved one person all of his life and was content,
even honored, to do so. And Helen loved him back.

The distant buildings of Towson peek over the trees, and farther
yet, Baltimore lies hidden to me here. But life is beginning again in
those places that formed me into this woman I've become, for good
or for bad.

I should pray. My father taught me to pray.

Jace stirs. "You awake, Hezz?"

I sit up and grab for my robe. "I need to get that turkey in the
oven so it's ready for sandwiches for the party this afternoon."

"What party?"

"We're having the end-of-the-year party for Will's class here,
remember? I've got a ton of stuff to do. At least I decorated the cake
already."

"Forgot. Would you like the shower first?"

"Nope. You go on."

"What kind of cake?"

"Triple chocolate with white chocolate buttercream icing."

"Mind if I take a piece to the office?" His mouth stretches into a
smiley ribbon. He closes his eyes and I stare at my husband. Most
women imagine that plainer women who've stolen a handsome man as
their own must feel smug and superior having scored an undeserved
hottie. Obviously, we've got brains or money or an extraordinary sense
of humor to have nabbed such a prize.

Let me say, it isn't as easy as it looks. I know what people think
when we walk into a restaurant. Tall, lean, good-looking Jace with his
wavy brown hair and smoky eyes, his easy assurance, his ruddy skin

warming up the room. They must wonder how on this green earth a little old roly-poly like me ended up with a movie star like him.

For the first ten minutes I'm conscious of myself in ways Jace has never made me feel. But he's just Jace, even in posh restaurants, placing his hand on the rounded waist that expanded with the growth of his child, smiling into eyes wrinkled from many afternoons squinting in the sun at swim meets, and laughing at my jokes that are only funny because of context, not content.

And they don't know that cucumbers give him terrible gas, that he can be a real jerk when he's sick, that he shuts down when he's mad, and that he still draws stick figures. They don't know that he doesn't call his parents nearly enough . . . that he gets upset about my spending habits, which I must admit are sometimes a little over the top. But it's too beautiful a morning to think about that.

I give his head a quick scratch. "I'll get you a cup of coffee, sweets."

Eyes still closed, he smiles. "I don't deserve you."

"Well, looks notwithstanding, that's probably true. Because I'm a good Christian woman, I seek an almost-perfection from the rising of the sun to the going down of the same. I volunteer at school; I once hosted a foreign exchange student; I color my hair, exercise at least three times a week to keep my temple from collapsing; I wear lipstick. Sometimes I wear two colors at once to manipulate the perfect coordinating shade with whatever Eddie Bauer or Talbots dreamed up for the season."

He squints. Why not continue?

"I tote a Vera Bradley purse with matching change purse, cell phone case, and makeup bag—which, honestly, I've never liked, Jace, but the Vera rage burned a couple of years ago at church, and I convinced myself a quilted handbag with a Noah's ark theme was not only a fine idea, but a potential witnessing tool, like a Jesus fish or a cross necklace."

"It's just a purse, hon." Jace leans up on one elbow. "You sure you don't want to shower first?"

"You know, I figured if I wore it steadily for three years, it would come to about ten cents a pop, and surely that's not bad, is it?"

Jace shakes his head, throws back the covers. "No, Hezz, it isn't." Under his breath he mumbles, "That purse is the least of it."

I wonder how long it'll take before he sees the new deck furniture. I'm glad I remembered to hide those bags from T.J.Maxx.

The coffeemaker is burbling like the creek on the west side of our property, the one that soaked Will clear down to his skivvies after he played in it at least four afternoons a week once the warmth of spring overlaid the fields and the woods.

Every so often that stream floods, and I am frightened for my son. Good reasons for this abound. Will was a wandering, curious tot with a certain "Don't you know I must be about my Father's business?" air about him.

Six thirty in the morning, and the forty-five minutes before I must awaken my son stretch in front of me like a sun-warmed path to the beach. I'm never alone, it seems, even with just one living child (and I wanted ten, but those thoughts are definitely for another day, or maybe next year). I feel so confined, as if my skin has thickened, hardened like the dried-up skin of a past-due tangerine, and inside this shell I'm fighting to be free, to be young and full of hope that I'm made for something more.

More than motherhood?

Justifiably so, the women at my old church would never understand these thoughts. Any woman who wanted more than motherhood wanted too much. But something inside me claws with puckered lips and shiny-bright eyes, believing it will drag not just me but all those I love right along with it onto a new roller coaster with longer drops to go speeding down but greater vistas from which to view the world.

I don't know how I know this, other than I've known it for years, known I was created to do something out of the norm; known that only one pregnancy out of five actually took because I wasn't cut out to be the mother of many nations; I wasn't destined to think that Elisabeth Elliott and her daughter have it all sewn up.

Gary and Mary Andrews fit into this somehow. See, right now

I'm living in a puzzle, the box lid having just been taken off, and I stare down onto the pieces, some clear, some hidden, and they work together somehow, but I'm just looking at them, smelling the woody pulp, and wondering, all the while knowing it's designed to do so, how in the world I'll make it all fit together and look like something real. Even the box lid sports no picture to guide me.

But first, the turkey.

Sliding the small bird out of the refrigerator, I lay the chilled pan on my soapstone counter. Just had to install those soapstone tops after a particularly enlightening episode of *Martha Stewart Living* on HGTV. Oven, 375 degrees. Rack in the lower third. Good. Poor bird, forced to give up its life for us. We'll eat every bit. After all, through no choice of its own, the creature sacrificed its life for our protein consumption, so how can I casually pitch it into the garbage without giving it some kind of meaning?

Thus the plethora of soups and casseroles that line the extra freezer in the basement; I long to give them away, but without a church home, who would I give them to?

Thus my weight problem.

But, honey, I can do more with a can of cream of mushroom soup than Paul McCartney ever could have hoped to do with two guitars, a bass, and drums. Although he did have Ringo to train. I have to allow for that.

I'd better vacuum a bit before we leave for school.

How do I live like this? The kitchen and family room alone spread out before me, larger than our first place down in Anneslie, a pea-sized second-floor apartment in an arts and crafts bungalow with a galley kitchen and a living room/dining room combo. But ah, the woodwork.

I insert the hose into the wall vacuum.

Less to vacuum there in Anneslie too.

Every year I think there must be more to life. And every year—despite a new car or a trip to a new land, new milestones and triumphs in my son's life, or a redone deck, a pool, a spa, or an entertainment system—I take stock and think once again, *I was made for more than this.*

But I love my stuff.

The hose jumps to life and I scrape the head back and forth over the cream-colored carpet.

Of course there's always church and God. And Jesus.

Something smells funny. Is the unit going up already?

Now Jesus, I get Him. I just wish I didn't forget Him when I open my eyes each morning and the day descends.

But church? Well, we left ours a year ago and still haven't found a place to settle. The praise songs had become so repetitive, the messages more of the same old "practical living advice" with a couple of Bible verses thrown in for good measure; and I was tired. Really, Jace and I were both just tired out. And there never seemed to be hope that a break was coming, that we wouldn't spend the rest of our lives doing this "stuff."

When Jesus said, "I will give you rest," I tend to think He meant the whole gamut, not just spiritual.

I finish the family room and the area rugs in the entry hall.

Jace enters the kitchen and refills his coffee.

"Jace, do you ever wonder what it was like for Jesus when He woke up each morning? Did He dread opening His eyes? Did He think, *Oh, Lord, all these people! People, people, people everywhere. How did it come to this? And why am I always the one who does the nice things? When was the last time anyone, especially one of these disciples, thought to do something nice for Me?* I have a feeling He didn't. He had no sin. He didn't carry around this darklight in His chest."

He pauses, coffeepot held midair. "Heather, are you okay?"

"Yeah. I just wonder about stuff like that sometimes."

"I'm a little worried about you. You seem really stressed."

"I'll feel better once the school year's done and this party is over."

"That fund-raising gala really took it out of you." He sets his mug down, walks over, and puts his arms around me. "I really love you, hon. You know that, right?"

I just burrow my face into his shoulder. I can't look at him when he starts making loving proclamations. If his professions are an accurate indication of his emotions, Jace adores me. So if he backs them up with candles and flowers and that sweet smile, why can't I believe him? With these sponge cake hips? This raggedy C-section scar? Come on, man! Where are your standards?

My hair is so greasy, and here I am snuggling into him. How can he stand it? "You know, Jace, with your looks, money, position, and exposure to the female kind in your practice, you could locate some remix of Martha Stewart with a little Gwyneth Paltrow thrown in for good measure. Some days I wonder why you don't."

"I don't know what more I can do to prove to you how much I love you, Heather."

He kissed me awake yesterday morning and whispered how much he loved me. When he got into the shower after I pretended to enjoy his lovemaking, I cried.

"What's wrong with me, Jace? Why can't I believe you? Why have I never believed you?"

"I don't know, Hezzie."

"It's not you."

"I know. I've always known that."

"It's got to be getting a little old."

"I'd be lying if I said it wasn't." He pours me a cup of coffee, and we stand on the side porch as the sun rises on this final day of school, peering through a misty sky, lighting the world as though nobody has given it permission and it doesn't want to overstep its bounds.

I turn around and refold myself into his tallness, and his arms surround me. I do love him.

"We need to get away together, Hezz."

"Yeah. Far away."

See, we fritter away our lives making enough to provide ourselves with four-star accommodations when we crawl home each night, and when all that isn't enough, when our bones are pitted and our muscles wasted, when our hearts are emptied out and imploded, we just want to get away from the reminders of our own foolishness.

My foolishness. Deep in my heart, I know this life on the hill over the lake is mine.

Jace never wanted any of this.

TWO

When Will went off to kindergarten, one mom did the Snoopy dance right at the end of the driveway as her last child climbed aboard the bus. There stood us first-time mothers crying our eyes to an angry, pulsating red, and Mary Jane, a veteran mom sending off her fifth and final, shuffled like Mr. Bojangles.

I understand now. In September my son will begin high school. And though I don't want to wish his youth away, I'll be dancing like Mary Jane did that day. School would be great if there weren't other children around being so mean and snobby and all. Just like their parents.

Will shuffles in, sleepy eyes weighed down by what looks like a dirty-blond Pomeranian atop his head. He lays his backpack against the desk. "Morning, Mom."

It's his birthday. We don't mention his birthday. After all, he says, he really had nothing to do with it, and if nobody is going to give me gifts as his mother, the woman who carried him for nine months, labored seventeen and a half hours, and went through major surgery to release him to the arms of the world, why should he get any? He simply showed up—invited, yes—but unable to accept or refuse. Fifteen years after the day he was born, I still can't wrap my mind around this eccentric soul. Now my heart is another matter entirely, of course.

I run my fingers through his hair. "Good sleep? Need a haircut?"

"Yes and no. I'll fix the eggs if you pour me a cup of coffee." He smiles with Jace's mouth and speaks with my father's voice, only a tad higher. Dad loved his grandson who inherited his artistic side. Dad

332

painted murals on my bedroom walls, changing them with my interests. Now a man who can paint fairies one year and butterfly brides
the next automatically qualifies as someone abnormally special.

Will opens the refrigerator door and leans down. Because we
decided he should repeat second grade, he's three or four inches
taller than most of the boys in his class, but probably weighs twenty
pounds less. "Want cheese in your eggs?" He speaks with his newfound man-voice. And he smiles again, sending the love of my father
right into the center of my heart.

"I wish you'd have known your grandfather better," I say.

"Me too. I loved going over there to spend the night. It must be
a bummer to have no parents living."

"Yeah." A big bummer.

And now I feel like going shopping again. I'm not stupid. I know
my incessant buying is trying to fill holes that purchases were never
meant to fill. But I just feel so much better afterwards. Jace can't
possibly understand. He's got the luxury of having living parents to
take for granted and a satisfying career that actually helps people.

Laney, another room helper, helps me get sodas together for the party.

"Heather, do you ever feel like running away?" She leans against the
counter, pulling the cans out of the plastic rings. She's pretty much
the only room mother I really relate to. Unfortunately, I haven't taken
the time to get to know her this year. That fund-raising gala took more
than my money, that's for sure.

Laney's gorgeous. Figure that out. "I want to run away five days
out of seven. It's those kids." Her oldest, Nicola, from her husband,
Cade's, first marriage, is in Will's class and looks like her real mother,
who isn't bad but is no Laney. The other four, who look like Laney,
are under five and include a set of twins. And she's pregnant again.
"Is that horrible?"

"No, it's understandable. We all feel that way sometimes." I heft
a bag of ice out of the freezer.

"What about you? Do you ever feel like that?"

"Sometimes I look at my Suburban and wish it would turn into a sporty import, top down, so I can drive her away with no planned destination, no seat filled by a warm body, no music on the radio, no familiar bends, or houses, or ponds, or service stations." I lean my forearm on the cold bag. "Just drive and drive and drive. Why don't you start on the vegetables?"

"Sure." Laney reaches over to a head of cauliflower and begins to slice up florets for the fresh veggie tray that Carmen, the head room mother who terrorizes the rest of us, insisted we have even though we all know there isn't an eighth grader alive who will voluntarily touch the stuff. "Where do you end up in your dream?"

"I don't know. I never get that far, I guess."

I lied. Somewhere at the other end of the journey awaits a spare white bedroom with a single bed, a student desk and chair, and a reading lamp with a pale yellow shade. On the other side of the bedroom door a Purpose sits waiting on a straight-back chair, gray felt fedora beside him on the mission-style occasional table, hands folded over the brown leather grip of a banker's satchel. Occasionally he glances at his watch and wonders when I will wake up and emerge from inside.

This from St. Matthews Day School's Volunteer of the Year!

But I want to drive away to that white shell of a room and sit on the side of the institutional twin bed with its beige bedspread, gazing out of the small window overlooking a vacant lot dusted with some gum wrappers, a soda bottle or two, and an old dish towel twisted and squashed like a braided donut left for a week in the box. I'd sit that way until I garnered the courage to open the door and talk to my Purpose sitting in his chair.

He'd squeeze aloft his hat, stand up, hold the hat in both hands, and clear his throat. "Good then, Mrs. Curridge. There's still plenty of time left. Shall we?"

So I follow him out the door of the boardinghouse and onto a city bus. We ride for a long time, and I fall asleep to the cadence of the tar lines crossing the road. When I awaken, I find he's carried me into a small, tidy abode with a galley kitchen and white walls. The cupboards only hold eight plates, bowls, glasses, and mugs. All white and simple with that Palmolive shine. Or wait, does Palmolive soften your hands while you do the dishes? I can never remember.

He shows me each of the two bedrooms, small bedrooms probably 10 x 12. Seven sets of clothing hang in each person's closet, easy clothing, mix and match.

"This way, Mrs. Curridge."

We walk through the living room to the sliding glass doors, and on the balcony sit Jace and Will in molded white plastic lawn chairs. Jace stands. "Welcome home. We decided to get rid of all the extras while you were gone."

I say "Amen" to that.

I pour bagged ice over the sodas in the cooler.

"Laney, do you ever feel like you're going crazy?"

"Only all the time."

"But you've got more of an excuse."

"Yeah, those kids."

"But you look so gorgeous."

She begins to place the florets on a segmented tray, haphazardly without a care for effect. I like it. "It's genetics, Heather. I'm not going to age well, I can tell you that. Thin faces are fine midthirties. But with these cheekbones, I'm going to end up looking like that Madame puppet."

I bark out a laugh. "For me it's one minute you're a smooth-skinned twelve-year-old; the next you look like somebody rolled you around in beer batter and deep-fried you to a puffy golden brown." Thanks to the tanning bed in the exercise room in the basement. I had to have it after giving my sunlamp away to a man from church suffering from depression. "Brown fat is prettier than white fat, I always say. I've avoided the bathing suit department for years. I lie and say I don't swim, that I'm photosensitive."

"I think you're perfect. And sexy too." She grabs the carton of grape tomatoes. "Hey, I think we're pretty good for each other. We need to hang out more."

"You said it."

Me. Sexy. The girl must have standards as low as Jace's!

She scratches her cheek and tilts her head to the side. "Do you have these kinds of conversations with everyone?"

"I try to limit myself to two a day." I shake my head. "No, not usually. They just seem to be happening more and more. I don't know what's wrong with me."

"Just wondering." She reaches for a head of broccoli and pushes back a heavy, wavy chunk of burnished hair. "So how much of this stuff do you think will be eaten?"

"At least half, because Carmen will eat it herself just to prove she was right."

Laney raises a single brow. "But she'll be sneaky about it."

"Exactly."

We keep on chopping Carmen's veggies.

I reach into the fridge for the red peppers. "I watched an episode of *Oprah* a few years ago about a woman who found herself allergic to practically everything. She ended up living in a tent in the middle of the forsaken desert, away from cleaning products, paper products, new clothes, varnished furniture, anything with chemicals in it."

"I saw that too." Laney picks up a cucumber.

"And I envied her! I kept thinking, *Now wouldn't I like to trade places with her for a couple of weeks.* I haven't read a good novel in fifteen years! Not since Will was born."

"I read poetry."

"Me too, Laney. All the bang in less than five minutes. Unless it's epic, in which case, who cares? I just flip over to the short stuff."

"My favorite poem is 'The Highwayman,'" Laney says.

"'And the highwayman came riding, riding, riding . . .'"

"Yep, pretty much."

"Do you ever feel like you settled, Laney?"

"Yeah, a lot. I love my family, Heather, I really do, but I've got my PhD in biblical studies, and here I am with all these kids."

"Wow."

"I know it's a choice I made. But talk about guilt. When I feel good about being a mother, I feel guilty about not using my degree. When I'm studying to keep up on things, I feel guilty about not being a good mother."

"It's a never-ending cycle."

"And at church they could care less about my theological training."

"Really? Why?"

"Because I've got girl parts, I guess. I mean, what other reason could there be?" She lowers her voice to mimic some unseen pastor or elder. "'With your training, Laney, you should really be teaching. How about taking the Primary class?'"

"No."

"I kid you not, Heather."

"We left church a year ago and haven't found a home yet. I don't know what it is I'm looking for, Laney. I feel lost. I'd honestly rather stay home, read the Sunday *Sunpaper*, and eat homemade sticky buns."

"You're not the only one. I'm seeing it more and more."

"Am I ungrateful?"

"No. You're tired. We're all just tired of doing all this stuff and feeling as fractious and unhappy as ever before."

Laney heads out to buy more ice. So the vacuuming's finished, I've dusted the furniture and the blinds, and now I just have to make sure the pool and the yard are in good shape.

Jace calls. "How's it going?"

"Almost ready. Just some last-minute things to take care of. To be honest, I'm kind of glad to be having something here. With church I could justify all this with the youth group and the ladies' groups meeting here, but it's been hard to live in a place like this just for us."

Church helped me justify this mammoth house. I mean, the

big-screen TV, the pool table, and the game systems were perfect for youth nights here on the bluff.

More. More. More.

How about a pool? Two years ago, there it finally lay, in blue sparkling California coolness, umbrellaed tables at the ready for the fellowship of God's people. Pool toys galore for the children—got those cheap at Tuesday Morning, though.

Built-in outdoor barbecue palace with a refrigerator and an ice-maker. Definitely a necessity.

"Still planning the tennis court, hon?" he asks. The tone is so slightly sour you'd only hear it if you'd been married to the guy for seventeen years. I pretend I don't.

"They break ground in July."

"Uh-huh. Hey, gotta go. I've got an afternoon surgery. I'll be home around eight."

I place the phone back in the cradle and head out to the upper deck leading off from the family room. Who could have told me that more, more, more is never enough, enough, enough? We have those dreams when we're tucked in those small apartments, thinking that lives lived in stone houses on hills overlooking lakes are surely free and easy. But those old days were exciting. I could put a gorgeous room together for under two hundred dollars, set a meal on the table for five bucks, buy a pair of jeans at the Salvation Army, and make the greatest skirts you've ever seen. Creativity proliferates in such circumstances, as I found in Jace's medical school years when we lived just fine all year on what we now pay for Will's tuition alone.

Great years, though, even with the limited income. How could I have known what a life we'd have when Jace first sat down in my chair at the hair salon for a buzz cut? Of course, I refused to clipper off those curls.

So, the deck furniture padding.

I open the doors to the pool house and start pulling out the golf-green cushions. This new furniture, more substantial, will last for years, I'm sure. A family from school told me about relatives who lost all of their furniture in a fire, so I gave them our patio furniture.

They picked it up yesterday. It was only a year old, so I didn't feel bad about handing it over as if I were giving away some second-rate castoffs.

Folks at school know me as someone willing to help out in such circumstances. It's really the only true ministry I've got these days.

Laney slips through the French doors. "I'm back. Here, let me help."

"Pads are in the pool house. Thanks for everything, Laney."

"Sure. I need the time away from home. I'll have to pick them all up soon enough. Are you sure you don't mind driving Nicola home after the party?"

"Positive."

At least my Suburban's good for something. I drive schoolkids everywhere. I'm the first pick for field trips because I always have drinks and snacks on board. However, I don't let the mean kids into my car. Will isn't the coolest kid on the block, and he suffers for it. I learned a long time ago that my being nice to the bullies does not make them behave any more nicely toward Will. So forget them.

The cushions distributed, I suggest a cold drink is in order. Cokes in hand, we settle on loungers by the deep end.

"So you had a life before all this, I'm guessing." Laney sweeps her hand over my vista.

"I had bigger dreams for myself, I suppose. I was a stylist, but I planned to major in business and have my own salon. I would have just called it *Heather*."

Heather.

A classy sign with simple raised gold lettering on a white oval, and tasteful heather floral arrangements to welcome my clients once they ventured inside. Good coffee available, fresh fruit and chocolate, wine in the evenings. Haircuts, spa treatments, community, a nurturing place in a busy world. "I miss talking to my clients, the other stylists, hearing the ins and outs of ordinary lives. It's all so big and important when it's somebody else's life, isn't it?"

"What happened?"

"I married a med school student."

"Well, at least he didn't dump you after he finished."

I raise my soda. "Here's to that, that's for sure. How long have you and Cade been married?"

"Six years."

"You happy?"

"Sometimes. I just want to get the child rearing over with. I miss the classroom so much, and here I sit with this belly out to here again."

"When are you due?"

"They say late July, early August. I lost track of when my last period was. And I refuse to get an ultrasound. My midwife doesn't like it, but she's a natural-type woman, so she understands."

"I'd say you have other stuff to think about."

I pull back up to the house around two thirty with a car full of kids intensely aware of the opposite sex, and ten minutes later their shouts ricochet off the waters of the pool and the slate patio. Two of the moms with lifeguard training stand on deck, chatting and getting browner by the minute. They look good in their suits. Not great. But darn good. Normally their volunteerism extends only to the sports program.

The girls have congregated around the edge of the pool, their skinny legs swallowed just below the knee by the water, chatting and gossiping while the majority of the boys, arms and legs loosely hinged, splash and dunk each other, hollering in their mid-change voices, thrashing about like clownish wildlife.

Will wants to join in, but he can't. He volunteered to man the grill, and Carmen is standing there looking over his shoulder. It's one thing to *be* the nerd; it's another to know you *are* the nerd. My heart breaks that he is the gangly, artistic oddball of the group whose voice changed sooner than the others. Yes, yes, I know he will do wonderful things someday, but that he's not welcome in this part of his world, a part I'm paying $20K a year for, mind you, makes me just plain angry.

And there's Ronald P. Legermin, the ringleader, whom I could absolutely strangle.

"I hate that child."

Laney whips her head around. "What?"

"Ronnie."

"So does Nicola. She can't stand him."

Whoa. I can't believe she didn't call me down for that one.

Carmen, dressed in the tropical theme of the party, pats Will on the back, then breezes in from the deck. Her skin glows like golden oak. "Burgers and dogs are almost done. Let's get the food out, ladies!" She clicks on her lime green slides over to my fridge, her derriere shaking like a Latin dancer's, and she yanks open the door. As she slides out Laney's veggie tray, a frown ages her brow. "Okay, then. Well. Heather, did you slice the turkey yet?"

"Yep. It's on a tray with the deli meats."

"And did you arrange it nicely? Please say yes." Laney reddens. Mercy, Laney, you're a PhD, for gosh sakes!

"Whether or not it's up to your standards, Carmen, I can't say." I point to the kitchen table where it's displayed. "Is that all right?"

She gazes over. "Oh yes. Relief. The cake is gorgeous too. You're almost professional at it, Heather."

Almost.

She clicks on over to the ice chests and peers in, nods—in satisfaction, I hope—then clicks over to the bathroom. She peeks her head back around the doorjamb. "Do you have any cleaning wipes?"

Laney and I exchange looks.

"I cleaned the bathroom this morning, Carmen."

"Really?"

"Are you that rude?" My hand flies to my mouth. Mercy!

Laney coughs into her hand.

Carmen reels backward. "Well, no, but I . . . well, I just thought I'd help out."

I cross my arms. Might as well keep going with it. I am losing it a bit after all, right? "Because I'm getting a little sick of your snide way of making the rest of us feel so unworthy."

Laney lays a hand on my arm. "Don't listen to her, Carmen. She's tired. She's married to a heart surgeon, you know, and they're never home." She squeezes.

"Right." I turn toward the refrigerator. Salad dressing. We need some for Carmen's veggies. Carmen clicks back toward the French doors.

I set the dressing on the table. "Do you think I'm losing it, Laney?"

"Maybe. Would that we could all lose it like that."

After Laney arranges the rest of the food, the kids file in, and Ronnie Legermin pushes his way through the crowd. I wish he wasn't so good-looking. His dark hair is richer than any color I ever applied in the salon, and his wide shoulders loom above slender hips. "I'm first. Get out of my way, folks!"

He shoves Will, who almost loses the platter of grilled meat.

"Hey!" I say.

Will looks at me with eyes that say, *Please, Mom. Don't.*

"Ladies first, Ronnie. Get back in the back of the line."

He stalks back, and soon the group of boys are laughing and pointing at me.

After setting the platter on the table, Will slinks up to his room.

Carmen claps her hands, her bracelets jingling, and gives out a list of at least ten instructions, ending with, "I just cleaned the bathroom, so you're all good to go."

That sneak!

A kid shouts, "Literally!"

Somebody, please, anybody, get me out of here.

Nicola loads two plates and disappears up the steps.

Jace arrives home after the crowd has filed away, all except Nicola, who's playing Super Smash Brothers with Will in the study. She's kicking his butt, and he's letting her with nary a clue. Jace throws his keys in a delft bowl placed on a half-moon table near the garage entry.

"How'd it go?"

"Good. They're almost all gone." I reach into the fridge for a V-8. "I'm going to run Nicola home in a while. She and Will are having a good time."

"Does he *like her* like her?"

"I think so." I hand him the drink.

"And do we approve?"

"Definitely."

THREE

An hour later, we drop Nicola off at that bustling city row house Laney makes a home by utilizing an enthusiastic palette on the walls and decent finds at Goodwill. Nicola, brilliant in math, receives a healthy scholarship to St. Matthews. Laney, baby on hip and another tugging on her T-shirt, invites us in for something to drink but is visibly relieved when we decline.

Her husband, Cade, slogs in from the kitchen, one of the twins, a boy named Reid, wrapped around his foot like a sniffling moon boot. "Thanks for bringing her home, guys." Cade peers with aquamarine eyes from a face pitted and scarred long ago by a youthful battle with acne. He's the same height as his wife, with a paunch thicker than the lenses of his glasses, and Laney loves him. Talk about an unstereotypical couple: a house painter/carpet layer and a woman with a doctorate together caring for a passel of children. He loves her more, though. There's always the one side of a couple who loves more. It's Cade in this case.

After the good-byes, we find ourselves lost in a crumbling downtown neighborhood. Jace fell asleep two seconds after I turned out of Laney's neighborhood in hopes that signs to the Jones Falls Expressway would appear. I still haven't figured out who loves who more in our case. I don't want to.

Jace's snore practically shreds the upholstery. He's so good-looking, and then this snore rips out. It's like Mickey Mouse cussing or something.

I should have brought Will. He wanted to come, but Jace and I spend so little time alone we suggested he watch a movie instead. So now he's asleep, and wow, what quality time this has turned out to be.

I pull over and nudge Jace. "Hey! Wake up!"

"What's the matter, hon?"

"Look. I got us lost."

He sits up. "Huh? How?"

"I've only been to the Petersons' once before."

"Do you have any idea where we are?"

"Last thing I remember is North Avenue."

"North Avenue? Why would you turn on North Avenue?"

I've got to admit, it's getting a little scary around here. "I was looking for Charles Street. I just sort of recall those wacky street-lights that line the road. But I think I turned the wrong way. So I went down a side street to turn around and bottomed out into this one-way street, and now I have no idea where we are."

"Okay. Pull into that gas station there and I'll get directions."

"It's got bars on the window. Let me drive to something else."

"Hezz . . ."

"Okay, okay."

Jace and I have switched male/female genes when it comes to get-ting directions. I am off the charts masculine, because really, if you drive on long enough, you're going to recognize something eventu-ally, aren't you? And I am the expert at taking long drives and find-ing my way back home again.

He hops out of the car, the anemic light from the awning over the gas pumps encouraging his light brown hair to turn a sickly sort of green, and yeah, look at how much more white glitters along his temples. Mercy, Jace! Getting to be an old man there!

A man saunters up to him in drawers with the crotch practically scraping the cracked pavement. He gestures in such a way that it seems he's offering something. Jace shakes his head and says, I think, that he just needs directions. He points over at our Suburban.

Okay, Jace, big mistake there.

"Hi, Mr. Drug Dealer, we're rich whiteys from the country just ripe for the picking!"

My scalp freezes as I watch the man, all of twenty-two, reach out and put his finger in Jace's face. Jace instinctively backs up. The man laughs, clapping his hands.

The radio is playing "Wake Me Up Before You Go Go."

I have two choices here.

Stay in the car. Jace would approve, wanting me to be safe; getting out would be a ten-regiment assault on his masculinity.

But he's a surgeon, not some tough guy.

He's brave every time he operates, but this is different, right?

Maybe if I just beep the horn. Or should I get out?

But before I can, he steals a glance my way, parallels his hand to the blacktop, and quickly slides it back and forth.

Okay. So stay put.

But I promised to stand beside him through thick and thin. I put my hand on the latch in readiness. My mouth dries out.

At least I can lower the music and roll down the window to hear what's going on, because like George Michael, I'm not planning on going solo either.

"I'm just looking for directions," Jace says.

"And I just want to see what you got to offer me for those same said directions."

"Are you threatening me?"

Man, his voice is really calm. Guess when you've stopped someone's heart with the full belief you'll start it back up again, this is mac 'n' cheese.

An inky Mercedes pulls up, blacked out and flat except for the chain motif around the license plate. Florida plates. Heaven help us, this is probably the big dude. Now the hair stands up at the back of my neck.

Cell phone! Cell phone! I'm an idiot! Cell phone!

I root through my purse as a very short, impeccably dressed man, his warm brown suit a shade lighter than his skin, slides out and walks over in a smooth, unhurried stride.

"Are you giving my man trouble here, man?"

Oh no.

I knew I should have cleaned out my purse. I thrash my hand around inside among the Noah's ark animals, feeling at least ten lipstick tubes, a can opener (a can opener?), loose change, hoping I'll hit the keypad and the phone will light up.

There.

And as I drop the phone into my palm, ready to dial, a new voice, female, pulls my eyes away from the phone and back to the scene.

"Ezekiel Campbell, you'd better leave that man alone!"

A woman taller than Jace strides into view, her nun's veil flying behind her.

The first guy holds up his hands. "Sister J, I was just talking to the man."

She turns to the Mercedes man. "You, you rascal, you get out of here."

"This is my corner, nun lady."

She doesn't flinch. "No. You'd *like* it to be your corner. I'm telling you, get in that dang sleazemobile and scram!"

"And if I don't?"

Her pale, wrinkled skin reddens, and she jerks her head toward Ezekiel. "Tell him what will happen, Zeke."

"She took in Knoxie Dulaney when his grandmother died. Practically raised him."

"Shoot."

"Yeah, man. You'd better get outta here."

The man holds a finger up to his lips.

Sister J points to him. "My corner. You got that?"

He steps into the car, shuts the door, and leans out the window. "How could a nun raise a devil like Knox Dulaney?" He drives off slowly, not in the scraping peel I expected.

"Go home, Zeke," the nun says. "You're better than this bull." And she kisses his cheek. She whispers something in his ear, and he shakes his head, smiles, then shuffles away.

I finally clamber out and Jace waves me over.

I run toward them. "Mercy! Are you okay?"

Jace whooshes out some relief.

I turn to the heroic nun. "Thank you so much!"

"No big deal." She waves a chapped, man-sized hand.

"Was that guy really dangerous?"

"Who, Zeke? No. He's just stuck. He's not such a rascal once he knows you. Now that other guy, I don't know who the heck he is. D'you see those Florida plates? His corner! His corner, my rear end!"

"Thank you, sister," Jace says. "I'd like to say I could have handled it, but that was way out of my league."

"Frish, but this place is out of most people's. Never mind that."

Frish?

"I'm Sister Jerusha."

"Jace Curridge."

"Heather."

Her speech hails from a more northerly location than Baltimore. Sounds like it grew up in the Bronx or someplace once upon a time, but I'm no expert on these things. And it kind of explains a nun using the word *bull*. Call me old-fashioned, but I didn't expect that.

Jace shoves his hands in his pockets. "Where did you come from? It seemed like you appeared from nowhere."

Sister Jerusha tilts her head to the left and points to a decrepit old hotel across the street. "There. I was almost home from visiting with one of my ex-clients when I saw what was going on. I was just about to go inside when I heard 'Wake Me Up Before You Go Go' coming out of your car. Frish, but I always loved that song."

Frish?

"Then I saw Zeke talkin' smack, so I waited a minute until that Florida boy pulled up. I may be sixty-five years old, but these boots are still made for walkin', if you know what I mean."

"You live there?" I ask.

"Run the place, doll."

A sign above the aluminum-framed glass doors reads "The . . . Hotel." The original name is covered over in electric blue paint.

"What do you do there?"

"What don't we do there is the better question. Meals—three a day. A nurse comes in once a week. Showers. Food pantry. Clothing center. Fourth floor we use for recovering addicts. Displaced women whether prostitutes or battered women—third floor. Families transitioning from homelessness—second floor. And then there's the big room where guys hang out during the day and have a meal or come in off the street on cold nights. We open that up when it hits below thirty-two degrees. Otherwise it's up to them to find shelter. City rules."

So she's given this spiel, what, at least a thousand times?

"Come on over and I'll fix you a cup of tea. I'm sure you could use something to calm your nerves after those thugs tried to put the make on you."

I look at Jace. It's late.

But he's all over it. "Good idea. If you don't mind."

"'Course not. Hold on, just let me tell Jaleel inside you're leaving your truck here for a little while."

She walks into the store.

Jace turns to me and blows out a whistle. "I pictured a bullet in my head more than once."

"I didn't know what to do. I was just about to dial 911 when the nun came running over."

"She's unbelievable, isn't she?"

"How tall do you think she is?"

"At least six-two."

"No wonder they listen to her."

The bell on the convenience store's door clangs against the glass. Sister Jerusha flies through like a bat. "It's all okay. Just leave that thing right there and follow me." Her glance slides along the Suburban. "Good Lord, that truck's a monster."

We cross the street, and she shoves a key into the lock of the double doors. "We lock up at nine in good weather. Plus, that's the curfew for our residents unless they have a work pass." She ushers us into a large room with pink-and-salmon-colored checkerboard floor tiling, strips of fluorescent overhead lighting, square tables, and chrome chairs. A long table stretches across the back of the room, presumably where the food is brought during meals, but I can't be sure. A desk sits perpendicular to the door, and an African-American man who must weigh four hundred pounds, with a head bigger than a Halloween pumpkin, a long thin nose, and one gold chain with a crucifix hanging around his forty-inch neck, says, "Good evening, Sistah J."

"Mo, this is . . . frish, but I already forgot your names, now, didn't I?"

Jace shakes his hand. "Jace Curridge. This is my wife, Heather."

Mo's hand swallows Jace's, and all I can think is, "Don't crush that hand! It makes lots of money!"

Pathetic but true.

Sister Jerusha tucks in a wisp of gray hair that escaped her veil. "What do you know about that rascal with the Florida plates? Big black muscle Mercedes?"

Mo leans back in the office chair, and I pray the springs hold. "Knoxie brought him on. Some distant cousin on his mother's side."

The hardened face of the nun softens for a second. "I don't like him."

"If he's working for Knoxie, he's not supposed to be likable."

"Have you seen Knox lately?"

Mo shakes his head. "Good riddance to bad rubbish."

"Don't talk about my godchild like that, doll."

"Godchild or not, Sister J, he deserves more than a name like that."

Sister Jerusha turns to us. "Knox went south. I tried, but what can you do? When his grandmother passed away, he was already fifteen. I was too little, too late."

Mo rolls his eyes. "You was a lot too late. He was already bad seed, and I should know." He taps the desk. "So you giving these folks the fifty-cent tour?"

"Heck yeah. It's payment for me saving their lives!" She laughs. Her smile blesses us with a loveliness previously unseen. Sister Jerusha was actually a beautiful woman in her day, I'll bet, very big but very beautiful. "Follow me. We'll start right here." She sweeps a hand around the room, empty except for two men in sweat suits filling out paperwork or something. Hard to tell.

"This room is a hodgepodge of scrap. The floor in these lovely designer shades came from the Dumpster at Color Tile, and the paint from the Dumpster at Lowe's."

Hmm. "Not a bad shade of blue."

"I know. Lucky for us."

"Is that right? You get a lot of stuff from Dumpsters?" Jace.

"You bet. We haven't been Dumpstering enough lately. But what can you do? I only have so much time in the twenty-four hours the good Lord gives me each day. You wouldn't believe the things you can find out by the malls, though. We're thinking of selling them on eBay to raise money for operational expenses."

She laughs. So do we.

"I'm serious, doll."

"What about government funding?" Jace asks.

She pushes through a swinging door, and we find ourselves in the kitchen. "Not a dime. We're privately funded." She is proud of that. "We're pretty much the last stop on the line for a lot of our clients."

Clients.

"Yep. We're here when all the principalities and powers have failed them and only Jesus'll do. God's Spirit keeps us humming."

The kitchen needs a good scrubbing. The stainless steel work-table is covered with crates of broccoli and some canned goods. The industrial stove . . . well, let's hope the Health Department doesn't inspect the place anytime soon.

"Kitchen. As I said, three meals a day, seven days a week. In the past ten years we've served over two million meals."

"Is that right?" Jace gazes at the Peg-Board holding colanders, spatulas, and other utensils. He's a gadget guy—can actually deep-fry a turkey if you please. "All that from right here?"

"The Christmas and Thanksgiving meals have become their own entity. Lots of volunteers during those times. And believe me, we'll take whatever we can get whenever we can get it. A lot of people doing what we do get all high and mighty about the holiday do-gooders. Not us! No sirree. If you show up, we'll put you to work, no questions asked."

"Where do you get that kind of money for food?" Jace.

"Almost all our food is donated. We don't buy anything except food for the holiday meals. Got to have turkey and dressing for the holiday meals—five thousand people we feed that day in four shifts. I make the stuffing myself. And I make a good stuffing. My mother's recipe, God rest her."

I readjust my purse on my shoulder. "Restaurants and stores donate?"

"You bet. It can get a little lean some days, and we have to do a lot of soup, crazy soup, and then some days there's caviar. It's a crazy way to run a place. Anyway"—she points to a doorway—"that's my office and my quarters back there. Nothing to sneeze over. Not even worth the steps it takes to get over there. Unless, of course, you're a collector of crucifixes like me or you have a thing for duct-taped recliners."

How could we resist a combination like that?

We head back out to the main room.

Depression hangs like an ocher fog. The plaster is so old the walls buckle and bubble and crack, and somehow sadness has oozed like black mold into those crevices to stay. I guess there's only so much hope, so much sweat that can keep it from taking over completely.

Sister J ambles over to a corner where a Bunn coffeemaker rests on a card table. "I'd marry this thing if I wasn't already married to Jesus." She laughs at her own joke. "It was donated by Jack Billing, who owns Baltimore Coffee. Boiling hot water anytime you want it. How about that tea?"

We nod and she plucks some chipped mugs from a nearby shelf, mine celebrating *200 Years! Bicentennial USA!* thirty years too late, and Jace's apparently a year-round tribute to Kwanzaa.

As she fixes our cups, she rambles on about all of the refurbishment that has taken place over the years, how the Hotel looks like Buckingham Palace compared to what it was when they held hands out front, praying to the Spirit for strength and declaring that redemption had come to this neighborhood. I had no idea nuns could be so spiritual. Who ever heard such talk?

Finally we sit down at one of the tables in the now-empty room.

"We're a Catholic Worker community."

"Dorothy Day," Jace.

She nods, brows raised. "You bet. You've heard of her?"

"Big time." He turns to me. "The Catholic Worker movement started in the Depression, hon."

"Some people call us leftist crazies because we hate war." Sister Jerusha barks out a laugh, then reaches into her pocket and draws out a white hankie she begins to fumble. "We call ourselves a ministry of presence. The first step is to be here, to be present. So anytime anybody wants to come in and just hang out with the clients in the main room, we relish that. You don't have to work your fingers to the bone in the kitchen, although we can always use an extra pair of hands. Our first step is to just be around."

"Interesting." Jace looks up at the ceiling. "Need some new tiles there."

"Heck, yeah. We need a new administrator if you ask me. I can only get so excited about facilities and fund-raising." She points to a set of steps to the right of where we came in. The newel post is long gone, but with some rubbed-down wooden carving and a bit of gingerbread, it's easy to tell it was once a hotel staircase. "I love being with the people. That's my thing, getting into their heads, seeing what's in their hearts, stealing them back from the devil. Ha! Anyway, upstairs it's like I told you. Getting late, so I won't take you up there."

"And you've been here ten years?" Jace asks.

"Eleven in October. We've also got the food pantry and clothing ministry like I said, around the corner in a warehouse. Plus, people can do laundry there. Got a phone there by Mo's desk for clients to use. We do a lot for the working poor too."

The working poor?

"Lot of 'em can't afford to install a phone line, so they can use this one. We try to provide those little things most people have learned to take for granted. Frish, but it's hard to get a good job if your clothes aren't clean, isn't it?"

"What about classes and job training?" Jace asks.

"Lots of that with the families in transition and our former street people upstairs. But as far as the homeless gang that comes in for meals most days, well, remember, we're the last stop on the line. We can only give them food and respect in exchange for a little bit of nothing. A lot of them don't want to be helped other than that, and God forbid we shove them aside because of it. A ministry of presence is what we do. I can't explain it any better than that."

I brighten. "And who knows what God might do in their lives in the future?"

Sister Jerusha shakes her head. "Oh, doll, I wish I had that kind of optimism left. Most of the downstairs folk die of overdoses or exposure or AIDS or whatnot. As I keep saying . . . last stop on the line. But somebody's got to be around for the least of the least."

"Thank you for the tour." Jace drains his cup, then stands up. "It's late, and we don't want to keep you."

"Thanks for coming over. I love showing people the place. And we can always use any help anybody's willing to give. Time is always of the most value. Money only goes so far."

She walks us to the door. A loud knock vibrates the aluminum frame. Sister Jerusha peers through the glass, shakes her head as she twists the bolt and opens the door.

A loud, shrill voice gushes over us like ice water.

"Sister J, I'm so sorry, I didn't mean to be late. I waited for the bus for over an hour."

"Don't lie to me, Krista. I can smell your breath. You know the rules."

She's seven months pregnant if she's a day.

"But I swear I'm telling the truth."

"Out. Back out there. Come back at eight for breakfast, and we'll talk then."

"Please don't send me out there."

"This is the fourth time, Krista." She turns to Mo. "Right, Mo? Four times."

"She's right. Now you know I can't let you by this desk, so come back in the morning."

Krista begins twisting a thread of expletives so foul even Jace raises a brow. Sister J and Mo remain like stone.

Mo stands to his feet. "Do I have to escort you out?"

Krista flips him the bird and backs out. "I ain't never coming back here. You love your rules more than you love people!" More cankered words and a jabbing finger at Mo. "You are no brother to me, sir!"

The door shuts her out.

We turn to face the pair of them. "Wow," I say.

"Will she be back?" Jace.

Mo sits back down. "Shoot, yeah. If not tomorrow, then the next day. They almost always come back. She's not herself right now. Krista's not all that bad when she's not strung out. In fact, she's downright sweet. You all be careful driving home."

As we swing through the door, I hear Sister Jerusha say to Mo, "Bread delivery will be a little late in the morning. Is the nurse coming?"

And we are already forgotten.

We practically run to the car, jump in, and press the lock button right away.

What a couple of milksops!

"Mercy, Jace!"

"Wow, some evening. Can you believe that place?"

"Can you believe you might have been shot?"

He turns the key in the ignition, the car engine humming a timely tune of departure. "I don't know. It all seems a little weird, like some contrived way Sister Jerusha gets volunteers. Wait for people to get lost, sic Ezekiel on them, and come to save the day so she can do a tour."

"Pretty much."

"Seriously, she's a whirlwind, isn't she?"

"I'm still reeling from all that energy." I turn in my seat to face him, adjusting the shoulder strap. "It's hard to believe one person can do so much."

"Right. I know exactly what you're saying." He pulls out of the gas station. Good-bye, Jaleel, who watches us from inside.

"And turning that girl back out on the street. I didn't understand that, Jace."

"Imagine trying to run a place like that and not have your rules mean something, though."

"Yeah, that's probably true. You know, we really should send them a donation, don't you think? Fix that ceiling, redo the plaster on the walls, put some decent shelving in the kitchen?"

"Big time."

We are quiet the rest of the way home, leaving the city behind and returning to the soft darkness of the hill over the lake where the only lights are those of the fireflies who've never seen Jaleel, Jerusha, Krista, or Mo, and probably never will.

Three days later we find ourselves at a large church inside the beltway, its campus spreading like jam over a twenty-acre plot. The band plays with perfection, its singers in coordinating outfits looking like they just came home from lunch at the club or a day at work downtown. Tasteful ficus trees dot the auditorium, spilling a few brown leaves on the understated beige carpet.

Everything is so perfect. Just so perfect.

Turning into the parking lot of Gibby's Restaurant, I say to my family, "Do you picture Jesus as perfectly coiffed or kinda messy?"

"Messy," Jace.

"Most definitely messy," Will.

"I'm kinda messy, at least on the inside. Is there a church out there where people can be messy?"

Jace pulls into a space near the back of the lot. "Everybody's messy, hon."

"Okay, then, Mr. Smarty-Pants. Is there a church out there where we can admit we're messy?"

"I'd like to think so."

Jace hates the church-shopping we're doing. But right now, at this point in my life, the thought of settling down with another bunch of Christians makes me want to scream. He wasn't tripping the light fantastic down the aisles either, if I remember correctly. It was such a big church, you see, the faithfuls working their fingers to nubbins so the other 75 percent could sit in the pews without feeling at all uncomfortable.

As far as I remember, the gospel isn't all marshmallows and cream. But who am I? Just another woman in Christendom who's trying to figure out why she feels so defeated all the time and is coming up with a long list of problems but a short list of answers.

Is it the church? Is it me? Is it Jesus?

We all go down for a nap, our bellies full of crab cakes, crispy fries, and a snappy coleslaw. But I do not sleep. I wait for Jace's ripping snore and tiptoe into Will's room. Yep, his nose-whistle assures me he's slumbering, dreams of Nicola probably sashaying across his pubescent brain.

Time for a drive. I resist the urge to drive by Gary and Mary's house. There's time for that tomorrow or the next day or the next. I just want to drive and find my little house with white rooms, white plates, and an 8 x 8 plot of lawn with white rocks in the flower beds and some angled Japanese shrubbery that points a jointy finger, saying, "Less is more, my friend. Beauty in simplicity is still lavish and full of grace."

Okay, maybe not.

An hour is all I safely own, so I turn right out of the driveway and head out on Jarrettsville Pike. So many whispering trees and staunch white fences, hay fields and horse pastures, still ponds and winding creeks. Hess Road beckons me onto its twists and turns, and before I even realize it or know quite how I got there, I am in the veterinarian's office parking lot and the Andrews's house rests in a puddle of shade from the oak trees surrounding its sides and back. And no one is home again.

FOUR

Well, at least summer throws most of Will's school and extracurricular activities into hibernation. We zip around like bees all year long, and now summer's arrived, no school play, no band practice, no Japanese. No. No. No. No art class. No fund-raisers and cleanup days at the school. No "cooking with kids" at the community college.

I love this.

Okay, except for swim team. That party's just getting started.

Lark calls. "Hey, Heather."

Lark is the closest thing I have to a best friend.

"Hey, Lark."

"Summer's begun. You ready?"

"Yeah. Pretty much."

"Bring Will down for lunch tomorrow. Leslie needs some fresh faces around here."

"How's your mother doing?"

"The cancer is progressing, unfortunately. Six months, they're telling us."

"Poor Leslie."

I can picture her waving a hand.

"Oh, you know her. She's not admitting anything is wrong. She hired a new housekeeper and is giving the poor person fits."

Yeah, they're loaded.

"Nobody can replace Prisma."

"Obviously. This is number five since Prisma moved. So you coming tomorrow or what?"

"Why not? We could use a drive down into the city."

"Good. See you around lunchtime. This new housekeeper's a great cook. Not that Mother appreciates it." Her voice changes, dripping with aged Southern honey. "'I'm sick of field greens, Larkspur. If everything's as bad as you all say, then please get me off this heart-smart stuff so I can enjoy myself to the bitter end.'"

"She's got a point, Lark."

"You may be right about that. See you around noon."

"We'll be there. Hey, who gets the Christmas stocking this year?"

"Don't know yet."

She's always embroidering a stocking. One a year. Intricate needle-work that leaves everybody guessing all year long who will be the lucky recipient.

Ha. Right. I wonder if it's for me.

Lark Summerville and I crossed paths a few years ago at a fund-raiser for her late father's charitable foundation, the Summerville Foundation. One of Jace's surgeon friends dragged us along. I experience a guilty pleasure at these sorts of engagements, I have to admit. I grew up staunchly in the lower realms of the middle class. Dad supported us in our little brick row house on Joppa Road in Towson where our neighbor transformed his small front yard into the formal garden of Versailles. I always knew what the male anatomy looked like, thanks to Mr. lo Fabro. But my dad's idea of a high time was a Colts game with buddies from work and dinner afterwards at Johnny Unitas's Golden Arm Restaurant.

She was trying to brush her crazy mane of kinky hair in the bath-room when I first saw her. I thought she was a child at first—she's that tiny. And as women sometimes do, we just hit it off, were laughing within thirty seconds and revealing our souls. I've always felt sorry for men because I don't believe that happens to them very often.

We ditched the fund-raiser and opted for tea at Starbucks, her treat.

I caught our reflection in the plate glass window of the storefront as we searched for a table outside in the summer air. With my height and weight next to hers, well, we'd have been the perfect choice for the casting director of *Of Mice and Men: A Female Review*.

Mercy! I was Lenny.

The tea was bitter yet weak, and I didn't care.

She pulled out her embroidery, that year's Christmas stocking, and we talked until Jace, after a frantic cell phone call, picked me up to go on home. Lark said, "Oh, lucky you. You get to go home with him. I get to go home to Mother."

I belt out a laugh as we travel down 695 toward Charles Street and the home Lark shares with Leslie, Leslie Strawbridge Summerville, a socialite's socialite in her day. That woman's royal bearing settles in a subtle cloud of expensive perfume around all who draw near, but according to Lark, she has mellowed a bit in her old age, or as Leslie herself calls it, her "dotage."

"What's funny?" Will asks. I tell him the story. Will likes to read. He gets literary references but fails to see how I could be Lenny under any circumstances. He likes the Beatles too.

"Does Miss Lark still play the organ, Mom?"

"No. She gave that up a few months ago. Had to because of her crazy schedule with her dad's charity."

Lark was the organist at St. Dominic's for years. She plays a mean organ. A raging river of an organ that will pull you downstream if you're not careful. How that little person can birth such resplendent sound from those childlike hands and feet is about as mystifying as a five-thousand-square-foot house on a quarter-acre lot. She rebelled against her parents' wealth and situation by impregnating herself via a wild boy from her posh set, running away from home to play keyboard with his rock band and then, after the divorce, running into the arms of the church.

I believe she looked at her music as God's open arms.

"Maybe she'll play something for you at the house." We fly under the overpass for York Road. I always fly places. I have to ease up on the gas pedal one of these days. Jace ribs me for the way I drive. And he's totally right. Not only do I drive too fast; I'm not really very good at it. I had two accidents in beauty school, one *not* my fault. Only the grace of God and an enervated guardian angel keep Will and me alive, and the other people on the road as well. When I see someone walking with a stroller alongside a busy road with no sidewalks, I want to yell, "Don't you know there are people like me on the road?"

I turn to Will; he points my gaze back to the road. "You glad school's out, bud?"

"Most definitely. I don't think my crotch could stand another month."

"What!" Oh, dear God. "What do you mean?"

"Wedgies, Mom."

"They give you wedgies?"

He just nods.

After what I sowed with Gary and Mary Andrews in school, I hoped to counteract any rotten crops that could be reaped by my own children. I volunteer every chance I get, show my face all the time like that bee that won't go away no matter how hard you bat the air.

"I'm sorry."

"I don't know what more I can do to get those kids to leave me alone."

"There's nothing you can do with kids like that, believe me."

"Were you bullied?"

"In the early grades."

"What happened after that?"

"Julia B. moved in. She liked me and she created a new regime."

"Oh. Were you one of the mean ones after that?"

"No," I lie.

"Phew. Good. I'd hate to think of my own mother like that. I think I'd lose all respect for you if you were once one of them."

Does Will suffer because of my sin? Does God say, "See how it feels to see someone you love ridiculed and ostracized?" He wouldn't do that to a good boy like my son, would He?

Maybe it's easier to ride past that house instead, begging for-giveness. From Gary and Mary and Will. And God. Again and again and again.

"Do you want to go to public school next year?"

He taps his fingers on his thigh. "No. They're jerks, Mom. One day they'll look back on what they've done, maybe when they've had their own kids, and they'll pay. I'm a big believer in justice if we only have a little patience."

"I'm sorry."

"And Nicola's cool. We're already planning to hang out all the time next year. She doesn't take anything from anybody. Especially Ronnie Legermin. He won't come near her!"

"That's good."

"Most definitely. Those guys have problems to begin with, Mom, if they keep having to reach down into another guy's drawers to make themselves feel better."

"Yeah, but it's your drawers." I really am going to talk to the prin-cipal about this.

Did I say I hated Ronnie Legermin?

We pull onto Greenway, a street in Guilford, one of Baltimore's old-money enclaves. Not that Lark's dad hailed from old money, but Leslie sure grew in a womb of privilege! Generations of money. Horse money, tobacco money, land money, trace-your-lineage-back-to-John-Smith money. Virginia money so old it hasn't had its own teeth for well over a century. Lark's dad, James Summerville, founded Baltimore Machinery Parts with a thousand dollars and his brain. Since he could never be old money on his own, he married it. And Leslie never let him forget it! Oh, that woman is a real stinker. But one of those lovable old stinkers who would drop everything to help you at first beck and call. Lark tells me she wasn't always this way.

In the three years Lark and I have been friends, Will and I have visited the house many times. Lark prefers rambling within the city limits, and the chauffeur—yes, chauffeur—would rather be gardening, so instead of inconveniencing him, she ends up catching the bus or a cab to most of her appointments. That's Lark in a nutshell.

We turn through the gate in the stone wall surrounding their city acre and pull up to the parking pad at the side of the house. Fashioned of local granite with an olive cast, the house on Greenway is one step away from a haunted manor house in which Mary Shelley would feel quite at home. Perhaps Percy as well. Talk about going against the flow, those two!

The door, slightly medieval and masculine with wrought iron hinges and a ringed latch, fools the first-time visitor about the innards of the house, and Lark once told me what I'd suspected to be true. Her father built the house before he met Leslie Strawbridge. She has never liked it and doesn't mind saying so. She calls it "my medieval monstrosity."

Inside, well, it holds everything you'd imagine a gracious Southern woman would deem worthy of her home. Impeccable. Expensive but not flamboyant like something you'd find in a casino or on the Trinity Broadcasting Network or, heaven help us all, in a *Yankee's* home. Tasteful reds, greens, and yellows, every stick of furniture an antique or handmade. No Pier 1 or Pottery Barn fare on Greenway. I doubt if Leslie has even heard of those lifestyle purveyors.

I yank on a cord leading to a bell mechanism housed somewhere in the stalwart facade. A Quasimodo bong shivers our eardrums. Leslie must hate that thing. As we wait, the sound of Charles Street traffic borne on the breeze of a waning morning caresses our eardrums. I've always loved the city for some reason.

Finally the door is jerked open, and there stands quite the most rough-and-tumble-looking man I've seen in a long time. Grizzled, he smiles, his missing left front tooth reminding me of the cook in a stereotypical western, only twice the size and with that Fu Manchu, a little more motorcycle around the edges. "Welcome!" And he bends at the waist in one of the most awkward bows I've ever witnessed firsthand. Come to think of it, I believe this is the only bow I've ever witnessed firsthand.

". . . Thanks . . . ?"

A voice calls from the stairway, and Leslie's slender feet in bone-colored Grasshoppers descend the runnered steps. "Lloyd! For goodness' sake, we don't bow around here. Who do you think we have visiting, the Archbishop of Canterbury? Just let them through the door, if you please."

Lloyd steps aside in his hiking boots. So this is the new housekeeper. I had pictured my grandmother or Hazel, the nutty housekeeper on the old sitcom I used to love as a tot. Mr. B.! Mr. B.!

Maybe I need a housekeeper.

"Hi, Mrs. Summerville." I hurry over and circle my arms around her bony shoulders. She smells like lemon balm today.

She kisses my cheek and pulls back. "I do enjoy a hug from you, Heather, and truth to tell, I'd rather visit with you than the Archbishop, but it's your boy I've been most looking forward to seeing."

All this in that buttered rum accent.

Will adores Leslie and throws himself into her arms. He accepts her warm embrace like a sort of tonic to the past year in school.

"Let me introduce Lloyd to you. Heather, this is Lloyd Harmon; Lloyd, meet Heather Curridge and her son, Will Curridge."

We shake hands.

"Lloyd started a couple of months ago. He thinks it's some kind of palace or something. You're not the first people he's bowed to like a darned footman."

Lloyd shrugs. "Sorry, Mrs. Summerville. I'm just a highway flagman at heart, I guess."

"But can he cook." She places a bumpy, simply manicured hand on his shoulder. "And we always watch *Wheel of Fortune* together, don't we? He's a whiz, I don't mind telling you!"

"So what's for lunch, Mr. Harmon?" Will asks Lloyd.

"Fresh salmon and asparagus with hollandaise. Wanna come help? I'll be grilling outside. And I'm just Lloyd."

"Okay. What are you marinating it in?" Will follows Lloyd back past the stairs, and I hear Lloyd respond, "No marinade per se, a spicy herb rub . . . ," and into the kitchen they fade, where they will become one in the nirvana of food preparation. Will has been out-cooking me since last Christmas.

Leslie tucks her arm through mine. "Why don't you come back out to the patio while we wait for Lark? She said she'll be down in a minute. Honestly, Flannery brought home a straightening iron and she's trying it out. I told her it would take more than a couple of min-utes to handle that head of hair, but"—she flutters her hand up in the air—"what does a silly old woman like me know about these modern beauty conveniences?"

Flannery is Lark's fabulously artistic twenty-seven-year-old daughter.

She leads me through the formal living room, where a fancifully carved organ—Lark's organ—looms in the shadows of abstinence, into the walnut-paneled family room complete with requisite plaid furniture a million years old. Although I could be wrong.

The brick patio supports a few new iron chaises, their celery green padding freshly placed. Oh, the colors, the life, the living going on before my eyes as birds bathe in the birdbath and a squirrel steals seeds from a birdfeeder across the lawn. I breathe in to the bottom of my lungs, believing with all my heart that the city fumes stop where their yard begins.

"Please have a seat."

I obey. For some reason, everybody obeys Leslie without ques-tion. As always, her clothing rests without pucker upon her slender frame: ivory pants and blouse, a light sweater in a heathery plum. Pearl jewelry and close-cut silver hair complete the flawless, classic senior-citizen ensemble. I'd hope to look as good at her age, but I don't look as good now!

"Now tell me how you've been."

"Heather!" Lark's voice streams through an open window upstairs. "I'm in the bathroom. How are you?" A hand waves from between the sashes.

"Fine!"

"I'll be down in a few!"

Leslie lays a hand on my knee. "So really, honey, how are you?"

Leslie owns the title to personal questioning with more certainty than her Bentley, which she refuses to drive nowadays, much preferring her granddaughter Flannery's old Toyota.

"Great. Good. Fine. Okay, I guess. Sometimes not so good. But fine. Really."

"Well, you've sold me on it." Leslie smirks, then crosses her legs on the chaise. "Oh, come now, Heather. Let's be honest enough to admit the truth, all right? I won't tell a soul. We're all playacting 80 percent of the time, aren't we?"

"What are we doing the other 20 percent?"

"We're either with someone very safe, or we're alone."

"But what if we're the unsafe ones?"

"Then you've got a far larger problem, honey."

Lloyd appears with a tray of iced tea, lemon and orange slices floating in the pitcher.

Leslie frowns. "Oranges! Lloyd, whoever told you to adulterate iced tea with oranges!"

"My mother did that until the day she died."

"Well, God rest her soul, then." Leslie picks up two glasses, hands one to me. "Bottoms up!"

Plain to see, Lloyd has already cracked the code to Leslie. He winks at me, and I thank him. I take a sip as he walks away. "This is pretty good if you ask me."

Leslie watches until the screen door shuts entirely. "It's ghastly, truth be told. But I'm not about to speak ill of the dead. Not at my age, anyway."

"Seems to me you've settled down, haven't you?"

Leslie wrinkles her nose. "I was a handful, certainly. Daddy relied on me quite a bit, Mother being the glorious drunk she was."

Mercy!

The dame waves it aside. "But I'm too old to worry about a woman like my mama. She's been dead too many years to lay the blame about much at her feet anymore."

The patio door slides open. Lark steps out. "Look!"

Leslie actually hops to her feet. "Goodness gracious, Larkspur. I don't . . . quite know what to say!"

"Isn't it pretty?"

In actuality, Lark looks like Cleopatra via shrink-ray. Did she really think straightening all that hair would make it lie flat and shiny?

Lark turns like a little girl in a swingy dress. "What do you think, Heather? Isn't it cute?"

"Well, it's certainly—"

"Holy mackerel, Miss Lark! What did you do to your hair?" Will emerges with a platter of raw salmon in one hand and tongs in the other.

Lark folds into laughter, then does the ninety-degree-angle Egyptian dance.

"Isn't it horrible?" Lark cries. "What was Flannery thinking?"

Leslie sits back down. "Thank heavens I didn't make a mess of that one."

A tension always seems to run like a fine thread between these two. It's my one beef with my friend. Doesn't she realize how wonderful it is to have a parent at all?

Lloyd grilled enough salmon to feed both of our families for two days. He divided up the spoils into Styrofoam take-home boxes.

"Wherever did you find those?" Leslie asks when he brings them to the table as we wrap up the feast with some hot drinks: tea for Lark and myself, coffee for Leslie and Will. I've never before seen Leslie Summerville embarrassed, but for some reason, the sight of those Styrofoam take-out boxes on her magnificent burled walnut dining table deepens the pink in her face.

"Costco, Mrs. Summerville."

"Oh, that Costco. I hate that place. It's the ghastliest store I've ever been in. In my day, shopping was a personal experience."

Lark rolls her eyes. "Mother, in your day, everybody came to you."

"And it was so much nicer that way."

Thirty minutes later, the two Summerville women wave us on. Leslie grabs Lark's hand and sags into her a bit as they turn and walk inside the house.

I start the car. "Four years ago they couldn't stand each other, Will. Now at least they don't crash on the rocks with every interaction."

"Maybe they both realize how little time they have left together."

"Let's hope so."

"Can we stop at Towson Art on the way home?" he asks.

"Sure." I take a right onto Charles Street. "I can't imagine having wealth like that."

"You'd never know Miss Lark was rich." Will pulls a small sketch-pad out of the glove compartment.

"No, not at all."

"Mrs. Summerville's a little bit what you'd expect." Next comes a pencil bag filled with drawing implements, his car bag. "But I like her!" Will rolls down his window a bit and spits his gum out. Dear Lord, please don't let it fly into someone else's car. "She's got great gams for an older gal."

I turn and look back at him despite my seventy-five-miles-per-hour travel speed. "Great gams?"

"Yep. I just call it like I see it."

Mercy! He would be fifteen now, wouldn't he? And she does have some great gams.

Still. "That Lloyd can really cook, though, can't he?" I jerk the wheel to the left, crossing two lanes to skid into the turn lane for Towson Boulevard at the last second.

Yes, I am *that* person.

Will draws a bold line with the side of his pencil point and he's nailed Leslie's jawline. "Most definitely."

I love him. As much as I love Jace and even God, I never realized that love like this existed until I had Will, and each year turns it into something so much deeper, I cannot begin to climb down into the well.

Knowing I wanted a dozen, God only blessed me with one. In a kingdom of children He might have given me, He was merciful enough to give me the prince.

I tell Will to clean his room before he watches TV.

"But you watched TV all the time growing up, Mom! You've even said so."

"I was a child of the '60s and '70s. We didn't know how bad it was for you."

"Please. I'll bet you watched at least four hours a day."

"Definitely. In the morning, after a soft-boiled egg on toast or cold cereal, I watched *The Little Rascals* with my father; after school I watched reruns of the old *Mickey Mouse Club*, *The Boys of the Western Sea*, *Speed Racer* via *The Captain Chesapeake Show*, and then *Gilligan's Island* came on before dinner."

"See? It's hardly fair, Mom."

"Wait, it gets better. By the time I made it to late elementary, *The Brady Bunch* came into the afternoon lineup. Then in the evenings, military comedies like *Gomer Pyle USMC* and *Hogan's Heroes* were on. I'd watch them with dessert, usually junket or 1-2-3 Jell-O. My dad always made dessert, believe it or not. He actually was a good cook."

"What about *McHale's Navy*?"

"*McHale's Navy* came on Saturdays. I hated *McHale's Navy*."

I still hate *McHale's Navy*. Everyone must hate it, surely.

"It is a little stupid." Will.

Come to think of it, I really didn't enjoy *Gomer Pyle* all that much either. I liked Jim Nabors, true, but that Sarge needed an enema or, at the very least, a big old Valium.

Will places his foot on the first of the steps leading upstairs from the kitchen. Yes, we have two staircases. Because I enjoy vacuuming steps so gosh darn much. The thought of that housekeeper returns.

"So what did Mrs. Summerville's husband do? What's that foundation you guys are always talking about?"

"He was a great humanitarian."

"In other words, he put his money where his mouth was?"

"Pretty much."

"Cool."

"Are you going to go back sometime to that hotel you and Dad found?"

"I don't know. Why?"

"I'd like to go if you do."

And he's gone. Will doesn't hang around for the pleasantries.

I decide to look up the Summerville Foundation online instead of just taking Lark's and NPR's word for it that it exists. An easy Google.

"Dedicated to bettering the human condition."

Yeah, I'm all for that. Who isn't?

But there's enough of that distrusting evangelical church lady in me that suspects any organization that uses such words. Are they . . . liberal?

I click away down the menu sidebar, suddenly privy to all sorts of poverty issues, wrongful imprisonment, torture, human trafficking, medical experimentation on street children.

Female genital mutilation and honor killing or mutilation by throwing acid.

And there's more.

Rape camps in California. Dear Lord, please. Some of these girls are only seven!

I shut my laptop.

And it had been such a nice day.

How does Lark do it? Day after day after day?

Well, her daughter's grown, for one thing. She's from money and has no financial concerns, for another. Lark doesn't live in the real world.

***

I wake Jace up in the middle of the night.

"You okay, Hezz?"

"I'm having a personal crisis. I think so, anyway."

"What is it, hon?"

"I saw Lark today and looked at the Summerville Foundation website. Lark does a lot to fight injustice, and I'm sitting here wondering how she does it."

"How do you think she does?" He's going to drift back at any second. I can tell.

"Her faith is very simple, I can tell you that."

His voice emerges thick. "Maybe because she's God's answer and she realizes that He has a plan for all these horrors, a plan of redemption and that He uses people to carry it out."

Maybe.

I focus on the lace edging of my pillowcase, such as I can see it in the darkness of the room.

"I've battled with God for years over the fact that if He is good, why do some children grow up without love, abused every day? Why do they pass it on when they know how bad it feels? Why are seven-year-old girls servicing dozens of men every day? And why do some of them, having lived such horrors, never even grow up at all, but are snuffed out before love has come?"

The snore begins. But I am not finished.

"I say I've battled," talking to the pillowcase. "I haven't really. I've only skirted around the issues because I'm scared that God will ask more of me than I feel like giving. Not so much time—I'm used to not having time. But my life, my comfort."

I look at my husband sleeping peacefully, a man strong in his faith who isn't cracked with fissures of doubt like I am, and I realize these are questions I must answer on my own. And I remember my father, a man who took a little girl without a mother and gave her the best childhood he could. He was my answer to the hand I was dealt.

FIVE

This morning I found I just couldn't stand my towels. So mismatched. Pretty, yes, but all those patterns and trims, everything from ribbons to ball fringe, unnerve me every time I open up the linen closets. I threw out everything that wasn't white. Well, actually, I packed it up for Goodwill.

All white towels. Peaceful, easy, uniform. Simple.

The good feeling lasted exactly nine minutes until I thought about the Summerville Foundation all over again. And I'll need to stop by the Linen Loft during swim team and fill in the gaps my purging left behind.

And I still haven't written that check to the Hotel.

So to cheer myself up, I bake a cake. Will took some misdelivered mail next door earlier in the day, and Jolly invited him for Salisbury steak and mashed potatoes—English peas from the garden too. Jace is working late, so I'm going straight for the dessert.

Pride may not be becoming, but I make the best cakes most people have ever eaten. No hunch on my part, this, because they tell me all the time. Why mine turn out so well using the same recipes as anybody else, however, is a topic for *Unsolved Mysteries*. Jace says I have "the gift of cake." Maybe he's right about that. It does seem a smidge supernatural, and they do look professional despite what Carmen thinks.

Sitting up in bed against the mound of pillows I bought from some ridiculous catalog, the same pillows that enable me to make the bed in five minutes as opposed to one, I dig into a slice of triple mocha cream cheese torte. Mercy, but this one turned out smoother than Lauren Bacall's voice. Cream cheese comforts your tongue like nothing else can. A cup of decaf coffee rests on my nightstand, the last rays of sunlight lying across the walnut surface. Can't do tea with chocolate.

When faced with the fact that seven-year-old Mexican girls are ending up in rape camps in Southern California, this all feels just a bit silly, not to mention full of denial, not to mention, and dare I say it to myself, downright sinful.

I set the cake aside and try to picture that little Mexican girl in the video clip online, try to remember Will at that age and the girls in his class. And as the tears begin to collect like salty mist, the phone rings.

The Mighty and All-Powerful Phone!

Its shrill alarm shatters the sun and the sweat and the tears. I may just be having a real moment with the Holy Spirit here, and what do I do?

"Hello?"

"Hi, Heather. It's Carmen."

"Hey, Carmen."

"Are you all right?"

I take a sip of decaf. "Oh yeah. Just allergies."

"Seems to be the worst season yet for allergies. And you know what they say about Maryland."

Everybody dubs her state as the worst allergy state in the U.S.

"Listen, Heather. I know you're really busy these days, so I went ahead and ordered professional bakery cakes for the welcome dinner for the new ninth graders and their families. Remember that new family that enrolled their child last year that owns that new bakery on Stevenson Lane? I thought we'd throw a nod their way, get them involved."

I pick at the Battenburg edging of my sheet. "Ah, they're doing it for free?"

"No. But they did offer a 10 percent discount." She clears her throat.

Okay, some things really are just funny.

"I hope you don't mind," she says.

"Of course not!" Of course so! My cake tastes better, I love doing it, and it's free. What is she thinking?

"They're delighted to help, of course," she says.

Help? No. It's a sale.

"I'm sure they are."

"Oh, good. I'm glad you're not offended."

"No. You know me, Carmen. Just glad to help out."

It's like the powder room to-do never happened! Or is this retribution?

My mask is pretty much superglued to my face right now. Mercy! I feel like I'm at church!

"I figured you'd be fine."

Just a thought, Carmen. Maybe a quick run-by first would have better served the overall grand scheme of your purposes. "Listen, Jace is due any minute. He had an emergency surgery this evening. I'd better go."

"Oh, sure. Thanks, Heather."

So I lounge here in my six-hundred-count Egyptian cotton sheets, look at my cake, and think about flour and eggs, cream cheese and chocolate, and it pretty much comes up short when compared to the doings of people like James Summerville, who not only wrote checks but rolled up his sleeves and dug ditches and spirited endangered human beings away in the night with no thought for his own safety. The stories Lark tells.

I call Lark.

"Hi, Heather!"

"Thanks for yesterday. It was really great."

"Mother loves it when you guys come. She feels a little useless in her dotage."

I bark out a laugh. "That woman in her dotage? What a crack-up. Hey, where are you going to church on Sunday?"

"I've been going to this small Catholic church. St. Peter Claver. I take a cab." Defiance weighs down her words.

"So are you jutting your chin out over the cab drive or the Catholicism?"

"Please. I was the organist at a Catholic church for years."

"The cab ride? Oh, Lark! Come on."

"Easy for you to say. You just get in your car and drive like a bat out of . . . you know where, Heather. And I have to fight to even get one foot out the door. Of course I'm defensive."

Lark lives inside her anxiety like other people would live inside their underwear if it were made of fiberglass insulation but somehow can't imagine wearing anything else.

"How about if I drive down and we go in the cab together?"

"Shoot, if you're going to drive all the way down here, you might as well just drive. I'm defensive, not stupid."

"What time should I be there?"

"Eight forty-five. Mass starts at nine thirty."

"Okay. I'll pick you up then."

"Why don't you want to go to your church?"

"We left a year ago, Lark. Too big, too busy, a lot of activity but not a lot of Jesus."

"How come you didn't tell me?"

"I'm still processing."

"Oh gosh, Heather, that sounds so jargony. Okay. I'll see you when you get here." And she clicks off.

When Lark's done talking, she's done.

I need to take a lesson from her.

SIX

My tea is pretty much fabulous. I normally go for spare, but today I started thinking about Gary and Mary and drizzled in I don't know how much honey.

"So what do you think?" I ask Lark. "Do you think I should take Will out of that school?"

"Beats me." Lark, looking out the car window, sips on the tea I brought her. To say her hair is downright massive this morning would be like saying Billy Graham did a little preaching. "I'd just start praying that something bad happens to Ronnie Legermin."

"Oh, Lark!"

"Seriously, though, Heather. Will is so gifted in art. What does that school have to offer him?"

"Not a whole lot."

"You might want to check out Baltimore's School of the Arts. I would have killed to go somewhere like that."

"It might give him an in when he applies to Maryland Institute."

"What about you? You know, I have no idea what your college major was, Heather."

"I didn't go to college."

Her brows raise, and I'd love to pluck those hamsters. "Really?"

"Why's that so surprising?"

"Well, you seem so, I don't know, prep school like."

"Nope, Joppa Road gal born to and raised by a plumber. I'm a trained stylist. I was pretty good. I was going to major in business and open my own place someday, but with Jace and medical school,

I found myself on a different path. I upped my hours in the salon instead of going to college." I pause for effect. "I sold Mary Kay, too."

"No way!"

"Yeah. I did well enough, and it was fun, sort of like being a cheerleader in high school long after the fact. It was cool while you were there, but a few years down the road it feels oddly embarrassing."

"Did you get the pink car?"

"No!"

"Sorry for not taking you up on the offer to do my hair. Why didn't you tell me you were trained?"

"It's a little embarrassing in my current circles."

"Oh please. All of our families started out humbly. Why that's such a crime I don't know. We all have to go to the bathroom and shave our underarms, you know?"

We are silent for a moment, sipping our drinks as we whiz by the brick row houses with their white granite stoops. Every once in a while the aroma of frying bacon from a restaurant wends its way into the car. Mercy, but I love bacon.

Lark taps her knee. "Well, maybe Mother doesn't have to shave her underarms." She turns toward me in a quick movement. "So if you could do anything you wanted to do, what would it be?"

"I don't know the answer to that question anymore."

"Look out!" she yells, and I swerve the truck back into my lane, waving with the zippy hand of apology to the pedestrian I almost plastered against my jumbo bumper.

Lark and I enter the small church, the smell of lemon wax high on the air. I've never been to a Catholic church before. The chapel seats perhaps seventy-five people, and there's no automatic projection screen that I can see. Some statuary, candles, a podium, and a broad table carved with Gothic arches embellish the sanctuary. The honey-hued wood, almost living despite the fact it was removed from its roots years ago, warms the sacred chamber where a trail of people dressed in white shirts with black skirts or pants now file into the choir loft. I watch with little expectation because, heaven help me, church hasn't done it for me for years. Yeah, there are a couple of praise songs that make me cry. But I used to look up at my pastor, who was ten years younger than me and light-years cooler, and most Sundays I heard, *Wok, wok, wokka wokka wok.* I was usually worrying about the turkey in the oven back home or wondering if everything was going okay in the Junior High Breakout Jam (yes, they actually called it that) where the kids learned all about the issues they were facing these days, not about being like Jesus, being wise, being loving, or, *gasp*, being meek.

That's right, folks, let's make it all about *you* and then go have pizza.

Still, I sent Will every week because I was too lazy and maybe a little too overwhelmed to take his spiritual education into my own hands.

Lark leads me to a back pew on the far left near a window with St. Francis of Assisi glowing in stained glass.

I sit in a rainbow glow pulsating through the window at my left, and I'm wondering who Peter Claver was and why he was canonized, and I'm hearing this congregation, mostly African-American, sing—

> *Lamb of God, you taketh away the sins of the world;*
> *Have mercy on us.*
> *Lamb of God, you taketh away the sins of the world;*
> *Have mercy on us.*
> *Risen Lord, you taketh away the sins of the world;*
> *Grant us peace.*

They draw out the word *grant*, rising upward on the scale, and the rest follows in a glorious crescendo until the word *peace* is sustained and resolved in a note of stunning power when sung from the lips of those around me and the choir in front of me, who all look upon Jesus as the suffering servant and take comfort from His birth in obscurity, His death on the cruel cross, and all of the poor wanderings, with no place to rest His head, that happened in between.

I watch and listen with expectation, caught up in the reverent hush that fills the sanctuary.

The sanctuary.

Oh, so that's why they call it that.

I was taught mostly to hope in the power of Christ's resurrection and glorification. Those are wonderful doctrines, but they hold little meaning if He didn't dirty His hands and feet, didn't get sick, didn't cry, didn't long to scream in pain and frustration but couldn't, not with the eyes of His children looking to Him to show them the way. He has grace on us because He gave Himself little.

Father Norman talks about what it means to be a peacemaker, and the concept is so new. A peacemaker? What about "Onward, Christian Soldiers"? Aren't we at war with those who oppose God? Put on the armor and all that?

"Jesus never once lifted his hand against the body of a living soul," the young black priest says, his skin smooth, his hands moving in punctuation. "My brothers and my sisters, we may be pressed, persecuted, and cast down, but only one Man, one Man, showed us the holy response. And the Lord Jesus Christ is all we have to go on.

"Pressed . . . but not crushed.

"Persecuted . . . not abandoned.

"Cast down . . . but not destroyed."

Amens bless his words.

Lark leans toward me. "It's a Baptist Catholic church."

"I love it."

And then we recite the creed and agree that someday Jesus will come again. But we are united in more than these beliefs. I'm not exactly sure what it might be. But that knowledge is newly secure.

I remember Sister Jerusha.

Jace and I lounge by the pool on the new furniture he still can't get over I bought. Will and Nicola swim in the pool, doing handstands, seeing how long the other can hold their breath. Her black hair contrasts with his hemp hair, her olive skin with his cream, and he's falling for her, dear Lord, I can see that a mile away.

"Jace, what do you think Jesus really meant when He said, 'Deny yourself, take up your cross and follow me?'"

"Jesus never minced words, did He?"

"That kinda bugs me about Him."

"I'm sure His contemporaries felt the same way."

"What does it mean to follow Jesus? Surely it means to act like He acted, walk where He walked, and love like He loved. But that seems like an extremely tall order, doesn't it?"

"Yeah, it does. It really does. I can't help but think of Sister Jerusha."

"Me either. I'm going to send a donation tomorrow."

"You do that." He looks down at his book and repeats in a whisper, "Yes, you do that." A minute later, he sets his book aside, and soon after I hear his car wind down the drive. Maybe I'm not the only one with a twisty life right now.

Man, I wish God wasn't starting to shake us up like this. Wouldn't it just be easier to care about stuff like dinnerware, golf, school uniforms, and getting to that new restaurant that just opened?

I fall into bed with no piece of cake at the ready. Nobody wants my cake anyway. "Oh no, mine's not good enough anymore, thank you, Carmen."

Mercy, these sheets feel good, all smooth and clean. And I just shaved my legs today too.

Jace sets down his Tozer book. He's a huge Tozer fan. Tozer all the time. He worships Tozer almost as much as those intelligentsia folks worship C. S. Lewis, like he's another incarnation or something. "What's that, hon?"

"Nothing. Just thinking about the cake for the freshman welcome dinner at school."

"As if you don't have better things to do with your time." He picks the book up again and settles his reading glasses on his nose. "Like buy more stuff."

"I'm sorry about the patio furniture. But those people really needed it."

"I'm not questioning your motives, Hezzie. I don't mind helping people, you know that. But where does it all end? I'm working as hard as I can as it is."

"Is this about the tennis court?"

"Partly. I have dreams, hon."

"We're not enough?" Okay, so that wasn't fair. And it was really lame. I hope he just ignores that, because he should.

"I don't want to talk about it right now. I've got two surgeries tomorrow, and when we argue I can't sleep."

"But this is important."

"Yes. And so is the money those surgeries will bring in. Much too important, if you want my opinion."

I want to tell him I'll cancel the order for the tennis court. But I can't yet.

I lean over and pluck *An American Anthology of Poetry* off my nightstand. We read in silence for a while.

He lays down his book. "You know, it's okay if you want to do something for yourself now, Hezz."

"What do you mean?"

"Maybe you need a bigger purpose?"

"What if I like things the way they are?"

"Then that's good."

"Right?"

"Right, Heather. Right."

"Just get back to Reverend Tozer, Jace."

"I don't know. You probably wouldn't like what he has to say."

Nope. I probably wouldn't.

Five more minutes go by and I'm reading some Poe; he lays his book down again. "Do you ever think your spending habits come from a lack of direction? I mean, your heart breaks over those websites and TV shows, and all you can think to do is write a check. Don't you want more?"

"You know, you're starting to bug me."

"Just food for thought, hon."

Five more minutes; a little Longfellow.

I lay my book down. "I'm sorry, Jace, about your dreams going unfulfilled."

"And yours haven't?"

"That's true, but I guess I'm used to taking care of things here, worrying about Will and you. I don't even know what those dreams are anymore. I used to think it was the salon. But now, well, I really could start one up, we can afford it, and I'm smart enough to get it running on a profit in the first year. I actually was thinking maybe when Will graduates from high school, I could do it. But now Sister Jerusha and James Summerville and Lark are throwing a big fat monkey wrench into my plans."

"You never told me you were thinking about opening up a salon."

"I know. Can you imagine? One of the area's leading cardiac surgeons married to a salon owner?"

He sits up. "You don't think I'd think that, do you?"

"No. But everybody else would."

"Oh, Heather. My gosh. I never realized."

"So yes, I'm trying to keep up appearances, I admit it. But please at least admit there's every reason why I should."

I cannot believe I'm throwing this back on him, like it's so uncomplicated, like he isn't partially right that I'm a bored suburbanite with no greater purpose than to make my life look like an episode of *Martha Stewart*.

He peels off his reading glasses. "Who convinced you you had nothing to offer in and of yourself? That you needed all this to make yourself worthy? Please tell me it wasn't me, hon."

"No, Jace. Never, never you."

"A tennis court isn't going to make you the picture-perfect country club lady."

"I know."

"In fact, if we have a tennis court and a pool, why do we need to be members in the first place?"

"Beats me."

"Right. We've got to figure something else out, Heather. I can't keep working these hours; you can't keep up this Jonesin' stuff, because at the end of the day, we're both still miserable even though we, quote, have it all."

"I know," I whisper.

He lies back down.

"What are your dreams, Jace?"

"Not tonight, hon. I've really got to get some sleep."

If that isn't the male version of "Not tonight—I have a headache," I don't know what is.

At 3:00 a.m. his pager beeps. He quietly pads downstairs to call the hospital. I follow him.

An emergency surgery. The lady he did a bypass on three days ago went into cardiac arrest. "I'm going to have to crack her back open, I think."

"Poor thing."

And three minutes later he's zipping down the driveway.

SEVEN

I dropped Will off at swim team practice and didn't feel like going back home, so I'm wandering down the aisles of T.J.Maxx, where a fabulous white sale has drawn in the bees of the cul-de-sacs in search of new looks for their bedrooms, baths, and kitchens. The prices are rock-bottom, folks. I fill up the cart with white bath towels, face towels, and washcloths, then head down the sheeting aisle.

Oh, why not? I'm tired of those brightly colored comforters in the spare rooms, and I know Sister J would appreciate them more than I do. One room holds two sets of twin beds, the other a queen. Today I'm laying aside the boldness of greens, reds, and golds and going for white down comforters and sheets so pure and crisp you'd think God sent them down like manna while you were asleep.

I load up another cart, then the car. Jace never goes into those rooms.

I feel like I'm going to throw up. I could take these things back right now.

But I don't.

Before I pick up Will, I drive by the old house on Joppa Road. The Versailles garden still anchors the block, and my old neighbor bends down onto his knees to plant . . . looks like impatiens . . . in a shady spot near the front steps. Next door, our house hides behind overgrown shrubbery and drawn blinds guarded from the outside by the same shutters, but now they shirk beneath peeling layers of black paint.

Some things change. Some things don't.

We pull up into the driveway. He's home!

I tiptoe in, arms loaded, and hurry up the stairs, dumping my booty into the closets, already thinking I've got to get the steaks marinating. I pause by his study door, cracked open an inch or two. His bass voice carries.

"Yes, Bonnie, I'm definitely interested, but I have more than a few details to work out here. It's something I miss, I can tell you that. I've never forgotten the ship."

Bonnie Reynolds, his old friend from the hospital ship, is apparently on the other end of the line. She has kept up with medical missions, something Jace did before he started at Johns Hopkins.

He didn't go to med school until he was twenty-six. After he graduated from college and earned his RN, he traveled around, worked on a Mercy Ship, and saw the world. He realized he wanted to be a physician, so he came back and I met him the summer just before he began.

"It's going fine. I enjoy surgery, but the lifestyle is eating me alive. I never saw this as my life. I feel like I'm living somebody else's life."

His dream.

"Heather's fine. She's really involved at Will's school and keeping up appearances here at the house."

That wasn't nice.

"But I can't blame her. She sacrificed for so many years for me. I told her she needs to start doing things for her own sake, but I don't know if she can, or if she even knows what that is."

Bonnie's an old friend and a dear woman. I guess he has always confided in her. She's also happily married, so no worry there. Still, I feel an itch of betrayal at the base of my brain.

"You're right about that. How can I pull her away from all this?

She and her dad just scraped by. Her things give her great comfort. That's definitely part of it."

It's true.

"I'll get back to you about Chicago. I just don't know how to tell Heather about all this. I almost did last night, but I just couldn't."

He stands up. I back away from sight but continue listening.

"I know, I know, Bonnie. Just pray for me, okay?"

Jace didn't want this life we have—all the stuff, the cars, the big house. It was all me, Heather Reeves, trying to get out of that little Towson row house for good, trying to run away from the life she really deserved.

All is still. My eyes opened rather suddenly and I felt the slick of mucus and a raw throat. Darn these allergies. I tiptoe to the bathroom, fumble in the dark for the Benadryl, and try my best to turn on the water quietly.

It sounds like Niagara Falls.

I swallow the pills and pad into Will's room, a testament to the fact that he has always been no frills. Dark blue walls surround a platform bed, a dresser, and a desk with matching hutch. On the walls hang his artwork through the years in craft store plastic frames. Simplicity and neatness, however, do not go hand in hand. I move aside some books and a pair of sweats to sit down next to his sleeping form on the bed.

You're something, bud.

I lay my hand upon the blanket resting atop his thigh, and he feels so warm and substantial underneath. So much to learn, so much to learn. He breathes, a gentle puff escaping his lips on the exhale.

I hope he won't get waylaid like we did. We owe it to him to show him there's more to life, but what is it?

What are we doing? Have we really drifted so far off course? We have it all, don't we? We get along, live comfortably. But what's it all really for in the long run?

And still, from here in my strawberry fields, I dream about that little shop every so often. I can smell the heather. Jace dreams too, of parched plains and dying people.

"Hezz?" Jace stands at the doorway. "Are you all right?"

"Yeah. Just thinking about things."

"Want a cup of tea?"

"What time is it?"

"Five thirty."

I stand up and cross the room. "Mercy, I thought it was a lot earlier. Yeah, tea would be nice."

"Why don't you go ahead and jump in the shower first this morning, and I'll fix breakfast."

A nice turnabout. I love that he never takes our arguments with him into the next day.

Ten minutes later, my hair still wrapped up in a towel, I sit down at the breakfast table. Jace's scrambled eggs enjoy their own renown. He overdoes it on the cheese, which is why they're so delicious. I sip my tea, steeped and black.

"You know, Jace, I think this is one of my two favorite moments of the day."

"The first sip of tea, huh? What's the other?"

"Sliding in between the sheets at night."

"And all the in-between?"

Mercy, that prickles.

I lean back to the kitchen desk and grab the handout from yesterday's service at St. Peter Claver. "Look at this, Jace. Look at all this church does to help people."

He sits down and takes the bulletin out of my hand. He holds it way out and his eyes scan the activities: crisis pregnancy clinic, food bank, mentoring, after-school tutoring, to name a few.

He grabs my hand, his eyes burning.

"I miss the hospital ship, Hezz. There was something so stimulating about that kind of environment. I felt closer to God there than I ever have anywhere else."

"I know."

"We were of single purpose, really committed to the suffering and to the gospel. I don't know if God has that kind of life charted out for everyone, but man, I miss that kind of hard-core commitment."

"We tend to fit the gospel into our lives and not our lives into the gospel, Jace."

"Right. We sure do." He lets go of my hand and picks up his toast. "That's what we've done, isn't it?"

I nod.

We eat for a bit and I feel so married. Those moments hit me every so often when I realize that I'd do anything for this man.

"Jace?"

"Yes, hon."

"Would things be better if we just settled down at a new church? Maybe that's the reason life feels so confusing."

"If the answer was that easy, the church would be saving the world."

"What's going wrong?"

"We've sold our souls by selling our time to the highest bidder."

I look around me, copper pots, soapstone counters, high-end furniture, and I know he's exactly right.

"This place is a far cry from the Hotel, isn't it?"

Jace nods. "This place isn't real, Heather. You know that, don't you?"

"I think I'm starting to figure it out."

I decide to give him a chance to talk about Bonnie. "I got a support letter from Bonnie awhile back. How's she doing?"

"Well, she and Rob are doing really well." He looks at the clock above the doorway. "Hey, I'd better get a move on. I've got to make early rounds."

EIGHT

Jolly's wife, Helen, collected dolls. Dolls in flapper dresses, tuxedos, Southern belle gowns, gowns with bustles, gowns with shawls, gowns with matching coats, hats, gloves, and parasols. Dolls looking through painted-on eyes or realistic glass orbs. And some of them are the most mutated-looking bits of porcelain and wax and plastic I've ever seen. Horror movie prop people, if they realized what a gold mine sat here on the bonnie banks of Loch Raven, would be knocking down Jolly's door.

Oh, but Helen. With her gleaming coffee-bean skin and her tight battleship gray curls, her smiling garnet mouth—well, you never wanted to leave her kitchen table. Especially when she made scalloped potatoes, fried fish, and biscuits. And her lasagna made you almost want to give up on life because it just had to be all downhill from there.

The walk to Jolly's house feels like an enchanted step back in time. Years ago, the daughter of the MacFees, the family who built our original house, and Jolly's grandmother convinced their fathers to lay down a stone path that meanders close to the drop-off down to the waters of Loch Raven so they could easily get to each other's house, even on rainy days. For some reason, though several families have come and gone since the days of the MacFees at the turn of the century, we've all kept up the path, kept the slate pavers clear. We even planted moss in between the stones several years ago. Several telltale signs of romance festoon the walk. I pass maple trees with initials carved into their trunks. A squat concrete bench that's now crumbling but which no one can find the heart to remove and a line of honeysuckle bushes that perfume the humid air surely supported a marriage proposal or two. A muscled wisteria vine that spills its morning-sky purple over the banks undoubtedly witnessed its share of stolen kisses.

I wanted to live right here all of my life. The waters of Loch Raven hold a great deal of mystique for me, a girl who grew up with a chain-link fence separating the concrete patio from the concrete alleyway behind the house. And I'd be lying if I didn't say the multi-gabled stone house hardly looks like it belongs to someone like me—someone who walked to school with the other kids wearing clothes from Two Guys, someone who vacationed for a week every summer on the Magothy River in a small sea-green bungalow with a rotting pier and a rowboat even my father couldn't propel in a straight line.

The euphoria lasted about two years from the time we moved in.

Jace is from a "better" family, to use the adjective in the most presumptuous of vernacular. But for some reason, he never seemed to notice that. And certainly they give the chintziest Christmas gifts I've ever seen. Give me Dad the Plumber any day, who saved up all year for a rousing buyout of Toys "R" Us. The fact that I laugh with Jace and reach for his hand is, he said, "something I never knew I needed so badly, and something I'd never want to live without again."

Jace's family belongs here on the shores of Loch Raven, but they're still tucked down in Hampton, a cushy late-'50s neighborhood that was *the* place for rich city folks moving out to the county. They still do martinis at five.

I push through Helen's rose garden and skirt the grape arbor.

Jolly is the last farming holdout in the area. His house sits back from the cliff. A real beauty—its Palladian windows line the front, and several grand chimneys poke through the slate roof for the many fireplaces inside. But as Jolly says, "It's just a big old farmhouse, you know."

I need people like Jolly speaking into my life with their actions, particularly actions like having the same sofa for the past thirty years or so.

He planted anyway this year, although he threatened not to when Helen died. We stood by Helen's grave and he said, "I do believe the life has gone right out of me." But Jolly not planting is like me not making cakes. It's simply what we do.

I open the porch screen door on the side of the house, cross the indoor-outdoor carpet, then rap on the kitchen door Helen painted a parrot green a couple of years ago.

The door swings open, and there he stands with eyes redder than the potted geranium he placed by the porch. He clears his throat and smoothes a hand over his hair, thinned out and looking as soft as a closely sheared sheep. "Come on in, Heather."

"You been crying?"

"Appears so."

I step into the kitchen that's so Helen. Pink walls and gray countertops complement pictures of rose bowers and gardens. A large square table with a white lace cloth covered by a sheet of clear plastic dominates the center of the room.

Jolly scratches a bristly, caramel-colored cheek. "Coffee?"

I pull out a chair. "You got some made?"

"Nope. But I was planning on making some sometime today."

He wasn't. "That's fine." He needs the coffee or at the very least something do to while I take up space in his echoing kitchen.

He turns on the faucet and half fills an aluminum pot with water. I feel the hollowness in his heart as the water smacks the cavern of the old coffee pot. I can't imagine losing Jace, something I don't take for granted, believe me. Doctors die younger, you know, the irony of which never escapes me.

Everything appears the same as the day Helen left it all to go to the hospital for routine surgery and ended up having a massive stroke on the operating table. Scary the way that happens. But Helen herself breathed life into her crazy possessions and even the very air in this old home. When Helen was alive, it just felt loved and taken for granted, haphazard and clean, a reflection of the lady who was a special education teacher for years and years.

They never had children, and I never asked why. With Helen gone, I doubt I'll ever know.

"Jolly, did your family build this house?"

"No. The original family fell on hard times after the war, and so my great-granddaddy bought it real cheap—after he'd been freed a good while. Grandpop Mercer had the Midas touch."

I reach for the *Field and Stream* sitting on the table next to the place he's already set for his next meal, coffee cup looking down in its saucer. "You getting your fishing license soon?"

"Yep. Even Helen's death can't stop me from doing that."

"She's probably jealous she can't go with you!"

He nods. "Yep, you're right there. She was a mighty fine fly fisherman."

"Jace said she was sheer poetry."

"Think Jace'll want to go out on the Gunpowder soon?"

"Definitely. So what are you going to do today?"

Jolly spoons some instant crystals into a couple of coffee cups. Ah, well.

"Jolly, you got a tea bag?"

"Yep, sure do. Want that instead?"

"If you don't mind."

"'Course not. Anyways, I'm going to work my garden and do a lot of mowing."

"Will can come over and help if you'd like. It's summer now, and he needs something more to do than play video games and swim."

"Like that boy. Sure. Send him on over."

He pours the hot water over the tea bag and the coffee crystals. Then he looks up at me. "I'm trying to keep on going, Heather."

"I know."

I take a picture of his face, storing in my mind that look of pain mixed with a somewhat hopeless determination. I love the lines of his face, the vertical folds of his whiskery skin, the droopy hazel eyes so different these days. I wish he wasn't sad. But with the life of love he lived, how could he be anything else? And I surely wouldn't want *that* taken away from him.

He blinks, then taps the tabletop. "But some days . . . well, you of all people know that Helen and I were a real pair."

"I do." Rarely did just one of them show up on our doorstep. If

Helen canned some beans, Jolly helped deliver. If Jolly thought some corn shocks might be nice to decorate for autumn, Helen carried over a pumpkin as well.

"Sure. Send the boy on over. Life has gotten a tad dull."

He sits down catty-corner from me. "On a good note, though, I've been selected to go to art school."

"Really?"

He pulls out a folded-up newspaper. "Look here. If I can draw this, I can go to this art school, they said." He winks. "I sent it in and they accepted me, surprise, surprise."

I take the paper. "Hmm. Looks like it could be fun."

"Why not? What else have I got to do?"

"Let me know how it goes. Will can help you, you know. He loves to draw."

Jolly winks again and points to the wall surrounding the now-defunct kitchen fireplace. Pictures Will taped up in a slapdash manner surround the chimney. "I gathered that a good bit ago."

We slurp our beverages in mostly silence—a little talk here, a little talk there, and despite the freakish dolls in the other room, the peace that Helen always brought to any situation still remains here in the old house.

"I sure did like the way she canned peaches, Jolly."

"She did a good job of it, didn't she? Helen never did much halfway, though."

"No, she sure didn't." My gaze slips over to the dolls in the other room.

"You know she bought the dolls she felt sorry for."

"I never knew that, Jolly."

"No, most folks didn't."

I want to hug him to me, but I can't make Jolly a project. Like I need one more thing to do. But I do enjoy sitting with him. How could a person not? Jolly is like your favorite chair. His 1930s existence makes my soul yearn: tending his garden, talking to the boys down at the old store on Jarrettsville Pike, the last vestige of Loch Raven in the old days before people like us began buying up the place.

394 @ QUAKER SUMMER

It seems like people in my parents' generation knew how to keep from overloading themselves. Or maybe they just didn't complain about it like we do. Haven't figured out which.

Jace calls me on my cell during my walk back home. "I was just on our bank account on the Internet. Five hundred dollars at T.J.Maxx, Hezz? Are you kidding me?"

"I'm sorry."

"Right. And here I thought our talk was a breakthrough. Man, Heather!"

"I said I was sorry, Jace."

"Maybe you should have thought *Sorry* before you walked into that store. Shoot, I'm being paged. I won't be home until late."

I slide some ground beef out of the freezer and lay it to thaw on a paper towel on the counter. My hands shake. Jace never gets mad like that. I hope it will all be blown over by the time he gets home.

Laney had her baby a few weeks early, and Will and I are going to deliver a meal. If her kids grow up to be just as nice as their mother, well, the world will be that much closer to what it should be. And isn't that important, God? To be around and raise decent children in a safe and loving environment?

Okay, so I'm crying and crying. I shouldn't turn on the TV this late at night, but I just couldn't sleep, and now an infomercial about what I can do to fight starvation in Africa is about to claw my heart right out of my chest.

I pull out my laptop, hop on the organization's website, and fill out a monthly pledge to help one child get enough food, clothing, and even schooling to hopefully grow up.

I'm feeling rather burdened, to use the church vernacular.

I bought the cutest outfit for a black-tie fund-raiser we attended tonight for the Make-A-Wish Foundation. All black with a touch of sparkle, it shaved off at least ten of my extra pounds. I'd just had my hair colored and styled it to look tasteful yet fancy. I try not to be overly concerned about my outward appearance to the point of obsessing, but you know when you've raised your personal bar. And believe me, church women can be so utterly obsessed by outward appearance it makes me want to just get old and be done with it. Maybe I should let all the gray hang out. My earlier years still haunt me, reminding me of how I never really fit in no matter how much I did, and following me to the clothing store all the time.

As a stylist, I could have worn all black, all the time.

My favorite rationale for excess Sunday fussiness is, "Well, I get dressed up and try to look my best on Sundays to give my best to God."

Jace, who was back to his old self when he came home last night, tied the bow tie for his tuxedo. "You look distressed."

"Ah, my. God was so impressed I had matching pumps and purse to worship Him, I'm sure. And when I sang "Shout to the Lord," He listened to my praise more than the poor schmoe up in the balcony with secondhand shoes, mismatched socks, and heaven help us all, faded blue jeans."

"You look beautiful, hon. A new outfit?"

"Yeah. It's new." I couldn't lie, now, could I?

"Pretty."

It's the guilt talking. I know he feels bad for yelling at me.

So I traipsed down the steps in my pristine high heels, smelling so fresh after a midafternoon shower, a very rare happening unless we're going out on the town.

"Whoa, Mom!" said Will. "Lookin' pretty good in that new dress!"

"Thanks, bud."

"Where'd you get it?"

"Nordstrom. And not the Rack either."

"Whoa."

Jace came down looking his typical dashing, easy self, the creep. He kissed my cheek. "I'm sorry." I tucked my arm through his and pulled him into the formal living room. "I dropped six hundred bucks between the dress, the shoes, the purse, the special bra, and the trip to the hair salon."

"Oh, Hezzie."

"At the time I rationalized it in a most stunning fashion. Ready for this? *Well, we don't have car payments. This is about the same amount as a car payment.* I'm sorry, Jace. I feel so out of control."

Jace, as usual, put his arm around me and didn't say a word. I knew what he was thinking, how he felt, how he feels. Can he not trust me with the truth?

"Aren't you mad?"

"Let's not talk about it. Let's just go and have a good time."

Which being interpreted means: I can't believe you did that, Heather. When will enough ever be enough? Do you even possess an enough?

And now here I sit in front of the TV in the family room at 3:00 a.m., eating New York Super Fudge Chunk ice cream, and if I figure it up right, everything I spent so I could look good and go give money to support a charity could, by my calculations, feed, clothe, and educate a child in Africa for almost two years.

Argh! Who wants to think stuff like this? I'm too busy. And we do enough, don't we? If I added up all the hours I worked for the church all those years, and that means working for God, I'm more than covered.

Absolutely more than covered.

I pick up the remote and click off the TV. Yes, enough is enough. I'm only one woman. I'll send off a check tomorrow. It's more than a lot of people would do.

"It's not your money we need. We need you. A ministry of presence is what we do here."

Oh, shut up, Sister Jerusha.

NINE

So I thought we'd try some smells and bells, as they say. We went to the early service at a little Episcopal chapel, stone with red doors and wrought iron hinges, and I swear, there must have been a memorandum sent out by the Archbishop of Canterbury around the turn of the century that made this a "must do." Prayers and Communion, no music, a tidy message of five minutes . . . and old people: men in jackets and ties, women in dresses and pantyhose. No smells. No bells. I guess they reserve those for the later service.

Or maybe they don't do that sort of thing anymore? I don't know much about Episcopalians.

Will and Jace sat in a peaceful quiet and went home to study more of Romans while I drove to Klein's to pick up something for lunch. Of course, it took me an hour and a half because I took the extremely long way home. I managed to steer clear of Gary and Mary Andrews's house. I did.

For some reason, Will let me sleep in. He left a note on the counter and headed next door to help Jolly with his art school assignment.

So I threw on some sweats from the old days and am now sitting in a special spot I always hope and pray no one else knows about. Many decades ago in the woods to the east of our house, an old lime kiln was carved into a hill. I keep meaning to find out the purpose of lime kilns, but so far I keep forgetting to look it up. But

I love sitting in the bowl of land that cradles it, and I know that at one time people came here for one reason or another to do that lime kiln sort of thing.

I spread out a blanket and lie down on my back, trying to summon up a picture of what life was like around here a century ago. Slower, kinder, more intimate with nature and people. Harder? Perhaps.

A June morning shouldn't be this chilly. But it rained last night after I turned out the light. Rained and rained and rained, washing away the heat, the humidity, the dust. It is stark. It is blue. It is clear. Simple.

I miss my father, his whiskey-voiced words, his gentle spirit, his gratitude for life's inherent blessings.

My dad used to bring me to Loch Raven Dam, and we'd watch the waters of the Gunpowder River flow over the graceful cement curve and out of the reservoir. Some evenings when the weather was nice, just he and I would drive out that way in his old Barracuda. I loved that car. We'd park across the road and I'd hold his hand as we crossed the street to the dam. My father had rough hands. Always warm. He loved to doodle when he was talking on the phone.

Carp the size of French poodles used to swim around behind that dam, and from the observation platform I'd throw bread in so those ugly fish might live to see another ugly day. I loved feeding those fish that seemed excited about a crust or two of stale bread.

I often think about the conversations my father and I had—Dad, the local history buff.

"There are towns buried beneath these waters, Heather," he said one day, forearms resting on the wrought iron railing, gray eyes looking out over deep waters.

I think I was about seven when he first told me.

"They built the dam, poured the cement, and unfortunately, at least from what I've heard, there's a worker buried in there."

"Oh no!"

"It always seems to happen when they're pouring the cement for dams, Heather. Somebody invariably loses their balance and falls in. Quite a few are buried in the Hoover Dam, if I recall correctly." And he put his hand over mine and squeezed a bit of comfort into my bones.

Looking back now, I realize there's metaphorical significance to this. How somebody always has to suffer so humankind can move forward. It feels so fallen.

Dad kept on with his story. "Once the dam was completed and they rerouted the river back to its original course, the water began to collect and rise. It took awhile to fill up the valley, but eventually it covered these towns up completely, and there they lie."

"Are there bodies still down there?" I asked him. I remember feeling the heat beneath my hat. It was cold that day, and he remembered earlier to tell me not to forget my mittens. I curled them around the railing.

He laughed a little. "Oh no, Heather. The people got plenty of warning. They were paid by the county for their property and they relocated. But"—he leaned forward, and his eyes sparkled like they did when he was up to something—"some people say that if the water flows just perfectly and you're standing in just the right place, you can hear a church bell ringing."

"A church bell. In the water!"

"Yes. Maybe someday you'll hear it."

And I've been listening for it ever since. Maybe someday, here on my hill above the waters, I'll hear the church bell calling to me.

Nobody knows this, but my father's ashes are in a container in an old hat box in my closet. He somehow would have understood my confusion these days. Dad understood the world was sometimes wonderful, sometimes frightening, but always broad in scope and wide open with possibility.

"Mom?"

I open my eyes, shielding them against the sunlight. Drat. "Will?"

He appears through the brush. "What are you doing here?"

"Just thinking." I sit up.

"Don't you love this spot?" He plops right down on my private blanket like he owns it or something. "It's my favorite place on the property." He lays his head in my lap.

Well, maybe it's okay if it's just him and me. "Mine too."

"Really?" He looks up into my face. "I thought I was the only one who knew about this place."

"Me too."

And it's good.

"Do you know what a limestone kiln did?" I ask him.

"I looked that up awhile ago. They'd burn limestone at a really high heat and ended up using the stuff that resulted to make plaster and mortar and stuff."

"Oh. That's cool."

"Yeah. Kinda strange that stone can be burned like that. I mean, who'd want plaster when you can have stone?"

"Plaster's easier to mold, and bricks without mortar are pretty useless."

He closes his gray eyes against the sun and folds his hands over his stomach. "Yeah. Don't ever go inside there, Mom. It could all come down on you."

"Thanks for the good advice." I keep quiet about the fact that I've been in there many times.

It's a pretty sad day when your fifteen-year-old is smarter than you are. I touch his hands, running a finger over the protruding knuckles. They were baby hands yesterday, little balloon digits, dimpled and supple. Dimpled and supple and sweet.

TEN

Lark always answers on the first ring, and I'm not sure how she does it with such dependability. She completes most of her foundation work from home and seems to be able to remember to take the cordless phone with her from room to room, unless, of course, there are phones in every room in that house on Greenway.

She's glad to hear from me. I can tell this because she doesn't ask me to get to my point even though, this time, I do have one. I've given up, you see, and figure I it owe to myself and Jace to at least see what's going on down there at the Hotel and not just throw a check at the problem.

The impish portion of me wants to prove to him I'm more than what he thinks I am, thank you, Mr. Hospital Ship.

I watch Will from my bedroom window as he and Jolly mulch the flower beds near the pool. "I'm calling for a specific reason, Lark. Do you know about Sister Jerusha and her hotel down somewhere off of North Avenue?"

"I've heard of her. Never been there, though. She's one of the Sisters of Charity, I believe."

"Jace and I were over there the other night. We got lost—okay, *I* got lost—and ended up getting a tour of her place."

"So what's this got to do with me?"

"There's something special going on there. I was wondering if you'd like me to come pick you up tomorrow; we can go out to lunch and then see the Hotel."

"It's a sad place, isn't it? I hear it in your voice."

401

I grip the phone and swallow. Jolly hands Will a rake. "I haven't been able to stop thinking about it since we were there."

"Okay. What time?"

Lark would outlaw crowds if she could. "How about eleven? We can eat early and then go over."

"Sounds like a plan."

Outside, Will says something, and Jolly begins to laugh, shakes his head, and lays a bony brown hand on my son's shoulder. I open the cupboard after hanging up the phone. Look at all those plates in various colors. Three sets, actually. Not one all-white plate in the bunch. Well, that's going to change too.

I gather up the old sheets, towels, and comforters and throw them in the back of the truck to take to the Hotel tomorrow. Maybe soon I can find nice white plates and take my old stuff down there too. Just white plates, a fresh surface every time, the food itself a lovely sight.

I don't know why excitement dances around inside me like Fred Astaire and Ginger Rogers, but for some reason, I can't wait to get back down to the Hotel. When Jace sees me doing this, he'll open up and tell me about the doings of Bonnie Reynolds and Co.

So I set out to bake a cake. A full-figured cake for the "clients" at the Hotel. And I'm going to decorate it too; diverse colors, bright as a populated beachfront, on chocolate icing maybe.

I open my favorite cookbook, *Let Them Eat Cake*, pour myself another mug of coffee, and start to flip through as I sip.

Devil's food. A family favorite.

Hot milk cake. Fabulous.

Lemon chiffon. I think I hear the Hallelujah Chorus.

So why pick? I'll make one of each.

Will slides into the kitchen on the wood floors, socks grayer than old wash water. Why he doesn't go barefoot like the rest of us is beyond my understanding, but Will is just Will and it rarely occurs to him to be anybody else. "What're you doing, Mom?"

"Gagging at the sight of those socks."

"No, really."

"Making up a grocery list for cake baking." I give him the scoop.

"Okay, you definitely need to do a chocolate mousse cake while you're at it. Hey!" He opens the fridge. "Can I get Jolly to come over and help? I think he'd like that. He was crying again yesterday when he didn't know I was looking."

"Sure. Go on over."

Will grabs a small plastic container of orange, well, liquid stuff, really, and pops it open. "What time?" He chugs the drink.

"I just need to run up to Klein's to get the ingredients. I'll be back in about thirty minutes."

"I'll get him. Hey, he's a pretty good sketcher too. You should see his bunnies. And I taught him how to do a killer robot."

I've got to admit it, Will draws great robots.

An hour later, both ovens heating up, Will and Jolly hack up baking chocolate squares and separate eggs.

"You're doing a good job there on those eggs, Jolly. I'm impressed." I begin measuring cake flour into four separate mixing bowls, and my hand will ache tonight after all this sifting.

"You know how Helen was on her baking days."

"I liked her." Will inflicts upon us the weird tongue motion he commits whenever he's concentrating on something like cutting or drawing or sculpting, and quite frankly, the face frightens me and I always hope and pray he doesn't do it in school but don't see how he could possibly avoid it.

"Everybody liked Helen," I say.

Jolly looks up. "That's the truth, Heather. I don't know of one person who didn't like Helen, and that's a fact."

Wish I could say the same about myself.

The little gray house with the diamond door comes to mind, and Mary Andrews's hair blows around all knotty inside my skull. I

wonder what she thinks of me. Does she hate me like she should,
like I hate Ronnie Legermin? And if I hate him, does that prove I'm
better than I was way back when, when demanding the social upper
hand was more important than anything else?

I can't believe what I said to her, what I did. I can't believe I was
so cruel.

"Almost done with that chocolate, Will?"

"Yep."

Jolly pushes two bowls before me, one containing egg yolks and
the other egg whites. "Mind if I make us a little coffee?"

"Not one bit. We can sip and talk while the cakes are baking."

Jolly stands with hands on hips before the coffeemaker. "Now how
in the world do you use the likes of this?"

Will jumps right in.

Fifteen minutes later after he takes a sip, Jolly declares, "I think I'm
going to get me one of those things. Will, want to head over to . . ."
He looks up at me. "Now where would I get a coffeemaker like this?"

Will pats his shoulder. "Don't worry, I know where to go. You ever
been to Target?"

"Well, now. I haven't had the pleasure."

"Oh, you're gonna love this place, Mr. Jolly. They have video
games and even gardening tools."

"That so?"

I'm watching something special right now: a fifteen-year-old
boy saving the life of a seventy-some-year-old man. Tell me God
doesn't care.

The cakes are perfect. Almost. The 13 x 9 lemon chiffon now measures 9 x 9 because I lopped off an end to send home with Jolly. Will
and I expressed ourselves in whatever way we saw fit, employing
every last decorating tip and dye I own.

I tell Will about the Hotel. He wants to go to lunch too. Big
surprise there.

"Oh yeah. Carmen called, Mom. She asked if you'd do the decorations for the freshman welcome dinner at school. She said to call back if it was no; if she didn't hear from you, she'd figure it was a yes. Then she went into a big spiel about you calling her back to get the color scheme, the theme, and something else. But I can't remember what it was. Cost maybe?"

"So much for not calling back."

"Yeah. She's a little high-strung, isn't she?"

"You think?"

I call her and get the details. Mercy—Carmen and her themes. We're going with a tiki party, and they'll give away the centerpieces to the new parents. Like these people need more junk.

Next call, the administrator of the school.

I look to the left and to the right. I'm not sure where Will is, but just in case, I tuck myself into the coat closet and shut the door. I crouch down at the end of the coats, leaning up against the wall, cupping the mouthpiece with my hand. "I have something I need to discuss, Mr. Maddock."

"Yes, Mrs. Curridge?"

"Have there been many complaints about Ronnie Legermin?"

"A few. Why?"

"Apparently he was giving Will, well . . . wedgies . . . almost every day last year. I just found out about it."

"Oh my!"

"I know. Is there anything we can do?"

"Certainly. I can't go into detail, but as I said, you're not the first to complain."

"And it won't come back onto Will at all, will it?"

"I'll do my best to protect him. But if it comes down to his father demanding the evidence, Will may have to come in and see me."

I grip the phone and crush it to my ear. "You don't think they'd retaliate with anything violent, do you?"

"No, Mrs. Curridge. Are you aware of Ronnie's situation?"

"Not really."

"His father's raising him on his own. His mother died years ago."

Oh great. Just great.

"Yes, ma'am. It's one of the reasons we were trying to give him a break." He sighs. "But if he's being physical . . . Well, you know as well as any other parent at St. Matthews that violence is something we simply do not tolerate."

"Yes, I do. Thank you."

Great. A boy without a mother. Life is never straightforward, is it?

I slip out of the closet and find Will in his room working on a watercolor. "Do you know about Ronnie Legermin's home situation?"

"Duh, Mom."

"Okay. I get it." I sit on his bed. "How do you stand it, though, even if you do feel sorry for him?"

"First of all, the guy's, like, four times the size of me. I really don't have a choice. It's the other things that keep me from hating him. Not that I like the guy or anything. He's still a jerk."

So okay.

I won't call Mr. Maddock back, though. Let the chips fall where they may.

Is that wrong?

I call Laney to arrange for Nicola to come spend the day later on in the week. So that's all set. After coordinating the necessary arrangements, I ask her about social upper hands. I've been thinking about that a lot the past few hours.

"What do you think, Laney? It just changes appearance when we're older?"

"I have no idea what you're talking about, Heather."

"Well, I was part of the cool crowd during a large part of my schooling. We worked hard to keep that upper hand, doing what it took to feel good about ourselves, be the best. Whatever that was."

"Okay, I'm tracking now."

"So as an adult, how does that look? Is it the nice car, the big house, the great clothes, the good schools? Is that the same thing, really? Only we let our stuff, our ability to travel and spend a fortune on our kids' education, speak for us?"

She's quiet.

"Are you still there?"

"Yeah. Uh, Heather, do you realize if I say yes what it is I'm saying to you?"

"Oh, right. Sorry."

"What do you think?"

"I don't know. I tend to think yes."

"Well, that could be," she says. "But honestly, I think people accumulate for different reasons. I don't know what yours is. And it could be a lot of reasons thrown together. Only you can say for sure."

"You're right."

We ring off and I wonder. I guess the only way to find out would be to start getting rid of stuff. Then I'd know for sure.

Okay, that's definitely something to think about tomorrow. Or the day after that.

Will and I stand on the pathway between our house and Jolly's. He places a hand on my shoulder and leans into me; the golden afternoon sun, warm and glowing like a welcome-home window in the dark clouds surrounding it, casts a vast circle upon the gray waters.

I tell him the story of the church bell and ask him if he's ever heard it.

"No." He whispers in a voice heavy with awe. "They drowned some towns?"

"That's what my dad told me." I never wanted to share this with anyone before. It was like giving away a piece of my father that belonged only to me. But it feels right.

"Wow, Mom. I wonder what they look like now?"

"I would imagine they're all decayed. Probably only the stone structures are even remotely intact. I guess. I don't even know when they built the dams."

The lake is always so peaceful. I love living on the water. It calms me. Everybody needs a calmer me.

"We're lucky to live here, aren't we, Mom?"

"Blessed is more like it." I examine his profile, remembering the days when the full curve of his cheek gave me no clue as to what the man would someday look like. Now many telltale signs occupy his superstructure. He'll have a strong, rounded, bullish jaw, not the bent, chiseled jaw of a model, but sturdy, dependable, and ready. His eyes will examine the world through their gray irises and recreate it in his own image. His nose will emerge below his forehead without indentation between the eyes. He seems to be hanging on to the fuller bottom lip.

I love staring at him. "Sometimes I wonder about who you'll be, and more to the point, what I'm doing now that will either stifle you or spur you to greatness."

He squeezes my shoulder. "You overthink this stuff, Mom."

"I don't know. I mean, maybe you'll want to be a simple man, a plumber like my father or a schoolteacher who grades all his papers during his free hours and comes home to work on his art."

"Maybe. I doubt it, but maybe. Although I would like to learn how to bend pipe. I could do some really cool stuff with that."

"But will I, the wife of a surgeon, the lady who lives in the big stone house on Loch Raven and vacations in places most people haven't heard of, will I be fine with that?"

He squeezes again. "Mom? You okay?"

"I guess. I'm just a little torn to pieces these days. I don't know where to set my feet anymore."

"Well, I'm here."

I turn to him, smile, and run the backs of my fingers down his cheek. "It's not your job to worry about me that way, bud."

"Hey, I worry about what I want to worry about!" He turns back to face the water. "So that Hotel place is really falling down?"

"It needs a lot of work."

He nods and shoves his hands deep into the pockets of his khakis. "I think I'm going to take a little walk." He steps away, walks toward the limestone kiln, then turns. "You know I don't need to live here, don't you? In this place?"

"Huh?"

He sweeps a wide arm. "All this. Don't hang on to anything for my sake, Mom."

And he walks away, hands in his pockets, posture loose and open.

I call Laney again. She says, "You still sound troubled."

"I'm just remembering things."

"Like what?"

"When I was a little girl, my father used to take me to a peninsula on Loch Raven that turns into an island when the water is high. We'd pack up a blanket, some books, and a transistor radio. If an Orioles game was on, we'd follow along, picturing Al Bumbry and Brooks Robinson. Tippy Martinez in later years. If the O's weren't on, we'd listen to WLIF's easy listening music and read. Sometimes we'd read the same book, our heads close together on the blanket."

"You guys were close."

"Very. We read at the same speed. He would turn the page just when I was ready, and I never had to say a word. It was always me and Dad, Laney. I was glad to have my father all to myself. I was glad my mother had died after she left us."

"Your mother left you?"

"When I was really little. And then she died a couple of years later, and I never had to worry about trying to get her attention, getting her to love me, chasing after impossible dreams."

"Maybe sometimes, Heather, we just keep chasing the same dream over and over again."

So fine, then.

I stay up until 2:00 a.m., a booklet of stickers in hand as I start to categorize my belongings by placing a coordinating dot of color: red for less than five years old, blue for absolutely necessary—and my definition of necessary is pretty extreme—I mean really necessary, like settler on the prairie necessary. Blue like the ocean or the sky necessary. Yellow for sentimental value, a yellow glow, a yellow light in the window leading you home. Finally, green for unnecessary. Green for "go." *Good to go.* So far, having gone through the living room and dining room, I've used up two yellows and forty reds, twenty-seven greens and seven blues.

The next morning Jace, towel around his neck and pouring a cup of coffee, asks what's going on.

"Just a sort of inventory."

He shakes his head. "Care to explain, hon?"

"Nope."

He leaves for work ten minutes later.

If he can be slanty about his Bonnie thing, well, so can I about this.

Will's all over the idea. "I mean, how much stuff do three people really need, Mom?"

"Oh yeah, mister?" I rip off some sheets. "Go do your own room and we'll see how excited you are about it."

He grabs the stickers, the challenge in his eyes. "Just you wait and see."

ELEVEN

Nothing cheers up a Marylander like a crab cake. Lark, Will, and I finish up lunch at Bo Brooks Crab House. On the deck, the breeze off the river ruffles our hair and clothing; my blue and white sundress flutters. I like clothing that flutters. Will licks the last of the shrimp salad off his fork, and Lark scams the final onion ring, dipping it into the mixture of mayo and ketchup she always jumbles together.

My excitement returns while trying to relay to Lark the work going on at the Hotel. Lark says, "I don't think I've ever seen you this excited before, Heather."

"And I've got cake!"

"Lots of cake," Will says. "Lots and lots of cake."

We pull up to the Hotel thirty minutes later.

Will looks around him, eyes like planets. He has never been in a bad part of town. Fifteen years old and he has never been in a bad part of town.

I park around the side of the Hotel, smack up against a Dumpster that looks as if a stiff wind blew it end over end like a tumbleweed at least a decade ago, rust growing like copper mold around every crack in the army green paint.

Lark climbs out and shuts her door. Will and I follow suit, and my son and I just stand there, eyeing the decay, the garbage, and a pair of sun-dried underwear and three gray-white tube socks. I wonder if he saw the used condom. His round eyes lock on my own. Drat, he did.

Lark moves forward. "Oh, come on, you guys. Stop acting all scared."

"Like you can talk!"

"Hey, at least I know to get off the street."

Two young men run up the road, shouting just as we round the corner. A well-dressed man in a European-cut suit hurries toward us from the doorway of the Hotel. "Come inside quickly, folks. Those guys are bad news."

He's a beautiful pale mocha, and intense, glowing eyes catch the sun in their golden irises. Hair cut close to his skull enables us to see a scar running along the right side of his head above his ear. That must be a hundred-dollar tie too.

"Thanks," I say. "I'm not down here much."

Lark jabs me in the ribs with her elbow.

He smiles. A dimple in his left cheek too. What a charmer! I'll bet he's one of the local pastors. He opens the door. "Believe me, I've been around here too much. It can get a little rough."

Will says, "You obviously don't live in these parts anymore, though, right?"

"Will!" I say.

The gentleman waves a hand. "No worry, no worry. No, I moved away a few years ago, but I find myself around here more than enough. I'm a big fan of Sister Jerusha." He smiles sweetly, warm eyes casting a generous, welcoming net and pulling us in.

I sneak a glance at Lark, who's standing there looking like her brain has flown out of her head. *Lark? You attracted to this man?* I sure wouldn't blame her if she was.

"I am too," I say. "Sister Jerusha is amazing."

"No doubt, no doubt. She tries to do her best by people."

"You should know, Knoxie." Mo strides down the stairs like a milk chocolate Incredible Hulk.

Knox Dulaney? Ah, yes, Heather Curridge charmed by a drug dealer. Just perfect.

Knox turns to us. "Ladies, young man, have a fine day." He nods his head politely and leaves.

"Bad news, the man is bad news." Mo sits back down at his desk. "Well, hey, hey, Mrs. Curridge. Escorted by Knox Dulaney himself."

"Good memory, Mo, and it's just Heather, believe me."

"And who you got with you?"

"My friend Lark Summerville." Mo shakes her hand and she snaps out of her trance. "And my son, Will."

Mo shakes his hand as well. "Fine young man you got there!"

"Good to meet you." Will.

I lean forward. "That was really Knox Dulaney? The drug dealer? I thought he was a pastor or something."

Mo laughs himself into a coughing fit. "Oh, that was a good one, girl."

I don't tell him I wasn't kidding.

"You lookin' for Sister J?"

"Yes. If she's got the time. I've got some cake in the car too, for dessert tonight if you need it."

"Hang on, I'll buzz her. And we always need cake." He picks up the phone and presses a button. "Retha? Sister J upstairs with you? Tell her that lady whose husband was almost shot by Knoxie Dulaney's no-good cousin from Florida is down here to see her." He listens. "Thanks." Looks up at us. "She'll be down in about ten minutes. There's a social worker up there with some of the women, workin' things out. You know."

"No problem. Why don't we unload the cake?"

Mo calls one of the guys hanging around by the television set playing, of all things, *Martha Stewart Living*. "Sly! You wanna come give Mrs. Curridge a hand here? She brought cake."

Sly jumps to his feet. "There isn't much I wouldn't do for cake."

By the time we settle the boxes on the worktable in the kitchen, Sly has revealed he is twenty-eight days clean from crack.

He runs a hand over his shaved head. "I'm just, you know, tryin' to get my body strong first, and then I'm going back to work. My brother-in-law gets a lot of work bricklaying, and I'm a bricklayer too, been bricklaying since I was that boy's age. But . . . got to get this body strong first. One step at a time. You know."

Sister Jerusha pounds across the big room. "I saw the cakes. Terrific! Frish, but I've never seen such pretty food here at the Hotel.

You've given us a first, doll. And believe me, that takes some doing."

Will looks at me as if to say, *Frish?*

After I introduce Will and Lark, Sister J invites us back to her quarters for a cup of tea. So robust, so mythic, she hardly seems like a tea person, more like a whiskey person.

"What's your last name, Sister Jerusha?" I ask as she points to the small couch. We all crowd in as she sits on an old La-Z-Boy, the side upholstery held together with duct tape as promised. I think about the lounger in our family room. She needs one far more than we do, and I saw a wonderful chair online last week that would replace it. Or maybe I don't need to replace it. Maybe Will and I can run it down next week. Ah, and I can't forget to get the bed linens out of the back of the truck before I go. And the towels and plates.

Crucifixes of wood, silver, brass, ivory, and plastic hang all over the walls. Jesus, Jesus, Jesus. It's important He suffers down here. It's important these folk see what He did in obedience so He could not only redeem but understand.

"My full name is Jerusha Bridget Mary O'Neill. I grew up in the church, and I'll die in the church. I, my dolls, am a walking cliché."

"My mom's a cliché too," Will says. "So no worry there!"

"Will!" I turn to him. But I have to laugh. "If I was twenty pounds thinner, you'd be right on the mark." A lot of the physicians' wives I know, stay-at-home moms like me, are teeny-tiny little Botoxed, faux-buxomed beauties. It would bother me, but Jace assured me he'd be mortified to be married to someone so artificial. "Do you honestly think a guy wants to hug someone with a plastic chest, Heather?" Gotta love the guy.

Okay, thirty pounds thinner.

Lark has remained quiet since we arrived, taking everything in.

"Did you help with the cake?" Sister Jerusha asks.

Lark shakes her head no. "I'm just here to see what's going on. Heather hasn't been able to shut up about this place since the other night."

I nod. "It's true."

Sister Jerusha pulls out her hankie. "You either love us or

completely want to avoid us. I don't see much middle ground, that's for sure. Some folks actually dislike what we're doing as far as the downstairs set. Say it's enabling people to stay in poverty." She leans forward. "But God's been with me every step of the way." Sits back in her chair, once again starts fiddling with the simple linen square. "If it wasn't for that, well, I'd have thrown in the towel long ago. Plus, it isn't like I'm Mother Teresa or anything. Someday they sure as heck won't be talking about canonizing a St. Jerusha!" She laughs a great, loud "Humph!" then points to Will. "You like ice cream bars?"

"Oh yeah."

"Hang on, then." She rises to her feet, tucks the hankie into the waistband of her skirt, and disappears into the opposite room. A few seconds later she returns, Fudgsicle in hand. She hands it to Will. "Our secret. I never share these with the clients." She turns to us. "See? A saint I am not. But what can you do?"

The phone rings beside her. "Hold on a sec." She picks it up. "Yeah? You bet. Okay, tell her to wait just a couple of minutes and I'll be right out." She cradles the receiver once more. "Krista, remember her? She's back. I told you she'd be back, didn't I?"

An overwhelming sense of relief gushes through me.

"So I figure you're back here because you're feeling either guilty or blessed beyond belief, and maybe even a little called. What is it?"

Is that what I sound like when I speak my mind? No wonder everybody's worried! "I just thought Lark here might be able to help out the Hotel."

Sister J turns to Lark. "We can always use help. In what way?"

"I run the Charles Summerville Foundation."

"The one on the radio all the time?"

Lark nods. "Yes. I'm his daughter."

"No kidding."

"No. Heather says a lot of work needs to be done around here."

"Heck yeah. Always. I need new plumbing, part of the roof replaced, a couple of new machines for the Laundromat, a ceiling in the main room, and that's just to get you started. But what we really need around here"—she turns to me and points—"is more cake like that. Capiche?"

Capiche? I thought she was Irish!

Of course, Lark understood right away and tells me so on the way home when I ask what Sister Jerusha meant by the whole cake thing.

She sets the Christmas stocking she's embroidering on her lap. "She's saying there are always people like me to throw money at problems, and we're awfully good at it. It was no affront to me, believe me, and we're very necessary. But you brought cake, Heather, made in your own kitchen, with a lot of love and care, made with your own two hands, and Will's hands too. You can see the difference, right?"

Tears nick my eyes, and I force down the throaty emotion that rises like sea foam. "Do you think the foundation will be able to help them?"

"I'll make a recommendation. I don't see why we can't help fix up the Hotel. But it's more than that. Did you hear her talk about her dreams for a youth center, a health center, a job training place right there in the neighborhood?"

"I'd help tutor!" Will says from the backseat of the car. Gosh, I love that kid.

Lark reaches back and baps him on the arm. "Problem is, the Hotel lives on heightened alert 24-7. They're providing a lot of relief, and even some help in getting people on their feet, but I know she wants to do more than that. The rooms are pretty depressing. Can you imagine trying to make a life for yourself in a 10 x 10 with cracked walls?"

After dropping Lark off, I turn to Will, who immediately points back out the windshield to direct my attention where it belongs.

Okay, okay.

"I liked that man Sly, didn't you, bud? I've never met somebody that newly off drugs before."

"Me either, Mom. It's not really what you think, is it? I mean, Sly's a real person."

"Everybody there is a real person."

"Did you see that Chinese guy with the long hair who just sat there staring off into space?"

"Yeah. Hard to tell if he was stoned or just burned out."

" 'Cause we know all the signs of drug addiction."

"You got a point there."

We continue the drive north to my little windswept paradise on the cliff, far away from Sister Jerusha's Hotel.

Will considers the landscape flying by a little too deeply, silent.

He doesn't realize how lucky he is that these moments, these new experiences, can fall on him like a virgin rain shower; that he doesn't have children and a house and a life that muddy the ground upon which the raindrops fall.

TWELVE

I want to keep dotting my possessions, but centerpiece construction begins today. Only a few days remain until the freshman welcome dinner is yet another meaningless experience for all concerned. Will helps me gather up the craft supplies we're using.

"Do I really have to go, Mom?"

"I have no idea how many people will show up. Mrs. Peterson said she'd be there, and she's bringing Nicola."

"Mom, this dinner is so lame, and you know it. Do you really think everybody will get all buddy-buddy because of it?"

"No. But we're a part of this school, Will. And we'll do what it takes to serve."

There.

Will slams some pipe cleaners into a bag. "Well, if serving's the real issue, let's just drive this stuff down to Sister Jerusha and those kids upstairs on the transition floor. All this is going to get thrown into the trash by the time next week rolls around anyway."

And he's exactly right.

This stuff definitely deserves a big green dot of unnecessariness.

Laney grabs a seat next to me. Of course, nobody has shown up but them and us. Figures. "This reminds me of church," she says. "Everybody can find time for the actual activity, but the setup and the cleanup are left to the old faithfuls."

"You said it. The baby's adorable." A teeny little Brooke sleeps in her car seat.

"At least there's that." Then she smiles. "I do love my kids, Heather."

"I know."

"Good. Just making sure you knew." She grabs a hair elastic from around her wrist, and in the time it takes to sneeze, she commits fabulousness in the form of a tousled up do. But with Laney, you just don't mind.

Will and Nicola sit at their own table, mind you, taping foam blocks into bamboo baskets and glue-gunning moss over the top. After that we'll set in a tiki statue and finish it off with a circle of silk dendrobium in white and pink.

We sit in the cafeteria, a multi-windowed room decorated in shades of gray and maroon, the focus wall adorned with the school's crest. More boring than a khaki trench coat.

Mr. Maddock, the administrator, approaches. "Hello, Mrs. Curridge, Mrs. Peterson."

We greet him.

"Thanks for all your help here at St. Matthews."

"Sure," I say.

"No prob." Laney.

He peers down at the car seat and smiles. "Another future student, I see?"

"Uh-huh. We'll keep 'em coming!"

He excuses himself, back to the grind and all that.

I pull some moss from a cellophane bag, considering Will's dead-on observation. These things will definitely be food for the dump next trash day. "Don't you ever wonder what it's all for anyway?"

"What do you mean?"

"This school. This life. We just try to make things better and better for ourselves, don't we? You've got the doctorate in theology, Laney. Isn't it a little skewed?"

"Yes, frankly, it is. But I haven't figured out what to do about it."

"Maybe that's not the theologian's job."

She rearranges the blanket of her newborn. "But maybe it is. It all starts with our view of God, Heather, who we believe He is, what we believe He desires. Why do we think we can divorce our everyday decisions from the desires of His heart?"

Mr. Maddock pokes his head in the room. "Mrs. Curridge, can I talk to you privately for a moment? It won't take long."

Two minutes later he gestures to one of the chairs in front of his desk and sits down in the other. "I wanted to keep you updated on Ronnie Legermin."

"Oh, yes?"

"His father had no idea his son was behaving in such a way."

I'd find that hard to believe, but hey, my dad didn't know about me.

"He'd like to talk to you personally and in private."

"Does Ronnie know this came from Will?"

"No. I told him it was a grapevine affair. Do you mind if I give him your number?"

"Not at all." Oh, man!

Well, I survived the centerpiece gathering with only one deep scratch on my arm from a wire flower stem. I drop Will off at the club for practice for tomorrow's swim meet. Three hours to myself, and a list of things to do unravels like a falling hem. I need to sign Will up for fall art classes at the community college, pay bills, figure out if I've got all Will's immunizations ready for high school next year, and I haven't ordered his uniforms yet, but, well, the wanderlust in me triumphs again. I really need to drive.

I pull out onto Blenheim Road and travel north. I always seem to travel north past the horse farms and the farm farms, past the hilly woodlands, the wide bands of grass, the nurseries, the sensible ranchers on their three-acre plots; the mammoth new mansions-in-a-minute that border old farm property.

I call Jace. "Are you doing rounds?"

"Just about to. What's up?"

"I'm driving. Just driving."

"You okay?"

"Just thinking about how I always seem to end up where I went to school. It's odd to think that now a lot of kids who grew up in the Christian school movement have reached middle age and even odder to think we're no different statistically—divorce, alcoholism, our likelihood to have a TV—than the products of the public schools. When I first read that in *Christianity Today* or someplace like that, Jace, I practically freaked out. And now I begin to look around me and I think there must be something to this."

"How so?"

"The divorce rate among my own graduating class is off the charts, and I know of at least three extramarital affairs. So if we're not any morally different than the rest of the world, why do we think we're so great, why do we think we've got the answers, why do we act like such know-it-alls? Shouldn't our love for Jesus make a difference in our behavior?"

"I'd like to think so."

"As far as I'm concerned, all we have is hope. And if I'm honest, it's probably all we've ever had that's separated us from the rest of humanity. Isn't that right?"

"I don't know, hon. It sounds a little simplistic to me."

"I really didn't think so either. But I can't come up with any alternative theories at this stage of the game. All I know is I can't go on avoiding the questions any longer."

"I don't think you should. I think you should ask all the questions you'd like."

I turn off the air-conditioning and roll down the windows. "It seemed like all the answers were found in that Christian school in those days, or so I heard every week in chapel. But those suggestions sure as pie didn't do a bit of good for Gary and Mary Andrews, did they?"

"Who are Gary and Mary Andrews?"

"I've got to go. I'll keep a plate warm for you at dinner."

"Heather, who are Gary and Mary Andrews?"

"Another time, Jace. I can't talk about it yet."

If he can't tell me about what's going on with Bonnie, I don't feel the least bit guilty about not sharing Gary and Mary with him.

"Hon, are you sure you're okay?"

"Gotta go."

I park across the street at the veterinary office parking lot. I watch the little bungalow, hoping that maybe this time somebody will step out. It's got to happen sooner or later, doesn't it?

On the way to pick up Will, I call Lark. Leslie answers. "Hello, dear!"

"Hi, Mrs. Summerville. I called to talk to Lark. Is she home?"

"No, she took the bus to a meeting across town." The mystified disapproval rises like a fog out of the earpiece.

"Darn. It wasn't important, I guess."

"Will I do?"

"Well, it's like this. I was just thinking about Phillip Carmichael from high school. And I think I had a revelation."

"Tell me about it."

"When I was in ninth grade, I made it into concert choir at school. The alto section. Phillip Carmichael was this slightly effeminate tenor who was a junior the year I was a freshman. I have no idea where he is these days. And actually, I'm not really sure his last name was Carmichael. I don't really remember his last name, if you want to know the truth. I hadn't thought about him for years until the other day when I ordered blue cheese dressing to go with my wings."

"I love blue cheese."

"Me too. One day, on choir tour, we were sitting in a Shoney's somewhere in Tennessee, and I was in my chef salad phase. I ordered chef salad all the time during my early years of high school. Loved them! Phillip said, 'I hope you don't order blue cheese dressing again. That really makes your breath stink, Heather.' We traveled hours and hours by bus, so breath made a difference.

"So I ordered Thousand Island dressing. And you know, it wasn't half bad. With some extra pepper to counteract all that ketchup, I actually liked the way it went with the strips of provolone cheese, the salami, the ham, and wedges of hard-boiled egg."

"I love a good chef salad too."

"In fact, I ordered Thousand Island dressing for years, because heaven help us, someone told me I had bad breath. But over the years I ate less and less salad, and by the time I was twenty-five— *ten years later!*—I realized that blue cheese dressing was still my favorite and so were chef salads and how foolish to have let Phillip Whatever-His-Last-Name-Is deprive me of my favorite dressing for an entire decade."

"Yes, indeed, it was. It's important to eat what you like, because there's always somebody out there who doesn't like it and will tell you so, Heather, and if they tell you so, they're not appealing and kind."

"Pretty simple, right?"

"'Elementary,' as the old man said. I think I'll get Lloyd to make me a chef salad for dinner. You put me in the mood."

"Good."

"Heather, are you all right?"

"I don't know."

"Was this really about salad dressing?"

"Of course not."

"Are you the Phillip in the story, or are you you?"

"Both, I think. I think I'm Jace's Phillip and my own Phillip."

"Oh dear."

"Was there anybody like that in your life, Mrs. Summerville?"

"My Aunt Regalia."

"Regalia?"

"Ghastly name. Family name, of course, dear. One afternoon our housekeeper made biscuits and I slathered on the butter. She told me thin is more important than delicious and that I was looking more delicious than a girl should if she wants to look like a lady. I haven't had butter since."

"How old were you?"

"Twelve years old."

"Humans can be a rotten bunch, can't they?"

"Oh my, yes, dear. They certainly can."

"Would you do something for me? Would you go downstairs and tell Lloyd to make you some homemade biscuits with butter?"

"You know, Heather, I think I'll do exactly that. And grits too."

Lark called me back at eleven. I slipped out of the bedroom and downstairs into the kitchen ready to unload.

"So everywhere I went today I saw cake. First off, Safeway displayed posters advertising a buy-one-get-one-free cake sale in their bakery. In Strapazza's window a sign said 'Italian Wedding Cake Here!' And then, I swear, four people said 'piece of cake' to me during a conversation. Four people."

"Whoa, Heather."

"I think God's knocking on my brain, but I'm not telling a soul except you. They'd think I was nuts. Almonds, most likely—arranged on a fluffy bed of buttercream icing."

"Does Jace think you're nuts?"

"A little. But he's keeping his own secrets."

"Bad ones?"

"No. Good ones, ones he thinks I can't possibly understand."

"Are you hurt?"

"Yes. I have to admit it. I really am."

"Is his secrecy justified?"

Why does Lark always have to ask the hard questions?

"Probably. But I'm not ready to do what it takes to bring it all out into the open."

"Don't let your life pass you by because you're scared, Heather. I did that for years, and it was horrible."

"You raised Flannery, didn't you?"

"Not really. Sometimes I think she raised me."

Will finds me in the night gloom of my thoughts and sits down without a word. Stands back up. Makes us hot milk with just the right amount of honey and cinnamon.

"Mom?"

"Yeah, bud."

"I heard your conversation with Miss Lark. Mom, I'm not the most spiritually mature person in the world, but are you really that thick?"

I can't help but laugh. "Yeah. I guess I am."

"Dad and I started into Isaiah. God cares about those people down at the Hotel. And this"—he waves his arm around my belongings— "this is sleaze in comparison. So is my school. So is, well, just about everything in our lives right now."

So tell me how you really feel, Will.

"I think maybe you're crossing over the line, bud. Your dad has worked hard for all the stuff you're so readily disdaining."

"Sorry." He squeezes my arm. "This is all driving you a little nuts. Do you realize that? I'm kinda worried about you."

"There are things about me you don't know. Torments you have no knowledge of."

"Like what?"

Like a little gray house where two dirty kids lived, one of whom I betrayed. "I can't go there yet. And don't ask me to, Will."

"Okay." He stands up and kisses me atop the head. "I love you, Mom. I'm sorry if I was hard on you."

I grab his hand and kiss it. "Just go to bed, bud. It's very late."

"Okay. Hey, take a look in the garage before you go to bed. I've got some stuff for Goodwill. I couldn't believe how many green dots I had. It was pretty bad."

"And you've already got them boxed up and ready to go?"

"Well, yeah. I mean, what's the point in keeping it around?"

THIRTEEN

Tomorrow the freshman dinner descends like a giant spider. I'm so torn by Will's words. He's an idealist, yes, and always has been, but this school isn't bad. The parents are interested in their kids for the most part; the academics are excellent. So they want tiki center-pieces. So what?

Carmen, raven hair spiking up around her head, runs up to me as I hang up tropical floral swags in the cafeteria in preparation. Tablecloths go on next, and then the oh-so-glorious centerpieces.

"Oh, Heather, I'm glad I caught you. You'll never guess what happened."

I'm dying to know. Um. "What?"

"The Whittings can't do the cake. Her mother was rushed to the hospital last night with a massive heart attack or something. Can you make the cakes? Please?" Her lipstick is always so perfect.

"For tomorrow night? Ten cakes?"

"I'm so sorry, I just don't know what else to do." And she doesn't have those little jaggedy cracks around her lips sucking up the lip color either. How does she manage that?

Maybe it's a sign. Maybe God really wants me to make my cakes for the school. I mean, the Hotel is all the way downtown, and with my driving . . . "All right. But can you find someone to fill in for me tomorrow morning for folding programs and setting up the sound system?"

"Oh. Uh—hmm. Uh—well, let me see. It's kinda short notice."

"Try."

426

She looks up at me, sea-blue eyes suddenly gone round. "I'll do it. Sorry . . . Heather."

Immediately I flinch under that horrid remorse that comes bowling along whenever I blow it and act all snippy. Carmen works hard; she doesn't need a smart aleck like me, even if she is a clod sometimes. And make no mistake, that was definitely cloddish. "I'm sorry. I just can't do both. Not with that much cake. I'll be baking almost all night as it is."

She rubs my upper arm. "Sure. I don't know what I was thinking."

I shake my head. "It's always something, isn't it, Carmen?"

"You said it."

"Go ahead. You got lots to do."

"Good luck!"

Carmen really is a good person beneath her control freak, tanning bed persona. She just thinks her thing should be everyone's thing.

"Hey, Heather? I'm sorry about the powder room."

"Me too."

I watch her click to her car, cell phone already up to her ear.

Will slides into the family room on his dirty socks, laptop under his arm. "So, Mom, I hate to tell you, but I think the church bell thing your dad told you about Loch Raven is one of those myths."

I pat the sofa. Here I sit, watching my favorite cooking goddess, Nigella Lawson, who actually eats the food she cooks, looking like she's ready to swoon when she stuffs rare steak dipped in béarnaise sauce into her mouth; she's probably a size ten, which in Hollywood sensibilities relegates you to the category of sideshow freak. I click off the set.

"Okay, burst my bubble, then. Where did you find the info, Mr. Smarty-Pants?"

He sits down and opens his laptop. "Here on this site."

"How long have you had those socks on?"

He points to the screen. "There are several towns under water, but

428 ® QUAKER SUMMER

the biggest one was Warren, Maryland. There was a big mill there, and a school, and boys' and girls' gymnasiums, a church. Lots of stuff." He scrolls down. "You need to check this out. But let me just tell you, when the City of Baltimore bought the town from the Summerville family—hey, do you think they're related to Miss Lark?"

I shrug. "Beats me."

"Anyways, the city bought the town for a million dollars, and before the water filled up the valley, they disassembled the towns."

"Really?"

"Yeah. Sorry. I like the bell idea a lot more. But I don't think it's true. Bummer, huh?"

"Definitely. I've been listening for that darn bell ever since I can remember."

"I'll bet. You want me to leave the computer here?"

"Sure."

Fabulous, then. I'm so disappointed I actually want to cry. I read on. Sure enough, all the buildings came down, and the stone from Warren was used to build a shopping center down in Anneslie where Jace and I first lived. A shopping center! I'll bet I know the one too, stone buildings with a storybook appeal.

Will's right. My way was better.

I call Lark.

"I can't stand on the cliff anymore listening for a bell that just won't ring, can I?"

"If I knew what you were talking about, I might be able to answer that question."

"I don't understand it either, Lark."

"Heather, have you thought about therapy?"

"I don't need therapy, Lark. I need a frontal lobotomy."

Today I placed a hundred red and green dots, ten blue, and one yellow. Only one thing out of 111 possessions had any real meaning for me.

There hasn't been a day in my memory I've felt comfortable inside my own skin with anyone other than my father. And while I love the Hotel, I was just too busy with my cakes for school this morning when Lark called and asked if I wanted to accompany her this coming Monday. Besides, I have to be honest, the second time I went down there and actually saw all the homeless people, I just felt, well, awkward, really.

Uncomfortable.

I call Jace.

"Can't I just be a champagne socialist, a benevolent patroness of the Hotel? If it's good enough for Lark, isn't it good enough for me? What would those places be like without the monetary support of people God has blessed financially? I could plan a fund-raising dinner. Something nice at the club. Carmen could give me loads of good ideas right off the top of her spikey-haired little head. I'd rather spend money on this stuff than all the stuff I buy."

He sighs. "If you say so, Hezz."

"Okay, just checking. Bye."

"I mean, if you're so set on spending to make you feel better, I guess this is better."

"I said bye, Jace. Mercy!"

I hang up and survey the cakes on my island, ready to be iced. I outdid myself this time. Maybe I feel there's more to prove as second choice. I've constructed the vanilla cakes like giant tropical flowers; I'll decorate the chocolate cakes as edible jungle islands. Thank heavens the dinner is in the evening.

Once again I pull out all my decorating tools from the appropriate bin in the pantry and gloat a little. It never gets old. Like Will enjoys the mere sight of his paints and clay, the pristine expanse of white paper, the square gray lump ready to receive the crushing blow of his grasp, I love the sight of that sugary golden canvas in front of me—knowing what I do will actually give the partaker a burst of energy and, hopefully, a moment of joy when that moist, sugary confection touches their tongue and for a split second they forget their cares. Unless it's my rum cake—two pieces of that, and you can forget your worries for an hour at least.

I have to admit, though, that I don't feel comfortable even in this role—the sugar mama of St. Matthews Country Day School. Do people look at my thirty extra pounds—okay, forty—and say, "I'll bet she eats this stuff at home too!" And on the scale of importance, does cake rate very high when considered alongside the likes of teaching, preaching, playing in the church orchestra, and cleaning the facilities?

I call Jace back. But his voice mail picks up.

"Do we really just need to get back to church? Do you think that's what's at the base of all of this?"

I hang up.

Ah, but I do enjoy these things here in my hand, the decorating bags, the various tips, and the icing colors . . . the colors, how I love to mix the colors into vibrant hues, dusky hues, pastels—I love all the colors. Who knew what that little cake decorating class at the community college would do for me?

But there's still time for this, and surely I need more confectioner's sugar, don't I? It's only 8:00 a.m., see, and I have to get out of the house right now.

Back in my bus route days, it was just a dingy old bungalow on the outskirts of the town of Hickory. Back in those days, nearby St. Ignatius Catholic Church wasn't the thriving parish it has become. Back in those days, Hickory Elementary hadn't yet experienced the slightly postmodern do-over that it sports now. Back in those days housing developments hadn't filled in the gaps between houses and farms and businesses like the Tractor Supply Company or Bill's Deli or the Hickory Inn specializing in broasted chicken and charbroiled steaks.

I long to pick up my cell phone and call Jace or Lark, or even Leslie. But I can't. Too much at stake. How about Laney? Can I trust her?

I dial her number, and she answers in a whisper. "Oh, hey, Heather. The baby's asleep."

"Want me to call back?"

"No. Hang on a sec while I walk outside and slide under the deck."

"Under the deck?"

"They won't find me there. They never have yet."

I hear the sliding door open and the muffled sounds of her stooping over to walk beneath her shoulder-high deck. "Okay, I'm sitting down now."

"I always went to the linen closet in the guest bathroom."

"Did Will ever find you?"

"Eventually."

"So what's on your mind?"

"I have to tell you about where I went to school growing up."

"Having another spell?"

"Ah . . . yes. I guess you could call it that."

"Okay, shoot."

"Do you think I'm going crazy? The others do."

"No, I have this feeling you're probably saner than you've ever been."

"I feel that way, in some fashion. I hope you're right."

"Heather, when God speaks, it usually sounds like the light's not on in the attic, usually counterintuitive from mankind's boring ways of doing things. So go ahead and talk. I'm hearing you. I really am."

I fiddle with my Vera Bradley change purse as I talk. "I rode this bus route to a Christian school from third grade forward."

"I went to one."

"I felt a little silly wearing those fundamentalist Christian clothes that made up the dress code; hated the fact they paddled kids; hated even more that my fifth grade teacher had drilled holes in his paddle and painted 'Mr. Stinger' in bright red letters across its surface and then this bee with a big stinger coming from his butt."

"You've got to be kidding me!"

"No. Oddly enough, it seemed normal, in a harsh way, true, but nobody wondered how a grown man could keep a paddle like that up on the blackboard ledge. Nobody wondered if he was actually abusing children."

"Can you imagine that happening at St. Matthews?"

"No, thank God. I haven't thought about Mr. Stinger in years!

Wish I hadn't thought about him right now. Who says times haven't changed for the better?"

"I'm with you. So did you have chapel service once a week like we did?"

"Oh yeah. And what I heard there contrasted with Dad, who took me to his church for worship and youth group. He led a men's Bible study as well. Had a very vibrant inner faith."

"My dad's like that too."

"Dad took long walks around town by himself and called it his praying time. Sometimes I'd catch him on his knees by his bedside. But I never let on that I saw him. His body seemed to be strung in anguish at times like that."

"How did you end up at Christian school?"

"My aunt offered to send me, and he wanted to protect me from the sex education at public school. He was the single dad of a daughter, you know? I'm sure he was pretty scared about raising me right."

"Understandable."

"So I ended up on this bus to the Christian school where I heard so much talk about persecution and how the world was going to hell in a handbasket, how the 'godless left' plotted to steal away all our rights like a thief in the night, but I rarely heard much about love, about basic human kindness. It was all 'us versus them,' and believe me, the transition from 'us' to 'them' could be found in a single breath if someone found out you wore shorts or liked rock 'n' roll music."

"Sounds about right."

"Laney, nobody ever took me and my friends aside and said, 'What you're doing to Mary and Gary Andrews is abominable, horrendous, cruel behavior. What you're doing to those poor children is so terrible that if you ever come to some moral grounding you haven't been spoon-fed, you'll never be able to forgive yourself. If you ever become a decent human being who adheres to a code of kindness and the law of love, you'll look back on this time of your life and cringe at your own inherent depravity. You'll pray that God is merciful and your own children won't reap their mother's cruelty.' Nobody ever said that. And so I drive by their house a lot, Laney."

"How bad were you? I'm assuming you were horrible."

"Yeah. I don't think I can even get out the words to tell you. And now I wonder if Will suffers because of it. He's odd, and the type of group I ended up in would have had nothing to do with a talented, sweet guy like Will. I worked hard to get into that group because I was ridiculed myself until grade five because of my weight."

"How did you end up in the cool crowd?"

"Julia B. came to our school, fresh from New York City with a go-to-hell attitude, and she decided she liked me. I slimmed down over the summer due to a crazy growth spurt. We rode the same bus as the once-popular crowd that Julia B. dethroned and then asked into her court, and I rode her train to popularity."

"And Gary and Mary became the brunt on the bus?"

"Yes, and everywhere else too. Julia B. cornered the market on insulting superiority. She had a nose for the weak, descending upon them like a wild animal, the queen of our pack. She left after eighth grade."

"What happened to you?"

"A lot of them forgave me when I changed my tune in high school after Julia B. left. I assume she spent her time wreaking havoc at some other school in Pennsylvania where her father was relocated. But Mary and Gary were long gone by then."

"Can you find them, Heather? Do you know where they live?"

"I know where they used to live."

"Well, start there. Oh crud, I hear one of the twins. Hey, can Will come down later on? Nicola's jonesin' for him."

I inhale sharply. "She really does like him, then?"

"She's nutso. And she should be. For a while there she took a shine to that Legermin freak, but I nipped that in the bud."

"What did you say?"

"I told her that if she insisted on liking a cretin like him, she'd have to do the family's laundry for a year. That shut that down."

"Oh, Laney!"

We ring off. Laney doesn't think I'm crazy.

Find Gary and Mary. Is Laney right? I stare at the small house, as humble as the home in which my father raised me, played Monopoly with me in the evenings, readied me for church. But I live on the hill now. Away from them all. I live above. Away. Above. I live on waters that have swallowed towns whole.

I guess a new owner fixed up the Andrews's house. Putty-colored vinyl siding overlays the old siding; the door, diamond-shaped window pane still set into its surface, is painted a shiny hunter green, and new white picket fencing has replaced the former rusted chain link. I pull into the gravel drive, the wheels of my giant car crunching so loudly as to be violating.

What went on here, Heather?

For a person can fix a house so it appears fresh and without stain, cover up the grunginess, paint the surfaces that experienced the abuse and neglect of the once-inhabitants, but these acts are absorbed into the very fiber of the wallboards, the studs, the foundation blocks themselves. I feel that, just like at the Hotel.

I negotiate a sidewalk freshly invigorated with interlocking pavers before I can think further and rap my fist on the diamond door.

"Hang on a sec! I'll be right there."

Okay, so she must have smoked a thousand packs of cigarettes a year. For the past seventy-five years or so. Maybe I should go. This was a stupid idea. And it wasn't even my idea. *Thanks, Laney.*

The door opens.

Mercy!

So she isn't one hundred. Midsixties, perhaps. Her homemade hair color—a purply red; how did she get that shade?—is pulled back into a bow the size of a train case. I haven't seen one of those since the late '80s. I almost offer to give her a free cut and color right there. "Sorry. I had to sign off on my computer. What can I do for you?"

"I was looking for someone who used to live here. Gary and Mary Andrews?"

"Sure." She pulls wide the door. "Come on in. My allergies are killing me." As her reddened, tilted nose attests. She leads me down a narrow hallway into a small kitchen painted a sunny yellow at the back of the house. I feel sick. Are they still here at this place? "Mary?"

"Oh, good heavens, no! I'm old enough to be Mary's mother. She's long gone. I spent a fortune redoing this place, you know. Ultra-seal windows, state-of-the-art air purifying system." She turns on me suddenly. "You don't have cats, do you?"

I shake my head.

"Good. Have a seat." She points toward a dinette upon which sits an arrangement of faux sunflowers, a napkin holder with one napkin between its wooden sleeves, a shot glass with Splenda packets, and one bambooesque place mat. "Would you like a cold drink? Iced tea, water, or Tab?"

Tab? Who the heck drinks Tab anymore? Might as well see if it's as bad as I remember. "I'll take a Tab."

Her eyes light up. "Another Tab fan! Swell!"

She opens a harvest gold refrigerator and pulls out a can. "Ice?"

"No thanks. I'll take it straight from the can if you don't mind."

"You're my kinda gal, all right. I'll have one myself, I guess."

I take a sip. Mercy, it's just horrid. But the nostalgia factor is sweeter than hard candy, hearkening back to a time when you had a limited amount of choices. Boy, those days are gone!

She sits down. "So you want to know about the Andrews kids?"

"You know them?"

"I knew their grandmother years ago when I was a pharmacist in town. She worked the register. Was there long before I was."

"Is she still alive?"

"I don't know. I haven't seen her for, shoot, about thirty years, I guess. We worked together for eight, I guess."

"Do you know Gary and Mary?"

"Xavier's kids. Delores's grandkids. Well, sort of."

"What do you mean?"

"At least I did know them once. Every once in a while Delores brought them in. Xavier was a wild one. He was in high school when

I first started working with Delores. Oh, she'd complain about that boy all the time. But you couldn't help but like him, you know?"

I nod.

"So he was always one to win the ladies. Had that flash in his eye. Good lookin' he was, really foxy."

Foxy?

"He shacked up with this woman, Sandy something or other. Maybe Cindy. Mindy! Mindy was her name. Had these two kids, Gary and Mary, when she started dating Xavier after they met at the oyster supper over at the United Methodists. He used to work on the grounds crew at that church."

I remembered an old gray pickup truck parked near the house. A dumpling of a pickup, putty thicker than the makeup on a drag queen's face.

I sip on my Tab. There are worse things to drink. Offhand I can't think of what they are, but I'm sure they're out there somewhere.

"So this Mindy got her hooks into him, they got married, and he adopted those kids, I guess. Not two months later, she was gone!"

"As in left?"

"As in hit the road, Jack, and don't you come back gone. Gone, gone, gone. And she left Xavier with those kids. Now Delores tried to do her best by them to be sure, put them in that Christian school up a ways. They didn't like it after a while, though, and asked if they could just go back to the elementary school. Delores said sure, the tuition was a huge sacrifice for her. Actually brought in mayo and lettuce sandwiches for lunch just to make do."

Dear God in heaven.

"And then one day Xavier announced he was moving to Michigan and taking those kids with him."

"He got the kids when they were how old?"

"Elementary school age. Didn't quite know what to do with them, I guess. Delores was always getting on him, but he was lost. Sort of a wild one anyway, and then to be saddled down with those two. It isn't any wonder he couldn't take care of them."

She leaned forward.

"Delores once confided in me that he wasn't all that nice to them, really. She tried to make up for it all best she could, but she was only one woman, divorced years ago, and she was living hand to mouth as it was. And honestly, they weren't her grandchildren. But that was Delores for you. A kinder soul I've yet to meet."

"So they moved to Michigan, you say?"

"Years and years ago. Delores followed them soon after. Xavier needed her."

"Why didn't they just put them in foster care?"

"I don't know, really, only that Delores had a strong faith and probably figured God brought those kids to them for a reason. That's what Delores was always saying. 'These things happen for a reason.' It could be the most horrible situation, and Delores would say, 'This happened for a reason.' Me, I think she was a little overboard on all that stuff; I mean, I'm as God-fearing as the next person, but Delores never seemed to question one thing about God, as if He'd come down and give her a good shake or something if she did. Sometimes I'd ask her questions about why God allows this or that, and believe me, being a pharmacist, I saw a lot of pain, and she'd say, 'Oh, heaven help us, Peggy, it's not up to us to question.'"

I let out a laugh.

"Now what's so funny about that?" the lady I'm figuring is named Peggy asks.

"If that was the truth, I'd be going to hell in a handbasket." Speaking of hell and handbaskets.

"Me too."

"I always feel guilty about questioning God like I do."

"Me too. What's your name?"

"Heather Curridge."

"Peggy McCall."

Kindred spirits, obviously.

I drain my Tab. "I won't take up more of your time."

"Oh, I was just chatting up my grandson. He's all into the Internet these days. It's kinda fun."

A few minutes later I'm back on the road, headed toward home and some cake decorating.

Michigan. Thank heavens Delores had the sense to name her son something outlandish like Xavier. I mean, really, how many Xavier Andrewses can there be in Michigan?

And did I really just down a can of Tab?

FOURTEEN

Everybody raved about the cake, but as usual the food committee, translate Carmen, overestimated the amount needed, and Jace, who met me at school after work, helps me load the leftovers into the car. And five of the centerpieces that nobody even bothered to take as a door prize.

"You outdid yourself tonight, Hezzie. That was the best devil's food you've ever made. And those monkeys on the jungle cake were really cute."

Jace, a heart surgeon, is so proud of me and my cakes. Crazy, isn't it? I just adore the guy even if I don't get to see him as much as I'd like. Because it's like this: when he is around, he's really around. I mean, a lot of women tell me that they never feel connected, that as soon as their husband gets home from work, he's either on the computer, watching TV, or playing sports somewhere. Jace probably spends as much actual time with me as their husbands do, maybe even more.

"And the flower cake was really tasty too."

I hand him a box. "The red velvet?"

"Your best yet."

"You always say that."

"You just get better and better."

I'd gag if he wasn't so earnest.

"Did you actually try a piece of each one?"

He nods. "Of course. What are you going to do with this stuff?"

"I think I'll drive it down to the Hotel tomorrow."

Will bounds up. "Hey, can I drive home with you, Dad?"

"Sure."

If I asked my son to ride with me, he would. But I don't. Jace has a BMW.

And yes, we really are walking clichés.

So I slam down the hatchback, climb up into the behemoth, and start her up. Off I go, up the road from Timonium north to my cliff-hugging home.

But instead of taking the main thoroughfares, I decide to navigate the skinny way home across Merrymans Mill Road. No streetlights guard this byway that cuts close to Loch Raven west of where I live. Yet so much roils through my brain, it'll be nice to just drive.

My cell phone rings. And darn it!

"Yeah."

"Yeah? What kind of greeting is 'yeah'?"

"Hey, Lark."

"Hey, yourself. Where are you?"

"Merrymans Mill Road. What's up?"

"I'm heading down to the Hotel on Monday to talk to Sister J a little further, and I thought maybe you'd like to go."

"Nah. And you already asked me this. This answer is still no, Lark."

"Really? How come? I thought you loved that place."

No. No, no, no. Here I am, dotting my possessions, driving up to Gary and Mary's practically every day, buying white things, and making crazy phone calls to my friends. Everyone but Laney thinks I'm losing it, and my own husband doesn't even trust me with his dreams. I'm no more fit right now to put a ministry like that on my plate than I would be to pack up and be a missionary in Tibet, if they even allow them there. No, Lark.

"No. I just can't do everything, Lark, you know? I've got my responsibilities with Will's school, and Jace's surgical schedule is nuts. It's too much if I put that on my plate too."

"Oh, okay. No problem."

"Besides, I'm going down tomorrow to take this leftover cake from tonight's school dinner. I thought maybe they'd like that." Right? Doesn't that count for anything?

Lark doesn't say anything.

"You still there?"

"Uh-huh."

"What did I say?"

"Heather, take a piece of advice from me. Taking the rich folks' leftover cake may not be the best idea. Just a thought."

"You really think they'll be offended?"

"Wouldn't you?"

"I don't think so."

"But you don't know what it's like to be them, now, do you?"

"No, Lark, I don't. Mercy, you're awfully socially conscious tonight."

Lark laughs. "Tonight?"

Thank goodness she has dispelled the tension. "Okay, point taken. But honestly, I just can't come Monday. I can't take on one more thing."

"Suit yourself. Hey, though, let's have lunch here at the house soon. Mother's dying to see Will again. She just loves him. And my brother Newley's going to come next time. He wants to see this child Mother keeps raving about. Believe me, Mother never used to rave about anybody, really. She's changed, though, since I've moved in."

"Good. I'll call you tomorrow when I'm home to set up a time for lunch."

We ring off and I'm still driving in the darkness. Mercy, I was so gung ho on that old Hotel, and now, now I guess I'm worried I'll get too entangled in the place. And, well, I'll only admit this to myself, but the clients are odd. I have no idea how I'd even relate to smelly, mentally handicapped people.

No. Not this.

Not right now.

I don't have enough time. Maybe I need to get away for a few days, listen to the Holy Spirit or something.

I draw a mental picture of the Spirit rolling His eyes, shaking His head, and drawing His cloak more tightly about His broad shoulders. I hear the Spirit's words: "If you need to take special time to listen to me, you've got too much to do, Heather."

I see Will shove the pipe cleaners into the bags, angry at the waste of time and maybe even purpose, begging me to work down there; I see Krista pounding at the Hotel door; Sister Jerusha's veil blows in the city breeze; Knox Dulaney smiles and Mo waves a hand in disgust; the Asian man stares into space.

And I taste cake. Cake, cake, and more cake.

But I love my life, don't I? I'm here on the hill for a reason, surely. Perhaps I just don't know enough about Scripture, haven't studied enough to know God's will. I need to get to Greenleaf and find a good Bible study book. Lord knows, I haven't faithfully penciled in my Bible study fill-in-the-blanks for years now. That Becca Mills is such an anointed writer and teacher. That's what the women at my old church used to say, anyway. I need to get back to church.

And what's that hopping alongside the road?

Hopping?

Brown and furry, powerful hind legs.

A kangaroo?

A kangaroo!

And as I narrow the gap between us, still stunned at his presence here in Baltimore County, Maryland, USA, he darts into the road. I slam on my brakes, swerve, and careen into the ditch, leaves and branches thwacking my windshield while I pray the gully isn't deep and those darn cakes don't ruin the interior of my nice car.

Part Two

The Long and Winding Road

FIFTEEN

What in the world? Where . . . ? Here I am. Hands, yes, I see them, feel them. Yes, I can wiggle my fingers, bend my wrist—but ow! A spot higher up on the arm smarts. Feet—those move as well.

For real?

Or do I only think they're responding? I'm in a ditch apparently; I'm still alive apparently, and apparently, if the hand upon which the moonlight is falling is any indication, there's cake all over the place, all over me. The devil's food, apparently.

A tiki statue smiles at me from the passenger's seat.

Is this what death feels like, though? Do you not realize it, having never before experienced it, unless you once intersected with the "white light," which I haven't? I might actually believe I'm looking through my eyes, but they are really closed for good now, and I don't have the prior experience to realize what's actually going on. Will I float out of my body now? Hit the roof of the car and then somehow pass through like tomato juice through cheesecloth?

I shift in my seat. Okay, ow. Surely your spirit doesn't feel pain. And my head ripples with some discomfort, not a sledgehammer of pain, just that feeling that, "Yes, I have a head, and I know this because it hurts right now." I turn on the interior light, look out the side window, and see not a proper window view, but grass smashed up against the glass, some of it golden strawlike summer grass, other blades clinging to spring. And one now-beleaguered blossom of Queen Anne's lace.

The car interior is hideous. Cake chunks splattered against almost every surface.

I'm practically lying on my side against the door to my left, okay, a forty-five-degree angle, tops. I try to lift up my body, and a wave of pain courses again through my left arm.

I close my eyes and wait it out. *Oh, Lord,* I breathe. *Oh, Lord.*

I sit in the shadows wondering if the guys have made it home yet. Something warm slides down the side of my nose.

Am I bleeding? Don't think about that, Heather. You hate the sight of blood, remember?

Try to get up again.

Same thing.

Mercy!

I turn off the engine, relieved there wasn't some '70s boiling car explosion, and why is it cars explode on screen all the time but rarely in real life? Not that I mind right here right now. I knew my driving would get me into trouble. Did my guardian angel finally throw up her hands in despair?

The shade. The silence. Like I'm in a vast room with the door closed and locked, lights out, good night.

My breathing echoes inside my head and all around me.

I run a finger beside my nose and taste it. Yes, blood and cake. Never thought I'd taste that combination.

Injured in the dark seems an extremely solitary place, and how am I going to get out of this truck? And should I do that anyway? Are you supposed to wait until someone finds you, or call 911? Maybe there is some sort of accident etiquette to which I've never been privy, having never been in a real accident before, which, I'll grant, is a miracle akin to growing a leg back. Yes, there was that fender-bender. And the time I slipped on the ice and ran into the guardrail. And that trucker who ran me off the road. I forgot about that one.

It's going to take one of those primal yawps to sit up and twist into any kind of position that allows some leverage, and then I'm going to have to push open the passenger-side door that will be extremely heavy at this angle.

Or I could crawl through to the back and flip open the hatchback. Hopefully those air pump tube things aren't damaged.

More silence. More darkness. Not a car goes by, and a third option has yet to raise its hand.

Okay, then. The hatchback.

But in the meantime, I twist in the seat and shift onto my good arm, the injured arm sending blistering messages to my brain, and here's to no head injury, right? I mean, it hurts, but surely if I'd sustained real damage, I'd be unconscious right now.

That pretty much wore me out.

Okay, just for another minute I'll sit like this. Wonder where Jace is? Is he worried? Should I call 911?

No way. Not yet. Not with this cake all over me. I reach up. Big globs of it infest my hair. Ah, this'll be cute. Maybe I should just call the Three As. That's good. By the time they get here, I'll have wiped off at least some of this gunk.

Deep breath and I hoist myself onto my knees, sort of. And in a gangly, spidery, slipping-down course, I crawl to the back of the truck, smashing cake into the seats and surfaces wherever my hands and feet land. So much for these pants too.

But who was I kidding with these things? Pink and green?

More tiki gods smile upon me. Actually, I think they're laughing their little brown heads off.

I pull up on the handle.

Locked.

Oh, for the love of all that's decent, why me? And who tripped the child safety switch?

I swear, my arm is glowing with pain.

Back I go, more pain, more cake, and I push the switch, disengaging all the locks on the truck. Mercy, this is too much. I'm so glad I haven't called anybody yet. Some things a woman has to do on her own.

Still slipping, still glowing, I return to the back of the truck.

I yank on the handle again, and up the door rises, letting in fresh darkness and the smell of leaves and woods and strong skids of tar.

Finally.

And I forgot my purse with the cell phone inside.

Drat. I just have to keep moving forward. I can't go back again. I'll get it from outside after I rest.

Now just a quick climb out of this ditch. I claw at the grass with one hand, trying my best to keep my injured arm still. I doubt it's broken, but man, I wish that fabled "numbness" would settle in, for heaven's sake. Hey, I do have a bottle of ibuprofen in my purse.

No way. Forward, forward.

I crest the top and lie down on my back.

Merrymans Mill Road? What was I thinking? Why must I always take these drives? Why must I always take the long way home?

Ah, yes! That kangaroo.

What in the world was a kangaroo doing hopping down the road? Well, no sign of him now, but with my luck, he'll return to give me a good kick in the head with one of his giant feet.

I stretch my neck back, tendons as tight as metal strapping, and see a light farther off in the woods. Maybe I can reach it. Maybe they'll have a phone. Maybe they're criminals. Maybe I've lost my mind.

But heaven help me, I have to go to the bathroom. I've had to go since right after I left the house this evening. Okay, so if I hold my arm against my abdomen, it's a little better. No time like the present, Heather. Let's get going.

I roll over and up, the world astir, my head spinning a bit, and whoa! Okay, breathe in, get past all those carnival lights behind your eyes. Wait for the stars to fade.

Breathe. I breathe.

Now gain your feet and forward march and all that manly persistence jargon. Maybe someone like Jolly lives where that light is. Somebody lonely who could use an interruption from a warm soul like me. Or an old couple who just made a pot of tea for the evening— something herbal and light, although they'd probably just as soon have Lipton's Decaf. Maybe they'll make me a cup, and she'll gently suggest I call the Three As while handing me a phone with the wire still threaded into the wall.

Well, add thorn scrapes and a bleeding scalp wound to devil's food cake, and you've got the makings of a zombie fresh from the grave in *Night of the Living Dead*, and I have to admit, those movies crack me up, even if they do scare me more than I'd like to admit.

Through the trees I see some movement in the yard, hear an old woman's voice saying, "Hurry up and take a poo, Oatmeal. I was ready for bed an hour ago." The voice, soft, kind, and patient despite the words uttered, brings to mind Michael Learned on *The Waltons*, and I do believe if that character grew into old age, she'd sound like this.

I push aside some brush, and there she is, as old as Loch Raven, which I can see over her shoulder—older probably.

"Hello?" I try to speak as softly as I can without startling her but still letting her know of my presence. "I just had an accident."

She turns. "Oh!" And immediately starts walking my way. "Oh dear, are you all right? Look at the dirt!" She walks without impediment, sure on her miniature, old-style feet shod in brown loafers.

"It's cake. I had cake in the back of my car."

Concern pulls down her wrinkled features. She must be ninety if she's a day, which means she's lived through everything that's come to matter to us nowadays. Which means there isn't anything I could say or do that would shock her. Well, that's a relief.

"Your arm. Are you in pain?"

"Yes."

"And your head. It's bleeding."

"Yes. And I did go out for a couple of seconds, I think."

She reaches out a bent hand, arthritis swelling the knuckles. "Look there. There's a knot and an abrasion too. You may have a concussion."

Over her shoulder, the back of the house, modern yet warm, reclines in a bath of floodlight. Walls of windows set in fawn-colored frames, stacks of river rock, and expanses of stained cedar create a lived-in sculpture. A wide chimney pokes through the flat roof to stand darkened against the stars. Will would love this.

"I feel pretty clear-headed, other than I forgot to check for the lock on the car door before I climbed to the back to get out. And my purse is still up by the front seat with my cell phone, and the keys are still in the ignition." Did I say I was clear-headed? Mercy!

"I'm sure everything will be fine. Most people don't travel down this road at night unless they have to. Let's get you inside and you can call home. Careful now. Oatmeal probably did her business, and while she takes her time choosing her spot, she does tend to leave it out in the open."

"Thank you."

Her close-cropped white hair hugs her head, and the porch light attached to an overhang at the side of the house illumines the rosy scalp beneath. A sweater covers her bones on this cool June night.

She yanks open the sliding glass door at the back of the house. "Liza! We've got company!"

Taking my good arm, this angel-lady guides me into a den, past some old modern couches, two bentwood rockers, and a stone wall with a darkened fireplace, and into a cheerfully lit kitchen. The plain wooden cabinets soar to the ceiling, and the gold counters provide a space for copper canisters, a white Sunbeam stand mixer like my grandmother had, and a carved wooden fruit bowl. In the center of the room, a simple, round wooden pedestal table supports a bouquet of peonies in a glass bowl.

"My sister and her late husband built this house over sixty years ago. He was an architect." She speaks with apology.

"I like modern."

"I don't necessarily prefer it. But there's no accounting for taste, is there? Liza's always been the artistic type, or at least she found herself in that colorful kind of company. Even after Alva passed away, which was years and years ago, poor thing, she still found herself at all the gallery openings and exhibits and such." She leans forward. "My sister's very active, very bold. Of course she's five years younger than I am, which might explain it."

As if that matters by the time you've reached this age. This lady is so adorable.

"How's that arm? Let me take a look at it now that the lighting's better."

She lifts my arm and presses spots here and there, asks me all the right questions. I try not to grimace.

"Well, it isn't broken."

"Are you a nurse?"

"Doctor."

"Sorry to assume. My husband's a doctor."

"Cut my medical teeth in the Korean War." She turns. "Liza, honey! Oh, I don't know where she is. But let me run and get an old sheet for your arm. I'll make up a quick sling, and then would you like something to drink? And you'll need the phone."

"I'm coming, Anna!" an elderly voice calls from somewhere down the hallway. "I'll be there in two shakes of a lamb's tail!"

"I'd love something to drink. Maybe a cup of tea?"

"Surely. And the phone is right over there." She points to a bone-colored plastic phone attached to the wall. "I'll be back in a jiffy."

I still have to go to the bathroom, but I'd better call Jace. I lift up the receiver and dial Jace's cell.

"Jace, it's me."

"Hey, babe," he whispers. "Will and I decided to go to the movies. I kept trying to call you on your cell phone but wasn't getting an answer."

"You're not going to believe this." I tell him about the kangaroo.

"I'll be right there."

"Whenever you get here is fine. Finish the movie. I'm at some-one's house. I probably should have called the Three As, but I saw a light in the woods and walked here. The lady who lives here is a doc-tor. She said my arm isn't broken, and she's off to get an old sheet for a sling."

"I'll come pick you up."

"Take your time, Jace, really. I'm fine. She's making me a cup of tea, and I just need to sit for a minute. Can I give you a call as soon as I collect myself?"

"Absolutely. We'll be on our way. Did you hit your head?"

"Yeah. It doesn't hurt that much though. I need to wash up. I've got cake all over me."

"Well, it sounds like you're in good hands, but I don't like the idea of that head, Hezz. Listen, we'll be there in about forty minutes. We're at the Senator. Some indie film Will wanted to see."

"Okay."

Gosh, I feel more frayed than a forty-year-old coat!

"What happened to the truck? Not that it really matters, but I thought I'd ask."

"Well, there's cake all over the interior."

"That's all right. They'll be able to clean it up."

"I hate that truck, Jace."

"We'll talk about that later."

"I don't know why I had to have it. It looked as big and stupid there in that ditch as it looked shiny and promising in the showroom. We only have one kid."

"We'll be there as quick as we can."

"Do I sound that bad?"

"Just a little out of your head. Let me talk to the doctor."

"Anna!"

She hurries in. "Yes, dear."

I hand over the phone. "My husband wants to talk to you."

"Of course." She holds the phone up to her ear as if both are made of glass, the way old folks tend to do. For half a minute they speak in the medical jargon I've learned to tune out, then talk about getting the car towed, and apparently I'm all taken care of. She hands me the receiver and zips back down the hallway.

Jace says, "Good, hon. Sounds like you're in good hands. Anna told me where you all are. I'll call the wrecker to meet me."

"All right."

We hang up and I head into the powder room, thankfully, right by the phone.

Liza, I assume, clips into the kitchen where I stand, cake still overlaying my person. "So you're Anna's patient."

"Yes, I guess so."

"Now a cup of tea is what you need. And don't ask for coffee. I ran out this morning and forgot to stop at the store."

"Okay."

"Right, then. First the kettle, and you need to go sit in the den there. The couch on the right is truthfully the most comfortable. Feel free to put your feet up on the coffee table. I'm sure the Eameses wouldn't mind."

The Eameses?

"Go on. Tea will be ready in two shakes of a lamb's tail."

"Thank you."

"My pleasure."

I haul my wounded arm into the den. My goodness, what a gal! As spicy as her sister is sweet, she exudes that artsy confidence of, say, a gallery owner or a museum curator. Her hair, a shining silver, is pulled back into a tight, chic bun at the nape of her neck. I'll bet she has worn it like that for years. And her skirt, black and slender, hugs her sapling frame. Only the flat silver house shoes attest to her age.

So she married her an architect. Seems fitting.

I can't sit! I'll ruin the couch with this cake.

Purposeful clankings sound from the kitchen as Anna returns holding a strip of snowy sheet with pink rosebuds scattered about its folds. "Let's get that arm stabilized. And I'm sure you could use some painkiller. I'll get you a glass of water too. Wait, you might like to clean up before I put this on. How did you get all that dirt all over you?"

"It's cake."

"Oh my, yes. I forgot already." The aquamarine eyes sink deeper in the smiling flesh. "It seems when I turned ninety it all started going downhill. Liza! Could you get a pair of Maria's lounge pants? And a shirt? This woman has cake all over her!"

"That's not dirt?"

"Apparently not."

"It's devil's food!" I yell.

"What's your name, honey?" Anna asks.

"Heather Curridge."

"I'm Anna, and that's my sister, Liza, in there. Let me show you to the bathroom, where you can take a shower. Your husband is delightful."

"Who's Maria?"

"Our great-niece who comes to visit occasionally." She turns the faucet inside a built-in tile shower and then faces me with an impish smile. "She only comes around because Liza's loaded!"

So a bit of cayenne mixes with that sugar.

"The water will be warm in a jiffy. Yell if you need me."

Liza sets a cup of tea on the kitchen table. "Right, then. Here you go. You must feel much improved sans all that cake."

"Definitely."

Anna bustles in. "The guest room is ready. My, this is a bit of excitement for us two biddies, isn't it, Liza?"

"Speak for yourself. I refuse to be a biddy."

Their eyes meet. Sisters.

Liza picks up my teacup. "Let's take this to the guest room and you can rest there in comfort until your husband comes. You've been through enough already without having to listen to our inane conversation."

"Speak for yourself, Liza. I refuse to be inane." Anna scrunches up her nose.

Maria's sweatpants are as soft and broken in as crushed rose petals, and as Anna ushers me into the velvety beige guest room, the down counterpane pulled down, exposing cocoa sheets, nothing but this arm impedes a comfortable rest. I won't complain about the Percocet either.

"Just rest."

I love being taken care of like this. I feel cozy, a scuffed fairy-tale princess finding refuge at a hidden cottage.

"Thanks for taking me in."

"Oh, honey, it's a pleasure. Would you like me to turn off the light?"

"No thanks. I'll drink my tea and maybe just read." I pick up a book on the nightstand.

She smirks. "That one will put anybody to sleep. But it's one of my favorites."

And she shuts the door quietly. *Pacificism and Biblical Non-Resistance.* Also on the nightstand, *Cyrus Pringle's Diary.*

What? She's right. This looks drier than my skin in February. And I'm tired.

SIXTEEN

Upon opening my eyes, I know the morning settled in awhile ago. What happened to Jace? The warmed air has burned away the night. The sunlight, welcomed by the wall of windows, gilds the room. Everyone should have a wall of windows, I've decided lying here.

Peace has come upon this place, and I'd love to know why. And how. And can I take some home with me?

I roll onto my side to sit up. Pain darts through my arm. "Ow!" I can't help but cry out.

A quick bunny knock vibrates the flat door. "Heather, honey, are you all right?" Anna.

"I just forgot about my arm and rolled onto it. Come on in!"

She enters without hesitation. "Let me look."

"Actually, it feels a lot better than it did last night." I lift it up by the shoulder, bend it at the elbow, then the wrist. "It's stiff, but that's all."

"You'll still want to keep it in that sling today, and an X-ray would be a good idea." She sits down on the bed. "So your husband came by last night. I told him just to meet the wrecker and check on you while you slept. We both agreed it was best to let you go on sleeping. Jace. Is that his real name?"

"Yes."

"I like it. Very different. Very 'cool,' as the younger set would say."

I smile at her. She's dressed in a pair of khaki serge pants and a short-sleeve pullover top in heather gray. Small pearl drops weigh down her delicate earlobes.

"He's a good guy."

"Yes. Used to work on a hospital ship, he said. I have a thing for men who care about others."

"Did you have glasses on last night, Anna?" Mildly hip rimless spectacles rest on the bridge of her nose.

"I still had my contacts in."

It's all I can do not to giggle. She's so old, so cute. And yet she's a doctor. Talk about un-cliché! Nothing like us Curridges.

She pats my leg. "I'm going to bring you in a nice pot of tea and a roll. Liza's helping me get ready for a meeting for clearness out in the den, so if you want to stay in here and rest, that's fine. Jace called early and said he'd be by, but I told him you were still asleep. He'll be here around one because of Will's swim meet, which he was going to 'blow off,' as they say, but I told him to go on ahead." She stands to her feet. "So you still have a few hours to rest."

"What's a meeting for clearness, Anna?"

"Oh, I belong to the Society of Friends. Quakers. A meeting for clearness is when an individual has a decision to make and seeks counsel from his fellow Friends. In this case, it's Adam, who's wondering which college he should attend this fall. He's been accepted to two, but he just can't seem to make up his mind. Nice young man."

"Is Liza a Quaker?"

"Not really." She laughs. "Depends on what day you ask. Liza could never be a wholehearted anything when it comes to organized religion. She takes Christ by the hand and hits the ground running each day. She dabbles in all sorts of denominations and ways to serve, and she certainly wouldn't get herself arrested for peace or anything like that, but she does the work of the cross."

"And you'd get arrested?" I couldn't imagine this sweet old lady being taken away in handcuffs.

"I've been arrested more times than I can count!" She waves a hand. "I know! Surely it's the last thing you'd expect. Why don't you sit outside? I'll bring your tea there and you can look at the water. I so love looking at the water."

I throw back the covers and pad to the adjoining bathroom. Over a simple dresser hangs a saying in calligraphy.

The Friends Peace Testimony
"We utterly deny all outward wars and strife and fightings with
outward weapons, for any end or under any pretence whatsoever.
And this is our testimony to the whole world."

From "A Declaration to Charles II," 1660

So she really believes all this? Wow. I don't know anybody, not
one single person, who would get arrested for their beliefs, including me. I've never even written my legislators.

On the dresser, my clothes are laundered and folded.

Five minutes later I'm sitting out on the slate veranda that anchors
the back of the house and extends around to the side I didn't see last
night. I believe there's a pool around there because I smell chlorine,
and a wringing wet Oatmeal just came running from that direction.
A wooden deck peeks from behind the other side of the house.

The dog plops down next to me on the warmed stone as I sip my
tea in the morning sunlight. The lake lies placid this morning, so
deep, so calm and mysterious.

And so devoid of underwater church bells.

I'm still disappointed.

Ah, but what perfect tea, rounded and smooth with a large dollop of honey and a smidgen of milk that removes any rough edges
whatsoever, if there were any to begin with, which I doubt. These
women seem to hide all the secrets of life inside deep magical pockets that hold things much too large for their dimensions. Living
ancient like this never appealed to me, but if I resemble these sisters,
may my trunk grow thick and my roots grow deep.

The open sliders usher the morning breeze into the den; screen
doors banish the bugs. The group speaks every so often, asking questions, I presume. Mostly they sit in silence. I suppose they are praying. I heard someone mutter something about discerning the will of
God and the leading of the Spirit.

"I only desire the will of God. But I can't discern God's from mine."
The young man's voice sounds so earnest. And he begins to summarize
before the small group of what, I surmise, are very trusted people
who've invested in him his entire life.

I shouldn't be listening.

Cradling my arm, I heft myself off the lounger and head down
the steps toward the lake. Oatmeal follows me, prancing in the grass
like a dancing wet mop.

The group stops speaking as I pass by. They appear normal enough.
Nothing like the Quaker Oats guy.

Oatmeal!

I get it.

I lean down and touch the dog's wet head, and she wags her stump
of a tail. I have no idea what breed she is, but maybe some Lhasa Apso
loiters somewhere in her assemblage. My grandmother had a Lhasa.

So I sit cross-legged on the grass and stare at the water, longing
for the bells and wondering if just maybe one of them escaped the
wrecking ball.

"We've got cake!" Anna laughs. She's found me.

"I don't think I could possibly eat a bite of cake, having worn so
much of it."

"Do come in, dear. Liza made it." She looks over her shoulder
and whispers, "It looks horrible. But it's got more chocolate than
Willy Wonka inside of it." She waves a hand, proud of her own
joke. "Come."

"I really don't want to disrupt what's going on. It sounds rather
serious."

"Well, then. I'll sit here for a while if you don't mind. Clearness
committees are always exhausting."

She bends down, slowly lowering herself beside me. "I may need
a committee to tell me how I'm supposed to get back up."

"I'll help you."

"With that arm?"

We laugh. "You're good for my soul, Anna."

"Thank you. I surely appreciate the compliment." She looks out over the lake.

"It's beautiful here."

"Jace told me you live on the lake too. Not many of us, are there?"

"No. We're quite the club."

"Oh, goodness, yes." She smiles, suddenly far away.

Her face lifts to the sunshine, gravity pulling away some of the creases atop her features. She was an interesting-looking woman in her day, I'll bet.

And why do I always try to find the young woman buried beneath the aging landscape? Aren't Anna, and Peggy McCall at the Andrews's house, and Sister Jerusha beautiful enough all on their own?

I don't know how much later, Anna opens her eyes. "I'll bet they're gone now. How about that cake?"

"All right."

"How about that hand?"

I help her to her feet. She chuckles at her own creakings and groanings. "Oh, goodness, I don't know if a body's supposed to go on this long." And she tucks her arm through mine. "I'm glad you've come, Heather."

She didn't say it, but I felt her next thought. *You are a troubled soul, dear, and maybe somehow, here at our house, you will find a measure of peace and light.*

Liza crosses her arms and looks at me as I take my first bite, and I know the feeling.

"Fabulous!" I pronounce.

"Right, then." She turns on her heel. "Anna, I'm going now!" she calls, grabbing her purse off a hook near the phone. "You be careful, Heather. I'm glad that husband of yours is coming to get you. Truthfully, I'm still not sure if you're all right."

"He'll give me a good once-over."

"Yes, Anna told me he's a physician too."

"Yes."

"Right, then. I'm off."

She's wearing jeans—yes, jeans—and a green blouse. Sensible shoes too. I didn't notice it last night, but she has a sort of Julia Child curve to her back. "Do you mind if I ask where you're going?"

"To the halfway house in Cockeysville."

"Halfway house?"

"For alcoholic men. I help the men clean on Saturdays. My late husband was a drinker like you wouldn't believe. He died young."

Mercy! Such candor.

"I'm sorry."

"Alva enjoyed life even if he did live it with such intensity. Anyway, that's neither here nor there after half a century. Needless to say, I've learned to live without him."

I can't help it. I bark out a laugh.

Liza smiles. "Bye now. And don't be a stranger."

And she walks away, so very different from the rest of the world, but somehow fitting right in. I'm seeing firsthand what it means to be in the world but not of it.

"Anna? Has she always been like this?"

Anna shakes her head. "The Lord came to her one day. That's all she'll say. I don't know what form He took, but I do know she recognized Him for who He was."

SEVENTEEN

Jace shuts my door and swings around to his side of the car. "Seriously, aren't those the coolest ladies you've ever seen?"

"Definitely. They were wonderful."

He shakes his head and puts the car in drive, and we head off into the woods that front their acreage. "Man, I'm glad you're okay. Your arm should be fine. It's heavily bruised, but if you want to see an orthopedist, I can arrange that. You've got good movement, but maybe we should get an X-ray."

"Let me just give it a couple of days."

He pulls out onto Merrymans Mill Road. "I knew you'd say that."

"Will okay?"

"Absolutely. He wanted to come, but I thought you'd be a little overwhelmed. His enthusiasm can be a little suffocating."

"I'm feeling a little overwhelmed in general these days."

"I could tell. Laney's husband, Cade, got him from swim practice. He's spending the day with them. You want to get some lunch? Just the two of us?"

"Definitely." Maybe he'll open up about Bonnie's request, whatever it was.

Jace chitchats about his new patient—an old blind minister named Carl whose daughter is actually married to the brother of Snap, the lead singer of Great Guns. "Remember them, Hezz?"

"We listened to them all the time in high school."

"So did we. Anyway, my patient's a wonderful man, second time for open heart. He's grieving the death of his youngest daughter from an accident a little while ago. He said, 'If you could mend that big tear right down the middle of my heart while you're in there working on those valves, I'd appreciate it.' I wanted to cry."

"What did you say to him?"

"I said I'd do my best, but only one person can heal a wound like that."

"How do people get through things like that?"

"I don't know. I pray to God we never have to find out."

"Still. I wonder if my faith would hold."

"As do we all. What would happen to our faith if it was tested, really and truly?"

"I don't know." I whisper the words.

And now we sit at a table for two at the Nautilus Diner in Timonium. After Liza's cake and my general cake garment of the night before, I will most certainly skip dessert.

"I'll take the moussaka, light on the tomato sauce." The waitress writes down the selection.

Jace orders the grilled salmon.

I guess when you see hearts literally encased in globby yellow fat, it's got to affect you somewhat.

The waitress asks if I want all the peripherals. Salad, soup, bread. No thanks.

For the first time in my life, I'm not really all that hungry.

I lean into the table after she leaves. "Something's very wrong with me, and all the long drives in the world won't fill the emptiness or shine a light or whatever it is I need. I realize that now."

"I've been thinking about things, Hezzie. Do you think you might want to try some medication?"

"For what?"

"Anti-anxiety, perhaps?"

"What will that do?"

"It will dull those scared feelings you're experiencing."

"Who says I'm scared?"

"You have. Not in so many words, but you have."

"I'm wide-awake for the first time in my life, Jace. I don't want to dull anything."

"Tell me what you mean by wide-awake."

"I'm comparing myself to three old women. Sister Jerusha in that rundown hotel, and then Anna, who actually gets arrested for her beliefs, and her sister Liza, who right now is cooking at a halfway house." Maybe dessert would be a good idea.

"Is this comparison a good thing?"

"I don't know."

"But maybe some medication will help you see things more clearly if the fear's gone."

"Who said fear is always a bad thing, Jace?"

He stares at me for a moment, then takes a sip of his water. "What can I do to help you see your way through?"

"I don't know. I love it there at the sisters' house. They told me to come back if I needed to. I think I might need to. I've been driving too fast, thinking too much, saying more than I should to anybody who will listen. I can't even begin to hear God speaking, Jace. And I have no idea what He'd say if He did."

"My parents have been wanting to take Will for a couple of weeks. I've got that seminar in Chicago the week after next, so I wouldn't mind the quiet in the evenings to prepare. I'll probably spend some time at the library too. Maybe you should take them up on their offer?"

"Are you sure?"

"Give them a call and see what they say."

Already I feel a little better. Not much, but any break from the routine that has become my life sounds like a good idea.

"So what's happening in Chicago?"

"Just a seminar for cardiologists."

As we listen to music on the way to the Curridges' vacation house, the recumbent farms of Delaware whizzing by, Will asks questions about the Sermon on the Mount. He's been reading the book of Matthew since school ended. He has too many questions.

We listen as he asks them, and I think about my life when weighed in the balance of the truth of Christ, drowning in the hard sayings of Jesus, and I think I'd just as soon keep my mouth shut.

"What does hoarding treasure really mean, Dad?

"What would it look like if we really didn't judge?

"Aren't preachers always asking people to make vows? To sign little pledge cards, although that's in direct opposition to the teachings of Christ? Or is it? Was that what He was talking about?

"How do we know what to throw out and what to keep? I mean, if we only pay lip service to His teachings anyway and they have no real showing in our actions, haven't we cast them, in all reality, into the dustbin?"

"The dustbin? Where did that word come from, Will? I haven't heard anybody use it for years. Other than my grandmother."

"I have no idea, Mom."

Jace grips the wheel, and I know his thoughts. All Christian parents pray for their children to be interested in the things of God . . . but fifteen and asking these questions? Will it do more harm than good?

And then the inevitable question I ask myself: "What kind of trust in God is *that*, Heather?"

"Love your enemies? If Jesus let His enemies crucify Him, what does that mean for us, Dad?"

"'Take up your cross and follow me,' Will."

I can't stay silent. "That's impossible."

Jace frowns. "He wouldn't have said it if it was."

"I know. But it still seems impossible."

Will leans forward. He always sits in the middle of the backseat. "But we have this book that shows us what God would do if He was human; what God *did* when He was human. Doesn't that count for something?"

"Then why does living as a Christian seem like such a mystery?

More books than I can remember on how to do this very thing have been passed around in churches."

And yet the very example we have, we pooh-pooh, saying, *Well, He was God. Of course He could do that.*

Jace breaks for a stoplight. "Maybe we don't live *for* Christ because we don't live *like* Christ."

"Right, Dad. And maybe I don't live like Christ because I've taken the Man out of Him, made what He did here so mysterious and unreachable that I've taken away any possibility of success in imitating Him."

Jace steps on the accelerator. "He wouldn't have told us to be like Him if it was impossible."

"You really believe that, don't you?" I ask.

"With all my heart. Although most days, I wish to God I didn't, Heather."

Sandals, a robe, a cloak.

No place to rest His head.

Friends, disciples. Followers.

"I proclaim good news to the poor."

Twisted and broken on a cross.

"Father, forgive them."

He could have called ten thousand angels, but He didn't. He lifted his face to the corruption, the power plays, the violence of His own creation and opened not His mouth.

I write these words on the back of an envelope from my purse and turn to Jace as we drive home from dropping Will off at the Curridges'.

"Can we do it, Jace? Can we really follow His teachings?" I have a feeling I'll be asking this question over and over for as long as I breathe.

"I believe we can, hon. We won't do it perfectly like He did, but that's where the grace comes in."

"Yeah, but I can really abuse grace."

"From your perspective, sure. But if there's an unlimited supply, how can you use up too much?"

"Still, a lot has been left undone in the name of grace."

He's quiet for a little while. Then, "It's a fine line, isn't it? I guess, for me, I'd rather use more grace for having tried and gotten it wrong than for not having tried at all."

That's it. That's it exactly.

"Hezzie?"

"What?"

"Nothing. Never mind."

The sisters are delighted I called. Anna answered the phone, and Liza picked up the extension in the kitchen and said they weren't surprised to hear from me and were glad to help in any way.

"In fact," Anna says, "I bought more of that cranberry tea you liked so much as an unspoken prayer."

Ah, I love that woman.

But before Jace drops me off, I hop on the Internet to locate the whereabouts of Xavier Andrews in Michigan. Okay, people search or something.

I hate this stuff. I'm just no good at it. I should have done this before Will left for the shore. He's a whiz at this sort of thing. But then again, I can't tell him what I'm doing, admit I was once Ronnie Legermin. Not after what he goes through.

I'd still like to take him out of that school, by the way. But no go! Especially not with Nicola in the works.

After thirty minutes of pointing and clicking, I find nothing on Xavier himself, but his mother, Peggy's coworker Delores, died in 1982, the year Gary would have been a senior. I locate the town, look up the local high school, and his name appears on the list of the 1982 graduates.

The name, so real in the black cyber-ink on my monitor, shoots a jolt up my spine. I quickly bookmark the site, shut down the computer, close the door to the office, and tell Jace it's time to go.

On the car ride over, I offer him one more chance to come clean on Bonnie. But again my husband will not trust me with his heart. Probably because he has already given it to me so thoroughly he can't ask anything of me anymore. I deserve this.

"Hon? What are the dots all about?"

I tell him the plan and the code.

"Oh, wow. We have that many meaningless items around?"

"Yeah. It's worse than even you thought, Jace. And don't say 'I told you so.' Please."

He places a hand on my thigh. "You going to get rid of any of it or just be thankful for what you have?"

I don't know.

What would Jace think of an all-white house?

EIGHTEEN

Anna leans over the railing, looking down at the creek. It rained last night, and the water, smelling of leaves and ozone, rushes beneath our feet, hurrying to join with the bay. We've stopped on our way to visit a friend of hers at the VA hospital in Havre de Grace. "And the other men too," she says. "A lot of the boys are there."

"Do you know them?"

"I do now. I just go to let them know somebody hasn't forgotten."

"But you hate war, don't you?"

"Yes. But I love people. I put many a man back together out on the battlefield, Heather. I've more than earned the right to hate war and still love our soldiers. It is possible to do both, dear." She turns to me. "Heather, why are you here?"

"I'm not sure," I whisper. "I think everybody thinks I'm going a little crazy."

She nods. And gazes back at the water. "Do *you*, dear?"

"A little."

"Is it a good thing or a bad thing?"

"God's speaking to me, Anna. I just don't know what it is He's saying. But I hear Him, like I hear the wind in the trees or that running water beneath our feet."

"Most likely you know it deep down already. No matter. God has plenty of time. It's one thing He's never short of."

"But I feel so muddled."

"Through the ages people who listen to the promptings of God have always been thought more than a little goofy."

And she begins to tell me story after story of saints who make my meanderings, my dots, my white items, my conversations, seem like a walk in the park.

Okay, so I thought the Hotel felt depressing. This VA hospital is the singularly most disheartening place I've ever entered in my entire life, and that includes airport bars, casinos, and beach bathrooms, not to mention bus stations, pawn shops, and the health department. Anna whirls from patient to patient like love potion in a misery cocktail, greeting each of them by name, a peaceful sweetness accompanying her simple act of knowing them: their names, their conditions, their birthdays. She hands out several cards.

Ah, Lord Jesus, all the suffering in the world. More walls of sadness. How have I lived so long without coming face-to-face with this? Have I purposely anesthetized myself, or was I programmed years ago to avoid the living tragedy? And does it matter now that my nerve endings have begun to awaken and my taste buds have matured to include the flavors of despair and responsibility?

Anna curls her arm through mine. "Come see my dear friend Bobby." She leans her head toward me and whispers, "I had a thing for him years ago. He was much too young for me, though."

She leads me down a hallway, still greeting each man who sits in a wheelchair along the path, introducing me like I'm Sophia Loren or something. I've never seen so many lost limbs or burn scars in one place. I'm grateful, believe me, but the heartache that petrifies my insides at what man does to man weighs down my footfalls. I walk more heavily. I feel my shoulders droop under the knowledge of their anguish, their lives lost yet still going on, these forgotten men.

Anna pats my arm, then swings me through a door.

"Bobby Stewart! You old rascal!"

"Anna Banana!"

Bobby lies in a bed. I assume he's paralyzed, but I'll have to ask later. His cumulonimbus hair is obviously the true testament to his personality.

"Bobby and I were in the same unit in Korea. He's a doctor as well."

"Used to be." Bobby raises his arms. No hands. "Left them somewhere in Vietnam and somehow can't finagle the time in my busy social schedule to go back and find them."

"He only wears his prosthetics for special occasions." Anna. "I'm old hat, obviously."

"Well, you wouldn't be. I keep asking you to marry me, Anna, and you keep refusing."

"Not to mention I'm twenty years older than you are." She laughs. "He was a real Lothario back in the old days, dear. Much too wild for my poor blood."

He jabs a stump in my direction. "So she roped you into coming along on one of her do-gooder rounds, did she?"

"I'm afraid so, Dr. Stewart."

Anna. "Heather's husband's a medical man too, you know."

"Oh yeah? What field?"

"He's a cardiac surgeon." Each word makes me feel like I'm dangling a luscious plum in front of a person with no teeth.

"Remarkable strides they've made in cardiology since my day." Bobby.

Anna sits on the edge of the bed. "Oh my, yes. Bobby still keeps up on the medical journals. He puts me to shame."

"Have to keep myself busy mentally. In between visits from old Anna here."

"You know you count the minutes until my arrival, Bobby."

He winks. "Pronounce me guilty."

"I talked with the Department of Veterans Affairs, and they said they'll look into your benefits, see if you can get into a different facility, but for now, I'm afraid you're still stuck here."

"I feel like I'm in prison."

"You are," she said. And she changed the subject, talking about happier times after the Korean War when they met downtown and danced the night away. "Of course, Bobby picked up a more willing partner, and I went home to Mother. Hardly fair."

Bobby only replied, "It depends on what your definition of fair is."

On the way home, I asked Anna, "Doesn't Bobby have family that can help him?"

"Not to the extent he needs, Heather. He never married, so he has no children. That we know of, anyway." Her laugh sparkles like a sequined scarf. "His only sister had a couple of kids, but they don't know him. She lives on the West Coast. He's most surely a forgotten man."

"Mercy."

"Terrible, isn't it?"

"How come you're doing all that stuff for him, though? He seems more than competent."

"Can you imagine the depression that has overtaken him? He's quite debilitated that way. Turn down that road there on the left, dear. Anyway, there's more than one way to support the troops, isn't there?"

"I guess it's pretty easy to wave a flag and mutter some words, isn't it?" I thought of my car flags when the war in Iraq broke out. But men like Bobby were totally off my radar. In some ways I wish he still was.

"We can cheer them when they go away to die for us, but most of us don't want to think about them when they come back and suffer the rest of their lives for us, do we?"

"I guess not."

"I've exposed myself to what happens on the back end the way not many other people do." She looks out the window, then turns to me. "And I've seen them die and suffer on the front end too. I appreciate their sacrifice for me, but I can't help but believe there's a better way to shore up our freedom. That we don't have to rely on the deaths of these precious men and women to do it."

I've never heard talk like this before. I don't even know what to think, really. But we don't have to agree on everything to appreciate one another, do we? I mean, my father was a Marine when he was young. "But God used death all the time to get His will done."

"Jesus didn't. And He's really all we have to go on, isn't He?"

Ah, my goodness, there it is, more of that vein Will has been thinking about. I don't know if I can handle all this deep thought. Lord, I came to get direction, not to become even more confused.

I continue on down the road, our speed consuming the fields and fences of Harford County. "Are you hungry?"

"Oh yes! I always eat a little lunch on the way home. Would you like to stop in Bel Air?"

"Okay. Do you have any place in mind?"

"There's a little tearoom called Tea by Two. I love their scones and watercress sandwiches."

"Definitely."

Anna tells me about her parents. Her father was a doctor at Johns Hopkins who specialized in pediatrics; her mother ran a local chain of supermarkets with *her* father. Anna and Liza grew up downtown in well-to-do Mount Vernon, went to all the best schools, had the greatest advantages children could have. "But always with a great attention to love and responsibility. My mother didn't always make life easy for us! Oh goodness, no. I was doing my own ironing by the time I was eight, and Liza and I volunteered at the hospital all the time or stocked shelves at the store. Mother was quite the woman."

We enter the tearoom and are seated at a table draped in white damask, a china sugar bowl and creamer holding down the center.

After ordering, I ask, "Did you grow up Quaker?"

"No. My father was an agnostic and Mother was too busy."

"How did you find Christ?"

"In a still, small voice."

And I can tell by her tone that's as much of the tale as she is willing to tell.

"I've never met anyone like you before, Anna."

"Well, you'll find if you open yourself up to the possibility that

God is found in locales you've never imagined; you'll meet Him in all sorts of faces and places you never thought possible."

"How do you know when you've heard the Spirit speak?"

The waitress delivers a serving tray loaded with three plates: sandwiches, scones, and cookies.

"My way of hearing may be different than yours, Heather. So it isn't for me to say. I don't want to put my fences around you."

"This isn't helping me any."

She raises her brows and lifts a tiny sandwich to her mouth. "On the contrary. One day you'll look back and see I did you the greatest favor I possibly could by keeping my mouth shut." She bites down into the soft white bread.

NINETEEN

I've settled into the same earthy, restful room. Peace. They talk about it around here, and I sense it in these walls and long to feel it inside of myself. How do they make it seem so easy? And is it easy? Can you truly feel at peace?

And is freedom the result of peace? Or is peace the result of freedom? I look around me and shake my head. I've always believed the latter. But now I'm not so sure. I want to be free. I want to be at peace. At present I am neither.

Then again, the sisters are in their nineties, and their peace arrived with a hefty price tag. The late afternoon sunshine casts the shadows of the hills onto the loch, deepening the waters, blocking the reflection of the sky. I can gaze out into the nature scene from where I sit on my bed. It's easy to feel peaceful here, really. Maybe that's their secret.

Ah, yes. I have much the same view from my bedroom at home, don't I?

But then, the answer couldn't have been that easy.

I slip my Bible from my suitcase and turn to Matthew, remembering what Anna said, what Jace and I talked about. Jesus is all we have to go on, really, as far as who we imitate, as far as what God looks like as a human being, and we're supposed to be like God, right? I'll start with Jesus. And I'll pay great attention to the red letters.

Teach me, Lord.

I don't pray these words through a great holiness. I pray them through a clawing sense of desperation. I don't want to run away anymore. I want to find my way right here, inside my skin, the skin of those I love so much, and the skin of those who have gone and are going before me.

Laney picks up on the sixth ring.

"Can I ramble?" I ask.

"Sure."

"I've spent most of my life in service to my family; first to Jace and his medical degree and then to Will. I don't regret that."

"But . . ."

"But I could have listened to the Lord more, Laney. I let my service to others drown out His voice. We can do both, right? Listen to His voice and serve our families."

"Yes. But usually we sacrifice one for the other when they're supposed to go hand in hand."

"What does it look like when a woman does both?"

"Well, don't look at me for the answers, Heather. My life is about as balanced as the federal budget."

Next I call Jace. "How's the prep work going for the Chicago trip?"

"Good. So how are you doing at the sisters'?"

Next I call Lark. I tell her about Jace. "I'm hurt. Should I be?"

"Maybe. But can you blame him? Really, Heather, have you thought of what that tennis court you're planning must feel like to him? You might as well put jail doors on the entryway and lock him inside."

Liza, dressed in midnight blue crushed velvet lounge pants and an ivory satin blouse, sets a record upon the turntable of the old stereo in the corner of the family room. The sounds of the Glenn Miller Orchestra and "Little Brown Jug" enliven the space, the piano's bass launching the piece, the throaty trombones grabbing the melody, the trumpets lying down on top for the breezy ride.

"I loved the way he sometimes played big band with a different equation, the trombones playing the melody so much." Liza claps in time with the song. "It's why you can always tell it's Glenn Miller."

Really? They did that?

I just nod, and she reaches out her be-ringed hands toward Anna, who walks into the room with a tray, our coffee mugs steaming on its teak surface.

"Come on, Anna, let's dance a little!" She wiggles her fingers.

Anna doesn't hesitate. She sets the tray onto the blond coffee table and snaps up her sister's hands, and they slide into a thrifty jitterbug, right through "In the Mood" and onto the depot in "Kalamazoo."

Their blue eyes sparkle, the notes settling upon their features like dew, their smiles stretching their faces young. Anna's short hair feathers in the wake of their movement, moving in the same direction as the hem of Liza's velvet pants.

I want to weep in the presence of these lives well lived. I'm witnessing the most beautiful thing I've ever seen, and I know it.

When "Pennsylvania 6-5000" disconnects, Anna sits down and takes a sip of her coffee. Black coffee. "So do you know how to knit, Heather?"

Okay, then.

"No, I don't."

"Then let's get started right away."

Liza lowers herself onto a rocker and draws out a crochet hook attached to a length of work about a foot wide and thirty or so inches long.

"A scarf?" I ask.

"How did you ever guess?"

Anna. "Oh, Liza!"

Thank goodness Anna is a patient teacher, because clearly knitting is as natural to me as American cheese. I've already knotted up the yarn a dozen times, knitted when I should have purled, and how can anyone possibly find this soothing?

"I think I'd better go to bed."

"I don't blame you." Liza.

"Liza! She's done a wonderful job for her first try!"

Liza winds the free length of yarn around the ball. "Tomorrow I'll teach you how to crochet. You may find that easier."

"Who said easy is the best way?" Anna.

Ah, a sisterly fight.

Now this is more like it.

"Please, Anna. People are either crocheters or knitters. It's that simple."

But Anna shakes her head. "You can do both, dear. I know it."

I hug them and head into my room for more Matthew, more Jesus, and hopefully a little more light.

"You do both, Liza. You just happened to pick crocheting tonight." I smile.

And the kingdom of heaven is like a mustard seed, a net, a hidden treasure. She who has ears to hear, let her hear.

TWENTY

"Mary! Mary! Dirty Mary!"

The children sing softly so the bus driver won't hear.

Mary sits in front of us, dirty blonde hair waving in clownish, kinky, matted chunks that jump up and down in the stream of air from the open bus windows.

It's always warm in my school memories. The bus windows always clicked open. The children always boisterous and yelling like police sirens.

Donald pulls a straw out of his pants pocket, wads up a bit of notebook paper, and places it in his mouth. He chews on it, letting the saliva soak into the very core.

He positions his lips around the straw, loads the spitball with his tongue, aims it at the back of Mary's hair, and blows with all the force he can push from his lungs.

The projectile whizzes out, lodging in the hair just above her shoulders. She doesn't move. She doesn't turn around or yell at us or even remove the spitty wad from her hair. Maybe she's learned that no matter what she does, we'll make her life miserable, and that in the end, we will always win. People like us always win.

I reach forward and push her head with my hand. "You're so gross, Mary. You're a disgusting, filthy little piece of nothing. You're nothing now; you'll be nothing tomorrow and clear into the rest of your life."

I stare up at the ceiling from the womb of my bed, breathing heavily, the dark air breezing off the loch and into my window.

I'm sorry, I'm so sorry.

I call Lark. It's 1:00 a.m.

"Hi, Heather."

"Do you have caller ID?"

"No. It was either you or Flannery, and Flannery's out of town at a gallery showing, so I figured it wasn't her."

"Were you up?"

"Uh-huh. Working on a proposal for some renovation supplies for the Hotel."

"You don't have someone to do that for you?"

"This is my backyard, Heather. So what's up?"

"I had a horrible dream. Something's happening to me, and I can't figure it out."

"Oooh, what a surprise."

"Let me wipe my chin a sec. A huge drop of sarcasm dripped out of the phone."

Lark laughs. "Just spill it. I'm wide-awake anyway."

"How come?"

"Mother had a terrible night last night, and I ended up sleeping until two this afternoon. My sleep schedule is all screwed up."

"Is she okay?"

"I think she's slipping. I won't be surprised if they find even more cancer."

"Will she go on chemo again?"

"I doubt it."

"You want to talk about it?"

"No way. Not at 1:00 a.m. I doubt I can process anything yet, and her doctor appointment isn't until next week, so I'd just be obsessing about something I don't even know is the case. So tell me about the dream."

I tell her the dream as well as other episodes of tormenting Gary and Mary. The way one of us would crawl up underneath the bus seats and slip something out of her book bag and throw it out the window. Or grab her lunch. Or cut a hole in her tights. The songs we made up, the many notes that said, "Take a bath" or "Brush your hair." The drawings of her, buckteeth sticking out with mile markers along them, or mice and bugs living inside her hair, dialogue bubbles saying, "Help! I'm stuck in here!"

"And that much would happen in a week! It was constant, Lark."

"Oh, Heather. You really did all that?"

"Yeah." And that wasn't the worst of it. But I can't even think about it yet, much less confess it to anyone.

"Wow."

"Were you ever made fun of, Lark?"

"A little, by the stupid kids. Never had all-out war declared on me, though."

War. Interesting metaphor.

"So why do you think I'm recalling all this now? I went for years without this bothering me so much. I mean, I always felt bad, but now . . . it's plaguing me."

"I don't know. Just sounds like God's doing a number on you in general. Cleaning you up inside and out, maybe."

And I always thought I was so squeaky clean. "Yeah, maybe."

"Get some sleep, Heather. Call me in the morning."

"Okay."

Squeaky clean or whitewashed tomb? I mean, honestly? No, I don't murder or steal or commit adultery, but inside, God knows I'm filled with unconfessed sin. Pride. A lot of pride.

A light knock.

"Come in."

Anna opens the door. "Are you all right, honey?"

"I'm sorry. I had a terrible dream and called my friend to talk about it."

"Oh, then. I was hoping everything was all right. It is all right, isn't it?"

"I'm having a crisis of guilt, if you want to know the truth."

"I always want to know the truth."

I believe her.

"I'll tell you about it over breakfast tomorrow." I'm sure she's tired, and it's so late.

"All right. If you change your mind, that's fine as well."

She sure knows how to take the pressure off.

"Thanks, Anna."

"My honor, friend."

"Anna? Did your pacifism lead you to being a Quaker, or was it the other way around?"

Anna leans against the doorjamb. "Quaker is actually a nickname, Heather. We are the Society of Friends. And even that is shortened. It was originally the Society of the Friends of Truth. Truth being Jesus. I met Jesus first."

"I thought I met Jesus, but now I'm not so sure."

She rests her hand on the doorknob. "Jesus comes to us in many ways, Heather. Don't discount your journey so far. He may be leading you down different paths now, but that doesn't mean your previous paths were rabbit trails, does it?"

"I guess not."

"God knows you, Heather. Every little part of you. Good night, my dear."

I check my cell phone for the time. A message came in earlier. I'll get it tomorrow.

Liza shakes her head. "My golly, you were awful, Heather."

Anna. "Liza!"

"Well, it's true! What did that poor girl ever do to any of you?"

"She obviously feels bad about it or she wouldn't be bringing it up."

"You're right." Liza lays her hands flat on the kitchen table. "Sorry. I'm not nearly as sweet as my sister."

I grip my coffee mug with both hands. "I've been trying to find them. So far, I'm up to 1982 in Michigan where Gary graduated from high school. But I'm wondering if I'm doing the right thing."

Anna. "Well, only you can say. Why do you want to find them?"

"I want to apologize, I guess. I want to see if they're okay, if my treatment of them, especially Mary, affected their lives for the worse."

Liza. "And if it did?"

"Then I want to try and make it up to them."

Anna puts her hand over mine and squeezes. "I guess all we can do is pray that what you're doing is coming from the Spirit."

"And if it's not, that you'll meet a door you just can't open and that'll be that." Liza.

That'll be that.

I wish.

But I'll move forward. I believe I must.

Anna stands up, scraping her chair backwards. "Just try to make sure you're not doing this for yourself, to assuage your own guilt and feel better. If that's the case, Heather, then you don't want to drag Mary through the pain again."

Heaven help me, but how Mary might feel never entered my mind. I guess I really haven't changed all that much, have I?

They've nurtured me for the past five days. We've knitted and crocheted, depending on which sister got to me first. And I'm not too bad at either of them now, after a great deal of practice. We listen to the breeze outside and not much else.

When Liza cooked, we ate classic French food like coq au vin or cassoulet or something exotic yet simple like Cornish game hen with truffles. Anna usually set out homemade bread and cheese with some fruit to round things out. Or perhaps a piece of fish and a steamed vegetable. Every morning, steaming oatmeal topped with sliced banana, laced with brown sugar, and surrounded by milk. Strong black coffee.

We walk sometimes and we sit and read, one sister beginning to hum, and the other joining in, and always they seem to stop at the very same place.

Blue moon, you saw me standing alone.

L is for the way you look at me, O is for the only one I see. V hmm, hmm, hmm, hmm, hmm.

I can only give you love that lasts forever.

And we work, scouring one room each day, gardening, raking, and canning food.

The humming is almost always off key but always exactly on the beat.

Will calls with a stockpile of information on the ecosystem of the Chesapeake Bay and "Mom, Grandma and Grandpa actually took me for a sail on a real skipjack. I got some great photos with the unbirthday camera you left for me in the suitcase. Thanks."

We chitchat, and I decide to tell him, "Sometimes I wonder if I've taken the right tack with the kids who've made fun of you in school. Well, maybe that's not completely true. I regret that I haven't found the right plan."

"You tried, Mom."

"I've tried everything I could think of, bud. I talked to teachers, the administration, the janitor. I talked to anyone who would listen. I also encouraged you to take it silently, and when that didn't work, to fight back, and when you came home with your blazer ripped, I knew that wasn't the answer either."

"I could have told you it was a bad idea."

"Why didn't you?"

"You're my mother. I figured you'd have an inside scoop on the perfect response."

Mercy.

"And I don't know why I didn't look harder for an answer somewhere else. Should I have homeschooled you? Should I have just sent you over to the public school? It couldn't have been any worse there, right?"

"Mom, I didn't want to go anywhere else. Don't get all revisionist on me. I was the one who asked to stay. And another thing—those guys are mean, but I've made other friends."

"But those kids are so popular. Don't you ever—?"

"Want to be popular? Sheesh, Mom. Those kids are the long-haul dorks. They'll get to be your age and they'll be insurance agents over the phone and they'll wonder what happened to all that popularity. They'll have done nothing special to speak of with their own lives."

Does he realize he could be talking about me?

"But what if that doesn't happen?"

"Mom, what goes around comes around. Nerds rule the world. Not the cool people. You know that. I mean, think Bill Gates, think Warren Buffet. Shoot, I'll bet J. K. Rowling was an utter geek in high school."

"Have you been talking about this stuff with your father?"

"Most definitely. Dad's helped me big-time to accept these things. I don't know why you think you have to wave a wand and make it all go away. Life is never perfect."

Lord, oh Lord. What do you have planned for this kid? And should I buy myself protective armor just in case?

How will he take it when I tell him I'm trying to find the Andrews kids and when I tell him why?

TWENTY-ONE

Liza's driving diverges from her personality as fully as Gloria Steinem's face from her political views. She crammed a fifteen-minute drive into forty, the queen bee leading an angry swarm of motorists down Paper Mill Road.

I am thirteen again, sitting in the front seat of our Barracuda as Dad drives to my grandparents' on the other side of town, or to church, or out to Loch Raven. His slowpoke ways, especially on the beltway, especially in a car that could blow the doors off most of the other vehicles on the road, made me more embarrassed than a woman caught gossiping in the church bathroom.

I can feel my own scalp.

Liza doesn't notice a thing. "So you must be fairly discontent with your life if you feel the need to get away from it all and stay with us ancients."

So tell me what you really think, Liza.

"Guilty."

"I see. Is it helping?"

"I don't know. We'll have to see."

"What's so unacceptable about your life as is? Your husband seems awfully nice, and you haven't mentioned your son in such a way as leads me to believe he's giving you trouble."

"No. Will's my buddy, and Jace is a good husband. Works a lot, but he's a good man. I'm not under the delusion that I can have it all."

"Really? Most people are, I've found."

I shrug. "Part of me is beginning to think of all my stuff like

486

weights, not anything that lifts me up. There's a part of me that would like to throw everything out and start over. Buy simple white plates and plain cutlery. Seven outfits. One church dress." I'm not about to tell her the process has begun.

"Why don't you do that? Just pare down to those things."

"I said there's a part of me that wants that. But having the trappings comforts me. I hate to admit it."

She takes the next curve with all the recklessness of a tuna salad sandwich on Wonder Bread. "That's why I've always loved my house. It was all created to work together without the need for more, more, more."

"Your husband designed it?"

"Yes, he did. Including the dinnerware and the textiles. Was quite the visionary." She turns to me, and I'm tempted to point out the window like Will does. "And he designed wonderful, affordable houses for the simple working man. Modern, of course. Functional. Inexpensive to heat. The neighborhood is down in Glen Burnie."

"Did you have children?"

"One. He's gone, though. I don't talk about him. His very death defames him, and I said I'd never do that."

"I'm sorry."

"We weren't talking about me. I'm not the type to let people off their hooks, Heather."

"I believe that."

"So what about church? You haven't said much about it, and I saw your Bible when I dusted your bedroom."

"We left regular church attendance last year, and I don't know whether it's my fault or the church's."

"Why does it have to be anybody's fault?"

"I don't know. Shouldn't it?"

"Maybe it's not about casting blame, Heather. Maybe you've got a different testimony to live out."

"Testimony?"

We turn into the parking lot of a newer building with a sanitary residentiality about it that screams, "Not a real home, but we're trying!"

She crawls into a space, shuts off the engine, and looks at me. "It's one of Anna's Friends things. I always thought of testimony as our story. How God came to us and how we recognized Him and decided to follow."

"Me too."

"But for the Quaker it's about the inward *and* the outward journey. For some reason, I always found it easy to fall into the trap that our testimony signifies all that we abstain from. I don't smoke, or get drunk, or fool around, so my testimony is good. But Anna speaks of her testimony as something more—her good works, her commitment to the community, to the least of these—like her friend Bobby. That all of this bespeaks a commitment to the light of the Spirit that lives inside her."

"She's a good friend."

"Certainly. So did your church encourage you all to move outward, or was it inwardly focused?"

"Mostly inward. I did much more for my church members than I did for my neighbors, if that's what you mean."

She places her hand on the doorknob. "Maybe God's simply flipping the equation."

"Putting the trombones on melody?" I ask, remembering Glenn Miller.

"Who knows? Might just be something to think about."

Liza seems more comfortable at offering concrete theories than Anna.

"And," she continues, "if God sent you here to be with us, He's obviously got some sort of plan. Of course, Anna's more cerebral and ethereal and mystical about all of it than I am, so she might disagree."

"You think?"

She leads me into the home for alcoholic men. The foyer is bright and clean, painted white with mass production artwork hanging on the walls; mostly Thomas Kinkade's unattainable regurgitations, and wouldn't Will the artiste have a fit? To the right, a set of steps, tan runner cascading down, leads to the upper floor.

We continue on through to a kitchen in the back. No one greets us. "Is the place empty?"

"Yes. Everybody works outside the home during the day. Unless, of course, somebody's sick, which isn't out of the question. Here." She reaches up, grabs an apron on a hook by the pantry, and hands it to me. "Get one of those big pots out and fill it with water. Set it on the stove to boil. I'm going to make pasta primavera."

"Do you have much contact with the men?"

"Depends. Not on Fridays. I just cook and put it in the fridge to be warmed up by whoever has KP tonight."

"Do they cook for themselves?"

"Usually. But Friday is a big night for them. Family can visit. I do this so they can eat, clean up, and spend time with their loved ones."

She turns on a radio, and we listen to classical music from the local NPR station, working in silence, working in peace; chopping broccoli and carrots, browning onion and garlic, grating cheese.

An hour later, a man in a mechanic's jumpsuit walks into the kitchen. "Miss Liza."

"Howie!" She turns, and I see a different woman. She rushes over and hugs him. "How are you? I haven't seen you in weeks!"

"Been workin' hard. Just came in to get my insurance card. Got a doctor appointment."

Howie possesses the lean frame of a whippet and the eyes of a basset hound.

"Are you all right, lovey?"

"Just a checkup. Been dry six months now." Satisfaction turns down the corners of his mouth. Ah, and there's the bulldog side of him.

"Good for you. Listen, I'll make you a sandwich in two shakes of a lamb's tail while you go get your card."

Howie retreats down the hallway toward the steps.

"I just love that man. If anybody deserved to drink, it was Howie."

But she offers nothing more, and I don't feel it's my place to know his story.

She hums Glenn Miller as she assembles a peanut butter and strawberry jam sandwich, her features younger and softer. This woman who buried a husband, buried a son. Her only son. My, but humans are resilient.

My cell phone rings, and darn it, but I'm right next to it. I really don't feel like talking to anybody. It's so lovely sitting here by the pool.

Legermin, Ronald.

I push the talk button. "Hello?"

"Is this Mrs. Curridge?"

"Yes."

I'm going to make him work for it.

"This is Ron Legermin. My son, Ronnie, is in your son's class. As I'm sure you're already frighteningly aware of."

"Yes. It's nice of you to call."

"Thanks for allowing me to. Mrs. Curridge—"

"Heather."

"Thanks. Heather, I just wanted to call and apologize for my son's behavior this year."

"It's been years, actually."

"I figured." He sighs. "I want Ronnie to apologize to your son."

"But then he'll know Will had something to do with it, Ron."

"I know. But I honestly don't think he'll repeat the behavior."

"Really?"

"Yes. Believe me, he's not having a great summer because of it. I'm so sorry. I had no idea. I've always thought parents oblivious to their kid's faults had no excuse. And I'm right."

"Why don't we just see how it goes at the beginning of the year?"

"Will you promise to keep me posted?"

"I will."

"I can't help my son if I don't know what's going on."

"I know. And I accept your apology, Ron."

"Thanks."

After saying good-bye, I look out over the chlorine waters of the pool. Just great. Now I'll have to wait until September to see how this is all going to shake out. But Will would rather be hung by his hair than have to endure a false apology from Ronnie Legermin.

Anna slides open the top drawer of the built-in buffet in the dining room. "It's all laid out in here."

It will take me all weekend to polish this silver. But ah, it's fabulous. Smooth and cool and sleek—artwork, really.

"Thank you, Heather. Our hands just aren't what they used to be."

"I really don't mind."

"I'm heading out for a bit, down to the market. I'm cooking tonight and I just feel like fried pork chops. Do you like fried pork chops?"

"Definitely."

"I realize this goes without saying, but help yourself to anything you need. All we have is yours."

"Thank you." I pull out the first fork. "These will go nicely with my china."

She holds a hand up to her mouth and giggles. "Oh, Heather. You crack me up, as the younger set says."

I watch her leave the room. I hear her gather her purse and keys. Listen to the front door open and shut, the car start, the wheels roll down the drive. I love Anna.

Liza's taking Oatmeal for a little stroll, so I put my cell phone on speaker and call Will down at his grandparents' house. He practically shoots electrical sparks through the airwaves, he's so filled with excitement.

"Mom, I did the coolest collage out of watercolor paper. Very abstract, but you can tell it's the bay right around here."

Jace's parents bought a vacation home right on the Chesapeake Bay years ago, and now they live there all summer long. I don't blame them one bit. It's my favorite spot in the whole world. Who can blame anyone for wanting to live on the water?

Will has plans for more, however. Make it a series about the needy, and he's going to show people from the Hotel drowning in the bay in front of vacation houses, and oh yeah, Grandma bought an Xbox for the place.

I don't comment on the irony.

He also thinks about things and feels and black is black and white is white. He's like Liza. He doesn't let people off their hooks either.

Will asks me about the Hotel. "Mom, have you thought more about it? Really?"

"A little." A lot.

"I mean, a kangaroo? You've got to see that as some sort of a sign."

"And what would that sign be?"

"How should I know? I'm not the one who crashed her car because of it."

"You crack me up." As the younger set says.

Jace next.

"Hi, hon."

"Where are you?"

"In my car on the way to lunch. Where are you?"

"In the dining room polishing silver."

"Is that right? How's that going?"

"Fabulous. I imagine it'll be very therapeutic."

"Did Anna talk you into it?" Jace has heard updates every day. He feels like he knows the sisters.

"How'd you guess?"

"I must be psychic."

I pick up the silver polishing cloth. "Hey, while you're there, I want you to do me a favor. Read Matthew 25 for me."

"Sure. Did Will tell you about his collage?"

"Yes."

"It could be Loch Raven and our house, you know?"

"Big-time."

"What about the sisters? How do they deal with living here in this area?"

"Shoot, Jace. Their house probably cost about $15K to build and has been paid off forever."

"Seriously. Ouch."

"Uh-huh."

"Why did Jesus have to raise the bar so high?" he asks.

"And how did you and I get so far off track?"

Jace clears his throat. "There are a lot of people who disagree with you about what you're thinking these days, Heather. They think the more you have, the more you must be doing something right because God's looking upon you with favor. That Christianity should be about safety for their families, a place to stay holy and pure."

I pick up a knife and wrap the polishing cloth around it. "I guess it's my definition of holiness that's changing, then."

"I'd better go. I'm at the restaurant."

I say good-bye and settle into the silence and smoothness of my task. Here I am, polishing expensive silver. Somehow these ladies know how to handle material possessions and social responsibility.

Still, I bet they haven't bought anything new for this house in decades. Liza loves the things she has. Maybe there's a key in there, loving the things you have, not the things you don't have. And I suspect she'd give it away if someone asked for it.

Of course, I do that too. Only to trade up. Lock Jace in more. And more. And more.

Am I punishing him for the decision I made to live my life for his? Is this a retribution of sorts?

I make another call to the contractor who's scheduled to build our tennis court next month. I cancel the plans. Maybe it's in the cards someday. But that day is not today.

Another message on the phone. I listen to Carmen asking me if I can host the new mothers' tea this fall and why didn't I answer the last call?

I open my Bible to Matthew 25.

When I was hungry, you gave Me something to eat. Thirsty, you gave Me something to drink. Naked and clothed Me. Sick and in

prison and you came to Me. If you've done it to the least of My brothers, you've done it to Me.

Jesus said that.

Oh, Jace.

I call him though it's midnight, but the phone just rings and rings,
and his cell phone switches right to voice mail.

TWENTY-TWO

Anna explains as we enter the building. "It was a Full Gospel church once upon a time, but as you'll see, we rearranged the pews and conduct our meetings much differently than the Gospels did. First, though, we'll go to Sunday school."

Good! Sunday school. That sounds normal.

We thread our way through the hallway and into the library. Mismatched furniture circles the room, and I sit next to Anna. As the group assembles, people choose the hard, uncomfortable chairs first, the couch and lounge chair the last to be taken. Interesting.

I've never seen this many pairs of sensible shoes in my entire life, and the man sitting next to me, hair sprouting from ears and nostrils, has the worst case of nail fungus imaginable. I can't stop staring at his hand curled atop his cane. Do I appear rude, un-Quakerish, an individualistic, hedonistic, warmongering person who doesn't care about the environment?

Mercy, just relax, Heather. You're staring at somebody's hands, that's all.

I expected a Bible study like regular Sunday school, but they talk about initiatives the Friends Committee of National Legislation should focus on for the next two years. The man leading the group reminds me of a friendly, silver-haired lion. Campaign finance reform, clean and verifiable voting procedures, global warming and fossil fuel dependency, opposition of the doctrine of preventative war, immigration, living wages, and poor working conditions. Defense of the rule of law by limits on executive power?

Health care.

AIDS here and abroad.

National security: diplomatic versus military solutions.

What next, abortion rights?

Apparently not. Nobody mentions reproduction.

This is the craziest Sunday school I've ever seen. But I like these people anyway with their simple clothing, dye-free hair, pristine beards. They've even brought in their own breakfasts, which don't include a bag with golden arches but rather consist of yogurt, a bran muffin, some fruit. No wonder most of them have a granola glow. By my count, seven elderly people, two in their twenties, one in his thirties, and four in their forties or fifties circle the room.

I wonder if they have youth group?

Of course my nose has started to run, and every sniff sounds like the winds of a hurricane here in the silent gathering. Most sit with their eyes closed, expecting a thought from God or waiting for someone else to stand and deliver the Spirit's message. At least that's what their literature says they're doing. Me, I'm just looking around, breathing foreign air, and wondering what they'd do if I stood up and shouted, "Praise the Lord and pass the ammunition!"

My shoulders start to shake with laughter.

Anna grabs my hand and squeezes. I just cannot stop. The harder I try, the more heat builds in my face, providing a greenhouse for the tickles. *Please, God, let me stop!* But it's not going to happen. Maybe if I just relax.

Okay, yes. Yes. Good.

Think of tragedy. All sorts of tragedy. I think of my dad. But he would have been chuckling too.

Yes, just let your mind drift away. Perfect. How about Carmen? Nothing funny there.

And then—

Anna's shoulders start shaking too. In fact, the entire pew is vibrating underneath our giggles. I'm ten again and I'm sitting next to Dad during the Eucharist and he's squeezing my hand, trying not to smile.

Finally we stop, just waiting for the beast to bite again, when a man stands up and says something about summer and the newness of life in his vegetable garden, comparing it to peace, its hopes, its dreams, its ability to work miracles, widespread and worldwide. My underarms and back are slick and my heart is happy. I don't know if I found God here, but I watched other people find God. I do know that.

All at once several people stand. It is over.

"I don't know, Anna," I say on the car ride home. "I think it would drive me crazy week after week."

"It's all right, honey. Obviously, it isn't everyone's cup of tea. Speaking of tea, how about a cup of that cranberry tea when we get home?"

And that is that. I know Anna won't ask me to attend with her. She'll leave it up to me.

Anna picks up a fork. "How nice to eat off of polished silver."

"Certainly is. Thank you, Heather. And the potato salad looks divine." Liza hands us all a napkin.

Sunday dinner today is my contribution to the culinary life of the house. Food is so essential here, so holy. I made up the potato salad last night because it's always better the second day. Before church I put a brisket in the oven swimming in the makings of a barbecue sauce with a teriyaki slant. We picked up fresh rolls on the way home from the service, and now an easy peach cobbler is baking to a bubbling ecstasy in the oven.

Yes, I love food. Sweets best if forced to make a choice.

The women eat with such daintiness. Honestly, I do feel a bit, well, oxish. Each generation seems to eclipse the one before it in size somewhat, and the sisters were small in their own day, I'm sure.

So I help myself to a skosh more potato salad to even out the meat on my plate. I do need to make sure it all ends up evenly for some reason. I always have. The problem is, the more you have, the more that needs evening up.

"So how do you know when it's the Spirit speaking to you?" I ask Anna. Again. Maybe I can browbeat an answer out of her, like the insistent neighbor Jesus talked about, knocking and knocking and knocking.

She wipes her mouth. "I'm sure Liza would answer differently. But for me, it's the Spirit if it leads you closer to God."

Liza nods. "If it leads you to act more like Jesus is how I might put it."

It's funny how these two women have such a drastically different slant on the same God. Anna relies on the Spirit, has such a gentle, ethereal faith that works itself out in the sadness of others. Liza has jumped in Jesus's arms and said, "Let's go, good buddy!" And they gallop off together in search of the most awful places where their presence will make the most difference.

Doing justice, loving mercy, walking humbly with God. That's the sisters. And isn't that in the Bible somewhere?

Can I be a little of both someday, Lord? Someday when I grow up? A little of Anna, a little of Liza—and a little of my dad. I want to be like my dad too.

Eleven days. Only three more left here at Alva's home, and the trill of panic vibrates inside. It will be good to see Will, good to see Jace, but if I could meet them in some new life where we walk into that small house with those white walls and just the clothes on our backs, I'd be the happiest woman in the world. I've been drilling Liza about modern architecture and its values, and I've got plans in my mind, a small house with built-ins for storage, but with a homey aesthetic that I find a little more appealing.

And no cause for dotting.

The silver is polished, and when I hold up a spoon, I'm greeted by a convex portrait of myself, large wide nose and mouth, little eyes, and a forehead sloping back like in the drawing of Cro-Magnon man. But the smile is wide because I'm proud of myself.

I took it upon myself to wash all the table linens and iron them as well. The sisters were delighted.

I call Lark from my bedroom. "I feel another string of thoughts coming on."

"Go on, crazy lady."

"After trailing around with the sisters to all their meetings and workings, I honestly don't know how they stay sane. I've always thought the people who I've journeyed with so long ignore the down-trodden portion of humanity because we're too busy with everything else, too tired, too preoccupied with our own families and our churches."

"You think?"

"And yeah, I have to be honest with myself and say I fall into that camp. When was the last time, before taking the cake to the Hotel, that I did anything for anybody who couldn't possibly do anything in return? But I think there's more to it. Maybe we're frightened that we'll bend beneath the pain we'll feel for others, that maybe we'll buckle under the atrocities some of God's creatures are forced to endure."

"And there are many," Lark says.

"And will the God we've worshiped blindly from our cushioned lives hold up under the stress of a world that's bloody and bruised, blind and broken with absolutely no hope this side of heaven, sitting literally before our eyes? Will we trust Him ourselves when it seems that others, with their lost limbs, children, sight, and families, seemingly can't?"

"I can't answer that for you. The question isn't 'we,' Heather. A lot of faithful people serve like that. The question is 'I.' Will *your* faith hold under that sort of pressure?"

"I don't know. Would I be so quick to shout 'Hallelujah' if my infant son just had his arms hacked off with a machete by a cruel soldier or Jace died because I didn't have the money for a doctor?"

"I don't know. I don't think I'd be doing any shouting. Have you been on the Internet again?"

I'm not ready to be sidetracked. I'm Liza. I'm Will. "We pray we never have to really answer these questions for ourselves, don't we? Because in those moments when we give honesty its rightful place, we don't know if our faith will survive."

"Is that all God is to you, Heather? The Bob Vila of this decrepit world?"

"Sometimes, yes."

"I've noticed something. It's people like us who think these thoughts, because we have the white-bread luxury to think them. Those who've experienced horror, deprivation, and loneliness tend to see God in ways we never could. And that, my friend, is something worth considering."

"Why?"

"Did you ever think that these people may actually have something to teach you? That it's not just about you going into the uttermost parts and being the big savior? That they have wisdom and grace to share that you'll know nothing about until you sit yourself down in front of them and get to know them?"

"Of course I haven't, Lark. I've already confessed I'm bereft about these matters."

"Okay. Well, think about it. God's like a grandmother who grew up in the Depression. He saves every little scrap of food, of tinfoil, of plastic wrap, and He uses it again and again for different people. I'm sure there's a ream of faithful wisdom you can gather from those you're running away from."

"In other words, it cuts both ways."

"Yes! You'll gain far more than you'll ever give. And it's okay to be selfish about it like that. Suck out all the juice life has to offer, Heather. I think God wants us to, don't you?"

"I do."

"Then why are you making yourself so miserable about your calling?"

"I've got a calling?"

"Oh my gosh, Heather. You actually had a kangaroo cross your path. What more do you need?"

"A notarized letter?"

TWENTY-THREE

I find her on a boulder at the bottom of the steep incline leading down to the lake. Liza sits with her back to the breeze looking west toward the Dulaney Valley Road bridge. Does she somehow hear church bells beneath the waters? No, Liza knows the truth.

I start down the hill.

Her profile speaks of granite and statues, things unforgiving and bald. The noonday sun bleaches her features to a flat mask. The high wind diminishes her.

When I'm not with Liza, my mind-vision of her is of a much younger woman. I remember her with darker eyes and dark hair and gauzy movements. And when she walks into the room, I'm always surprised by her age and her well-planted feet.

She hears me approach and turns. She doesn't welcome me. "It's my day, Heather."

"Anna said." I stop halfway down, holding on to a sapling to keep from tumbling forward.

"I'd prefer to be by myself."

"You don't like to talk about him."

"No."

"You'd rather keep him to yourself."

She looks back to the waters. "Yes. It's easier."

Liza's only son died fifty years ago at the age of fifteen, Will's age. It was one of those stupid things, Anna said, that could have been easily avoided. Lou had always been a good swimmer, and why he chose to go out that night into Loch Raven nobody knew. The lake wasn't for swimming, and he knew that. Anna said that Liza only once admitted to finding a bottle of gin at the edge of the yard. Alva died only a year later.

Somebody's burning leaves somewhere, and the smell of autumn veils the summer day, anchors it for the grief-filled memorial.

Sometimes telling somebody you'll pray for them seems almost disrespectful, like saying, "This is a mountain you can climb." Sometimes some mountains are too high to ever get over, so I slide down the rest of the path, lay a hand on her shoulder, squeeze, kiss the silver smoothness of her head, and climb my way back to the house.

Anna and I sit on the couch together, holding hands and praying silently for Liza.

The sunbeam falling through the sliding glass doors lies on us warm and comfortable like a quilt from the dryer; the clock on the mantel holds a microphone inside. All is thorny and itchy, woolen and flax. But she keeps her hand in mine. Warm hand. Our perspiration mingles, and she holds tight. Doesn't she know the rule of prayer hand-holding? When you start to get uncomfortable in the grip, you either squeeze lightly twice or wiggle your fingers a bit. And then the other person is supposed to let go. Vice versa: if you feel this being done to you, you let go right away.

I've done this several times, and she's either ignoring me or too deep in prayer to notice.

Ah, Lord, I wish I could lose myself in prayer like that.

I close my eyes.

Two hours later, I awaken. And Anna still prays for her sister.

She opens her eyes.

"When will she come in, Anna?"

"After dark. We'll be long in bed. I'm glad it's not raining today. I always pray the weather will be mild for her."

The day progresses as we move about under the weight of remembrance, cooking our meals, washing our sheets, doing the crossword puzzle, and finally, watching *Jeopardy!*

"You think she's all right, Anna?"

"No. She will never be all right. And hasn't been all right for fifty years, Heather. But then, none of us are really *all* right, are we?"

No, I guess we're not.

This morning Liza and I traveled downtown—I begged her to let me drive, and she did—to the Church of Holy Peace near Essex. First of all, we were two of four white faces in the mix. Second of all, I've never seen people actually running around the sanctuary. I usually feel a little strange when I want to lift up a hand to worship, but folks were actually running around the sanctuary. Needless to say, I lifted both hands and wasn't the least bit embarrassed. It liberated.

The pastor, who hopped on her high heels, danced about and sang in a sing-song, "The Lord is good. Let me hear you sing it with me. The Lord is *good.*"

And the congregation joined in as the band encouraged them with the one-two gospel beat. "The Lord is good. The Lord is good."

"Sing it out, y'all!"

Oh, Lord, she was beautiful in her violet two-piece dress with just a hint of sparkle up top.

"The Lord is good," I sang, looking around me. But lost in their own praise, nobody noticed me.

Liza simply sat with her eyes closed, drinking it in like a desert flower. And in that crowd of Christians, even that was understood.

On the drive home I asked her how she'd found the place.

"I'm a nomad Christian, Heather."

"But what about finding a church home?"

"I have a church home, with the men at the halfway house."

"Is it the same?"

"We are all God's people, Heather. My church is *the* Church. I don't have many years left and want to be with as many of God's people as I can."

Jace and I sit on the patio outside the family room. The sisters putter about the kitchen, tickled to have a dinner guest of the male persuasion, and isn't that sweet? Earlier during breakfast before church, Liza patted the corner of her mouth with a napkin. "Now, Anna, men like beef. We'll have a rib roast, twice-baked potatoes, and a green salad."

"Then I'll do the dessert. Apple pie with butter crumb topping à la mode."

"Right, then. I'll throw the roast into the oven before we leave."

I almost spit out my coffee. No argument? Mercy!

Jace shoves his hands in his pocket. "So here's the deal, Hezz. Will wants to stay with my parents for another week. I think it might be good for you, if the sisters don't mind, to stay here until he's back. I think rattling around at our house, with what you're going through, will be the worst thing for you. My surgical schedule is crazy tomorrow and Tuesday, and Wednesday through Sunday I'll be at that conference in Chicago. Believe me, though, it'll be better after that."

Will it?

"What's the conference about again?"

"Just a surgical thing."

"Can't you be a little more specific?"

"It's pretty generalized, hon."

"Then why a conference on it? Aren't they usually pretty specific?"

"Not always."

Man, Jace! Fess up, okay?

But another week with the sisters? Like I even have to think. "Let me ask Anna and Liza."

"I already did. They said it was fine."

So what's all this about? Does he want to get rid of me for the week, or keep me with the sisters because they're a good influence on me, or is this something he thinks I need? For such a nice guy, he's driving me nuts right now.

And it stings a little. He has never kept a secret from me before. That I know of.

Mercy.

"Wanna walk down to the water?" I stand up.

"Good idea. By the way, Carmen's trying to get in touch with you. She's called the house a bunch of times."

"I know. I just can't go there right now."

We slip and slide our way down the embankment and settle on Liza's rock. We don't say too much. Who says much when the ship you're on begins to pull away from the dock and out into the harbor?

"Do you miss the hospital ship, Jace?"

"More than I can say."

"I canceled the tennis court."

"No kidding!"

"Nope."

When I kissed him good-bye an hour later, still no confession about Bonnie.

I tell Anna. "Is this a problem?"

"Oh dear. The fact that you can't come out and ask him speaks to something far deeper."

TWENTY-FOUR

We picked our own. Now that really does make sense after having been with these women, nonstop, for the past two weeks. It's really not quite the same to climb in the car, drive down to Klein's or Safeway, and pick up a flat of strawberries from California or South America or some exotic place with a strange-sounding name, far away over the sea.

The farmer, Dave Bittner, helped us pick the berries as we zig-zagged down the rows. Young, energetic, and somehow drawn to the sisters just like I was, he chattered about his kids, his crops, and all the plans he had. He talked about land and soil and rain, about roots and seeds and leaves, all these things God makes. And this is his life. Not ideas that remain ideas. Not postulations or prose. Dave Bittner must scrape the very planet from beneath his fingernails each night before he picks up an ear of corn and bites down with his calcium teeth.

Yeah, that sure beats the Safeway.

And now clear running water thrums into the stainless steel kitchen sink. Liza gently places the berries in to soak, although, you guessed it, they were grown without pesticides. Still, dirt, no matter how clean, isn't something most people want to eat.

Okay, yes, there's that odd man who pops up on TV shows every once in a while who eats dirt. But he only proves my point.

I begin cutting off the tops. We're making jam for all the ministries the sisters support: the home for marginalized women down in Randallstown—unwed mothers, battered women, undereducated women, pretty much anyone with girl organs who needs a hand and wants to get on with her life. The alcoholics' home, of course. And I'm sure Anna will take some to her Quakers and the Vets. I ask if I can make some for the Hotel, and they are delighted by the suggestion.

I bask in the holiness of these berries. I eat one, worshiping in a very taste-filled, texture-filled way as it slides down my throat, the natural sugars defining the moment, the sweetness a gift from heaven.

Liza pops one in her mouth too. "The best part. Sneaking tastes."

"I agree."

Anna told me not to ask Liza about Lou, and though I'm eager to know how she's doing, I refrain. Anna so very seldom gives concrete suggestions, I know this must be something I'd be wise to listen to.

"Liza, how do you keep going with all this? Don't you ever feel raw from dealing with so much heartache?"

"Well, Heather, if it was about me, I suppose I would."

"Even so. A person can only take in so much."

She starts to mash the berries in a pot over low heat. "Now there's your mistake."

Anna would never say something like that. I like it. "How so?"

"It's like this. I don't just take in, dear. More comes out of me than goes in. It's why I give, have really made a life work out of it. When you take so much in, it can fester inside of you, knotting up your muscles, your psyche, your stomach, your nerves, even your soul. You've got to find some way to get it out. So when I give some jam, or make a meal, or talk with the men down at the home, I'm giving away some of my doubts, my fears, my own sin, and the sin of others that I know about."

"I don't get how that helps."

"As long as good is happening, God is there."

"But isn't He in the pain too?"

"Yes. But in the pain I lean on Him. In the good, somehow, I participate with Him in a way that binds me to Him and Him to me in a different way. He allows me to partner with Him during those times, and I find that to be the highest honor He could ever bestow upon an old sinner like me."

I pick up another berry. "And then become like Christ Himself, who wasn't content just to say things, but to touch people, heal them, eat with them."

"Be with them. Jesus showed up, Heather, at the weddings, the funerals, the meals, the stonings, the healings, the crucifixions. We tend to forget how straightforward it can really be."

"Liza? Do you ever wonder if you would have remained with Him in Gethsemane, along Calvary road, and at the foot of the cross?"

"All the time."

"I do too."

"The only answer I can give to it is to ask a question. Am I there now? Right now with Jesus? Am I walking the road, praying in the garden, taking up my cross? If I can't say yes to that right now, how can I begin to answer the other question? Do I have the right to even ask it?"

"I often wonder how Jesus actually saw this world as worth dying for."

Her brows raise. "Oh my! Wouldn't you die for your son?"

"Of course."

It's all so simple with Liza.

She measures out sugar. "But most of us are only called to live for God, His world, our children, His children, aren't we?"

I raise my brows. Oh, so that's all it takes?

She smiles her saucy smile. "Easier said than done, I know. But honestly easier done, in the long run, than undone."

Lark picks up on the first ring. "Hey, Heather."

"How do you do it? You always pick up right away." I take a sip from my nighttime cup of tea.

"I'm scared I'm going to miss something important, maybe even life-threatening for somebody else, all because I didn't get to the phone in time. I used to have a toll-free line, 1-800-I-Pray-4-U, and I've been paranoid ever since."

Honestly, she's a bit wacky, which is why I love her.

"So what's up?" she asks.

"Did your father set up his foundation before or after he came to faith?"

"Before."

"Why?"

"He loved all the folks. The people in his factory, the people he met on his travels. He saw them as real people, with hearts and minds and lives to live. After he found Christ, he spent a lot of time in the Prophets, Heather. Particularly Isaiah. His life verses were Isaiah 58:6–8."

"Isaiah 58, you said?" I fish for a pencil in the nightstand.

"Yep."

"Thanks."

"Try Micah 6:8 while you're at it. It's the do justice, love mercy, walk humbly with thy God thingee."

"You're a veritable font of Scripture knowledge tonight, Lark."

"Well, I had to make sure I wasn't doing all this stuff for nothing. A lot of Christians play down good works like it's some smelly thing that only people from mainline denominations rely on to work their way into heaven. People who aren't really close to God in the personal devotion-slash-refrain-from-sin type of stuff."

"I know. Which is one of the struggles I'm having."

"People's souls may go on forever, but I think God wants us to help their bodies and spirits here right now too. And not just Christian people."

"Thanks. I'll look this stuff up."

"I mean, it's hardly an either/or situation, now, is it?"

"Not if you say so." Whoa, Lark.

"Okay. Go to bed, Heather."

I decide to check my messages. Oh my goodness, two more from Carmen. The new mothers' tea. The new mothers' tea. Does she never give up?

TWENTY-FIVE

Of course it takes us twice as long to get to the Hotel with Liza driving, but we left in plenty of time. Anna waved us off, clutching her own purse to head out to the Veterans hospital. Five jars of strawberry jam rest in a basket on my lap.

Though Liza may have lost her road speed, she should get a medal for her parallel parking. With two cake boxes in my hands, one in hers, we clop our way down the broken sidewalk alongside the Hotel. The jam hangs in a basket from the crook of my arm.

Mo sees us after we round the corner and walk past the plate glass window near his desk. He gains his feet and slips over to the door, flipping it open wide. "Well, here she is, and with some more of that cake!"

"Hey, Mo."

"And you brought along a friend, I see."

"This is Liza Stephens."

Mo takes her cake and sets it on a nearby table. The small, gentle movements of this mammoth man fascinate me. "Krista," he calls. "You mind helping these ladies get these cakes to the kitchen?"

She stands up without a word and walks toward us. It's the young woman who was locked out a few weeks ago. Grabbing Liza's boxes, she jerks her head toward the door at the back of the room. "Come on this way, y'all."

She doesn't seem too happy about this, but it gives me time to examine her from the back. Her black hair is piled into some intricate, wavy do, and two large hoops dangle from her ears. A tattoo

511

screams "Playgirl" across the back of her neck. Ah, her creamy skin looks like soft velvet beneath those words.

She's no longer pregnant. I wonder where her baby is.

"How's the baby?" I ask.

She pushes through the swinging door and into the kitchen. "You can set them right here on the table. And how do you know about my baby?"

"I was here the night Sister Jerusha wouldn't let you in because it was after nine."

She shakes her head. "That woman can be a witch."

"We all can," Liza says. "I've never seen a bigger one than myself." I laugh.

Krista tilts her head to the side. "I guess that's true of me too."

I nod. "Me too."

"So my baby been taken away. She in foster care and here I am. Just tryin' to figure some things out. Anyway, you wanna see Sister J? She back in the office."

"If she's got time."

She leads us through the kitchen to the back hallway and knocks on the door to Sister Jerusha's quarters. "Sister J! It's that cake lady and a friend of hers."

"Come on in!"

She sits with that suave, well-dressed man, whose sculpted face, exquisite and fine, breaks into a smile. "This is my godson, Knox."

He nods at me. The drug dealer strikes again. And that smile. What an intoxicating smile.

"Knoxie, this is Heather Curridge and—"

Liza puts out her hand and Knox takes it. "Liza Stephens."

"Pleasure to meet you." He turns to me. "Pleasure to see you again, Mrs. Curridge."

"Heather. Please."

"Of course."

He kisses Sister J on her cheek. "Better go, Aunt Jerusha. Don't you be too hard on these ladies. You know how you can get."

Sister J beams.

Mo would be scowling right now if he saw this, I can tell you that.

Once again Sister J gives the tour. She loves giving the tour, it's evident; cheeks flush, voice rises in excitement. And as you can imagine, Liza and Sister Jerusha are like oil and vinegar. Not really mixing, both too strong and too different, but really, made to go together in a way that would make whatever they would land on just that much better.

After about an hour of hearing them talk about the missions they've worked in, mutual friends, and how on this green earth they've never met up before this, I head out to the big room to watch TV with Krista.

"You like this show?"

She nods. "Martha Stewart—the woman understand more than anybody know. Especially now that she been to prison."

"You been to prison, Krista?"

"Spent a few sleepless nights in jail. Back in the day when I walked the streets. Then I got pregnant with Kenya and took off. I'm from Chicago. Moved down here to live with my aunt. Just got through a week of rehab. Three more to go, and Sister J gonna work on getting Kenya back."

"Did you graduate from high school?"

"No. I like to get my GED. But I got to get me a job. But I can't get a job without my GED. Not a good one, anyway."

"How old are you?"

"Seventeen."

I turn back toward the screen. "Now I'd like to be able to cut up a chicken so easily."

Krista waves a hand. "Oh, that ain't nothin'. I can do that with my eyes closed. My grandmom taught me all sorts of things about cooking."

"Well, that's a skill right there."

"I got bigger dreams than that, ma'am."

"My name's Heather, by the way."

"People tend to think people like me don't have big dreams."

Mo calls over. "Krista! The van's here."

"Gotta go. Three more weeks and then maybe I can figure out what's next."

And the horrible, privileged part of me doubts she ever will. I hate this creature, arms crossed and head down, that lives inside me, this part that knows nothing about the Kristas of this world and wishes she would, by golly, just pull herself up by her bootstraps and make something of herself. Enough people from the "hood" have done that very thing, right?

Lord, I believe. Help Thou my unbelief.

Five days remain, and I need another project. The sisters' deck could definitely use a fresh coat of paint. So I ask them at breakfast about taking on the task.

Anna sets down her toast. "Why, I think that's lovely, Heather. Are you sure you want to do something so ambitious?"

"I enjoy that kind of work."

"I like the idea." Liza.

"I can get the paint and start this morning. Did you have a color in mind?"

"No. Why don't you pick?" Anna.

"Any color I want, Anna?"

"Any color you want." She places a firm hand over her sister's.

Liza raises an eyebrow.

So now I'm standing in line at the paint store with a tub of primer and a five-gallon container of cobalt blue paint—high gloss. I don't know why I'm choosing this color. Maybe to see if they really mean what they say, if these women really are who they say they are when it comes to their own things.

I mean, a lot of people do things for others, but it's hands off when it comes to their own space, their own property. And I can't blame them.

But these sisters? Time and a lot of blue paint will tell. I call Laney and tell her what I'm doing, and she laughs for at least five minutes.

Okay, one minute.

"Heather, you are such a brat!"

I call Will, who asked all about my trip down to the Hotel. "I'm telling you, Mom. This is it. You've got to volunteer there."

"How can you be so sure?"

"I just feel it."

"What about all the stuff I do at your school?"

"They'll find other people to help. There are lots of moms who don't lift a finger. They work all day, right?"

"Uh-huh. But what if I like doing all that?"

He laughs himself silly. First Laney, now Will.

Mercy, of all the possible kids, I had to get one like this! I don't know if I can take his pressure much longer. Changing the subject, I find out he's been fishing with that skipjack crew and making ten bucks an hour. Mrs. Curridge comes on the line and says, "He's as brown as a berry, Heather."

Another message comes in from Carmen as I talk. I've got to, got to, got to call her back. Tomorrow.

Jace left for Chicago and his nebulous "conference."

The Towson Library is always a good place to do a little research. Maybe I can find Xavier Andrews before heading back to the sisters.

The young woman at the research desk eagerly accepts the assignment. Which is a nice change. She's new, looks fresh out of college. "I like a challenge every once in a while. And we have plenty of directories available."

"Somebody told me he relocated to Michigan, and that's the last place I have."

With her height and long cinnamon hair, she really should be a model, not stuck here in some library in Maryland.

"Michigan? Let's see." She turns to her computer terminal and starts clicking away despite long shell-pink nails.

"I've already been on the Internet."

"No offense, but I'm really good at finding things on the Internet." I smile and raise my hands. "Don't let me slow you down."

The building remains familiar. "I remember coming to this place as a child. Saturday nights, just my dad and me. We'd park in the lot out back that's the parking garage now, and then wind our way up the ramp walkway." The giant concrete cylinder of a lobby caused quite the design controversy when it was built. The librarian says nothing. "My dad would drop the books off at the circulation desk: a Zane Grey or Louis L'Amour and perhaps some photographic essays of the West, maybe some local history book; and my Little House or Nancy Drew books. Ah, I loved that Nancy Drew. Did you?"

"Uh-huh."

"She had it all together, didn't she? Her own car, a hairstyle, and a best friend."

"Actually, I was a Goosebumps fan."

Mercy. "Sorry. I'll stop babbling."

"No prob."

I try not to think about the fact that I miss my father like he died yesterday, and normally I can go on, but today, here at the library where we spent so much time, I feel it rush me down into a vortex. After he died, Jace and I moved into the big house on Loch Raven, the big house needing so much to fill it. So much time to spend picking out drapery and upholstery fabric, landscaping options, a new driveway.

She raises her hand off the mouse. "Aha! Here he is. Xavier Andrews, Grand Rapids, Michigan. Tax records. Owns the house, apparently. At least he did in 1993. It's the latest documentation I can find. So far."

She swivels her chair a bit and writes down the address and phone number. "You want me to keep looking?"

"No thanks. I'll take it from here and see what happens."

"If you don't mind my asking, why do you want to find him?"

Wow, that was a librarian faux pas. I like it. "To apologize."

"That's refreshing."

Just for old time's sake I check out a coffee-table book of the photographs of Ansel Adams. My dad would be glad for it.

"I've got it, I've got it, I've got it!" I step lightly into the house. Anna is on her hands and knees wiping the baseboards in the foyer.

She sits back on her heels. "My, you look happy!"

"I found Xavier Andrews's phone number. In Michigan."

"And did you get the paint?"

"Yes."

"So when will you call?"

"I don't know. Soon. I guess. I'm still sitting on your question as to my motivation."

"The answer will come, Heather."

"How can you be so sure?"

"I'm ninety-two years old, honey. Some things you just pick up along the way."

TWENTY-SIX

Liza's shadow falls across the deck planking. "Oh my! That's quite the blue color, isn't it?"

I've painted only two boards. "I thought the cobalt would be pretty with the green of the trees."

Liza looks upward and nods once. "And it adds a postmodern flair to the modern. Just a tad. I think my Alva would approve. He wasn't a man who got something stuck in his craw ad infinitum, you see."

"That's a good thing."

"Certainly. Alva had vision. Shame he couldn't get through the day without a drink."

"I had an uncle who was an alcoholic. Nicest guy, though."

"There wasn't a better man than Alva Stephens. He wasn't a mean drunk, either, and always handed me the keys. But it got to his liver anyway. We just didn't know things in those days like we do now."

"That's for sure."

"And there are plenty of mean drunks too."

"I know. My aunt was a closet drinker, but we all knew when she'd tied one on, no matter how much she brushed her teeth and sucked on breath mints. I hated Thanksgivings at her house."

"Right, then. I'm off to go pick up Anna."

"I thought she took her car."

"Yes, she did. But I need to post bail."

I set the brush on the paint can. "Post bail?"

Liza sighs and places her hands on her hips. "She went and got herself arrested again. That makes fifty-two times." She shakes her head.

"I think she gets a kick out of it, if you want to know the truth. Which makes me wonder if she's getting any brownie points at all!"

"I was wondering where she went to. She was gone before I woke up. I'll just stay and keep working."

"Oh, please do. Truthfully, it's not like this is a big deal anymore. But what is she going to do when baby sister's not around to bail her out? That's what I'd like to know."

I don't want to think about the world without either of these two women binding its wounds.

"Was she demonstrating against the war?"

"What else? When I heard on the news a few years ago the president declared war, all I could think was, *I'll be running hither and yon after Anna now!* And now I have to drive all the way down to DC."

Which could take days, if I know Liza.

The clock on the piano in the living room chimes noon. They'll be home by dinnertime, I'll bet. I root through the refrigerator and find a roaster and, glory be, some asparagus and pearl onions. Ah, I can already smell the meal. Chicken slow roasted with herbs and garlic and pearl onions. Steamed asparagus.

I check the pantry.

Yep, egg noodles. Buttered egg noodles with fresh parsley; a nice hearty dinner after the jailhouse.

Mercy!

They return around five thirty. Anna has a sheepish glow; Liza looks like she's whiled away the day in a hornet's nest, hair frizzing out of its normally sleek bun.

"That I-95 is going to be the death of me!"

"You and everybody else on the road around you," Anna quips.

Well, Anna!

"Not a particularly peaceful response from someone who just got herself arrested in an antiwar demonstration, Anna."

Anna winks in my direction. "Liza's driving would make even the president go to combat just to get away from her."

"Well, come have a glass of wine. Dinner is almost done. I chilled up your favorite Chablis, Anna."

"I'll take a martini." Liza. "I'll fix it myself."

She walks through the foyer and back into the family room to a small liquor cabinet next to the sliding doors.

"You want ice?" I call from the kitchen.

"Thank you, no."

I pour Anna a glass of wine, and she sits down. "I hope you don't mind if I just rest here while you finish up. I'm exhausted."

"Were you treated all right?"

"This time. DC police are used to us, honey."

I pull the chicken out of the oven to let it sit before carving. "Why do you do it, Anna? Aren't we as Christians supposed to obey our rulers, Romans 13 and all of that?"

"Not when they are going against God."

"You believe we are?"

"With all my heart."

"I just don't know about any of this anymore." I set a pan of shallow water on the cooktop to steam the asparagus.

"Well, that's good. It's when we believe we have all the answers that we find ourselves in trouble." Anna's voice curves with humility. I never knew people like her really existed.

"Besides, my father was a Marine."

She smiles into my eyes. "I'm sure he was a fine soldier, Heather. A fine man."

"Anna, have you ever seen a kangaroo in these parts?"

"No, dear. Why do you ask?"

"One hopped across the road the night I found you all. He was the reason for my accident."

"Oh my! Lucky for Liza and I, he did just that."

"Lucky for you?"

"Yes, dear. You're teaching us many things."

The onions. I scoop them into a serving bowl. Ah, browned and caramelized. I could pop one into my mouth right now if no one was looking.

I'm afraid to ask exactly what it is they're learning from befuddled Heather Curridge. "Like how a deck looks when it's painted blue?"

She pauses and looks me in the eyes. "Yes, Heather. Exactly that."

"What would you think about yellow railings?"

She takes a sip of wine. "Now that, my dear friend, would be going a little too far."

"Yeah, I figured."

Liza strides through the kitchen and pours her drink down the sink. "Sometimes I forget we're not too old to be stupid." She looks up. "Right, Alva?"

She sits next to Anna and watches as I carve the roaster, then bowl the asparagus and the noodles. I serve them their meals, and this is my privilege.

TWENTY-SEVEN

My clothes, freshly laundered and folded in tidy stacks at the bottom of the bed, smell of the dried lavender Anna tucked between them. I lift my suitcase out of the closet.

They'll arrive soon, my family. All will be layered inside this brown leather case. But more than clothing, shoes, and toiletries will accompany me back home.

I tread over to the window, pull aside the curtain, and look out over Loch Raven. I swear I hear a bell chiming. An airy ring of promise, a signal saying, *Come and worship.*

Oatmeal sleeps on my bed. She's been sleeping with me for a week now. She's a young dog, and I cringe at the thought, but someday she'll need another home.

Liza enters the room. "Ready to go?"

"Just finishing up."

"Mind if I sit with you?"

"Not at all."

She lowers herself into a chair formed of black leather straps and chrome piping. "Ah, Breuer. Now he could design a chair."

"I have to admit, it's unexpectedly comfortable."

"We're sad to see you go."

"I'm sad to leave."

"And happy?" She crosses her legs, ankles bare beneath the hem of her moss green pants.

I scoop up the stack of shirts and shorts. "I've missed my family."

"Naturally. We'll miss you, Heather. You've been a delight to us old gals."

Next the nightshirts and unmentionables. "Ah, yes. I keep forgetting you're old."

She waves a hand. "So do we. That's why you've fit in so well. What will you do once you get home? Other than taking care of your family, of course."

I place my work tennies along the back of the bag. "I have no idea. I'm a little frightened. I'm not sure I'm the same person I was when I left."

"Certainly you are. You just have some extra bits now."

I sit on the bed across from her chair and fold my hands in my lap.

She reaches out and jostles my knee. "You really are worried, aren't you?"

"Yeah."

Liza arises, sits next to me, and places an arm around my shoulders. "Heather, you're facing new things about yourself and the world around you. You're choosing to no longer ignore what's been staring you in the face all along. That's a courageous act, my dear. One not a lot of people are capable of handling."

"I don't know if I can see it through to the end."

"And what might that end be?"

"I have no idea."

She takes my hand with her free hand. "Right. For once I'm with my sister on the obscurity angle. You only have to commit yourself to tomorrow; you can decide about the next day when it comes."

"I don't know if I can live like that."

"Oh, Heather. We're always living like that. Each day we choose to go on, whether we realize it or not."

"There's truth in that."

"Of course there is. And you will go on and go forward. I have every confidence in you."

I shake my head. "But how can you? I'm a mess."

"God took you aside, Heather. He was here with you, don't you think?"

"Yeah, I do."

"Do you have any reason to believe He won't go with you from here on out?"

"No good reason."

"God won't fail you." She squeezes my shoulder and kisses my face, her lips so soft and fragile. I feel the warmth of it travel from my cheek down through my limbs. "You have our prayers, for what they're worth, as well."

"They're worth a great deal. More than you'll ever know."

She stands to her feet. "I know a lot about the meaning of prayer, dear. More than I ever hoped I would." She places her hands atop my head and kisses it, blesses it. "And you're hardly a mess."

She leaves the bedroom, her pain tucked somewhere inside, her love shimmering on the surface like water beads after a summertime rain. A soft hint of her perfume lingers in the air around me. I press it down into my clothing.

The grille of the Suburban glints in the sunlight as the car turns into the parking pad. Two seconds later, Will jumps out of the back and runs to me, slamming himself into my arms, burrowing his head into the base of my neck.

I'm still in love.

Jace next, hands in pockets, sidles up. He hugs me with that fleecy warmth, a calm, still hug that he holds until he steps back and says, "Wow, it's good to see you. I missed you so much."

The sisters stand on the steps by the front door and welcome my guys. Anna shows Jace the suitcase sitting in the foyer, and he loads it into the car. Oatmeal skitters around Will's legs, and he scratches her ears.

Liza pats an imaginary errant hair back in place. "We hate to lose her. But I'm sure you'll be glad to have her back."

"Oh yeah!" Will.

"Absolutely." Jace. "Thank you for taking such good care of her."

Anna smiles. "Nonsense. She took good care of us."

Jace takes my hand. "She's got that way about her, doesn't she?"

Liza points to Will. "Now how old are you, young man?"

"Fifteen."

She looks at me. "You take good care of him, Heather, you hear me?"

I hug them as quickly as I can to get it over with. I want to go home, but I don't want to leave them. "Why don't you come live with us?" I ask.

"Can you imagine?" Liza. "Us two? Always bickering."

Will. "Oh, we don't mind."

Anna lays a hand on Will's shoulder. "Well, you never know, then, do you?"

We climb up into the truck.

Liza shuts my door and I roll down the window. "My, this is a big vehicle. You drive this thing?"

"Yes."

"Goodness. How brave."

Jace starts the engine, then backs up.

We all yell good-bye as we head toward the street.

"Go in peace!" Anna cries, picking up the dog and cradling her in her left arm.

And Liza reaches for her sister's free hand.

They stand there, linked together, waving fragile hands, wishing goodness for me and my family from their stalwart, ocean-sized hearts.

I lie on the couch. Say what you will, but overstuffed furniture, while not sleek and clean like modern, just feels good. I'm going to switch the blue dots from the living room set to this one. Jace sits down and hands me a cup of tea.

I shift to a sitting position. "Thanks for dinner. It was really good."

"Grilled hamburgers are a real culinary feat."

"Yours are." I sip my tea. "How's Jolly? Have you seen him?"

"Yes. He looks a little rough. How old do you think he is, hon?"

"I don't know. Seventy? Seventy-five? It's hard to tell with African-American men. No offense, Jace, but they age better."

"I'm a little worried. I tried to talk him into an appointment with Brad, but he balked. Maybe you can talk to him."

Brad is one of Jace's friends from med school.

"Maybe he's just not eating like he should. But I'll give it a shot."

"Right. Even for just a checkup. Now finish that tea, and I'll give you a back rub."

A back rub? How can I refuse?

A few minutes later he's massaging my shoulders. "Jace, we've got to talk about Chicago."

"Hold on, I didn't tell you. I had two procedures on people from the Hotel last Monday. Can you believe that? Sister J visited one of them while I was there. She said she figures I've done several surgeries on her clients. I guess our paths never crossed."

"No kidding."

"Right. I just found that a little eerie."

"Me too."

"So you had a good time with the sisters, huh?"

"Chicago, Jace. What were you really doing there?"

"Why are you so interested in Chicago?"

I blow a stream of frustration from between my lips. "Urrrrrr! I overheard your phone call with Bonnie, okay?"

He stops the massage. "Oh."

I'm trying to think of something to say. Nothing comes.

Then he lays his hands back on my back. "Does that have something to do with the tennis court being canceled?"

"Yes." I sit up.

"Oh, hon." He puts his arms around me, but I'm not having that. I move away from him.

"Why did you keep this all a secret? Don't I deserve to know what you're thinking?"

He reddens. "You're spending my paycheck as fast as I can make it, and I don't know how I can keep it all going and still do mission work on the ship."

"Is that what you want to do?"

"It's what the conference was about. In a year they're losing their cardiac surgeon. But there's no way I can take a year and do that, now, can I?"

"What about Will and I?"

"You all can go with me. We'd be a little cramped, but can you imagine the experience it would be for Will?"

"What about the Hotel?"

Confusion lowers his lids. "I don't understand."

"I think I'm supposed to be there, Jace. But if you say it's the ship . . ."

He takes both of my hands in his. "We've got a year, hon. Let's see what kind of miracle God's got in store before we worry about how things are supposed to be in the future."

I lay my forehead against his chest. "I'm sorry for chaining you like I've done. I never realized what all those purchases were doing to you. I just thought you loved your job, and the money was good, so where was the problem?"

"I do love my job. Just not where I do it."

"I'll put a buying moratorium on myself."

"I can't tell you what a relief that would be. It was really starting to affect how I felt about you."

"Really?"

"Yes, because it seemed that all my hours working myself to exhaustion were taken completely for granted. Every new thing we didn't need felt like a slap in the face. But yet I wanted you to be happy. I don't know how to even explain it, hon."

So I sit back against the couch and tell him about my dream. Mr. Purpose and the little white house. How the dots fit in. A small, practical little home for the three of us. Will's permission to leave this hill. This time, though the hour is late and all I can hear is the thrum of the air-conditioning unit and my own voice, Jace doesn't fall asleep.

"You're not just saying what you think I want to hear, are you,

Hezz?"

"Nope. This is all me."

After he goes to bed, I walk to the banks of Loch Raven and weep for my father and let him go a little more, my memories flung over the dark waters to come back healthier and dressed in smoother raiment, white and neat and with no extra yardage.

Yes, it's time.

I hurry back inside, pull down the attic door, open up the box, and place my hands around the urn. *Okay, Dad, you ready?*

In the darkness I slip down to the water. He must have been scared having to raise a daughter on his own. He must have wondered why such a load was placed upon his shoulders. And yet he never flinched. Never once. He loved me.

Oh God, how my father loved me.

I don't fling the ashes, but, crouching low like a little mouse, I tap them from the container and into the night-blackened waters. Just him and me.

TWENTY-EIGHT

On my nightstand a note from Jace says, "Carmen called.

"Carmen called again.

"Again.

"Again.

"Again."

Oh great. I never did call.

I unpack my suitcase and lay the lavender on my dressing table. I feel something thin and cold at the bottom. Pulling it out, I smile at the sight of the sisters' silver fork. Around it a ribbon is tied, and attached to it, a note.

> *You are our dear friend. We will miss you. Thanks for brightening our days.*
>
> > *Love, Liza and Anna (and Oatmeal)*

I drop Will off at swim team practice and swear to myself I'll call Carmen on the way home. But to my dismay, she comes charging over to the car. "Heather!"

"Hi, Carmen. I am so sorry—"

"I've been trying to get in touch with you for weeks."

"I know. I was away."

"Lucky for you. Do you realize I've put you in charge of the new mothers' tea?"

"Well, I didn't think I'd agreed."

"Oh great! Now I've got to find somebody else."

"I'm sorry."

"I heard you were staying with those two old biddies over on Merrymans Mill Road."

"Well, they normally refuse to be called biddies, but yes, Liza and Anna let me stay with them."

"Life goes on, Heather. I've been picking up your slack."

"There are other women in the school, Carmen."

"Oh please. They're worthless."

"I can't do the tea. I've got other volunteer opportunities."

"Such as?"

"A homeless shelter downtown needs help right now."

"But what about your own son?"

"Will isn't exactly a baby anymore."

She crosses her arms. "You know the school does so well because of its volunteers."

"Yes. I didn't say I wouldn't ever volunteer for St. Matthews. I just can't take on so much this year."

"Then I've got my work cut out for me. I've got to go."

I watch her walk to her car, cell phone once again plastered to the side of her head, her other hand whirling about in angry circles as she talks.

The light has changed. The afternoon has obviously waned. Golden blinds block the low sunrays. What a lovely nap that was!

I pick up my Bible, and there it is, tucked in between the pages of Galatians, Xavier Andrews's phone number in Michigan.

Sunday afternoon is a good time to call, so I pluck the phone on the nightstand and dial the number before I can change my mind.

A cracked voice, churlish and clipped, answers. "Yeah."

Okay, then. I can do this.

"I'm looking for Xavier Andrews?"

"He hasn't lived here for a few years."

"Do you know—"

"Yeah. Used to work for him. What do you want with X?"

"I've been looking for him. I've got something I need to discuss with him regarding his wards. Do you know where he lives?"

"He doesn't have a phone. Went and bought some land in the most god-awful place in Minnesota you ever saw. Cold. Lonely. Nothin' out there but this crazy old lodge. We all thought he was crazy."

"Can you give me the name of the nearest town?"

"No, but I know he's somewhere near the Boundary Waters."

"Thanks."

I hang up on him before he can hang up on me.

I write the words *Boundary Waters* on a slip of paper. Fabulous— Minnesota. Remote Minnesota. It might as well be Guatemala.

"How's your mom?"

"She's in bed today. Very tired."

"I'm sorry."

"She'd love a visit."

"I'll bring Will down tomorrow morning."

"Great. Come early for breakfast."

Lark and I are eating a cell phone lunch together; she's out on the patio at the Medieval Monstrosity, and I'm sitting at the picnic table by the pool. I tell her about further locating Xavier and that I'm thinking about making the trip to northern Minnesota.

"Better you than me," she says. "Let me ask you a question, because I've been thinking about it a lot. Did you ever once do anything nice for Mary, or even act nice or something?"

"Only one time did I ever treat Mary Andrews as a human being loved by God."

"What happened?"

"My dad, for some reason, agreed to drive Mary home from the big Christmas basketball game, alumni versus the varsity team. I don't know how it happened, and I wasn't all that curious back then.

"So I slid in the front seat and Mary sat in the back, and Dad asked her all sorts of questions, and Mary answered with 'Yes, sir,' and 'No, sir.' I said nothing. It was easy to see Dad liked Mary, and as he continued his questioning, I found out that her mother had grown up not two blocks from Dad. He actually knew her when she was a little kid, and had babysat her a couple of times.

"When she got out of the car to go into her house, I smiled at her and she smiled back.

"And then, when January second rolled around and she climbed on the bus after Christmas break, she looked at me with hopeful eyes. I turned away.

"I made myself greater than God."

"It's easy to do."

"I haven't told you the worst of it."

"Darn. I was hoping we could put this all to bed, that I could shake some sense into your head. What happened, if you're willing to say?"

I've got to start over. I've got to throw myself into a place where there's nothing but an empty me, a full God, and a lot of people who need Him in a way I never have. Maybe this is a good first step.

Easier said than done, right? But as Liza says, easier done than undone.

"Okay, the fact that my dad babysat her mother, that they grew up together, was information I could not afford to get around school."

"So you were just as socially unsure then as you are now?"

Ouch. "Mercy, Lark. Can I finish?"

And I told Lark about the scheme. How my friend Rich, and Julia B. of course, cooked it up one morning on the bus. I sidled up to Mary and told her Rich liked her, and did she like him too?

Mary nodded, looking almost pretty. I knew if I had said that about any of the boys, Mary would have nodded. Just the thought of being liked by any boy would render her completely in love with him. Step one was out of the way. Rich hung out with Mary on the playground for a couple of days before the big math exam that would finish out second semester, just before Christmas.

Now Mary didn't get great grades, except for math. Rich convinced her to let him cheat off of her. She would have done anything for Rich. And Julia B. and I were acting all buddy-buddy, even inviting her to sit with us at lunch.

During the exam, Mary was supposed to look over at Rich's paper, see which answers he got wrong, and pencil in the answer on her scratch paper. It had to be this way so it looked like she was hell-bent on looking off his paper. I slipped out of my desk and walked up to the teacher and whispered, "I think Mary's cheating off of Rich." Then I just as quietly made my way back to my seat.

Five minutes later, the teacher stood over Mary's desk. She was taken to the principal's office and suspended for three days. She gathered her books to sit in the library until school let out, and she looked at me like she knew. I felt like Simon Peter when the cock crowed, but really I was Judas. On the bus ride home, I hissed in her ear, "If you *ever* let on that our parents grew up together, you'll get more of this."

"Wow, Heather."

"And she got a zero on the exam, and the only A she had went down to a C. Three days later after she served her suspension and came back to school, she got on the bus with a bruised cheek and marks around her forearm from what looked like someone gripping her hard. She was terribly uncomfortable in her seat."

"You think her dad beat her?"

"Yes. I never wanted to admit that before. She was beaten for cheating she didn't even do. And I just laid on some more blows. I knew it, Lark. I knew it then. Looking back as an adult, it's even more clear."

"You should find her, then."

TWENTY-NINE

Before I gave birth, my periods lasted nine days, and my cramps felt like a giant snake snuck up behind me, sank its teeth into my backbone, and tried to suck my uterus through it—and now my periods are a light five days with no cramps. Before I gave birth, I'd get the worst canker sores about two weeks after my period; now I only get them when the toothbrush slips and goes crashing into my gums. Before I gave birth, I had mousy brown hair. Now it's a rich dark brown, a dark baking chocolate brown, not that anybody'd ever know it after my buck fifty trips to the salon.

As payment, I lost my waistline, my smooth thighs, and the ability to drink large glasses of orange juice without calculating the calories.

It's worth it, I guess.

Usually. But I stand in front of the bathroom mirror as I slip on my nightgown and want to cry.

And Jace is so looking forward to this?

What is wrong with the man?

Music starts to play in the bedroom. A little Barry White.

I laugh. Barry White? The man is too much. Well, if we can't make it sexy, maybe we can make it fun.

I lost my sexual desire years ago, and I've looked for it everywhere. Remember that miracle cream someone touted on *Oprah* a few years back? That did absolutely nothing. Supplements? Nope.

It's not like I don't try or anything. I want more than anything to desire lovemaking.

Afterwards, Jace reaches over to the bedside table and takes a sip of water. "Would you like to head down to the Hotel with me tomorrow? I told Sister J I'd stop by and check up on those patients."

"I'm on it."

"You really ready, Hezzie?"

Yep, I really am. "I'll tell Sister Jerusha tomorrow."

Mo swings an arm like one of the *Price Is Right* girls. "And look at this. Those Summerville people did it right! We've got carpet, we've got paint and plaster, we've got new ceiling tile. Now all we got to do is round up the volunteers to install it, and we'll be sittin' pretty."

Two large rolls of carpet, cases of ceiling tile, and paint cans assemble nearby with little thought to arrangement. Behind the serving table parks a heinously ugly roll of padding that looks like a thousand sponges got in a tear-'em-up fight in front of a steamroller.

"Fabulous!"

"I can hardly imagine this place fixed up." Will.

"I know that's right. Hey, you all here to see Sister J?"

Jace nods. "I'm here to check up on a couple of patients."

"Uh-huh, that's right. I'll call 'em down."

I step forward. "Is Sister Jerusha in?"

"Naw, she gone to some seminary somewhere for some downtime. Some crazy Catholic-silence thing. Be back tomorrow."

Drat. I'll have to call her on the phone and tell her I'm all hers.

"What about Krista? Is she around?"

"She sure is. I'll call her down."

Mo starts making his calls. Jace looks around. "Maybe we can help find some volunteers. Your friend Laney at school, Hezz. Doesn't her husband lay carpet?"

"Yeah."

"Maybe me and the guys from the old food-basket ministry at church can replace the ceiling tiles and lay the carpet. Redo the plaster too."

"I'll bet Carmen and I could round up a group of ladies from Will's class to help. If she'd even take a call from me."

Jace puts an arm around me.

"I hate it when I burn bridges like that."

Krista walks down the stairs. "Miss Heather!"

"Dang, you look good!"

She turns. "I got it all cut off! You like it?"

"I do."

Her hair is shorn close to her head. She looks so sleek.

"Jace, remember Krista?"

"Absolutely. How are you?"

"I'm good. Good."

"Great."

"Dr. Curridge! Your patients are on their way down." Mo.

Jace turns on the kind professionalism even as he turns toward the first patient walking down the stairs.

As long as he's turning, I turn toward Krista. "How about we go get something to drink?"

"Okay."

Will looks at Mo. "Can I stay here with you?"

"If it's all right with your mother."

I shrug. "Sure, if you don't mind."

"Wanna play dominoes?" Mo asks Will.

"You'll have to teach me."

"Sit down, sit down, sit down." He drags a chair to the desk. "And learn from the master."

A few minutes later Krista and I sit on a bench on North Avenue, right near the Great Blacks in Wax Museum. The row houses along this stretch, some of them four stories high, sat pretty and proud back in the day, I'll bet. Beautiful woodwork probably hides behind drywall or heavy layers of paint inside those homes.

"So what's the news? Are you still going to rehab?"

"I'm just going to regular meetings now."

"Are you hopeful?"

"I guess so. It's hard, though, you know? Living there at the

Hotel. If I could just find me a place, just a little place with my own refrigerator and a stove where I could make up a stew or some beets—I love buttered beets—a little room with a pullout couch and room for a crib."

"An efficiency apartment?"

"Yes, ma'am. Nothin' much, just a place I can make my own. There's women at the Hotel acting like they know all that and more, and if they do, what they doin' there? No, ma'am. I just want to have a little place to call my own and still be accountable to somebody. I got to have that. I know I can't figure this all out by myself, but I'm about to go crazy there!"

"I don't know of any place like that."

"Me either."

It's amazing how different Krista is now that she's clean. I grieve to imagine her heading in again and losing all hope of getting Kenya back.

I reach into my purse and pull out a little calling card I had printed up when we moved into the house on the hill. "You know what, if you ever need anything, just call me. I'll drop everything."

She takes the card and doesn't say anything.

I want to fill in the gap and expound on my offer, but something tells me to let it be.

Mo trounced Will in several games of dominoes, and Will is determined to best him next time.

Jace examined some extra patients who heard there was a doctor in the house.

I actually had a conversation with Knox Dulaney just as I slipped back inside the Hotel. Krista took one look at him and hurried up the steps.

So here's the crazy thing. I've never before communicated at length with a criminal, but he's so cordial. I can't understand that, but I do understand how Sister J can't forsake him. He's lost. So very lost, and a piece inside him knows it.

"Sister Jerusha told me about my man giving your husband trouble awhile ago. I just wanted to apologize."

What do I say? It's okay? I mean, this isn't your standard situation. Oh, sure. It's okay if your enforcer or whatever they call these guys was ready to rough up my husband. No prob.

He smiled. "It's awkward. It's okay. Listen, when I walk in here, I lay everything else aside."

I nod. "Okay."

"Will you be coming back?"

"Yes. I wanted to talk to Sister J about that today."

"Well, do me a favor. You keep an eye on her, won't you? She burns the candle at all three ends."

"I will."

And then he left. And I swear, when he walked out that door, the delicate planes of his face hardened into walls of concrete. He slipped into the backseat of a black BMW, and it sped off as he closed the door.

Even now, I can't believe I interacted with a drug dealer. How can he come into that place knowing he's the reason a lot of those people are there in the first place, hooked on his drugs, scared to be anywhere else?

First of all, I don't buy that he casts aside his criminal persona. His presence intimidates people. When I asked Sister J about this a few weeks ago, she said, "He's Jesus too, Heather. As far as I can tell, Jesus didn't tell me who and who not to love. He told me to love them all."

She's a better person than I am, that's all I can say.

Jace climbs into bed that evening. "I think I'm going to go to the Hotel every other week. Maybe take JoAnne from work. The problem is, a lot of the residents there don't have time to get to the health department. One man I looked at is working three jobs. But I think I'll go in during the evening next time, after people are done working."

"What about prescriptions? How are they going to pay for what you write out?"

"Leave it to me. I've got some ideas."

I slide my Bible off my nightstand. "I think we both need to read Isaiah 58 every night for the rest of the summer, Jace."

"Go ahead and read out loud. I'll listen from here."

And I begin shading in a life that, up to this point, has felt very much like a line drawing.

I'm certainly going to look up real estate prices there on North Avenue. Surely one of those houses, or several of them together, could be made into a community home for women with living spaces just like Krista longs for. Privacy and some accountability both available. And cakes. Cakes are always good.

During the middle of the night I sit up straight. I dreamed Jesus came and led me out of the basement of an old stone church on fire, up through a rubble-strewn sanctuary. We climbed upon hewn stone blocks, up through rugged beams, sun beaming in strips through the latticed roof, leaving all the smoke and ash behind. And the rubble. And the debris.

And He never let go of my hand during the climb.

Then He left me, covered in the warmth of His breath.

THIRTY

I went and sat with the sisters for another shot of wisdom yesterday. For three hours we sat, each of them asking a question for clarification every so often. When will you volunteer? How will this affect your family? Mostly we sat in silence and I looked at them, Anna sitting with her hands lying like gloves in her lap, Liza with her arms crossed, staring at the copy of a Calder mobile over the dining room table.

Inside, a question erupted. *Will this hurt Will?*

And another question skidded up beside it, wanting a fair shake. *But what would hurt my son more?*

Meanwhile, the sisters sat in silence.

Do I want him to be raised to seek his own comfort and well-being, both physically and spiritually, or do I want him to be raised to seek the physical and spiritual well-being of others, especially those toward whom God feels such a tenderness?

Children learn best by example.

The sisters still said nothing.

And in the giving, my son would receive more than a ho-hum church life could ever offer.

The decision was finally made for good.

It is time for Jace and me to follow the desires God has placed in our hearts. In our hearts, both of our hearts. At the same time. This stunning display of God's love is something I don't deserve. We move forward, hand in hand, steps in unison. How beautiful is this?

So now it's time. Time to set my husband loose like a rock in a sling-shot toward that ship. Time for me to follow Sister J around for a while to figure out just what it means to really care.

Something happened in the silence. I don't like to call it a vision, really, but I saw my house on the hill glister before my eyes in a flashcube moment, the hill in negative, house crumbling and par-tially hidden by ivy.

Deep in my heart, I know my days on the loch are numbered. And they are numbered for all of us. In this, I grieve. Yet I know riches come in many forms, and God, who works in paradox and always has, will give us something far greater than a new tennis court in return.

But first I need to show up.

So with the first scent of a waning season in the air, I call Sister J from the bright blue deck of the sisters' house.

"Hi, doll. What's up?"

"I want to be a regular volunteer at the Hotel. As soon as Will goes back to school."

"You bet. Is cake part of the bargain?"

"Absolutely. What days would be good for me to come?"

"Any day. You pick. We aren't choosy."

"I was thinking Tuesdays and Thursdays. Will goes back the first Tuesday after Labor Day."

"Sounds like a plan. What do you want to do here?"

"Whatever you want."

"Doll, don't ever say that to a mission director. You don't know where you'll end up."

"I'll bring some cake down sooner."

"Good. Everybody loves your cake."

So that's that. I'm locked in. But there are some things to take care of first, I think.

Everybody loves my cake. How nice.

While I'm paying the stack of bills that accumulated, the doorbell rings.

I peer through my living room window curtains onto the entry porch. Ah, yes, it's Carmen. Fabulous. Probably come to ream me out for the other day. Should I pretend I'm not home?

I mean, really, we do that sort of thing all the time in one way or another. Maybe not literally, but the incessant answer of "I'm busy" to the perennial question of "How are you?" is pretty much saying, "No, I can't do another thing, so don't ask."

A pot of coffee is brewing, though, in preparation for a nice, cozy, sofa-sitting surf of REALTOR.com. Must be a sign. Besides, I left the garage door open.

I walk to the door and open it. "Carmen! This is a surprise!"

She rearranges the shoulder strap on her purse. "I'm sorry I'm just dropping in like this. I'm on my way to the doctor's office and I could have called, but, well, it's been awhile since we've really connected."

"Come on in. I just put on a pot of coffee a few minutes ago. It'll be ready in just a sec."

"I've only got a little bit of time. I promise I won't ruin your schedule."

I see it all!

Carmen is scared! This incredible responsibility rapes her calendar, gnaws her soul. It's stealing her life. Meetings and groups and events to arrange in such a way that parents will love it, feel appreciative for the school, give money, and keep the cogs a-greased.

But who appreciates Carmen?

She's frozen in the headlights, people!

But she has superglued the Happy Christian mask to her face. Even though I don't know if she's a Christian or not, I'd recognize that mask anywhere.

Poor Carmen.

"Have you had lunch?" I escort her back to the kitchen.

"No. I meant to make a sandwich before I left, but you know how that goes."

Not really. I always carve out enough time to eat, unfortunately. "How much time do you have before you have to leave?"

She checks her watch. "Twenty-five minutes."

"Have a seat." I slide out one of the counter stools by my island. Then I pour her a cup of coffee and fix it just the way she likes it, barely sweet, lots of half 'n' half, and I know that because I know these things about the people I'm involved with. I've always prided myself in knowing these things.

She sips. And sighs. Sips and sighs.

I dig through the snack drawer in the fridge. The Snack Drawer. Haven't yet figured that one out. So I use it for lunch meats and cheese. And tortillas.

"I'm going to make you a wrap, Carmen. Roast beef, Havarti, tomato, and horseradish sauce sound good?"

"Are you kidding? Can I have two?"

"Definitely."

I gather the cellophane bags holding these, truly, wonders of the world, and Boar's Head knows how to do roast beef, don't they? Cream Havarti too. The crimson tomato, compliments of Jolly, bursts as I drive the knife into its juicy flesh.

Ah, I love summertime. I slather the piquant white sauce on the tortillas.

Carmen sets down her cup. She does everything with a crisp thrift. Love her baby tee. Pale pink with pansies across the bosom. Matching lips too. "I'm getting together room mothers for the fall, and I was wondering if I could count on you this year, just to arrange the babysitting for parties and such."

It's an olive branch. I know it. I long to take it, but who am I trying to fool? I'd just be prolonging the inevitable. I lay on the cheese. "I don't know, Carmen. My schedule is filling up."

"It would only be one morning a week at the most."

The roast beef, the tomato. "Some lettuce?"

She nods. "So, will you?"

Roll up the sandwiches and slide the plate to her. "I don't know if it's a matter of *will*, per se, Carmen. It's more like *can*."

She picks up a sandwich. "Oh?"

"I'm going to volunteer downtown a couple of days a week while Will is in school."

"You mentioned some homeless thing." She puts down the sandwich. "Where downtown?"

"Near North Avenue. It's called the Hotel."

"Is it a Quaker thing?"

I shake my head. "No."

"'Cause those crazy sisters are Quakers, you know."

"Sister Jerusha who runs the place is Catholic."

She winces. "You're going to work for the Catholics?"

"They're doing good things down there, Carmen."

"Still." She takes a staunch, Protestant bite of her sandwich. "I grew up Catholic. It did nothing for me."

I'm going to let that slide. Not because I feel superior in my ecumenism, but because I believe her. I shrug. "I grew up Lutheran. Want some chips?"

"Sure. Thank you. And here we are with our children at an Episcopal school."

I make my own sandwich in silence. On the CD player in the living room, Will plays some obscure band called the Psalters. Crazy Jesus music. He's out there reading a cookbook on Texas grilling. Someday he's going to start investigating the meat industry, and we'll all suffer.

"So are you going to spend all your time downtown, then?" Carmen asks.

"Most of my volunteer time, yes."

"So, then, the school can just take a backseat now?"

I wince. "I'm just trying to figure things out."

"St. Matthews has always been the place for rational, well-educated people and their children. Maybe it's not the place for your type to begin with."

"That was pretty nasty, Carmen."

"Well, neither of us is one to mince words."

She puts a chip in her mouth, chews, and takes another bite of sandwich. I turn my back and pretend I'm going to the fridge for something, anything to give her some thinking space. Surely something looks promising. Ah, there. Pickles. That's convincing. I grab the jar.

And I do love sweet pickles.

She lays down her sandwich. "I'm sorry. That was over the line. Why now, Heather? Why all this all of a sudden?"

"I don't know. I feel like I'm being called out, Carmen."

"I don't even know what that means. Are we that horrible to you?"

Horrible?

I walk around the island and sit on the stool next to her. "Is all this . . . well, I don't know what to call it other than drama . . . because of me personally or because you'll have to find someone else to help out with school?"

Her eyes grow round. "I haven't really analyzed it. I thought maybe we were friends. Sort of."

Mercy! Friends? Carmen and I?

"Carmen, have you ever once called me and suggested that we go out for coffee or something?"

"Well, no. But neither have you, Heather."

"I know. I'm just a little floored by the friendship thing. You seem too busy for friends."

"Yes. I hate that about myself. I've been trying to work my way into favor with people my entire life, and all I do is end up pushing them away."

"You haven't made one real friend at St. Matthews?"

"No. Have you?"

"Laney Peterson. She's a good lady."

She finishes up her sandwiches, and we chat about safer topics like the new diner in Cockeysville, and isn't it great at Curves?

I walk her to the door. "I'm sorry I can't help out this year."

"I'll just call somebody who's more interested."

I wince again. So unfair, Carmen. "I gave my life to this school for years, and if I got ten thank-yous in that time, I'd be shocked."

She bends. "I'm sorry. I'm overcommitted and overextended and

I've got to find people. I don't know how it's all going to survive this year if more people don't step up to the plate."

"I'm sorry too."

"I don't know why I took the position as volunteer coordinator. Stupid." She rubs the bridge of her nose. "Well, I hope it goes well downtown for you, Heather. I really do."

I don't believe her.

And then she looks up into my eyes, her brown eyes peering out of prison bars. "I really, really do," she whispers.

I hug her. She hugs me in return.

"I'm sorry, Carmen. I just need a little time. That's all I'm asking."

"Okay. You got it. But if we need cake?"

"I'm still your gal."

THIRTY-ONE

I once heard someone say that we only change when staying the same becomes even more frightening. Well, I don't know if that has anything to do with this car; I only know I can get rid of it. I've come to hate it so much. The Suburban. Irony at its finest. First of all, it's not a suburban vehicle at all; it's a country vehicle. Got a farm? Get a Suburban. They should have called it the Countryboy or the Ranchhand.

It deserves at least a thousand green dots on it.

So here I stand in the car lot. I just want a wagon. A station wagon. Like a 1960s mom. This is cute, a streamlined white Saturn wagon. Oh, it'll be the talk of the country club and not in a good way. They'll be wondering if we took a hit on the stock market or stood on the wrong end of a business deal. Actually, it'll be kind of fun to see what happens.

Actually, we might want to quit that darn thing. Jace doesn't even play golf, and it sure is an expensive way for Will to swim. More green dots.

I page Jace, who calls back during the test drive. "I'd like to trade in the Suburban. Right now."

"Where are you?"

"At the Saturn dealer. Well, actually, I'm on Warren Road, test-driving a wagon."

"Aren't they kind of small?"

"It's the midsize. I want to trade in the truck, Jace. Right now."

"See how much they'll give you on the trade. You may actually walk away with some money in your pocket. But yes, I think it's a good idea." The relief he must feel shakes his voice a little, or is it skepticism? Is there truly a light at the end of this tunnel labeled *more-more-more*?

Of course there is. Because I say so.

I didn't walk away with money in my pocket, but it was almost an even trade. They gave me a zippy little wagon for that big old truck. I'd say I came out on the top end of the deal.

And it's a stick shift. I haven't driven a stick shift since my days in beauty school. I drive by Robert Paul Academy where I trained. The best cosmetology school in Baltimore by far. I stroll by the windows, watching the students work on their mannequins, looping and pinning fancy up dos. I smile and wave at a pretty, petite young woman bobby-pinning a curl in place. She finishes her task, smiles, and waves back.

I was you a long time ago, I want to say to her. Right now, I don't feel as far away from that as I used to.

On the way home I drive up Merrymans Mill Road and slow down in front of the sisters' drive. In the corner of my eye, a patch of yellow catches my gaze. A maple tree just begins to shrug off its slicker of green. My father once said as we stood on the banks of Loch Raven right before school began, "Heather, it's my sign, that first patch of yellow. My sign that summer is ending."

Thank you, ladies.

I do not turn into their drive, but continue on, back to Will, to Jace, to a promise that something golden will spring up from the lovely green garden my life has suddenly become, a garden planted in fertile soil, ready to nourish a greater purpose.

Mr. Purpose has offered his hand, I've placed mine in his, and we're riding along to someplace I've probably never dreamed of.

I laugh at myself. Sentimental, optimistic little fool that I am.

Part Three

I'll Follow the Sun

THIRTY-TWO

I'm whizzing down I-83 in my little wagon, past the numerous apartment complexes, the defunct mills now transformed into upscale lofts, the old London Fog factory, Stieff Silversmiths. The windows open, my hair is twice its normal size, and will God keep me out of the police radar since I'm headed down to do good works?

Ah, no.

At least that's what I'd bet if I had to.

Will's off to school, steps airy and expectant and ready to make tracks in Nicola's direction. The summer of Nicola. Let's hope it lasts throughout the year.

Of course, I'm waiting to hear how Ronnie Legermin behaves.

I've already called Lark, who cheered me on in her Larky way.

Will said, "Go get 'em, Mom! Was I right or was I right?"

Jace packed me a lunch complete with a Ho Ho and a carton of chocolate milk, obviously throwing his medical knowledge out the door. "You're going to do great, hon."

But for now, Unsearchable Riches, my favorite Baltimore Jesus band, sparkles at sixty miles per hour, their happy honky-tonk rock on my car stereo providing a spot-on soundtrack for the wind, the sun, and the speed of my wheels. And I want to throw back my head and laugh because I'm free at this very moment.

I love Mo. I realize this as I push my way through the door, so excited to see him. I also realize I don't know Mo's story, and just how he came to be sitting at this desk.

"Mo!"

"Heather! Yo, girl!"

"How are you today?"

"Good. You're one brave lady, that's all I got to say."

"Yeah?"

He shakes his two-ton head. "You got any grubbies with you?"

"Just what I'm wearing."

He examines my garb. "Can they be replaced?"

"There's not too much that can't be replaced. Well, if it's inanimate, that is."

He jerks his head toward the kitchen. "Health department cited us. That kitchen needs to be scrubbed top to bottom."

My stomach sinks. Yeah, I admit it. I had visions of chopping veggies, opening cans, skipping from big pot to bigger pot like a pixie, waving my magic spoon, creating fabulous meals from whatever anybody happened to bring by.

Drat.

"Point me at it."

"No need. You already know where the kitchen is."

I smile at him, and he knows.

He pats my arm. "Baptism by fire, girl."

"You said it."

I hoist my purse up on my arm. "Okay, then, wish me luck."

He raises his brows. "Oh, you need more than luck."

I gather as much air into my lungs as possible and move forward. One step. Then another. And then another.

Sister J's office door is open. I peek my head in. "Sister J?"

"Hi, doll. Come on in. Ready to work?"

"Yep. Mo filled me in."

She laughs, that grating hack. "I'll bet he did! You sure as heck can't clean in those. Go back to the clothes closet and pick out some of the used duds. No sense in ruining your good stuff."

I bristle. "No, no, no. I really don't mind."

"I insist." She looks at me, no-nonsense eyes. "Go pick something out. Doesn't matter what."

"But—"

"Now!"

Okay, okay. What is this? Some sort of bait and switch? The crusty yet nice nun turns into a hard-nosed mother superior?

Remember, Heather. Remember why and remember Who and who. There, that nice, righteous-sounding thought should see me through, right?

I head back out into the kitchen, into the main room, and over to the clothing room. They're all free, these clothes. But those who come for them can take only five at a time. I've heard Sister J's spiel three times now, so I know. The room sits devoid of clients. Ceiling high, windows grimy. I breathe in.

Oh, Lord, I've never put on someone else's clothing in my entire life! Other than my cousins' hand-me-downs or good friends' clothes. I don't know where these have been. Have they been washed? I pick up a pair of jeans.

Did someone urinate in them at one time? I close my eyes and sniff. They smell clean. But . . . how many people have slid their legs into these, and who were they?

I bow my head.

Help me.

I look up. Maybe a shirt would be a better first pick.

Sweaty underarms. Unseen dribble from a slack mouth down the placket, perhaps? Looking around, I see the ghosts of bodily secretions in neon colors on every garment. I see dirty people and poor people.

I see black people.

Oh God!

And my own prejudice confronts me in this garment I hold in my hand. All the thoughts I never allowed front and center, all the fears that never found their place.

Help me, God. Please help me. I don't want to be like this.

I stand. Frozen in the frigid pool of my own sinfulness.

A hand squeezes my shoulder. "Miss Heather?"

I turn. Krista. I hold out the jeans, speechless.

In her eyes I see time and pain and understanding, though heaven knows, I don't how or why she should, or would.

"Can I help pick you something out?"

I nod.

"What size?"

"Fourteen."

She starts at the pants table. "Mo told me you gon' be scrubbing the kitchen today so you want to be comfortable." She lifts up a pair of painter pants. "Here. Sturdy too."

I receive them from her.

She walks to the shirt rack. "I know color don't matter cleaning the kitchen, but we have to look good, all right? I think blue is your color."

"Why are you doing this?" The words slip out.

"You need me to."

"I do." I whisper the words.

She pulls out a blue blouse, blue the color of the Aegean in a travel poster for Greece. "Now that will go with your eyes. You go change in the bathroom."

She hands me the shirt and leads me out of the room, into the main room. "The bathroom is right before Sister J's door."

"Thank you, Krista."

Krista shrugs. Then she smiles. And she sees me for exactly who I am, a do-gooder white lady come to save the world.

Only she's the one who's going to save me. But I don't think she knows that yet.

Maybe Jace was right about medication. I cry in the bathroom. Who do I really think I am?

Sister J peers at me as I walk into her office. "Good choice."

"Krista saved me."

"She's got that in her. It's why I'm so hard on her. Okay"—she hoists herself to her feet—"come on in and meet Jimmy, our cook."

"There wasn't anybody in the kitchen."

"He's probably having a smoke outside."

Sure enough, Jimmy sits on the alley stoop, smoking a cigarette. He wears one of those caps that look like somebody cut the legs off a pair of pantyhose. His height makes me feel like I'm eight again.

"Jimmy, this is Heather. She's going to help on Tuesdays and Thursdays. Said she'd clean your kitchen for you. Wanna show her the supplies?"

"If you say so."

He takes one more draw, crushes the smoke beneath his sneaker, and rises to his feet. He walks by without looking at me, shows me the closet crammed with half-full bottles of every kind of cleaner known to broom closets. "There you go."

"Thanks."

Sister J heads back to her office. "If you need me, just holler. Jimmy, what's for lunch?"

"Soup!"

She rolls her eyes, shakes her head, and flies away, her black veil last to leave the room.

Jimmy turns away from me, and I grab a bucket and some rags. And Mr. Clean. I need a guy like Mr. Clean right now.

He points to the far wall. "Utility sink's over there." And he disappears.

I feel so otherworldly. So out of place.

But I fill the bucket and begin to scrub the baseboards.

Four hours later, I'm only halfway through the kitchen. I've seen more roaches and roach carcasses, more grease, more primal yucki-ness than ever before.

I change my clothes. Mo isn't at the door.

I leave.

My trip home is quiet. Windows up.

It wasn't what I thought it would be.

Not even close.

THIRTY-THREE

Sitting on the edge of his seat, Will listens and shovels in mac 'n' cheese without even chewing. I don't know how he does that. It makes my throat close into that gagging feeling just watching him. But there is something cool about it in that "boy" way. He keeps looking up at me, saying, "Sweet," every few seconds as I tell him about my day. Jace isn't home.

I almost want to turn on him and say, "Don't you get it, Will? I had a lousy time. Jimmy was rude and I spent a disgusting day scrubbing a bunch of disgusting surfaces and didn't even finish the disgusting job. A ministry of presence? Yeah, right, Jerusha."

He caught the demeanor of the thoughts in my expression.

"Didn't you have fun, Mom? You did, didn't you?"

How can I do this?

"No. It was the most humiliating experience of my life. I hated almost every minute of it."

Will bows his head. He's trying to hide the tears that always gather when he's had a horrible day at school or disappointment strikes like the clapper of a bell.

"But I'll go back Thursday."

Will looks back up. "Really?" He sniffs. "After all that?"

"Yeah. I've got to. If I don't finish that kitchen, they'll shut the place down."

A voice inside me says, *Those people will survive without you.*

"But life is about more than surviving."

"What did you say, Mom? Never mind, I heard you."

"It's that voice inside me telling me I don't have to go back, bud. That those people have it better than a lot of people in the world."

"Better than us?"

"Yeah, I get it."

He shoves a forkful of macaroni between his lips and grins a noodly grin.

"Gross."

I load up my own fork and we talk about his day at school. Ronnie Legermin broke his legs in a freak hang-gliding accident the day before school started and won't be back until at least Halloween.

Loser that I am, I actually high-five him on this. Poor Ronnie, right? I wonder how Ron's dealing with it? Maybe I have a lot to learn about compassion after all.

I put the positive spin on the day with Jace. He looked so tired when he pulled in around ten, I couldn't bear to burden him further. Besides, it'll get better, right?

Mo's eyebrows rise up so high I wouldn't hesitate to call it a wonder of the world.

"So you want to hear my story, huh?" And he laughs and laughs and laughs. He laughs so hard I think he's going to fall out of that chair, which has definitely lost the tone along its spine.

Pulling out a handkerchief, he actually wipes his brow.

"Never mind," I say.

"Good girl!"

I walk toward the kitchen, and he says, "Hey!"

I turn. "Yeah?"

"You all right, Heather. I can't believe you back here today."

"Don't give me too much credit, Mo. There's always next week."

And he starts laughing again.

The big room is filled with folks. Panera sent over a huge trash bag full of bread, bagels, and pastries clients are picking through. Neighbors too, I think. And there's some pretty good stuff in there—croissants too! I wonder if anybody'd mind if—

Heather!

We all love a good find, don't we?

I came prepared today. Tuesday's outfit is laundered and ready to return to the rack. I dressed in an old pair of jeans and a T-shirt from Ron Jon Surf Shop. Yeah, did I mention I tend to keep stuff?

"Hi, Jimmy." Jimmy's arranging a tray of cling-wrapped, day-old blondies and muffins that have a decidedly Starbuckian look to them.

He looks at me and nods. Turns back to his work.

"Sister J in?"

"Nope."

I stand there and wait for a possible explanation.

Nope.

Right, as Jace would say.

I pull out Tuesday's bucket, the colonial blue Rubbermaid with the plastic tube missing from the handle. Luckily I don't have to drag it far, or bye-bye, circulation in my fingers.

Mr. Clean again, and just for kicks, I add a couple of caps of Pine-Sol, mix it up a little, make it interesting. The water falls warm into the bucket, sudsing up the cleanser, and I place my hand beneath the stream. I close my eyes and feel the comfort of the hot wetness.

Okay. I can do this today. I made it through last time; I can do it again.

"I think I'll tackle the stove today."

Jimmy rummages through the large glass-front refrigerator, then snatches up some oranges in a red net bag and places them on the worktable. He looks at me and turns up the radio. I have no idea who the artist is. It's rap. I know nothing.

Well. Good, then. Maybe at least the tempo will keep me moving.

I pry the iron grates off the gas burners and throw them in the utility sink, stopper it up, and pour in plenty of dish detergent. The hot water flows again. It will take several hours to soak off that grease, and Jimmy will be making the soup soon.

We'll see what happens.

And the scrubbing begins. Wouldn't you know it? I forgot my rubber gloves. "Jimmy? Are there any kitchen gloves?"

He turns up the radio, and something the artist is doing sounds like a fly buzzing around.

I can't take him personally. He doesn't know me, right?

Or does he? More than I even know myself? Surely women like me have come and gone.

Time will tell. He's got to be thinking that.

But he heads around the corner to the pantry shelves and returns with a box full of tuna cans and several loaves of bread. "We'll have us a cold lunch." He starts opening cans with the industrial can opener attached to the worktable.

Krista walks into the kitchen with the creamer and sugar bowls in her hands. "These are all out."

"Creamer's gone." Jimmy.

She shakes her head.

Jimmy turns to me. "Folks bring by ramen noodles, green beans, white beans, black beans, pinto beans, kidney beans. They bring by canned soup and day-old bread. But you know what? We really, really need us some creamer."

It's nine o'clock, and I am exhausted. Finally the stove glistens. So do the refrigerator and the sinks and every corner of that downcast kitchen. Bring it on, health department.

Sister J came through, said hi and chatted for a bit, and spent the rest of the day in meetings.

I had a different picture of all this.

Surely there's some good I can do near home? Maybe visit a nursing home, read to the blind, grow a garden and take the produce to the elderly somewhere?

At least they'd appreciate me. Wouldn't they?

And I feel so white, rhythmless, and uncool. Sort of like a bleached whale whose only trick is to roll over and wave with her fin in the midst of dolphins that jump high into the air and turn somersaults. Floating ungainly, out of her element, while the dolphins ignore her existence and scornfully gaze upon her mass.

On the way home I stop at Costco and pick up a case of creamer.

I also noticed Jimmy has to cook with very little oil. I put a huge jug of olive oil and one of safflower oil next to the creamer, pay the cashier, and head on home.

So Will loves Pink. I know. A little girly for a boy, but I'm glad he ventures out from Led Zeppelin every once in a while.

Yeah, yeah, yeah. While Pink will never win the Brio award for good Christian girls, she doesn't compromise her standards—whether or not you think her standards are proper, she does stick to them! I like that about Pink.

I like her music too. Spunky, hip, full of groove.

I know all the lyrics to her album *Missundaztood*. It was in my car CD player for two years.

"Doctor, doctor, won't you please prescribe me somethin', a day in the life of someone else, 'cuz I'm a hazard to myself."

I am so there.

So when "Get This Party Started" blares from Jimmy's transistor on Tuesday, I can't contain myself. And it isn't like he's in the kitchen anyway.

I boogie my way around the stove, a mess again after the weekend, wiping, flicking my rag, wiggling my behind in time to the music. Singing as loud as I dare, but not close to as loud as I can, "I got lotsa style with my gold diamond rings. I can go for—'"

"Aww! Caught you! Caught you singin'. And dancin'! Ha, haaah!"

I whip around, feeling like somebody opened the door to the restroom stall by accident.

Jimmy stands in the doorway, shaking his head, his face rent by a smile.

"You caught the rhythmless white girl. I'll try not to scare you like that again."

"That Pink. She my *girl!*" He claps his hands, bends double, and laughs some more, swinging his head from side to side. "You all right, Heather."

He disappears out to the stoop to smoke a cigarette.

Something happened after that. Jimmy talked to me. Told me about his cocaine addiction, his association with a famous dead rapper, how he came to be cook at the Hotel because Mo caught him sneaking in to sleep in the storage room and offered him work. A few years ago he led a Bible study in the home for alcoholics he stayed in, and he'd love a good study Bible. I'll bring him one next Tuesday.

And when I cut away the rot from a case of oozing tomatoes that came from only heaven knows where, I experienced euphoria like I'd never known. I knew that at that moment I was doing the holy will of God. I was exactly where I was supposed to be; it was holy and good and just. Merciful—to me, the chief of sinners—and humbling. I shouldn't have been privy to such blessing, such favor from God as to serve right there, right then. He called me out to do this, and I deserved none of it. I could have been in my house at this moment, sitting on my plush couch with a cup of warm tea, a Bible in my lap, and a study book beside me begging God to make me whole while doing none of His dirty work. But no. I cut rot off tomatoes in a roach-infested kitchen off of North Avenue.

It didn't get any better than this.

Sister J walked into the kitchen just then. "What are you so happy about?"

"I can't believe I get to be here."

She rolled her eyes. "Believe me, you'll get over it." And disappeared. But I saw a hint of a smile before she turned away.

I loved where I stood. I loved the sink. I loved the stove. I loved Jimmy and Krista and Mo. I loved.

I loved.

I love. In a bigger, broader way than I ever have before. I realized Lark was right. God wants us to care for the poor and the lonely and the sick, not just for their sake, but for ours. Because in this, we become like Him, growing a bigger heart than we ever thought possible.

It wanted to burst from my body.

I wanted to tell everybody. I wanted to shout it from the housetops. God makes it all work together, folks! It's redemption time, and will you come to the well and drink deep? You'll get far more than you could ever give. Don't die in the desert of your Christian radio, Pottery Barn lives.

A cop pulled me over on the way home, and I swear he thought I was drunk, the way I was smiling.

"Do you know how many times you swerved over the lines, ma'am?"

"No."

"Five times to the right, four to the left. I thought you were drunk."

"I'm on my way home from volunteering at the homeless shelter." Would that extend me a warning and not a ticket?

He shifted his feet. "It's obvious you're not intoxicated, ma'am, but I must say, your driving is atrocious."

Well, I could have told him that!

I couldn't wait to tell Jimmy about it. And Mo. Oh yeah, he'd get a good laugh.

THIRTY-FOUR

Jolly has been delivering something from his autumn garden or his orchard every day. He's trying so hard to get over Helen, or at least to find a place to set his feet between the time they hit the floor in the morning and rise above it at night. He and Will are establishing a poetic friendship. An old man, a child, and so much to figure out on both of their parts.

I actually found time last night to read some Dylan Thomas.

Sister J thinks Jolly grows the best peppers she's ever tasted. I told him folks at the Hotel don't get enough produce, and Jolly scratched his cheek and said, "That so? Well, I believe I can help out a bit there." He's already planning a vegetable garden twice the size next year.

Jace fell in bed last night and said, "Well, Bonnie's ecstatic we're even thinking about it."

"What did she say about Will and me?"

"Not a problem as long as she can put you to work too."

"That's Bonnie all right. Nicola's going to have a fit."

"They're quite the number, huh?" He doubles his pillow and shoves it under his neck.

"Definitely."

"So it's looking quite dotty around here. You almost finished categorizing?"

"Yep."

"And then what?"

"I'm going to put all the yellow stuff in one room and reevaluate the blue and green."

"What about the house?" he asks.

"What do you mean?"

"Blue dot or green?"

"I think you know the answer to that."

"You want to start looking for something else?"

"Not yet. I was thinking that a tennis court would be a good investment for resale."

"What?"

"Just kiddin', sweets. Just kiddin'."

I'm always shocked and overcome with thankfulness when Will walks in the door after school in one piece. The lady I carpool with, well, let's just say that if my bad driving is a cup of Folgers, hers is a triple espresso. She ran over Will's foot last week! Of course, he thought it was hilarious.

"It didn't hurt at all, Mom. No harm, no foul, right?"

Normally we meet in the kitchen, break open a bag of chips, and munch for a while. He tells me about his day, and I listen. Then homework time.

Can I say I haven't been this happy in years? I'm watching my family with new eyes, new hope, my own sense of purpose, present and future, mingling with theirs like the hands of long-lost friends clasped in reunion at the train station. And I'm so thankful these days! Put yourself on the thin edges of society, and you'll see how paunchy you really are!

The garage door slides up. Will's home.

He sets his backpack in the middle of the floor and starts taking off his shoes.

"Bud, how long has it been since you've changed your socks?"

"I don't know. Can I have a soda?"

"Sure. How's Nicola?"

"Unbelievable. Man, Mom, she's perfect."

Ah, remember the days?

"Why don't you invite her over tomorrow? We'll cook out. I don't have anything going on."

"Cool." He swigs his Sprite. "You know, it's been kinda nice not being caught up in church so much like we used to be."

"I know. But I kinda miss it, don't you?"

"Some. You know, I think Miss Laney's getting tired of the rat race too. Maybe we can do something with them or something? I mean, the woman has her PhD in the Bible! We could learn a lot from her, you know?"

"You're a genius."

Jace helps me with the dishes, our butts sort of swaying in tandem in front of the kitchen counters, and we catch up on our week. He usually swings home a little early on Fridays and we eat a family meal together. Will made homemade ravioli along with a homemade mess.

I turn on the tap and start scrubbing the pans. We work together in silence, listening to Will practice his trumpet. He has a very mellow tone and could play jazz, I'll bet, if he wasn't such a rock 'n' roller stuck in the '70s like his father.

"I've been thinking," I say a few minutes later.

"About what?" Jace scrubs the spattered cooktop.

"I need to go away for a little while."

"Again?"

I look at him sharply. Turn back to my task. "I need to find Mary Andrews. Xavier was last in Minnesota. But he's in a remote area. The Boundary Waters. Ever heard of that area?"

"Great fishing spot. I went there in college. Hon, what good is this going to do?"

"It's Will. This year has been a turnaround. He's doing well, the stupid jerks are leaving him alone, he has the fair Nicola. I've got to make it up to Mary if she's not all right."

"Maybe you'll just open up old wounds."

"I've got to do this. Isn't there anything big in your life you regret, Jace? Things you wish you'd never done?"

"Not really, hon. But I can think of a lot of things I regret that I should have done, but didn't."

"Please understand this."

"Go ahead, then, hon."

"Just think, in a year from now, Jace, we might be sailing on a big old boat."

"I can hardly believe it," he whispers in my hair.

I wonder how many Jaces are out there. Men and women held behind in their calling because their spouses hold on to their ankles in one way or another, refusing to let them step out.

She pushes a light brown dreadlock crisscrossed with some kind of yarn over her shoulder. "And so I just parked my butt right there in the middle of the road. Almost got hit by a coal truck as it rounded the bend. And man, did he give me what for! Cussed me up one side and down the other, and I gave it right back to him."

I'm chopping onions and listening to Ashley talk about her latest protest. Her partner, Scott, stands there listening. He's the quiet one.

And talk about liberal! Oh my gosh! I swear, they're practically communists. Carmen would have a field day. But here they stand next to me chopping carrots at the Hotel.

I always thought people like this were evil. That's what the radio guys say. Well, sort of.

Then she starts in on her religious convictions. Or non-religious convictions. "God's doing a poor job if there is a god. Look at this earth! It's a stink-hole!"

She just keeps on chopping.

"Don't you think man's made it that way?" I ask, thinking that's a pretty good question.

"Of course I do! Which is why there can't be a god, if this god won't lift a finger to do anything about it."

I shake my head. "Why are you here, then? If it's all so pointless?"

"I didn't say it was pointless. We got ourselves into this mess. We're going to have to get ourselves out of it."

I've met more than one Ashley down here. I ask Sister J about it before I leave.

"What do you make of that?"

She sits down in her chair and settles a worn copy of the Douay-Rheims on her lap. "That's the crazy thing. Here God's using her to make things better, and she doesn't realize it."

"But God's using her nevertheless."

"He's not as choosy as some people tend to think He is. I've seen it over and over again down here. Frish, but I never turn away a pair of helping hands. It would be like turning away Jesus. And Ashley's a good person, doll. She needs to keep her mouth shut more than she does, but she's young. She'll learn someday the world isn't hanging by a thread waiting to hear what she thinks."

"That's a good attitude to have."

"We can't be picky here. And God's got Ashley here to be served as well as to serve. We can't forget Jesus shows up in all sorts of forms, even in people that don't give a rat about Him." She opens her Bible. "So we haven't had cake in a while."

"I'll take that as an order."

"You bet. If that's what it takes. Now let me share this verse with you. Have a seat. 'I thank my God upon every remembrance of you.'" She looks up. "You're doing a good job, Heather."

It was all I needed, just for her to take a little notice.

Yeah, I'm not that holy yet.

THIRTY-FIVE

Carmen corners me in the bathroom at Will's first band concert of the year. "Hey, freshman moms are doing a lunch bunch on third Tuesdays this year. Do you want to come?"

Don't these people have anything better to do with their time? "I can't. I volunteer downtown on Tuesdays." Drat, why Tuesday?

Brenda, who lives about a mile from me, applies a fresh coat of lip gloss. "Oh, come on! You can skip for one day, can't you?"

"Well, there's this girl down there. Krista. She and I always sit together for a while and talk. And I hate to let her down."

Laney, gorgeous Laney with five kids tucked in a town house, rubs my arm. "You knock 'em dead down there."

"Can we do it another day? My schedule is clear every day but Tuesdays and Thursdays."

Brenda purses her lips. "Let me work on that. Maybe next month we can switch it."

I head out of the bathroom, and Krista steps forward, looking scared and out of place. I invited her to go out to dinner with us and head to the concert. "Ready to go in?" I ask.

She nods. "Can I take this coffee in?" She holds up the cup.

"Sure. Let me get one before we sit down." The Booster Club is selling refreshments, and God bless those parents! They're hard-core.

A few minutes later we sit near the front at Krista's request. "I want to tell my grandmom everything about tonight. She be so happy I'm actually out with good Christian people."

A white turtleneck covers the "Playgirl" tattoo.

I grieve for her if her definition of good Christian people includes me!

The phone rings Sunday night. "Heather, it's Laney. Let's go out for coffee. I've got to get out of this house. These kids are about to drive me nuts."

I can see her standing there, her strawberry blond hair pulled back in a clippie, a sponge in her hand as she swirls it on the counter.

"Sure. I want to run something by you anyway. Wanna meet somewhere?"

"I'll come pick you up."

An hour later we're sitting at Starbucks. Yuck. But hey, this chai latte is pretty good! I may have to start coming here if they serve drinks like this.

"Thanks for doing this, Heather. I swear, I was about to become abusive."

Okay, so Laney doesn't wear a mask, and I *love* that about her.

"I've been there. Will went through the most horrible stage at seven. If you can't tell, he can be a little self-righteous."

"A little?"

"I know. But it would be worse if he didn't care about things. At least that's what I keep telling myself."

We both sip our drinks.

"Look, Heather. There's been some talk among the women at school about you."

"I figured. Carmen especially, right?"

"Nothing bad. They're just worried."

"Really? None of them have come to me with these concerns. Except Carmen. Which isn't surprising."

"That's for sure. Carmen says it like she sees it."

"I mean if they were worried about *me*, wouldn't you think one of them would come talk to me?"

"Oh yeah! Definitely."

"I mean, it wasn't like we were all the best of friends or anything."

"Oh, please. It's a gossipfest. I'm not worried about you, but I want to hear what's going on with you down there."

"I just didn't want to wear my good deeds on my sleeve. I mean, you're the Bible expert; you know more than anyone it's not what I'm supposed to do."

"Well, I'm asking you, then. As your friend. I've been praying for you ever since you started volunteering."

"Really?"

"Yeah. I can't believe it either. I'm not much of a pray-er, if you want to know the truth. I mean, I can go for several days and it's like 'Shoot! I haven't prayed in forever!' But God just keeps you on my mind."

So I tell her everything. The good, the bad, the boring. The funny and the sad. "You know what, it's the times that make me laugh and the times that make me cry that keep me going down there."

"Shoot. It's like that raising children."

"Definitely."

"Only nobody's going to end up in a shrink's chair someday if you don't show up. Well, I'm happy for you. I think it's great. I figured you must be doing okay at it since your crazy calls stopped."

Laney's right. Interesting. "Sorry about those."

"Are you kidding? I loved them! Actually, if I didn't have all these kids, I'd be right there with you."

"You've got your own 'least of these' right now, Laney."

She shakes her head and picks up a napkin.

"There's another reason I'm staying away. I've become so judgmental inside. I see all these women who have everything in life, and not only do they not reach out past the gates of the country club, but they act so miserable and wounded all the time. Like they're victims or something when God is blessing their socks off. Believe me, I'm one of them and I'm trying to change, but it's so easy to fall back into the habit."

"I know."

"It's hard for me to hide my feelings, so I just stay away."

"Yeah, but when you do that, it's easier to objectify these women. And they're people too. With their own pain."

"You're right, Laney. I know that."

"And you know, maybe some of them would actually like to help out too. Have you thought about asking them?"

"I did wonder if anybody would want to help paint the main room, but I didn't want to impose on them. Everybody's always so busy."

She begins rolling up the napkin. "I think it's worth a shot. You can't blame people for being farther back in the journey than you are, Heather. I mean, it took a kangaroo to get you on the road, for heaven's sake!"

Mercy, she's right.

"Maybe, Heather, you're supposed to be our kangaroo."

"Well, if that's the case, you're going to have to step up your prayers, Laney. I mean 'pray without ceasing.'"

"I can't do much outside the home, but I can pray. If I remember to. Man, don't you wish all this was easy? Some people make it look so easy."

"I honestly don't think it's easy for anybody. Some people are better actors than others."

She drops me off at home fifteen minutes later, and I hug her as we sit in the car. "Thanks for reaching out, Laney."

"Hey, you gave me a good excuse to get out for a good cup of coffee."

"No really. You have no idea how much I needed that. I've been isolating myself, I know that. I just have to learn to navigate these new waters."

"Well, you're not alone. Hey, and you pray for me too, okay?"

"I will."

See, it's like this. When God shows up, you never know what form He's going to take. But when it's Him, if you're at all awake, you know it.

"Laney, I've been meaning to call and ask you this. What would you think about our families starting a house church? Will came up with the idea, and it's all the rage, you know."

She barks out a laugh.

"Think about it. We shouldn't let your education go to waste a second longer than we have to."

She grips the steering wheel. "Really? Are you serious?"

"Definitely. Jace thinks it's a good idea too."

"Wow. I mean"—she presses her hand to her forehead—"I mean, I just figured God didn't want me to . . . well, didn't want me anymore . . . to serve Him like that . . . Oh, I don't know what I'm even saying, Heather."

She cries a cupful of very complicated tears.

I wave Laney off and turn toward the side of the house and the entrance in the breezeway between the kitchen and the garage. Someone sits on the porch bench.

"Jolly?"

"Hello there, Heather." His voice sounds sanded thin.

"Are you all right?"

"I just brought over some apples." He holds up a bucket. "And I just can't go home. I can't go back there, I miss her so badly."

He's been crying again. For a long time if I'm not mistaken.

"Come on inside. I'll make us a cup of tea and set up the guest room for you. You stay with us tonight."

"I'd appreciate that."

Jace, Will, and I gather around Jolly, and soon we're all drinking tea and playing a game of Trivial Pursuit. Jolly wipes us clean on the sports category. "I had no idea you were a sports nut," I say.

"Yes sirree. Helen and I never missed a game of anything if it was on the TV."

They must have enjoyed a lovely life. Really, really enjoyed it.

Will lays down *zaibatsu* using a z already on the board. On a triple word space. "Oh yeah. Oh yeah."

Jace bares his teeth. "No way. It's Japanese, and I have no idea what it means."

"It's a large Japanese business conglomerate." He leans back and crosses his arms over his chest. "And it's English."

"No way. It's a foreign word, bud."

I love watching this. It's only a matter of time before Will tallies those points onto his score. Hasn't Jace figured out what a pushover he is?

Jolly sips his tea, clears his throat, and looks down at his tiles through his pink half-glasses, Helen's old ones, of course. "Seems to me if a boy knows such a word rightly exists, he should get some points. I say give him half for even knowin' it."

"Done!" says Jace.

Our eyes meet. He knows I realize what a bargain he just got.

Will collects seven tiles from the brown plastic bag. "Hey, you were a topic of conversation in the cafeteria today, Mom."

"Figures. What did I do now?"

"You had to bring that girl to the concert, didn't you?" He smiles. "That's what the moms were saying. It was hilarious. You know the girls can imitate their moms dead-on!"

"You mean Krista?"

"Yeah." He dons a feminine affect. "'And she paraded her right up to the front. If she wants to slum it, fine, but does she have to rub everybody's nose in it?'"

Jace rearranges his tiles. "That's my girl. Making waves."

Will. "Yeah, boy. You should have heard Missy. She said her mom was talking about it with the other women."

Missy. Brenda's daughter.

No wonder Laney called.

"You must think you're so holier-than-thou, they say. And it's not only that—they heard the mission is Catholic. You're halfway to being a heretic too."

Mercy!

"I'm sorry, Will. I didn't think you'd be bearing the brunt."

"Me? Oh yeah, right. I think it's great. I mean, come on, it's not okay for you to bring Krista, but perfectly fine for them to talk behind your back, right?"

Well, honestly, I can't fault them there. Not really. I've done my share of gossiping. But somehow, when you're the one doing it, it just doesn't seem all that bad.

After settling Jolly in the guest room, I riffle through the day's mail and come up with a letter to Will. From Ronnie Legermin. Oh no. Bullying goes postal. I take it up to his room and hand it to him. "What's this?"

"Oh, cool."

"You want to explain why Ronnie Legermin is writing you?"

"I got a card from him two weeks ago. He apologized, which was totally crazy, you know? I mean, I never saw *that* coming!"

"Was it genuine?"

"Heck, I don't know. So I wrote him back and said, "Yeah, I forgive you," and all that sort of thing. No big deal, really. So I guess he's written me back."

"Well, open it, then."

"Okay, Mom. Sheesh. Can't I have a little privacy? I don't go asking to read your mail, do I?"

Okay, okay.

Liza outdid herself. A baked rockfish garnished with parsley and lemon rests on a simple marigold platter.

Anna sparkles in a new lime green sweater. "And don't you just love the gold trim around the wrists?" She twists her wrist back and forth.

"I do. You look wonderful."

"I know it's silly, a woman my age, but I couldn't resist it."

Liza sets down a bowl of buttered broccoli. "It was from Kohl's,

Anna. Nobody should feel guilty about buying something at Kohl's."

They've prepared for my coming, set out their best, and I feel as though I'm Christ Himself come for dinner. And knowing the way they think, I guess I am. "I could have brought my own fork."

Anna hugs me. "Do you use it?"

"Every day."

Liza updates me on her ministries, Anna as well, and she hasn't been arrested lately, which is a relief. I worry about her.

Liza sets down her fork. "I'm so glad you haven't forgotten us biddies."

Anna arches a brow but says nothing.

"Well, I do have an ulterior motive. Do you still have the plans for Alva's houses in Glen Burnie?"

Liza gasps. "Of course! Why?"

"I think we want to build one for ourselves, Liza. Sell the big house, live sensibly, cleanly."

"Like a true modernist would!" She smugly throws back her shoulders. "Right, then. They're in the study. This is quite exciting for me, you know. You'll have to keep us informed every step of the way."

"Oh, I will, Liza."

Anna lays a sweet hand over her sister's and smiles into her eyes. "I told you they'd be useful someday, dear. Dreams like Alva's don't deserve to die off completely."

"Anna, you were right, and this time I don't mind saying so."

THIRTY-SIX

Sly, the man who first helped me take my cakes to the kitchen, hasn't been around the Hotel very much. I ask Mo about this. Mo shakes his head above a bright red sports jersey. "Aww, Sly's using again. He's ashamed. I don't think he'll be back for a while."

"Where does he hang out?"

"Patterson Park. And do *not* go there by yourself, Heather. Don't be crazy. I see that look in your eye."

"Okay."

I should have reached out to Sly more instead of hiding back in the kitchen. The regret slams into my stomach.

Knox Dulaney breezes through the door. "Mo!"

"Knoxie." Mo doesn't smile.

"Now, man, don't do that to me. Is Aunt Jerusha around?"

Mo jerks a thumb around to the back.

A few of the guys sitting at the tables playing checkers or watching TV shift uncomfortably in their seats.

Knox disappears through the swinging door.

"Mo, I don't understand it. Krista told me how bad that man is. There isn't a month goes by that someone isn't dead because of him."

"He's bad news."

"Why does Sister J put up with him?"

"She loves him. Lord knows, she tried to bring him up right. But you know, sin is a dictator. Knoxie wanted fortune and respect."

"But it's fear, not respect."

577

"Not on these streets."

"But isn't respect earn—"

"Don't even try to understand it, girl."

"Okay. Well, I've got some cake in the car." I turn toward the tables. "Anybody want to help me bring in the cake?"

"I will." A man I've never seen, or perhaps never noticed, stands up. His words are quiet, hunched a little like their creator.

"Thanks."

We walk down the street to the car. "I'm Heather, by the way."

"Teddy Jamison."

"Have you been at the Hotel before?"

"I come and go. I try and find work when and where I can."

"What do you do?"

"I paint murals. That's my work down there on Lexington Street. Near the market on the parking garage."

"I've never seen it."

"Take a look sometime."

I open the back and load his arms with boxes.

"Sometimes I do sidewalk drawings for some spare change."

"Are you trained?"

"No. Just always knew how to do it."

"Do you take on commissions?"

"If I think I can do it."

I shut the hatchback. "I've always wanted a portrait of my son. It doesn't matter what medium."

I relieve him of some of the boxes.

"Sure. Just bring in some pictures. I'll do charcoal or pastel."

"I love charcoal."

"I'd appreciate it if you'd get the supplies too."

"Okay."

We're almost to the doors. Mo opens them and we deposit the cakes in the kitchen. Teddy disappears. When I deliver a fresh urn of coffee an hour later, he sits with the others, watching *The Price Is Right*, eyes glazed over, hands lying empty on the table, the memory of a syringe printed into their palms.

Oh yes, Knox Dulaney was here. One way or another he has that effect on people.

I'm scrubbing the oven again. Footsteps approach and a pair of expensive brown shoes comes into view. Nothing preppy or staid. Lots of European style.

I lean back on my haunches.

Knox smiles. "Hello, Mrs. Curridge."

"Hi. And it's just Heather."

"I just wanted to say thank you for coming down here. Aunt Jerusha has a hard time keeping volunteers, as you might imagine."

I drop my rag into the bucket and stand to my feet. "She's her own gal, that's for sure."

I know he's Jesus to me right now, but every time I talk to him, I feel like it's the first time.

"I'm regretful about my reputation to you."

"Yeah, I'm pretty much scared to say anything right now, Mr. Dulaney."

He nods. "No doubt. It's all right. You probably think I come in here to intimidate the clients."

I can feel my eyes widen.

"Ah, I read your mind," he says.

I nod.

"I don't do it for myself. I do it to let anybody know if they mess with my aunt, they'll have me to deal with."

"It's obvious you have a great deal of affection for her."

"She's saved my life more than once. Continues to. I try to help out here, keeping her safe, donating."

"She takes your money?" Mercy! Why did I say that?

"Yes, she does. You know what she says? She says, 'I'm not going to take the one good thing you actually do away from you.'" He chuckles. "I heard you brought cake today."

"Yes, I did."

"May I take a piece with me?"

"I'll wrap it up for you." Everything inside me screams, *Don't do it!* But a deeper voice asks, *Can you love as radically as Christ does?*

Yet as I tear a piece of foil off an almost-empty tube, I feel as if I'm doing something wrong and I wonder which voice is right.

But Christ never held Himself at arm's length, did He? He'd share His cake with Knox.

I might as well get it over with. On the drive home I plug my dead cell phone into the car charger and dial Carmen. She answers, thank goodness. I don't want to prolong this agony with the inevitable "Tag, you're it!"

That line has got to go.

"It's Heather, Carmen. Do you have time to talk?"

"I'm a little busy right now. Bart has a science project due tomorrow and I'm up to my elbows." Bart's ten.

It's two thirty. Will's going to Nicola's to study.

"Why don't I come over and help?"

"Would you? That would be great."

Half an hour later I sit with her at her kitchen island working on the project. I'm taping together construction paper cylinders to wrap around glass jars filled with water. We're going to drop in a thermometer and set them all before a heat lamp to see how quickly the jars heat up, comparing the temperature rise to the colors of the paper.

Or something.

Just hand me the tape and I'll be fine.

"Where's Bart?"

"He's got a game."

And here we sit doing his science fair project.

She looks at me, waiting for the inevitable "This is lying" speech, but I hold up my hands. "I can't say I haven't done the same thing myself."

"It's pathetic, I know. Okay, I'm setting in the thermometers. The water should all be at room temperature, so we'll let them get to the same level and then put the paper sleeves over and shine the lights. Want a cup of coffee while we wait?"

"Sure."

"I just got this wonderful machine that grinds the beans and makes a fresh cup in about thirty seconds."

Wow. It's great. Frothy and silky going down. I think maybe I should get one, but . . . get thee behind me, Satan!

"Carmen, I came over to set things right between us. I know there are a lot of hard feelings between me and the other women right now. And I know, believe me, I know it's my fault. I've been really caught up in things."

"It's true."

"I also want you to know I didn't parade Krista up front. She really wanted to sit there."

"Oh, that was just Brenda saying all that. You know her."

Of course, the obvious next question is why Brenda's gossiping criticism gets excused as "just Brenda." But now's not the time.

"Anyway, I just want to get things right. I can't jump back into all my positions, but I don't want to isolate you all either."

Carmen pushes the button and makes her own cup.

She sits down. "I guess I haven't been all that supportive. You've just always been in such a leadership role, Heather. And then to remove yourself."

"Can I tell you my story?"

"Maybe that would be a good idea."

So as we turn on the lights, write down data, try different light-bulbs, I tell her everything, just as I did Laney.

She pencils in the final temperature of the lightest cylinder. "I can understand a bit more. I think."

When I leave she hugs me at the car. "Be careful with that drug dealer down there. You might get shot or something."

"Maybe you'd like to come down with me sometime?"

She folds her arms across her chest. "Let me check my calendar." Then pulls me into another hug. "Of course I would!"

After having picked up the building plans from Liza, I pass my drive-way and turn down Jolly's lane. Almost six o'clock. The light is fading, but it's easy to see he still loves his land. Fall mums bloom, brightening their square foot of dusk, lining the driveway with the promise of a nice person waiting at the other end.

All lights in the old home are off, save the kitchen, and the yellow bulb over the porch shines in silent hope that maybe someone will ease his loneliness.

I hop out of the wagon, bound toward the door, and knock, anticipation hovering in the air around me.

Why didn't I think of this before?

He yanks open the door, and a smile peps up his face. Jolly pushes the screen door forward. "Heather! Why, come on in!"

"Guess what? I've got a great idea!"

"Oh, now?"

"Yes. I'm heading off to Minnesota to find a man named Xavier Andrews. I'll tell you why later. But he lives in some remote area called the Boundary Waters and you can only get there by canoe."

"Heard of it."

"At least I think he lives there. Anyway, would you like to go with me? I'm leaving in about a week, before it gets too cold. Would you like to go?"

"Yes."

I look both ways, lean forward, and put my hand against his forehead. "You're not sick, are you?"

"No. You could have invited me to the moon without an oxygen tank and I'd have said yes to that too. I need a change of scenery, Heather. The sooner the better. Now Helen would say that's okay."

"She definitely would."

"Next week, you say?"

"Wednesday. I'll book your ticket along with mine."

When I tell Will, he descends into a full-blown sulk. "Man. You have all the fun, Mom. Going to the Hotel and being with Mo all the time, and now you get to go away with Jolly. It sucks being in high school."

THIRTY-SEVEN

Sister J stands with Mo, her handbag hanging from the crook of her arm. They both look a little stricken, a little angry, a little fearful.

"What is it?" I ask.

"Krista's disappeared again." Sister J. "She hasn't been back for three nights. Her stuff is still in her room. Nobody's seen hide nor hair."

"Where are you going?" I set my purse on Mo's desk.

"I'm going out to look for her. I'll see if Knox has heard anything too."

Mo tsks.

"Now don't you start with me! You know as well as I do that Knox knows more about what's going on in the street than you and I put together, Moses Weaver." She turns to me and jerks a thumb at Mo. "He's a rascal."

"Can I go? I just need to use the bathroom."

"You bet. It might not be pretty."

"I want to go."

The feeling of dread that pooled in my gut as soon as Sister J uttered the words "Krista's disappeared" begins to coagulate. Dear God in heaven, I hope she isn't dead! Sister J leads me out onto the street.

"Let's try that flophouse right there. LaQueesha lives on the first floor. She's tried to look out for Krista, but what can you do? We'll cut through the alley. Be careful not to step on the syringes; they can go right through your soles if you're not careful."

Mercy!

"And don't touch the walls if you can help it. Stay away from that cat carcass over there. Hold your nose."

Now I know why I've never gone down these alleys. And I could forgo the tour spiel if Sister J wouldn't mind. She looks right at home, though, I have to admit. I'll bet in her eyes, this is just the patio of the Hotel.

A brown door, paint scratched through, seems to be the only entrance around here

Sister J knocks. "This is LaQueesha's entrance. Nicest apartment in the building. The rest are like closets. But where else you going to live for fifty bucks a week?"

The door opens and a woman wearing a robin's egg blue sequined cowboy hat stands in the doorway. "Sistah J? How you doin'?" She swings the door wide. "Come on in! It's been too long, uh-huh."

"Heck yeah, it has. This is my friend Heather. She's a volunteer."

"Come in, come in, uh-huh."

We climb the three concrete steps and enter a dim hallway lined with frames surrounding copious cutouts: ovals, squares, and each one contains a school photo, a snapshot, or a ticket stub. She leads us toward the front of the building, past a couple of bedrooms—one set up as a prayer room with a kneeling bench and a crucifix—a bath, then a kitchen, all lined up along the corridor. And pow! Into the front room we emerge like spelunkers from a cave. Heavy venetian blinds accordion near the tops of the tall, narrow windows, and almost everything is light blue, matching LaQueesha's outfit, a sky blue mohair poncho over a shimmery tank top, jeans the denim god must have exhaled onto her, and turquoise cowboy boots with silver heels and mirrored decorations.

LaQueesha must love hoops! Ten heavy gold hoops lower each ear farther down beside her thin neck bound up with necklaces of gold and silver. Bangles, rings accent her graceful hands. She jangles and smells like peaches. I wasn't this feminine on my wedding day.

"Have a seat, have a seat. I'm just about to head downtown to the beauty parlor, uh-huh." Hands land on hips in a slouchy, runway fashion. So slender too. "Can I get you a ice tea?"

"Thanks, doll, that sounds good." Sister J sits on one of those wicker fan chairs Pier 1 sold back in the '70s when it was more the garage sale of the Orient than a trendy boutique anchoring upscale strip malls. This one is decorated with crystal beads that catch the sun coming through the window and throw tiny rainbows on Sister J's cheek.

"You look like a saint in that thing." I choose a seat near her on the couch, a cream-colored leather sofa running the length of the room. "Nice!"

"I love my couch. Now some tea for you too, uh-huh?"

"Please."

She walks into the first doorway off the hall.

Sister Jerusha taps her nose. "If anybody knows where Krista is, it's LaQueesha."

"What's her story?"

"Her grandmother owned this building. LaQueesha is one of the smartest businesswomen I know. Keeps the building up better than most landlords around here, although I wouldn't want to spend a night here if I didn't have to. Other than here at her place. Now this is styling, isn't it?"

"It's amazing. So nuns like a little sparkle when left to their own devices?"

"This nun does."

"Do you ever bemoan the fact that you've led a life of poverty?"

"You mean that I missed out on all the good things of life?"

I shrug. "I guess."

"Not one bit. Don't know any different. I went into the convent when I was nineteen. I was the youngest in my family—fourteen children. We didn't have much, but nobody abused us or neglected us—of course, we only expected a few minutes a day from each parent, so we had lowered expectations. So I don't know what I'm missing. And you know there are all sorts of good things in life. Maybe not things, but people, and places, and deeds, and families, and children. You know, life itself."

She folds her hands across her stomach and sighs.

"And then some days, you get to sit in LaQueesha's apartment and have some of her iced tea." She raises her brows. "Uh-huh."

"I heard that!" LaQueesha steps out of the kitchen with a tray of tea glasses rimmed in gold. She laughs. "I've tried to rid myself of that 'uh-huh' for years, and I just can't."

"It's who you are, doll." Sister J reaches for a glass and sips. "Ahh, best iced tea in Baltimore."

I take mine, sip, and by golly, she's right! "What's your secret?"

"One mint bag in with three regulars. Does it every time. Lots of sugar, uh-huh, and got to put in a good amount of lemon."

I raise my glass. "I'll remember that." Even Leslie Summerville would approve of this brew.

LaQueesha sits next to me. "So what brings you round today?"

"Krista's disappeared." Sister J sets her drink on the glass coffee table.

"Again?"

"Yeah. I thought she was gonna make it this time. I really did."

Our host's brows knit. "Oh, Sistah J, I wish I was as hopeful as you, uh-huh. But I seen that little girl for a year now, just struggling every day, and if you can't help her, I don't know who can, and the dear Lord knows that's the truth."

"Have you seen her, then?" Sister J leans forward. Her upper lip quivers so slightly I can hardly believe I noticed. And it hits me. She loves this girl. She loves Krista more than someone like me is able to give her credit for.

"No. I'm so sorry. I haven't seen her for a week."

"Any talk?"

"No, but I been busy, you know, uh-huh. I'll ask around."

Sister Jerusha leans back. "Something about that girl pulls at my heart, LaQueesha. God's marked her. I can see it like I could on you, like I can on Knoxie."

LaQueesha just nods and turns to me. "Sistah J was the first person to realize I could sing, Heather. I sing all over the place now, uh-huh, for Jesus too."

"Sister J, can you really see God's mark on people?"

"You bet I can. Don't know how or why, but there're some that get a special mark from God to do great things."

LaQueesha points a finger at her. "Now I seen you get it right nine times outta ten—yes, I have. But I think you missed it with Knoxie, Sistah. You have most definitely missed it with that man, uh-huh." She wipes a hand in disgust. "And you and I are the ones left picking up his pieces, we are." She points to me. "You stay away from him, Heather, if you know what's good for you. Don't ever talk to him outside the Hotel. Ever. You hear what I'm saying?"

I nod.

Sister J sighs. "It's good advice. I love my godson, but he's a dangerous man. What can you do?"

Is there a mark on me? No way am I going to ask. Both answers contain major drawbacks.

An hour later after various interviews on the street, including Zeke with his droopy pants, we return to the kitchen.

"I loved that lady! She's wonderful." I raise a bag of bread off the yellow plastic bakery tray and set it on the worktable. Garlic bread to go with Jimmy's "minestrone," which means cans and cans of vegetables dumped into water with some bouillon cubes, macaroni, and kidney beans. Donations have been on a diet lately.

"You gotta love LaQueesha. I'll be in my office if you need me, doll."

She turns and trudges through the doorway, flips on the lamp, and shuts the door.

Sister J is the Atlas of the North Avenue area. It's easy to say, "The poor aren't my responsibility. They got themselves there, they can get themselves out." And most people do say that, if not by their words, then by their actions. But then people like this woman give their lives, like Jesus did, to whoever will reach out and take them. Not because they deserve it, but because she has so much life to give away.

Serving God makes little sense down here at the Hotel, the last stop on the line for many people. But there has to be that last stop, doesn't there? And Jesus is here too. He can't help but be.

I had so many theories there on the hill, and none of them felt like bone or bled like skin. None of them were once an innocent little baby who cried out in pain or laughed in amusement. None of those ideas looked out of eyes glistening with the wet of life, looked out over used syringes and condoms and men like Knox Dulaney, eyes filled with anger because any other emotion costs too much.

My bed feels better and better these days. I'm preparing to leave for Minnesota in just a few days. Already it's almost too late in the year for the trip we're making, but it has been a warmer fall than usual up north, so Jolly and I may be just fine.

Jace climbs into bed looking like a once-wet dog now dried by a trek in the hot sun and ready for a long lie-down on the porch. I don't know how he does it. "How you doing, hon?"

"Tired. What you got going tomorrow?"

"Actually, a lighter day. And I'll go to the Hotel for a couple of hours in the afternoon."

I curl my fists around the top of the sheet. "Krista disappeared and we can't find her anywhere."

"I thought something was bothering you when I called earlier. No idea where she is?"

"LaQueesha's going to ask around."

He leans up and looks over at me. "LaQueesha?"

"Yep. She loves blue."

"Hopefully they'll find her soon."

I lean up on my elbow. "Why is it so hard for some people, Jace? I mean, here you've got kids born into the right family, all the right circumstances, and the only reason they amount to anything is because their parents buy their way out of their troubles until they're old enough to get with the program. And then you've got the people who come into the Hotel. I swear, they're not that different. They just never had the cushion."

"No. You're right there."

"I wish I knew what the answer is."

"If you figure it out, tell the world." He smiles. "You're the answer, Heather. Surely you see that, don't you?"

And yeah, I'm just one woman and all that. But maybe he's got a point.

Okay, he does have a point.

We can only change the world by changing ourselves. I guess that's always the very first step. Sister J tacked a Gandhi quote above her desk. *"Be the change you wish to see in the world."* Michael Jackson sang about starting with the man in the mirror. Good thought, even if the messenger creeps me out. And Jesus, my Jesus, said, "Inasmuch as you've done it to the least of these, you've done it unto Me."

Why must it be so simple yet so difficult?

I lie in the darkness listening to Jace's deafening snore and staring at the ceiling.

My grandmother, God rest her, used to say this to me.

Only one life t'will soon be past.

Only what's done for Christ will last.

Granted, she enjoyed a platitude spirituality, but she raised my father, so she did something right.

So here's the bottom line. Do I want to stand before God's throne and say I kept a clean house, I made sure my child was athletic, musical, artistic, and got good grades, I was present at all the important church activities, and I changed the oil in my car every three thousand miles because I was such a good steward of my blessings?

Is that all I will have to show for the gift of life?

Dear God, I hope not.

I won't be able to sleep with the hound dog next to me, so I throw back the covers, tiptoe downstairs, and pull out a fresh spiral notebook. It's inventory time. One column for blue dots, one for green, and one for yellow. And I begin to take a closer look at my possessions.

I set out the cereal boxes, bowls, spoons, and milk on our island. Gone are the days of bacon or sausage, eggs and biscuits. No creamed chipped beef or French toast.

And they're surviving just fine.

Who knew?

Will enters the kitchen and pours himself a cup of coffee. He takes it black. I wish I was half as cool as he is. Now if I could just get him to remember to put deodorant on every morning, we'd be doing even better.

"Did you put deodorant on?"

"Sheesh, Mom! Of course!"

I cock my head, and he sets down his cup and runs up the steps.

Okay, so he's not above the occasional lie. But neither am I, especially when Carmen corners me.

He rumbles back down the steps a minute later. "Okay, there. I was just prophesying before." He grabs the box of Cocoa Krispies and pours some into a bowl. "So what's going on today with you?"

"Last-minute trip preparations and then I'm going to take a quick run down to the Hotel to drop off a few things." Okay, more than a few, but they're going to sell some of this stuff on eBay.

He pours the milk, then, grabbing the bowl and spoon, heads into the family room.

I take a mental inventory of the purged items. Christmas China, sixteen place settings by Lenox. That'll fetch a pretty price, and honestly, does having holly and bows around your food make it taste any better? It would be one thing if this stuff had been passed down, but all my dad ate off of until the day he died was Corelle.

"And you know!" Will hollers from the couch. "I was wondering if you could maybe change one of your volunteer days to Saturday. That way I could come with you."

"You've got a lot going on Saturdays, bud."

"I know. But I've been thinking about it for a while now."

And he clicks on the TV to watch *Good Morning America*. He loves that show.

THIRTY-EIGHT

This morning the Petersons and the Curridges met at Patterson Park. In broad daylight. Near the pagoda.

Laney opened up the Scriptures, we shared Communion, Jace played his guitar, we prayed. Afterwards we ate cake and drank iced tea made with LaQueesha's special mix.

Church happens, I learned today. It doesn't always have to be programmed and planned, pulled out of the Body like a splinter from raw flesh, leaving bits behind to fester in its wake. The Holy Spirit put in a visit too. I know that because I'm a Christian, and sometimes, we just know these things.

Jolly brews me a cup of Red Rose tea. We sit at his kitchen table, opera music filtering in from the hi-fi stereo in the den.

"I never knew you liked opera, Jolly."

"Helen hated it. So I figured I might as well dig out my old seventy-eights. That's Caruso right there. Isn't he something?" Jolly's face lights up. "My father loved opera."

"Mine hated it!"

"Maybe he should have married my Helen."

"Okay, Jolly." I reach into my purse and pull out his ticket. "Here's your flight itinerary. I'll pick you up on Wednesday morning at 4:30 a.m."

He raises his brows. "That's cow milking time!"

"I know. But we have to be at the airport two hours before our flight these days with all the security."

He flips open the flap. "That so? Never been on an airplane before."

"Nothing to it. It'll be fun to do together. Now is there anything you'll need? We'll have to take a canoe ride to Xavier's place. The girl at the library found out the general proximity of his parcel. So you'll want to pack warm. Do you have a suitcase?"

"I do. In fact"—he points toward the door—"I'm already packed."

An army green duffle bag rests on the floor.

"Oh, Jolly. I'm so glad you're looking forward to it as much as I am." I can't help myself—I throw my arms around his neck and give him a giant hug.

"Now, now!" he says. "Now, now!"

"You're just a treasure." I pull back.

"I was wondering if I might come with you down to that hotel of yours sometime. See if they might need an extra pair of hands."

"How about tomorrow?"

He scratches his cheek, the scritch-scritch of his stubble sounding like small maracas. "Well, now. I think that can be arranged. Of course, I'll need to check my overflowing social calendar first."

I do believe I see a sparkle in those eyes. Tiny, yes, but right there.

"Hey, Jolly. What happened to most of the dolls?" At least three-quarters of them didn't show up for duty today.

"I sent the ones I've always disliked to a doll museum. Helen's gone, Heather. And I never found her compassion for those ugly things."

"I don't think she'd mind."

"You kidding? She'd have had a fit."

I dial Carmen. "Hey, girl!"

"Heather! How are you?"

"Good. Listen, I've got a proposition for you."

"I haven't had one of those in years."

"Me either. So here's the deal."

I tell her about the paint from the Summerville Foundation just sitting there. "What do you think? Would the women of St. Matthews want to take a day and paint? It would be good PR for the school."

"Oh my gosh, yes! Are you kidding?"

My eyes blink of their own accord and my head is thrown back with the force of her enthusiasm. "Really?"

"Absolutely. You know, it's not that we don't care, Heather. We're clueless, not callous."

Well, that sure sounds like a different song than what they were singing awhile ago. I like it.

"Okay, then! Well, good. I'm going away for a week to find an old friend, so let's plan for something after that?"

"Great. I'll get the buzz going."

See, Carmen's not so bad. I don't know why I have such a hard time giving people a chance.

Okay, she deserved every bit of it, but still.

Jolly called at least four times today and came over twice, body taut with anticipation. His one duffel found a mate who came to the marriage with brand-new clothes from Target. Will is trying not to let his natural excitement show through the unnatural sulk. I watch him inspect and approve Jolly's purchases, see the longing in the movements of his sensitive hands, and I'd love to take him out of school to come with us. But I can't let him witness what might happen. It's my penance, my sin, and my time to face the consequences.

"Mom?" Will corners me in the bathroom, where I'm packing my travel bag. "I need to know why you're going."

"I don't know if you can handle it, bud."

"These people have a strong hold on you. Something's wrong. I think I need to know."

I take his face in my hands. "Will, a long time ago I was a terrible person. I'd rather you not know the ins and outs of it."

"Were you in school?"

"Yes."

"Can I ask Dad when you're gone?"

"I think that would be better."

"You know I'll forgive you whatever it is."

I kiss his cheeks. How does he know he has something to forgive?

THIRTY-NINE

Jolly and I climb out of the rental car, a soda can with bike wheels and barely upholstered seats. I've never seen car floors without carpeting before.

"Sorry I went so cheap, Jolly."

"I feel like I been on roller skates."

Me too.

"Sure was glad to get out of Duluth, though. I hate cities." He opens the trunk and starts pulling out our bags. "This'll be a nice little escapade, surely."

The drive took about six hours, Jolly talking about Helen, pointing out vegetation and naming it by botanical name and common name, never failing to express his delight at a well-planted field, a beautifully kept farm.

"Now that's a barn!" he said over and over again. "I always did favor the white barns for some reason."

"I like purple."

"I don't strictly find that hard to believe."

At the end of a flagstone path illumined by footlights with rusty iron moose ears sprouting from either side, a log cabin lodge sits against a star-filled sky. On a deep, wide porch, yellow light falls on settings of bent willow furniture.

"Who gets to run places like this? Who gets to live like this?" I ask.

"The lucky ones. That's for sure."

A young man with russet hair, a puffy beard, and an orange

sweatshirt proclaiming that the Mssrs. Abercrombie and Fitch have indeed taken over the world opens the door. "Ms. Curridge?"

"That's me."

"Have a good trip?" He walks behind the counter.

Jolly sets down his bag. "Yes, we did. Good drive. Pretty country."

"And you're Mr. Lester?"

"Yes, I am."

He turns toward a key cubby, just like in the movies. Pulling out two keys, he says, "Breakfast can be anytime you like. Eggs, bacon, that sort of thing."

"We'll want an early start. We're looking for a man named Xavier Andrews. I'm going to need a guide."

The young man shakes his head. "I've never heard of a man named Xavier Andrews. You know where he might be?"

"Runs a camp or something." I pull out the map the librarian printed off for me. "Somewhere around here. You all have the best guide in the area, right?"

"Let me call Ralph. He's the guide you're talking about. If anybody's heard of this man, Ralph will have."

The gist of his call is that Ralph hasn't seen Xavier Andrews in a couple of years, but yes, he runs a remote camp about twenty miles from here and as far as he knows, Xavier's still there.

Twenty miles? Mercy! I thought I was at least in the ballpark.

"It's a place for the hardiest of sportsmen. Ralph can't guide you tomorrow, but his nephew Grandy can. He grew up on these waters."

"Sounds good."

"He said he'll come by at 7:00 a.m. It'll take two days to get there."

Jolly and I stare at each other. He's thinking, *Is that right?* And I'm thinking, *Two days!*

The young man continues. "He said you'll paddle mostly. You'll have to camp for a couple of nights. We've got clean sleeping bags and all the gear you'll need. Grandy'll bring a couple of tents. I'll be honest, other than Ralph, there's no better guide than Grandy."

"Well, I guess that tells us what time breakfast is, then," Jolly says.

"You'll want to eat hearty. We'll pack up a cooler, too, if you'd like. Water. Two days there, two days back. You'll need the supplies. Grandy'll bring some things too."

I nod. "Thanks."

Jolly and I stand in the hall near our doorways.

"I had no idea, Jolly. I'm sorry. I just thought I'd come up here and find him easy. I don't know what I was thinking."

"Where was that last vacation you all took?"

"An all-inclusive resort in Belize."

"So there you go. It'll be fun. I needed an adventure, Heather."

"Well, we'll get one. I feel kinda stupid, very unprepared."

"Is that so? Well, he didn't seem to bat an eyelid, now, did he?"

"No, that's true."

"So stop thinkin' you're so dang special, girly."

I laugh. "You want to drive down the road and get a little supper?"

"To be honest, I'm exhausted. I'd just soon tuck in."

"Me too."

I love Jolly.

Tonight as I settled between plaid flannel sheets, I was thinking about the truly happy people I've known in my lifetime and how few there really have been, which seems so very sad. Miss Virginia was the crossing guard in our neighborhood when I was in first grade. I didn't start in at Christian school until second.

A joy shone from inside of her that made us kids want to be around her. And never once was I scared coming out of school, because Miss Virginia would be there, and she'd call me 'baby' and smile, her gold tooth gleaming. Nothing ruffled her, and even the mean kids smiled at her when they walked by.

Miss Virginia was happy, so therefore, Miss Virginia was safe to be around. I wish I thought of her more after I grew up. I want to be a Miss Virginia. I want to be safe—that place where people can fail and still be loved. Heaven knows, there are enough exhorters, enough admonishers, enough people with a lockdown on life, enough people who can tell all of us what to do and why and sometimes even how. They don't need me.

I rub some moisturizer into my hands. Raspberry.

But I want to be the person around whom people don't have to do a thing to be loved. Perhaps all of humanity can't fill that role, and maybe there's only room for a few of us on earth or all would be chaos. I don't know. But as I see it, there's definitely room for more Miss Virginias. And I aim to fill her shoes.

Tomorrow we'll be canoeing into the wilderness. I've never been in such a remote area in my entire life. Isn't that strange?

We set out in slim light, bellies full of a farmer's breakfast, as Jolly, rested and ready to go, called it. He sipped that coffee and gave out a long "Ahhh. Now that's good, strong coffee."

"You like it strong? I never had a strong cup at your house."

"It was hard on Helen's stomach."

The home fries were loaded with caramelized onions and cheese, and I ate almost a full plate, with Canadian bacon and a bunch of grapes.

I'm excited about the journey, but I really don't want to have to go to the bathroom out in the middle of nature. That's pretty much my single reservation here. Pathetic, I know.

Jolly sits at the front, I'm in the middle, and Grandy sits in the back, paddling, steering, saying nothing. We all paddle, and I think, *Two days of this?* Actually four days with the trip back, but I'm not ready to go there.

It surely makes whatever forgiveness I receive from the Andrews family, if I am even awarded it, hard-won. Even with this, I realize it's not enough penance. Not even close. For I remember the times we cornered Mary in the girls' restroom and smeared lipstick all over her face; I remember the time Julia B. and I told her the next day was red day and she showed up in red and the rest of us wore blue; and I remember Bryan stealing her lunch bag, opening it up, and displaying the contents to everybody in the cafeteria with a running commentary. "Ah, yes, the stinky egg salad." Or "Oooh, bread and margarine. The lunch of champions." After a while, Mary stopped bringing lunch, stopped eating lunch. Gary just sort of kept to himself—a silent pariah.

I can't tell Will this. I make Ronnie Legermin look like a saint.

I'm sure tomorrow my muscles will be screaming. I paddled several hours, although Jolly and Grandy were benevolent and took on most of the load. I even fell asleep for a little while as the waters slid by and we passed colonies of trees, their roots twisted through the banks, clinging to the earth, their upper surfaces carpeted in moss. But I didn't sleep for long. I didn't want to miss the great carved walls of rock, so ancient, looking as if the finger of God himself reached down and dug through the stone.

Pine trees lined the shores of the lakes we paddled through, open in the bliss of spaciousness, and they seemed to be guarding secrets inside their lineup. We haven't seen anybody since we left.

Grandy's a nice enough guy, but he carries some sort of heavy burden. Twenty-three and has lived back here all his life. I don't know what happened to outline him with a thorny crown, but I do know something did. With some people, I guess that's all you can know.

The men set up camp, and heaven knows where we are. They share one tent, and I'm lying here in the other. We had Spam and beans for dinner. Grandy brought out a travel guitar—I'd never seen one—and plucked some pretty strains. Jolly took over—never knew he could play—and we sang crazy songs like "You're in the Army, Mister Jones" and "I've Been Workin' on the Railroad." For a moment, Grandy's face cleared, and it was good.

Maybe that's part of redemption. Simply giving people the opportunity, even briefly, to allow their faces to clear and to be living for just one nice thing. I believe that's why I bake cakes.

And then Grandy had to ask why I was so bent on finding Xavier Andrews. Here's an example of when the truth can be a mistake. He told me he was a Gary Andrews, and nice try and all that, but the deed is done. Gary won't want to be reminded of all that anyway.

He's probably right.

He said if I was smart, I'd turn around.

But smart is Jace's department, not mine.

Hopefully tomorrow I'll see Xavier Andrews. I feel like the journey's really just beginning.

We actually had to carry the canoe about a hundred yards over land from one entry point to another. This is the most fascinating area I've ever been to. I can understand why people come out to places like this to find God. I never could before today. Out here you're so incredibly small inside the glove of His immensity and His beauty.

I saw some beaver dams and a few of the critters themselves. They're the cutest little things.

FORTY

My muscles don't scream, oddly enough, but surely tomorrow they'll voice their displeasure loud and clear. It is a chilly day, although Grandy assures me this is incredibly mild weather. Ice is beginning to form around the edges of the lake we camped by. By mid-October it can feel like a Maryland winter in these parts. I'll take the Maryland winter, I'm assuming, based on his description of what happens around here during the cold months.

I hate cold. I think that's what makes me happy about the Hotel. It's a place where people can go to get warm. Those nights will soon be coming. The city regulations say shelters can only open when the nights are below freezing. I can't imagine spending a night on a thirty-three degree street.

Now this morning, I almost could. A loon's call awakened me, that mournful warble that cut right down into the filling of my soul. When I climbed out of my sleeping bag . . . well, I dove right back in and dressed completely inside. I must have looked like a cartoon of two cats fighting in a sack.

The lodge loaned me a warmer parka and gloves and a hat. Thank goodness I remembered to bring some long underwear and thick socks.

So I dressed and met the men for some of Grandy's oatmeal, and glory be, a bull moose walked by not forty feet away. What next? Wolves?

I ask Grandy that very question.

"Sure, we got 'em. Timberwolves, coyote. And bobcat and lynx."

"Is it safe?" I ask.

Jolly coughs.

Grandy hands me a bowl of oatmeal. "Just sit still. They'll catch a whiff of your scent and most likely realize you're not a threat and pass on."

Those two words, "most likely," weigh about a thousand pounds. Just eat, Heather, why don't you?

The trees and their gnarled roots slide by, our boat lubricated by the water and the silence of Jolly, who's thinking about Helen, and Grandy, who's thinking about his childhood, I suppose. I'm thinking how the years go by so quickly and we sail right by so much, failing to recognize the intricate glory of it all.

Sometimes we fail to notice a shadow darting through trees and jumping over the river just out of our gaze, until one day, we realize how precious these years are, how more precious the next ones will be, and how we'd better confront the shadow if we want to live in peace.

That's what Anna does. Liza too. They live confronting the shadows. They know it does no good to ignore them.

Lunch consists of peanut butter and jelly sandwiches and some chips. Bottled water.

"Just another hour," Grandy says. He pushes his hand through his dark curly hair, and it stands up like a flame. "We'll probably want to make camp at Xavier's tonight and head out first thing in the morning." And then he shakes his head.

I sadden him even more.

That's the thing about sin. It's the gift that keeps on giving, as they say.

Perhaps Gary or Mary will be there. Of course, I've considered that thought, but Gary is forty-two by now and Mary forty-one. Surely they're not still with Xavier, are they?

No. That just can't be right.

True to Grandy's word, we pull up to the camp an hour after we resume our journey. A small dock juts into the rock-rimmed lake, thick legs reaching into the mud, and the men tie up the canoe.

Grandy jumps up onto the pier like the nimble youth he is, darn him. Nobody ever prepared me for how silly and ungraceful you feel when you reach middle age. Jolly climbs out next. Well done! But it takes both Jolly and Grandy to help me onto the boards.

A pebbled trail leads into the forest.

Grandy says, "I'll wait here with the boat."

I turn around. "Thanks. Jolly? How about you?"

"I'll go with you, but leave you to have your conversation alone."

I've never known a more thoughtful person. As I continue down the path, a little shrew runs across. Jolly stays beside me, and when I take his hand, he tucks it in the crook of his arm and places his other hand over mine.

"Thank you," I whisper.

He nods, a little teary. "It's just good to hold a warm arm in my own again."

After just a minute the trees thin out into a clearing, and in the middle sits a cabin that makes the lodge look like a five-star hotel: logs blackened by time and weather, porch sagging, whorls smoking out of a river rock chimney, scattering the aroma of a wood fire.

"Okay."

"You'll do fine."

We step up onto the porch, the floorboards, soft and forgiving, moaning faintly.

I slide off a glove and knock on the door, the chill wind·nipping my skin with chiseled teeth.

Footfalls echo and my stomach drops.

I squeeze Jolly's arm as the door opens.

A man bent with scoliosis, waiting for rain under a thunderhead of gray and white hair, raises his brows. "Oh? Can I help you?"

"Xavier Andrews?"

"That's me. You all come to stay? We close at the beginning of October, but you can camp in the clearing if you'd like."

"Thanks. I actually just need to ask you a couple of questions."

Hard to believe this hermit was once the ladies' man Peggy described.

"Come on in. It's sure getting cold."

He swings the screen door wide, and we find ourselves in a living room filled with old furniture, lots of Naugahyde and plaid. Dust swims in the rays of sunlight streaming through a side window. Sadness in these walls too.

"Nice fire," Jolly says. He followed me inside, and I am grateful.

"A guy needs one on a day like today."

Jolly holds his hands toward the blaze. "So you going to winter out here all by yourself? My, that's something!"

"I been doing it for the last five years. Plenty of wood and water. Supplies laid up. It's not so bad. I do a lot of reading. I'm real busy in the other months with the canoers and fishermen and the like. It's a fine little break."

Xavier seems like a nice man. His voice still resounds with the warm suppleness of middle age. According to my calculations, he's in his midfifties now.

"How about something warm to drink? A cup of tea? Or some coffee? I put a pot on not long ago."

No electric lights, just gas lamps with some ferocious-looking fabric wicks illumining the room. "How do you cook here?"

"Got a propane stove."

"I'd love something warm," I say. "If the coffee's made, that will be fine."

"Fine by me too." Jolly.

He heads back through a doorway to the kitchen, and I sit down in a chair near the fire. Feels good. "So what do you think, Jolly?"

"Seems fine to me."

"I'm nervous."

"You'll do all right, Heather."

I hope I'm not adding yet another nail to this coffin of a situation. I'm under no delusion that this trip, this need to find these people, is by my own goodness. I lived for years without thinking about Gary and Mary. Now it's time to clean up my act, and God's helping me with the details. He needs to continue to help me, that's all I can say, because I have no idea where all this will lead. And Anna's question of whether or not this is for myself and my own feel-good needs screams like a cat between my ears.

He returns with a couple of mugs in his hands. "Here you go."

Black. Just assumed, I guess.

I'll take anything warm at this point.

"So what can I do for you all?"

Jolly points to me.

I clear my throat. I haven't practiced the question. I should have. I should have worded it carefully, written down a variety of options. But I didn't. Perhaps I didn't want it to really work out. What I really wanted was to find this camp deserted, Xavier gone, the trail ended, and that's that.

"I went to school with your kids, Gary and Mary."

He closes his eyes. "Oh, which school?"

"Bel Air Christian."

His face darkens. "Oh."

"I need to find them."

"Why's that?"

"To apologize."

He sits down on a straight chair and flattens the fluff on top of his head. "Truth is, I haven't seen Gary or Mary in years." He looks up, eyes moist but not overflowing. "I never knew how to handle those kids. I don't think I even knew how to try."

Jolly clears his throat. "Do you know where they are?"

"Last time I heard, they was somewhere near Amarillo. Gary hit the road as soon as he graduated high school and took Mary with him. I only heard from him once, and that was to sign over my rights to Mary's guardianship."

"Did you sign?"

"Uh-huh, and I was thankful to do it. Gary's a strong one. Now Mary. Oh, dear God." He tears up again. "If you'll excuse me. I've got some things to attend to. On second thought, you're welcome to bunk here for the night."

Jolly helps me to my feet. "No thanks. We'll just head on back."

Xavier leaves the room with only a nod. We depart from Xavier and his sad cabin on faraway waters. I guess we all escape one way or another; only some of us have more to escape from, sending us farther out and deeper in.

We turned around and set up camp a bit later than yesterday so we can make it back to the lodge by nightfall tomorrow. I paddled more often today despite the fact that my arms and shoulders finally feel like someone's trying to pull them apart with each stroke.

Something about being out here in the wilderness settles my soul. I can see why people yearn to retire somewhere remote, just live their lives in peace without their own expectations or anyone else's weighing them down.

I quickly slide myself into the sleeping bag and turn on the lantern.

If I could rationalize it as a way Jesus would have lived, I'd do it. He may have gone off to refresh Himself, but He always came back around. At least in His man-skin He did. I sure wish He'd come back around right now.

FORTY-ONE

I drop Jolly off and have to wipe away the tears as he lets himself into that lonely old house. The heat blasts out of the car vents, but even so, I wonder if I will ever feel warm again. Naturally, the cold hit like a slap-boxer on that last day. Jolly and Grandy took it like men.

I am not a man.

If anybody had wanted to see a woman complain and act like a delicate hothouse flower, they would not have been disappointed. Grandy almost pushed me out of his canoe. And surly? Mercy!

The Jacuzzi tub awaits. Now if I could blue-dot that thing, I would! I open the car door, yank my bag from off the backseat, and head inside.

Jace and Will practically trample over each other after I open the door.

"Mom!"

"Hezzie!"

We hug and kiss, and Jace, already having heard all about my chilly bones via cell phone, flips on the electric teakettle. "Hot chocolate all around!"

Will flips it off. "Dad, you gotta use milk if it's going to be worth drinking. I'll do it."

Jace grabs the sugar canister and hands it to Will. "I want to hear all about the trip."

"Me too!" Will. "I can't believe you camped out for three days. That's amazing. You!"

Okay, got it, Will.

"I liked it, actually. If it wasn't for the cold. We should all do that sometime."

Jace. "Big-time. I will remind you that I've been trying to talk you into it for years. Are you saying I was right?"

"Sometimes we just need to have things foisted upon us before we can really appreciate them."

"Ah-hah."

Will measures out the cocoa into the pan. "Dad gave me the basic story about the Andrews kids."

"Yeah."

"Gosh, Mom. On one hand I can't believe you were one of them, but on the other, it kinda gives me hope, you know?"

"I'm sorry."

"Yeah, well, you're a nice lady now, and you take up for the weird kids at school."

"You all are not weird!"

"See what I mean?"

"I thought you'd be angry at me."

"Why? You've only been great to me. I mean, if you were still one of those *ladies*, like some of them at school who've never gotten out of the mean girl phase, it would be different."

The phone rings. It's Laney.

"Hey, Laney. How are you?"

"Up to my eyeballs, but what's new there? Hey, I heard about the service project the women's committee is doing. Very cool."

"Did Carmen start promoting it?"

"Oh yeah. In fact, she's been calling everybody personally. She's totally on board."

"That's great!"

"Just thought you'd want to know. And I'm signing up too. Cade said he'd take off work that day."

"Thanks, Laney."

"Hey, you got it. So see you tomorrow, then?" she asks. "We're meeting at my house."

"Oh, you have no idea how much I'm looking forward to it."

Lark calls as I drive downtown Tuesday morning. "Hey, come by and pick me up. Mother's driving me crazy."

"Is she all right?"

"She is woman, hear her roar, Heather. She's been reading a book that's driving her crazy, and yet she won't put it down. Said she's always wanted to read *Gone with the Wind*, and so before she dies, that's what she's doing. Only she's already taken up with Melanie Wilkes, and poor Scarlett can't do one thing right."

"Wasn't that kind of the point?" I've never read the book myself.

"Beats me. But you should hear her yelling at that woman and Margaret Mitchell besides. I can't hear myself think."

"Sure, I'll swing by. See you in a few."

So this is a nice little sparkle to the day.

While Sister J leads Lark up to the transitional floor to show her what needs doing, I sit on a stool by the worktable in the kitchen and cut the black spots off of ten heads of broccoli. Cream of broccoli soup tonight with cheese that came in from one of the grocery stores, along with some outdated tubes of poppin' fresh biscuits. I'm almost tempted to take some home with me.

Honestly, I think Sly, who turned up last week, went Dumpstering and found this loot, but I don't want to ask for sure.

I hear Mo holler from his desk, "Now don't you be disturbing that nice lady back there, Knoxie."

Oh great. Why me? Why does he always want to talk to me? All I can think when I'm talking to him anymore is that I'm jeopardizing my family by even being around this guy, like if I'm caught in some kind of drug war and I die, then Will is left without a mother, Jace without a wife, and then who would be around to get rid of the green-dotted merchandise?

But then I remember that only the grace of God, in a general sense, keeps us all from being murderers and thieves.

"Heather Curridge."

"Hello, Knox. Pull up a stool."

He does, darn it. I was hoping this would be one of his breeze-throughs.

"What are you up to today?" I ask, then clap my hand over my mouth. "Forget I said that."

"Well, actually, I've been doing a little soul-searching. A very little, but any improvement is good."

"So what has your search dug up?"

"I was thinking about why I am the way I am. It's not like a five-year-old ever dreams of doing what I do."

"What did you used to want to be?"

"A fireman, of course. Then a policeman."

I hoot out a laugh.

"And then I suppose I was around ten years old when I found myself out on the corner and realized it was either us or them, and them was a lot richer and more powerful. It wasn't a hard decision for me, unfortunately."

"I'm sorry for you, Knox."

He picks up a broccoli floret and examines it. "How do you make up for it once you've done so many things to so many people?"

I tell him about Gary and Mary. The trip to Minnesota. His soulful eyes close. "It would take me the rest of my life to try and make up for my sins like that, unfortunately."

"Can you think of anything better to do with it?"

"Pray for me," he said.

And I assure him I will. "I already have been, in fact."

On the way home, I tell Lark about him. "Now what got into him? What's happening inside that man?"

"Who knows?"

"I saw the side of him that Jesus loves, though."

"That's good, Heather. I hate to say it, but I don't think you're through with him. Not by a long shot."

The three of us pore over five different floor plans from Alva's port-folio. I spread them out on the empty dining room floor. Yep, empty. The table and chairs, sideboard, and china cabinet brought twenty thousand at auction. I had no idea they were such good pieces when I bought them from an antiques dealer awhile back. Obviously he didn't either!

"Wow, Mom. These are great. Are we really going to do this?"

Jace. "Yeah. We're going to sell this place just before the hospital ship goes out, and this will be built when we're gone."

"Have you found the land yet?"

"No," I say. "But that will come. We have awhile to decide."

We all agree on the same plan, the Guggenheim. Lots of win-dows, three small bedrooms, and a wide-open space that envelops the kitchen, a family room, and a dining area, all on different levels under the same stretch of ceiling.

"And it will be done in white," I say.

"No arguments from me." Jace.

Will says, "As long as I can do my room in whatever color I want, I don't care what you do with the rest."

Teenagers.

Will points to a figure in the lower right-hand corner of the plan. "Look, this went for seven thousand dollars back in the '50s!"

Jace and I both gasp, then burst into laughter.

Will settles a hand on an indentation in the carpet left over from the buffet. "How much did you get for the dining room furniture again?"

Mercy!

FORTY-TWO

November is one of my favorite months because it brings my favorite holiday, Thanksgiving. The spirit of gratitude revolutionizes, so human in the good sense of what is human. I believe we are at the highest pinnacle of being completely human as God designed us when we are most grateful.

Will is grateful today because I'm letting him take off school to come help.

I have to remember to pick up the Thanksgiving turkey on the way home from the Hotel. Carmen really played this day up big. We'll be finished with that room in no time.

We pull into the school parking lot at quarter to eight, and judging by the look on her face, Carmen is anything but grateful right now. She storms toward me across the tarmac. "I'm so mad I could spit!"

"Why?" I'm doing all I can not to laugh. Carmen has been snippy, bossy, angry, but the expression on her face can only be categorized as outrage.

"Five of us, Heather. There's only going to be five of us . . . counting you!"

"That's okay. Will's here too."

"Okay, six. But still no. It's not okay. I'm beginning to think you were right about this stuff. Maybe we should keep this sort of thing to ourselves. Nobody wants to help anyway." She stomps her foot like a five-year-old, and I want to hug her.

"Don't listen to me about anything, Carmen. I'm finding out I don't know much about pretty much everything. And it'll be okay.

You did what you could. Some listened. Most didn't. Isn't that usually the way?"

She looks over at the school, shrugs. "Well, when you put it that way, you're exactly right. I don't like it, though. I mean, it's one thing to not show up when you promised to decorate the gym, but to paint a homeless shelter? After you said, 'I swear, I'll be there bright and early tomorrow morning, Carmen'?"

"Who else is coming?"

"Laney, who's more excited than you can imagine."

Knew that.

"Olive and Betty Hayes."

"Betty Hayes? She's eighty if she's a day!" Her daughter Olive has a son in Will's class.

"I know. She sidled up to me at the basketball game and said she still had a great painting arm."

I clap. "That's wonderful! Are they meeting us here? We can all drive down together if you'd like."

"They'll be here any minute. We can take my van."

"Sure. Can we stop for coffee on the way?" I wrinkle my nose. "The stuff at the Hotel is pretty bad. Jimmy doesn't make good coffee, and I don't want to tell him so."

"Sounds good to me."

Betty and her daughter Olive arrive together, both swimming in large khaki pants and loose men's shirts. These two define the word *delightful*. Betty lives with Olive and her family these days and does all the grocery shopping and makes dinner too.

"Hellooooo!" Betty waves her hands and scoots toward us. Betty smiles all the time.

Olive shuffles right on behind her. "Hey, guys!" She holds up a tray of drinks. "Thought I'd presume you'd all like some coffee."

Of course. Yes, the Hayes women are just the type. Why don't I ever think of Olive when I think about the other moms at the school?

Olive hands me a cup. "I remember you telling me you like those chai teas a couple of months ago."

"Bless you."

"Skim mocha, no whip." She hands another cup to Carmen.

Laney screeches in, executing one of those mind-boggling, high-speed parking jobs you see every once in a while, the driving antithesis of Liza. "Is that coffee?" she hollers as she extracts herself out of her old Windstar. "Because if it is, I'll take it!"

Nicola jumps from the passenger door. Will shoves his hands in his pockets and walks toward his real live girlfriend. Okay, I have to admit I'm relieved. When your son's a misfit, you do tend to think, down in the whispery portions of your mother-mind, that there isn't a girl alive who will actually appreciate him.

Laney looks as if she spent the night running through the forest. Her hair porcupines out from her scalp, and her clothing twists askew around her reedy body. "I swear, I'm going to leave at 6:00 a.m. next time I get a day off. It took us fifteen minutes to say good-bye. 'I'm only going for the day,' I kept saying to Hannah over and over again."

Olive holds out the gold. "I wasn't sure what you like, Laney, but I assumed with your slender figure you could afford anything. So I got you a whole-milk white chocolate mocha."

Laney sips. "And you figured perfectly."

"I didn't realize Nicola and Will would be here. Sorry I didn't pick them up a drink."

Laney shakes her head as she sips. "No prob. Thanks, Olive. How much do I owe you?"

Betty. "That look as you sipped was worth every penny."

Carmen claps her hands. "Let's go, then! Giddyup or something like that."

We all climb into her van, every one of us happy to be there, feeling a bit like we're heading off to summer camp. And that's why it was only us. Some jobs God reserves for those who are delighted to have them because He knows that's pretty much going to be the only reward coming anyway.

I pat Carmen on the shoulder. "See? It's all going to be fine."

Her eyes crinkle in the rearview mirror, and she turns on her CD player. The strains of Glenn Miller's "Tuxedo Junction" fill the space.

Betty smiles. So do the rest of us.

Mo hollers. "Ho! Here they are! Lookin' ready to do some business!"

Betty holds up her paint roller and gives it a victorious shake. The others do an equally endearing motion, and I swear, my face will split like a tree under lightning, my smile's so wide. Will and Nicola hold hands.

My old people meeting my new people.

I take a mental snapshot of their lovely female faces.

Mo picks up the phone. "Sister J? Paintin' crew's here!" He hangs up after her response. "She'll be right down. There's some coffee if y'all want some."

We all hold up our cups.

I chuckle.

Mo raises his brows. "Yeah, Jimmy's not the best at coffee, is he? Next time, though, you be bringing one for me, all right?"

I make introductions, and Mo shakes all the women's hands. Will introduces Nicola, and Mo acts like he's just met a princess. My son looks ready to zing even as Laney looks like she's going to pop like a balloon rising toward the trees. She gazes around in a state of almost wonder, and I have no idea what's going on inside her head. Carmen just looks ready to get to work.

"Big room," she says.

"Definitely."

She turns to the other women. "So I thought we'd have a bigger crew. Do you want to make two days of this, or stay until we finish the job?"

Olive sets her box of supplies on one of the tables. "We came to paint the room. Let's paint it."

Carmen points at Laney. "You're the one with the little kids. What do you think?"

"If someone lets me borrow a cell phone, I'll call Cade."

Olive says, "I'd better call home too. Sam has indoor soccer, but you know, he can miss it for once in his life."

I point to the pile of supplies. "Well, then, let's get ready. The stuff is over here."

Jace and the boys did a great job patching the walls last week. Looks good.

It has already been well established that we all know how to paint. The drive down was filled with our years of exploits in covering walls. Betty once painted a room puce; she took the prize for boldness. Laney doesn't need tape—good for her—she can cut in around the ceilings and the baseboards; she took the prize for finesse. Carmen used to paint for money in college; she took the prize for smarts.

Fabulous, right?

Olive never could see paying good money to a painter—after all, how hard could it be?

Yep, we are the chosen ones.

Nicola and Will still hold hands.

I dunk a wooden stir stick into the paint and begin to swirl. "Now that you're teaching our churchy-thing, how do you like it?"

Laney picks up a bristle brush. "I love it. I'm finally doing something with the gift God gave me. It's a responsibility, though. I really don't want to lead anybody down a wrong path." She grabs the can and heads over to the ladder.

No wonder cakes are my gift to the world. I don't want anybody listening to me at all. Way too much responsibility. And what I've figured out for today may not even stand the test of a twenty-four-hour time span. All I can do now is cling to Jesus. I wouldn't want to be in Laney's shoes any more than I'd like to be at the bottom of Loch Raven.

Laney's talking and joking with people from her perch where she cuts in the paint around the new ceiling, way more at ease than I am with the clients. I just watch her as I roll on the green paint, following the trail of Olive and Carmen—the tapers of the baseboards. Betty's ahead of them cleaning the baseboards we'll coat with a thick white lacquer. Trim's my favorite part.

Will and Nicola are holding hands.

Laney understands how people are sinners. Everybody, everybody,

everybody. And she is no respecter of persons, herself included. At least that's my guess.

Sister J walks in. "Frish, look at you all!"

I set down my roller. "You like it?"

"You bet. Well, thanks be to God and all that good stuff! So introduce me to the gang, doll."

And I do.

Sister J touches her nose. "Jimmy's cooking up a special treat for lunch just for you all. Soup!"

We laugh.

"No, really. Obrycki's dropped off some crab cakes last night from a canceled catering job."

Carmen says, "I love crab cakes!" then claps a hand over her mouth. "Wow, that was loud!"

"Who doesn't love them?" Laney.

Sister J. "You bet. Every once in a while, the Lord throws us a bone. And if it comes in the form of a crab cake, so much the better."

Something happens to our little group. We solidify into a community, a single purpose ahead of us, a goal in sight, a small journey we agreed to take together. And that precious euphoria of doing good together reaches out and ties us close.

I love that feeling.

You know what I think it is?

God smiling.

Yep, nothing profound, just a few humans in relation to God and each other doing holy work that will bring themselves no benefit other than the joy of serving others. Now this is church.

A few minutes later, Sister J pokes her head into the room. "Heather? Got a minute?"

"Okay." I follow her back to her office.

"Not much news on Krista, doll. I thought you'd like to know. LaQueesha heard she got into some black Jaguar the night she disappeared. But that's all we know."

"Poor Krista."

"She's a baby doll. I'm still praying, though. Are you?"

"Oh yeah. I can't get her off of my mind."

"That's right. See, God knows where Krista is. And we know where He is, so it makes this silver triangle. At least, I always picture it that way. Anyway, thought I'd tell you."

"Thanks."

"Thanks for bringing down that crew. Nice gals."

I nod my head. "They're the best."

Carmen stands in line with her plate. "I feel guilty about taking one of these crab cakes. Maybe we should go out and get our own lunch."

I lay a hand on her sleeve. "Your presence here matters. It's not about you taking the food, Carmen. It's about you giving your presence."

"Are you sure?"

I laugh and so does Laney. "Sheesh, Carmen, you don't want the folks to think you think you're too good for them, do you?"

Carmen's face trims down into a look of horror. "Oh! I didn't think about it like that! Okay." She shakes her head. "This is all so new. I feel really uncomfortable."

Me. "I know! You should have seen me my first few weeks here. It was horrible."

Her brows rise. "Really?"

"Ah, yeah. *Really*, really."

Of course everybody ends up sitting together. "No, no, no, ladies, we go out two-by-two. Let's spread out."

Olive looks unsure, then says, "There are five of us."

Not counting Will and Nicola, who are still holding hands. They did manage, however, to pry themselves apart in order to mop the kitchen floor and clean the glass on the front doors.

"You're right! Okay, how about Laney and you and your mom. Carmen, wanna sit by me?"

"I'd love that, Heather."

Laney says, "Hey, I'm fine on my own." And she walks over to the table of the filthiest person there, Akbar Reynolds. His real name isn't Akbar. I don't think anybody knows what his real name is. He's a schizophrenic. And he smells like a litter pan on a humid day, and honestly, I just gag and gag if he's within ten feet of me. But with all the diapers Laney changes every day, I'm sure she doesn't notice.

She starts talking his ear off, and a few more people join her, a middle-aged couple—she bleached blonde, he with a long curly ponytail—and a street guy named Brill who left a good job and family for heroin. They're laughing like crazy within five minutes.

Good heavens, some people are just naturals at this stuff! God should have called Laney, not me.

Then again, God called Moses, and Aaron was the one who could do the talking. Because there are a million miles between what God *should* do and what He does.

"You gals are great." Hands on hips, Sister Jerusha looks around. "I can't get over how you've been at it all darn day, with hardly a break!"

Betty waves a hand. "Us old girls still have it in us."

Sister J points at her. "You said it, doll."

Carmen says, "We appreciate the opportunity."

"Anytime. Believe me. An-ee-time. So how much longer do you think you have to go?"

"Another two hours," Olive.

I look at my watch. Seven o'clock. "Tomorrow, nobody'll know what hit them, it'll be so pretty in here."

"Already is. Okay, don't let me slow you down. I'm heading upstairs to the Bible study for the addicted men. Jimmy's leading tonight, and he's always good."

Carmen's eyebrows raise, and she looks at me. After Sister J exits, she puts a hand on my arm. "Addicted men?" she asks.

"Yes."

"Do they ever have those types of studies for women?"

"Yes, in the mornings."

"Okay." And she walks away, picks up a paintbrush, and sets to work on the trim. Second coat. And I'm standing there with my mouth open, wondering who in Carmen's circle needs such a study.

We all set to work on the second coat of the trim. Betty and Laney on the windows, the rest on the baseboards, and oy! My back will be singing the blues and the greens tomorrow.

Will and Nicola are not holding hands; they are threading curtains onto rods I'll hang in place next time I come down.

Knox Dulaney steps through the front door. "Hello, Mo!"

"Not a good time, Knoxie. We got these ladies here doing good charity works."

He holds up a hand of peace. "Not to worry. Not to worry. Just came to see Aunt Jerusha. She here?"

"Upstairs at the Bible study."

"Hmm. I think I'll take a pass." He laughs. Mo waves him on.

I shake my head and can't help but smile. Man, I wish I didn't like him. Why do I like him? He's a horrible person! "Hey, Knox."

"Ah, the good Heather. And bringing more good ladies with you." He shoves his hands in his trouser pockets and gazes around. "It looks good in here. Nice colors. Bringing a little county to the hood."

I wince.

"Well, I'll be going. Just thought I'd stop in."

I wonder how many people he's killed.

Glass shatters, metal crunches. I jump at the sound. What's going—

"Watch out!" Mo's shouts provide a baseline for our screams as glass shards spew forth before the ramming hood of a car crashing through the now-twisted front doors. The room envelops the entire car as it screeches to a halt, the smell of oil and burnt rubber imbuing the air.

All I can think is, *Thank God we were on the trim, thank God we were all at the edges of the room!*

"Will!" I scream, and the two kids run over.

"Don't move!" Two olive-skinned men jump from the car like crickets, hopping in agitation, and are they high on something dangerous? I'm terrible at judging nationalities, but they're not black, and one points a gun at Knox and yells something I cannot understand. He shoots at the new ceiling over Betty's head. She screams and cowers as plaster falls at her feet.

Obviously Knox has stepped on toes, expanded his territory where it wasn't meant to go.

Dear God in heaven . . .

I'm in the middle of an all-out drug war!

Oh Lord, oh Lord, oh Lord.

I put one arm around Will and tuck Nicola behind me.

The slow motion begins, two more men emerging from the backseat, and we're a breath away from dying, aren't we? Isn't this the type of situation where people . . . more guns are drawn, a kind of rifle . . . where people open fire, spraying bullets like water? And the words rise in pitch and volume, complexions are heightened to a flaring crimson.

Laney is as pale as a china plate. She's thinking about "all those kids." Staring at Nicola, telling her *Stay put* with her eyes and the grim set of her mouth.

One piece of me is bolstering up Will; the other is being boned by fear, its razor teeth pulling back layers I never knew existed. *Don't let my baby boy be hurt. Don't let this be it.*

Knox yells back in that same language.

I'm wondering about my life, knowing it's in these guys' hands and I can't even understand a word they're saying. And why do I have to be standing right next to Knox? If they shoot—

The other women press themselves to the walls, fear paralyzing their faces into blanched masks.

The first man out of the car steps forward, babbling his language and waving his pistol; he points it at Will, then at Knox, at Will, then at Knox. God, no. *Please don't let him shoot my baby boy!* Not the child who drew me a million robots. Not the boy who hugged me countless times without my asking, who keeps me in check.

Flicker, flicker, back and forth, and he's laughing now, a fast, sassy, *don't screw with me and yet I find this all extremely invigorating because I'm a coldhearted killing machine* laugh. More words.

I pull Will closer into my side.

"Don't move, lady!"

But don't you see? This is my child. I stayed up a bundle of croupy nights, sitting on the closed john in the bathroom while steam from the tub faucet billowed around us, mingling with our sweat, soaking us in a fine, warm descent. I couldn't breathe, but he could and that was the point.

Back and forth, the gun moves.

Don't you see? *He is the point!*

He laughs again. I look at Knox, at the fear in his eyes. And I know the other man will shoot. I know it like I already saw the movie.

Knox yells, "No!" Steps forward. Flings himself sideways, in front of Will, as the man pulls the trigger.

Knox pushes us onto the ground and falls on top of me as another shot blasts from the gun.

I am jarred with pain as my bones, compressed beneath his falling weight, grind into the floor. And Will. Will crumples against the old tiles, salmon and pink, found in a Dumpster. "Will!"

"He's shot!" Knox. "My, God, the boy is shot."

I scream and push Knox off of me. "Will! Will!"

The color has drained from his face. "Mom, I'm okay. I'm not dead." I lean over him.

And the gunmen scream at me, but I do not move. I look at them with all the hate I've ever known and I turn back to my son. The sound of sirens falls upon us. And the men, they're turning back around. No more shots fired, right? No more.

Another blast sounds as they shoot at the light fixture in the ceiling near Mo's desk; sparks fly.

"No more. Oh, Will," I whisper. "Call an ambulance!" I scream.

Shot? Blood? I close my eyes. No, I don't want to see blood right now. Not my baby boy's blood. My baby boy. I open them again and hold his hand as his eyes close.

"It's okay, Mom."

The men jump back into the car, back out through the glass, and squeal away, the crunch of tires over glass sounding in our ears.

My brain flounders in a knee-deep puddle.

No more shots. No more shots.

They're still gone. *Please stay gone.*

"Heather, are you all right?" Knox's voice enters my ear like the prow of a ship through the fog. And then.

Will. "I hope that guy gets a flat tire from all that glass."

Knox smiles, wincing in pain.

The women gather around us, pale, ghostly. Carmen shakes.

Laney shouts, "Call 911. Will's bleeding!"

"Already done it," Mo hollers back, thumping over.

Nicola and Will hold hands. Blood seeps through the shoulder of his shirt. I kiss his cheek. "It'll be okay, bud."

Folks are running down the steps from upstairs. I hear Sister Jerusha's shouts from behind them.

Laney holds Knox's hand. The dealer looks over at Will.

"Shouldn't it hurt more?" Will asks him.

But before he can answer, he loses consciousness, and I sit next to my only son, my fifteen-year-old son, waiting for the ambulance to come.

Sister J's face appears. "Oh my God, Heather. Will, doll, you're going to be okay."

"He's unconscious."

"Hit in the shoulder, thank God. It could have been a lot worse. Here." She reaches into her skirt pocket for that hankie she fumbles with. "Apply direct pressure."

Around me an amphitheater of faces above bodies spattered with paint and concern protect us from the rest of the world.

FORTY-THREE

Having a notorious drug lord at least try to save your son's life makes you wonder about a lot of things. Like what clicked inside of him to leap in front of Will? Was it God who did that, and does that mean He's got good plans for Knox? Or just for Will? Am I supposed to pour more of myself into this man's life now when the whole episode was his fault in the first place? I'd be a fool to think a hardened individual like Knox Dulaney is just going to turn around like that. Right. Like he really felt concern for Will.

Now that the adrenaline is gone, an anger remains that I can't begin to process until we leave this bedside and the hospital behind. I can tell you one thing, I'm not going down the hall to visit Knox Dulaney. He can suffer all by himself as far as I'm concerned.

Will sleeps in the hospital bed. The bullet has been extracted and he hasn't yet awakened. But I have deeper questions than the ones about Knox Dulaney. Jace sleeps in a chair beside me. It's 2:00 a.m. and there's nobody awake to call. So I ask them to myself.

Am I not doing the right thing by coming downtown? Isn't this partly my fault? Wouldn't God at least protect my son considering I'm trying so desperately to live a Jesus life? Can I expect some sort of divine intervention when it comes to stuff like this, and if I can't, what does that mean? Do I really have what it takes?

"Hezzie, go to sleep."

"I was asking that out loud?"

"You sure were, hon."

Will's eyes open. "So I'm figuring I don't have to go to school today."

"You're a nut." I reach for his hand, relief flooding me, filling the gaps behind the dam of doubt that he would come around at all after surgery.

"Hey, I'm living to tell the tale."

Breakfast arrives, and he sifts through the liquid diet all the while asking Jace about the particulars of his surgery. "It was a pretty straightforward job. You've got some physical therapy to do, though, bud."

"What about Knox Dulaney?" he asks.

"Had his spleen removed. He's in far worse shape."

"Good," I say.

Will pushes the tray away. "Knox is here, right?" We nod. "Do you think I can walk down to his room?"

So, I didn't quite expect that. "No way!"

Jace sits forward in his chair. "I'm not sure that's a good idea, bud. Who knows who may come into that room?"

"Just for a few minutes."

"You shouldn't get up," I say. "Right, Jace?"

"Well, actually, hon, a little exercise is a good idea."

"Jace!"

"I'm sorry. It's true."

"Please, guys? And alone. Mom and Dad, you're great and all, but I've got to do this by myself."

"What do you want to see him so badly?" I ask.

"Mom. Can I go or not?"

Jace and I exchange an hour-long conversation in a glance. "Yes," he says. He touches my thigh. "In the medical sense, it's pretty minor, Hezzie. He's fine to walk down there."

Jace helps him step into a pair of sweats, then stand to his feet. He curls his hand around the IV pole, hands that seem to have become those of a man overnight.

"You okay?" I ask.

"Yep."

He walks out of the room, arm in a sling, face forward.

I look at Jace. "I'm dying to be a fly on the wall."

"Heatherrrrr . . ." He picks up the morning paper. "Actually, so am I."

"What do you think he's saying?"

"Well, with Will it's hard to say. But I can tell you this, we'll never know unless he decides to tell us."

"I'm going down to get a cup of coffee."

"Oh, that's convenient—you'll have to walk by Knox's room."

"What number is it?"

He sighs. "403."

I stand up and grab my purse. "Want something?"

"Yes. I could use the caffeine to clear my brain. Man, I just don't know what to think about all this."

"Me either."

I walk by Knox's room and quickly glance inside as I pass. Will sits in the chair, leaning forward, and Knox looks stricken. Not in a mountain-falling-on-you way.

The man is in for the battle of his life; it will make last night look like an afternoon at Chuck E. Cheese. And Will is leading the charge in a still, small voice. Mercy, but I wish I was more like my son.

Sister Jerusha arrives after the lunch shift at the Hotel. "I'm going to knock Knox's block off."

"Say that three times fast."

She hoots.

Will says, "He's right down the hall."

"Yeah, I know. But I just wanted to stop in first. Seems to me you're more of the victim than that rascal is."

"Oh, I don't know." Will shakes his head. "His injury is far worse."

I drag another chair next to mine. "Knox had his spleen removed in the middle of the night. I can't say I feel too sorry for him."

She nods. "Knox made his choices. I'd have moved heaven and earth to get him into a good college, on a good path. He knows that."

Leave it to Sister J to take away a drug lord's excuses and still love him.

She holds up a handled brown paper grocery bag. "And guess what I brought?"

I shake my head.

"Cake! And guess who helped me make it?"

"I have no idea."

"Come on in, doll!" she yells.

And in the door walks Krista.

"Krista!"

"Miss Heather!"

"Oh, girl, I am so glad you came back."

"Me too."

She hugs me lightly, and she smells so good.

"So where were you?"

"In Chicago."

"Really? How did you get there?"

"It's a long story. But I'm all right. I'll save it for the Hotel."

"I'll remember that."

She opens her eyes wide. "Oh, you will."

Sister J excuses herself to go visit with her godson.

Jace walks in with hot drinks round two from the coffee bar in the hospital lobby. Kristas is playing cards with Will, and really, she's still a kid, just two years older than he is.

"Krista! Would you like some coffee?"

"No thank you, Dr. Curridge. Are you comin' down to the Hotel soon?"

"In a week and a half, but I can come sooner if you need me to."

"I do."

"I'll be there the day after tomorrow."

She looks at me. "I got to make it work this time, you know?"

"Yeah, I do. We'll help you."

We sip our coffee, and Sister J walks in. Jace hands her a cup. "I saw you from the hallway."

"Good man." She sips, screws up her face. "What the heck is this?"

"A white chocolate raspberry latte. Will suggested it because Mo told him you love raspberries."

She sips again. "Hmm. Not bad once you know what it is. Thanks." She pulls out a little Bible. "I swore off Kings and Chronicles a long time ago. How about a little of that rascal David?" So she reads to us from the Psalms and reminds us, "Following Jesus isn't something we do because it's easy or even prudent. Sometimes it makes no sense at all."

"But then, God Himself being stripped of His clothes, beaten, tortured, and crucified makes no sense either," I say.

Sister J points at me. "You got it, doll. You've really got it. Will?" She takes his hand. "You were doing the work of the Lord yesterday. Sometimes we get scars from that, but someday they'll be badges of honor, stars in our crown."

I don't think I've ever been more proud of my son.

"What do you think, bud?" I ask. "Do we keep up at the Hotel?"

"Most definitely, Mom."

Jace smiles. I hear his thoughts, and to me they sound a lot like Jesus, who never promised loving Him would be easy or even secure . . . but free? Ah, yes. We shall be free indeed.

FORTY-FOUR

I stand on the deck, just under the eaves, my fleece robe pulled tight against the thin mist. The loch lies in peace, its waters barely visible through the low fog. Car headlights emit a cotton glow as they cross the bridge heading north. The waters seem to recognize that now is not their time.

Jace slides out through the doors and presses a mug of tea in my hands. "Nice nap?"

"Yeah. Really good. I'm glad to be back home. I hate hospitals. No offense."

"None taken."

"He's going to be all right, isn't he, Jace?"

"Yes, Hezz. I think you'll find he'll be better than he ever was."

"Why's that?"

"Life has become more precious. That's always a good lesson to learn."

"Still. Won't he be scared now?"

"Only if we let him be. I think the best thing we can do is continue on the course. It's like falling off a bike. Best to just get back on."

"I guess. I still have a lot of questions to ask God, but I'm so tired. Maybe they'll come tomorrow."

"You aren't too cold out here?"

"Just a couple minutes more. I'm remembering this place. It's safe here. When we leave, we may never feel safe again."

He puts his arm around my shoulders and draws me close. And he waits until I'm done, capturing the view I loved for so long. "We were never safe here, hon. Our souls were in greater danger than any bullet could extend."

"My head knows that. But so much of me cries out to stay."

"I know."

A wind blows through the empty, late-autumn trees, branches clacking softly, the almost dead revived through the breath of other.

I turn. "So you seem like you've got news to tell me. Is everything okay?"

"Maybe you should be sitting down."

"Oh no. What is it?"

"Hon, I found Gary Andrews."

FORTY-FIVE

"Let's go in, Jace. I'm cold."

He ushers me through the French doors. I sit on the couch, and he hands me a throw. "Where is he?"

"Just over in Howard County. He works for the Department of Health and Human Services."

"Are you sure it's him?"

"Pretty sure. I phoned him yesterday from the hospital and acted like I was from the alumni association of your old school."

"You didn't! Jace!"

"I know, but he bought it. He said he went there but wasn't an alumni."

He sits down next to me and pulls some of the blanket onto his own lap. We rest our feet side by side on the coffee table. "So I apologized for taking up his time, and that was that."

"What did he sound like?"

"Nice. Regular. You know, just a regular guy."

"Did he sound bitter or anything?"

"No, Heather. He didn't."

The call lasted two minutes tops, but my hand glistened with the sweat of two games of tennis in ninety-five-degree weather. I walk into the kitchen where the guys sit, ready to eat the meal Jace made. He really sets up a good chicken pot pie.

Two pairs of eyes question.

"He said he'd meet me."

"Yeah!" Will.

Jace sits back in his seat with a dramatic sigh of relief. "That's great, hon. What did he say?"

"He was very nice, actually." I pick up my napkin and sit down. "He remembered me, but I had to explain my way back into his memory. It was really weird. And really mortifying to have to say, 'I was that mean girl who used to sit halfway back on the right side of the bus.'"

"Is that right?" Jace. "Wow."

"I know. I'm relieved, though."

"So when are you meeting him?"

"Next Tuesday after he gets off work. He works flex time, so we're meeting early at the Hamburger Hamlet."

"Would you like some support? I could probably get Rick to cover my appointments."

I pick up my fork and look at each one of them. "No, but thanks. There are just some things a person has to do on her own."

Will picks up the serving spoon. "Let's eat."

Saturday afternoon Jace pulls up in front of a four-story townhouse, a looming house wider than most. "We're here!"

A For Sale sign hangs in the front window.

I look at him. "Is this what I think it is?"

"What do you think it is?"

"A possible home for the Kristas of this world?"

"Do you think it could work?"

I feel my heart race. "It's in the right location."

"The Realtor should be here in a few minutes."

I turn to Will in the backseat. "Are you okay to do this?"

He nods. "Yeah, Mom, I am."

It's like a narrow castle. Of course it's been cut up into apartments, eight of them, and maybe that's just the ticket. I'd dreamed of lofts, but why not one-bedrooms? Then if there are one or two kids with the ladies, there will be more room.

Woodwork hides beneath a thick crust of paint. The windows were replaced sometime in the '60s, I think. And the linoleum floor peels at the corners. Still.

"I think this could work." The first floor could have a gathering room and a training place for, well, all sorts of things, I guess: parenting, computer skills, ESL classes . . . hairdressing?

Well, why not? I still have a lot of contacts in the business.

Jace turns to the Realtor. "Are there any offers pending?"

The real estate agent, her sensible brown coat open to reveal a houndstooth suit, taps her day planner. "Not at this point. But you can't be too sure with these places. I wouldn't wait long."

"We'll get back to you tomorrow with an offer. Pending inspection, of course."

"Of course."

When we pull away, I can't believe it. "There's so much to do! We'll have to get some sort of funding, find a director for the home. Oh, man!"

My cell phone rings. It's Lark.

"He showed you, right?"

"Right."

"He made me promise not to say a word."

Jace.

"Just so you know, Summerville's on it. That place is going to need extensive renovating."

I breathe a sigh of relief as I end the call. "Ah, fabulous."

I turn to Jace. "This is amazing. Do you really think we can do this?"

"Would you like to?"

"I really would. Krista needs us to."

"Then yes. Absolutely, I do."

"What about the ship?"

"I'm figuring we get this up and running and stick to the game plan."

"I like it."

For the first time in many years, I'm glad I'm not some glamorous, skinny, glossy lady. I can't imagine showing up to ask forgiveness of somebody looking like life never dared touch me in a way that left a mark.

So here I stand in the entryway of Hamburger Hamlet. I hate Bethesda and pretty much anything right around DC. But I've never eaten a bad meal here, and they do a decent fudge layer cake.

I chose a simple khaki-colored wool skirt, a cranberry pullover turtleneck sweater, and mid-heel loafer pumps. My hair hasn't been colored since the beginning of the summer; it's too long, and I have to admit I look a little frumpy. He'll probably be glad to see I didn't turn out so well.

My purse hangs from double fists in front of me.

All of the bodily trippings one might imagine assail me. Dry mouth, heart beating like a Japanese drummer, brow a little sweaty. But he's meeting me, right? He could have said, "Let's just forget it. This is really creepy coming out of the blue." He must have turned out to be a pretty nice guy to agree to this.

A man in a barn coat, wire-rimmed glasses, and a ball cap walks in. He takes the cap off immediately to reveal wavy, dirty-blond hair. Computer programmer.

Nope.

Two women in ski jackets, high heels, and work skirts. Data entry or customer service.

Definitely nope.

Another man with white hair so thick there's no need for a hat, though the weather did turn quite cold yesterday. Charcoal gray overcoat. Financier.

Nope.

The door opens yet again. It's about five 'til four.

A grandmother, her daughter, and the grandbaby.

Cute, but nope again.

Maybe I should sit down and wait, or go to the bar and order something to drink. Or maybe not. If I'm not here when he comes, he may leave. But if I appear too eager, he might think I'm a stalker or something.

The door opens and he walks in.

Yep, it's Gary, loud and clear. He looks exactly the same. The wide cheekbones, slight nose, winged eyebrows that, seeing them as a functioning adult, are just beautiful. Without the overlay of dirt, Gary is handsome.

He smiles. "Heather Curridge?"

I step forward. "Yes."

"Now I know who you are! Heather Reeves, yes! I was remembering someone else."

"Probably Julia B."

"That's it."

"I'm surprised you came."

"It's pretty intriguing. Wanna go sit down? We can catch up and be more comfortable. I'm starving."

"Sure."

Now one would think I am relieved at this point. He's nice, accommodating, welcoming. But in truth my shame is utterly complete, having looked in the face of the person I sinned against and finding nothing but kindness.

I've never been lower.

The hostess seats us in a booth, the low, mellow lighting welcoming and yet offering me some sort of cover.

He really looks great. A wee bit overweight but in that nice-guy-who-wears-it-well way. His dark, straight hair, parted on the side like before, sparkles with a sprinkling of gray, and his brown eyes dance.

Now that's new.

"How did you find me?" he asks.

I told him about Jace.

He laughs. "That was your husband? Well, I was convinced. I mean, live in DC for long, and all people do is call for donations. Guess I don't have to send anything, then, huh?"

"Apparently not."

"So let's cut to the chase. Why in the world would you contact me after all these years?"

This should be easy, right? I've been working up to this for months. I've weathered canoes and forests, surly river guides and rental cars. "I wanted to apologize."

He shakes his head. "What? For the stuff on the bus?"

I nod. "And in school."

"You mean you've carried this stuff around for thirty years?"

"I guess so. I think so. I mean, it didn't start to really haunt me until about ten months ago. I was horrible, Gary. Especially to Mary."

"You've been watching too much *Jerry Springer*, Heather."

"I hate that show."

He smiles. "Me too. Look, I'm not saying what you did was right, but we were treated a lot worse right in our own home."

"But you all left so suddenly. What happened?"

"My grandmother just couldn't afford to send us anymore. She got laid off, and that was that. We all went up to Michigan—her brother lived there—so she could get work. I graduated high school, went to junior college in Amarillo, then got my degree from the University of Texas. But I always wanted to come back to Maryland. So I did."

"Are you married?"

"Was. Divorced now, but it's one of those situations where it's for the best."

Everybody says that.

"Any children?"

"A little boy. He's twelve."

"I have a fifteen-year-old boy." I tell him a little about Jace too. "But what about Mary? Whatever happened to Mary?"

I knew it was going to be bad. I could tell by the way he got quiet and folded his hands around his water glass.

"Heather, Mary's dead. She died years and years ago."

"What happened?"

"Some stories have crazy twists and turns. Mary was pretty beaten up by you guys, I'll admit it. But when we moved north, there was this lady next door who took a shine to her. She got her braces, permed her hair into some sort of style that looked good. You know, that"—he wiggles his fingers around his head—"sorta Farrah thing that was going on back then. Remember?"

"Uh-huh."

"She turned into a beauty."

"I'm honestly not surprised."

"Oh yeah. So she vowed she'd never be ridiculed again. And she got in with the fast sort of crowd. Dated a guy with a motorcycle, and to be honest, I couldn't blame her. Xavier, he did a lot of things he shouldn't have to her. If you get my drift."

I nod.

"Of course, I did what I could to protect her, but I had to work and go to school and couldn't be there all the time."

"I saw Xavier not long ago."

"Really? Where? On that river?"

"Yeah."

"You went all the way out there to find us?"

I nod and the tears gush and I cannot contain them and in the middle of the Hamburger Hamlet, darn it, in front of Gary Andrews, darn it, I weep and I weep and I weep.

"I'm sorry. I'm so sorry."

Gary scoots next to me on my side of the booth and puts his arms around me.

And isn't this rich? God, You are crazy. You know that?

I've finally calmed down. Gary has returned to his seat. We've ordered.

"Are you sure you don't want something stronger than coffee?" he asks for the second time.

"No thanks. I've got to drive back."

The waitress arrives with his soup.

"So do you mind finishing Mary's story?"

"No, not at all. Anyway, she ended up dropping out of school, getting into drugs, just a mess, Heather. I mean, it's the age-old story, you know. Some kids escape it unscathed and go on to live regular lives, and others never make it out."

"How did she die?"

"She OD'd. I took her to Texas with me after I graduated, but she couldn't kick the drugs. I honestly don't think she meant to OD. She was wild, and maybe sometimes a little crazy, but never suicidal. Not Mary. She was determined to make up for lost time."

"What about that neighbor? Wasn't she there to guide her? Before you moved?"

"No. She died of cancer not long after Delores passed away. Mary was seventeen. I think that was something else that tore my sister apart. Some people never seem to get any breaks, right? Mary was one of those people."

I drive too fast. Tears blur my vision, and I wipe them away with the back of my hand over and over. I call Laney.

"If salvation was all there is to it, perhaps God would just catch us up to heaven once we came to faith. It sure would seem easier that way."

"But He doesn't, Heather. That's pretty well established."

"So maybe we need to be there to give people those breaks. Not everybody seems to deserve it, and certainly, I don't. But I got that break through my dad, through Jace, and now through so many others, right?"

"Right, Heather. Are you okay? Where are you?"

I tell her.

"Oh, my friend."

Mary, Mary, where you going to?

Mary, Mary.

"But sometimes it's just too late, isn't it, Laney?"

Sometimes there's no way amends can be made, mangled piles of frayed rope retwined. Sometimes life must remain fragile, and sometimes forgiveness, while always sought, cannot be achieved. Amends cannot be made.

Mary, I'm sorry.

I'm so, so sorry.

It's all I can say. And nobody hears.

Do they?

Peace cannot be obtained. At least not about some things. Not here. Not now.

I pull off at the rest area on I-95 between Baltimore and DC, grab Will's car sketchbook and a graphite pencil, and scribble a note. Half an hour later Mo lets me into the Hotel.

"Yo, Heather! Kinda late for you ladies to be out and about."

I reach into Noah's ark and pull out the letter. "Could you give this to Knox next time he comes in?"

He eyes the paper with suspicion, then takes it from my hand. "If you say so."

"Sister J in?"

"She took herself an early night."

"She deserves it. I'll bet she sleeps like a rock, doesn't she?"

"Oh yeah."

The room is full. "Thirty-two degrees?"

"Just fell."

"Good."

I hurry back to the wagon, slide inside, and press down the lock button.

None of us really deserve forgiveness. Least of all Knox. Least of all me. But maybe in offering it to Knox, I'm giving Gary the greatest expression of gratitude for his own forgiveness I could possibly give.

Will would agree. Most definitely.

FORTY-SIX

At 5:00 a.m. Christmas morning the phone rings.

I lean across Jace and answer.

"It's Krista, Miss Heather. I'm about to run away again. I'm about to use and I know it. I know all the signs. It seems I get to this point of getting my feet underneath me, and then I throw it all down the garbage chute."

"I'm coming down to get you."

"I'll be ready."

"Stay inside the Hotel until you see me pull up. And pack a nice amount of clothing."

Jace touches my arm. "Would you like me to drive down with you? We'll be back by seven. And we can open presents then."

"Okay. I'll leave a note for Will in case he wakes up and wonders where we are."

Anna and Liza arrived around two for a big Christmas dinner. I left the sweet potato casserole and green beans up to Krista, and oh my goodness, she really can "throw down in the kitchen," as Jimmy says.

I called Sister Jerusha and told her Krista was with us. She said, "Merry Christmas, doll. You're a keeper. I still say I'm right about my God marks."

Mercy.

A pile of presents stood at the ready for Krista when we got home. Will had opened up ours carefully, picked out the ones we thought Krista might like, and wrapped everything back up again. When I saw the watch Jace obviously bought for me glimmering against her dark skin, I was happier than I ever dared to hope. It only deserved to be blue-dotted because it sat on her arm.

And when I saw the look on Krista's face, I thrilled. But when I saw the look on Jace's and Will's faces, I realized that God has big plans of grace and giving, shining light in the darkest of places, and my little family was being given the chance to be right there in the middle of it all. Could a Christmas get any merrier?

Bye-bye, house. Bye-bye, swim lessons and baseball. Bye-bye, tennis court and dinner out. Hello to so much more.

Perhaps some people can do both. Live high on the hill and down on the streets at the same time. But as Jace has always told me, "When you do something, Hezz, you dive in completely."

Flannery drove Lark and Leslie up, and Will, the creep, got the Christmas stocking. Carmen called to wish us a Merry Christmas. Then Laney and even Olive and Betty. We were tried by fire, I guess, bound together and purified in some way. I love these women. I really do.

Will and I stand in the snow at the cliff over the loch, looking behind us every so often to watch our tracks fill up with the falling snow.

We both suddenly look at each other.

"Did you hear that?" I ask.

"What? Yes. Did you?"

"Uh-huh."

"Mom, this is freaky. I heard a bell. I really did hear a bell."

"Me too."

We hold our gloves up to our faces and laugh.

"Did you really hear a bell?" I ask.

"No. But that doesn't mean we can't keep listening, does it?"

"Not at all, bud." I tousle his hair, put my arm around him, and pull him close.

If we listen for the church bell, really listen, we hear it chiming all around us, all the time, in every place the breath of God blows through like a silent breeze.

My ears are ringing with its music.

ACKNOWLEDGMENTS

Many thanks to Ami McConnell, Erin Healy, Rachelle Gardner, Claudia Cross, and Don Pape. Special thanks to Claudia Burney, who read the book in its original form and gave me the help I needed. And much gratitude to Ginny, Judy, Aaron, James, and Robbie at the Catholic Action Center, a ministry to the poor in downtown Lexington, Kentucky. Family and friends, of course: Lori, Jennifer, Chris, Marty, and Leigh; the good people of Communality who teach me the ways of Jesus and the ways of justice every day. As always, I appreciate my own family: Will, Ty, Jake, and Gwynnie. Here's to surviving an incredibly difficult year together! I especially want to thank my friend Heather, who cheers us on in our crazy ways.

READING GROUP GUIDE

1. Heather is struggling through two major dramas in this book: coming to grips with her past and the evil she perpetrated against Gary and Mary Andrews; and grappling with her future as she seeks to understand what is important and what her role should be in this world. How are these two themes related, and why are they happening at the same time?

2. What is the significance of Heather's flair for making cakes? Do you think Jace was right when he said she had "the gift of cake"?

3. Why did Heather get in the car and drive aimlessly around? Was she really aimless? What was she looking for?

4. How do Heather's spending habits reflect any behaviors of your own? What do these habits tell us about ourselves? What do we really want?

5. Which characters in the book impacted you the most? Which did you like the most?

6. Which character reminds you the most of yourself, and why?

7. What scenes or lines did you find particularly powerful, and why? How do they relate to your own life?

8. Why does Heather feel so insecure about herself with Jace, even though he clearly loves her?

9. Heather struggles between loving her "stuff" and knowing somehow there must be more to life. How is this similar to any of your own struggles?

10. What do you think is the main theme of the book?

11. What did this book say to you about church? About the church as a whole? About following Jesus and doing as He modeled?

12. Anna and Liza are the kind of characters who make you wish you could meet them. What purpose did they serve in Heather's life? Have you ever had anyone like them in your life?

13. Why is the character of Knox Dulaney so troublesome to Heather? What does he show us about ourselves?

14. This book is populated with a variety of interesting characters, including Sister Jerusha, Jolly, Lark, Laney, Carmen, Jace, and Will. How does each of these people contribute to Heather's transformation?

15. Heather is so concerned about appearances that she doesn't want to open up a salon for fear it wouldn't "look right." How does our concern about "what others think" keep us from pursuing our dreams and even following God's will?

16. Working at a place like the Hotel can be dangerous and even life-threatening. Would you do what Heather did and keep working there, bringing along your children as well? Why or why not? Do you think God requires us to put ourselves in harm's way in order to help where we're needed?

17. Heather's transformation began with her having thoughts and feelings that made her think she was going crazy. Have you ever had this happen to you or seen it happen in someone else? Why is it often true that when we really start listening to God, others may think we've gone nuts?

18. What do you think would have happened to Heather if she had not "coincidentally" found the Hotel? What might have happened in her marriage?

19. What was the significance of the church bell underwater? Why was it so sad for Heather to lose the idea of the bell ringing?

20. After reading this book, did you feel convicted or motivated to change your actions or habits in any way? What behaviors do you want to change? What do you think you really *will* change?

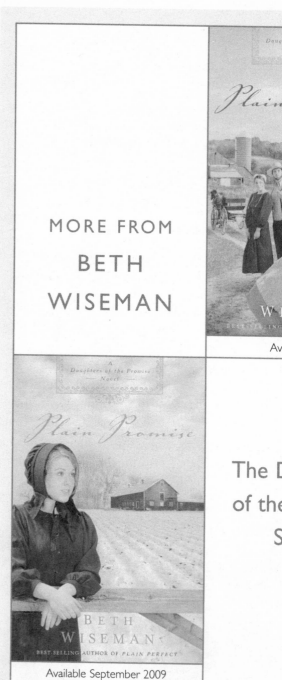

MORE FROM
BETH
WISEMAN

Available Now

Available September 2009

The Daughters
of the Promise
Series

MORE FROM
LISA
SAMSON

EMBRACE ME

believing is seeing

LISA SAMSON

Available Now

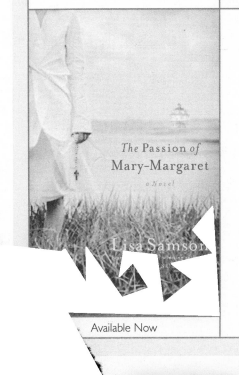

The Passion *of*
Mary-Margaret

a Novel

Lisa Samson

Available Now

THOMAS NELSON
Since 1798

Lisa Samson is the award-winning author of twenty-six books including *Quaker Summer*, *Christianity Today's* Novel of 2008, and *Justice in the Burbs*, which she co-wrote with her husband, Will, a professor of Sociology. When not at home in Kentucky with her three children, one cat, and six chickens, she speaks around the country about writing and social justice, encouraging the people of God to "do justice, love mercy, and walk humbly with God." She loves nothing better than sitting around her kitchen table, talking with family and friends, old and new.